THE NURSES
OF STEEPLE STREET

Welcome to the district nurses' home on Steeple Street, where everyone has a secret...

Ambitious young nurse Agnes Sheridan had a promising future ahead of her until a tragic mistake brought all her dreams crashing down and cost her the love and respect of everyone around her. Now she has come to Leeds for a fresh start as a trainee district nurse. But Agnes finds herself facing unexpected challenges as she is assigned to Quarry Hill, one of the city's most notorious slums. Before she can redeem herself in the eyes of her family, she must first win the trust and respect of her patients and fellow nurses.

THE NURSES
OF STEEPLE STREET

THE NURSES OF STEEPLE STREET

by

Donna Douglas

Magna Large Print Books
Long Preston, North Yorkshire,
BD23 4ND, England.

British Library Cataloguing in Publication Data.

A catalogue record of this book is
available from the British Library

ISBN   978-0-7505-4379-8

First published in Great Britain by Arrow Books in 2016

Copyright © Donna Douglas 2016

Cover photography by Jonathan Ring except background © Alamy
by arrangement with Random House Group

Donna Douglas has asserted her right to be identified as the author of
this work in accordance with the Copyright, Designs and Patents Act,
1988

Published in Large Print 2017 by arrangement with
Random House Group

Magna Large Print is an imprint of Library Magna Books Ltd.

Printed and bound in Great Britain by
T.J. (International) Ltd., Cornwall, PL28 8RW

Acknowledgements

Tackling a book about district nursing in the 1920s was something new for me, so I'm grateful for the help I've received along the way. Special thanks goes to Matthew Bradby of the Queen's Nursing Institute for all his assistance and for allowing me access to the archive of *Queen's Nurse* magazine, which I found extremely helpful in piecing together the day-to-day life of a district nurse. If you're interested in the history of district nursing, I would definitely recommend a visit to the QNI website: www.qni.org.uk

Thanks also go to my agent, Caroline Sheldon, and to the terrific team at Arrow – my editor Jenny Geras, Kate Raybould, Millie Seaward, and not forgetting the amazing sales team, especially Chris Turner and Aslan Byrne.

Finally, thanks as ever to my husband Ken for his endless patience and good cheer as our lives descend into chaos close to deadline. And to my daughter Harriet for reading all the chapters hot off the press and giving her disarmingly honest opinion. I may not always like it, but she's nearly always right.

Dedicated to the memory of Digby Clark

Chapter One

The District Nursing Superintendent was late for their meeting.

Agnes Sheridan sat straight-backed on a chair outside Miss Gale's office, her feet tucked underneath to stop them from tapping impatiently on the tiled floor. On the other side of the hall, a large grandfather clock ponderously marked the passing minutes, reminding her how long she had been kept waiting.

It was really too bad, she thought. She had arrived precisely on time for their meeting at three o'clock, and had even gone to the trouble of taking a taxi she could ill afford from the station, just so she wouldn't be late.

The skinny little maid appeared from the kitchen and scuttled towards her, head down, eyes averted. She never said a word, but had been patrolling the passageway at regular intervals ever since she'd opened the door to Agnes.

As the girl slid past, Agnes cleared her throat and said, 'Excuse me. Do you know how much longer Miss Gale might be?'

The maid froze, her eyes bulging in her thin face. She looked like a terrified rabbit.

'She's gone to see t'Miners' Welfare,' she mumbled in a broad Yorkshire accent.

'You've already told me that.' Agnes did her best to be patient. 'I just wondered how long–'

11

'I've summat on the stove,' the maid blurted out. And then she was gone, darting back the way she'd come, tripping over her own feet in her rush to get away.

'Well, that's nice, I must say!' Agnes muttered as the kitchen door slammed shut at the far end of the passageway. She had come all the way from Manchester, and hadn't even been offered a cup of tea.

She looked around, trying to get the measure of her surroundings. The passageway where she sat was long and narrow, with steps leading down to the kitchen at the far end. At the other, sunlight streamed through the stained-glass window above the front door, scattering brilliant diamonds of colour on the tiled floor. In front of Agnes was a door with an engraved brass plate reading 'Susan Gale – District Nursing Superintendent'. There were other doors leading off from the hallway too. One of them stood open, and through the doorway Agnes could see settees and chairs arranged around a fireplace, with bookshelves to either side and a piano in the corner. The nurses' common room, she imagined.

There was a telephone on a small stand beside the front door, with a message book open beside it. Further along, the faded wallpaper was covered by a large noticeboard, to which various lists and rotas had been pinned. Below that was a set of a dozen pigeon holes, mostly empty but a few stuffed with uncollected post.

Agnes took some comfort from the familiarity of the scene. It reminded her of the nurses' home at the hospital in London where she'd trained.

Perhaps this wasn't going to be so different after all, she thought.

A crash came from beyond the kitchen door, shattering the silence and making Agnes jump to her feet. She was just wondering if she should investigate when a door closed on the floor above her and she heard the stomp of heavy footsteps.

Agnes looked up to see a woman coming down the stairs towards her. She was in her mid-forties, solid rather than fat, her large body enclosed in a fitted dark blue coat. Wisps of greying hair escaped from under her neat hat.

Before she could speak, there was another crash from the kitchen, followed by loud cursing. Agnes flinched but the woman barely seemed to notice.

'Pay no attention,' she said briskly. 'It's always the same when Dottie's cooking. I s'pose you're the new nurse? Miss Gale said you'd be coming today.'

Agnes straightened her shoulders. 'That's right,' she said. 'I'm Agnes Sheridan.'

'Agnes, eh? Does everyone call you Aggie?'

Agnes winced. 'I prefer Agnes, if you don't mind,' she said.

'Do you now?' The other woman looked her up and down, an amused twinkle in her beady dark eyes. 'Well, Agnes, or whatever you want to call yourself, I'm Bess Bradshaw, the Assistant Superintendent. Miss Gale says I'm to take charge of you while she's away. So you'd best come with me.'

She led the way down the passage and pushed open a door marked 'District Room'. Agnes followed her into a large, sunny room lined with cupboards and shelves containing various items of

13

medical equipment. She looked around, taking it all in.

'This is where we keep our supplies,' Bess Bradshaw answered the question before Agnes had a chance to ask it. She picked up a large black leather Gladstone bag, set it on the wooden counter and undid the clasp. 'Each time you go out on your rounds, you'll need to check your bag to make sure you've everything you need.' Her Yorkshire accent wasn't as broad as the maid's, but it was definitely there.

As Agnes watched her holding up a bottle to the light to check its contents, realisation slowly dawned.

'Surely we're not going out to see a patient now?' she asked.

Bess looked at Agnes, the same mocking twinkle as before in her eyes. 'Where did you think we were going, down the park to feed t'ducks? Pass me the boracic powder, will you? It's up there, on the top shelf.'

Agnes reached for the glass bottle and put it in Bess' outstretched hand, her mind racing.

This wasn't right. At her old hospital a new staff nurse would have to undergo a thorough interview with Matron and be fitted for her uniform before she was allowed anywhere near the wards. And yet here Agnes was, barely over the doorstep before she was being let loose on the patients. It seemed a very haphazard way of going about things.

Was this what district nursing was all about? she wondered.

'Shouldn't I wait for the Superintendent?' she ventured.

'The Superintendent is in Wakefield, having a meeting with the Miners' Welfare Committee. She'll not be back while teatime, and I daresay she won't be in any mood to see you when she does get back. Miners' Welfare always puts her in a bad mood.' Bess Bradshaw checked another bottle, then put it back. 'And I'm to look after you, and I've got a call to make, so you'll have to come with me.'

'But—'

'You've come here to train as a Queen's Nurse, haven't you?' Bess cut her off.

'Yes, but—'

'Well, there's no time like the present to start, is there?'

Agnes looked down at herself. 'But I haven't even got a uniform.'

'Oh, stop fretting, lass! It's a willing pair of hands I'm after, not a starched collar. Now, frame yourself and let's get going.'

Perhaps this isn't such a bad thing, Agnes tried to tell herself as she followed the Assistant Superintendent out of the house. Bess Bradshaw was quite right. She had come to train as a district nurse, and the sooner she got started, the better.

After all, she reasoned, it wasn't as if working on the district was likely to be too difficult. She was a qualified nurse from one of the best hospitals in the country. She could certainly manage to give a few bed baths and change dressings.

But her nerve almost failed when Bess disappeared around the side of the house, only to emerge a moment later wheeling two bicycles. She propped one against the wall and nodded towards

15

it. 'There you are, lass. Your chariot awaits.'

Agnes stared, appalled. 'You want me to ride that?'

'Well, you could walk, but it'll take you a fair while.' Bess was already walking away, wheeling her bicycle up the front path. She stopped at the gate and looked back over her shoulder. 'What's the matter? Don't tell me you've never ridden one before?'

'Well, yes, but...' Agnes examined it suspiciously. The bike must have been at least thirty years old, a real old boneshaker, rusting and ramshackle.

'Then get on it and start pedalling! There's work to be done.'

It was a long time since Agnes had ridden a bicycle, and then it had been along leafy country lanes with her brother and sister when they were children. Nothing had prepared her for the narrow streets of Leeds. She clung on grimly as her bicycle juddered over the cobbles, convinced it was going to break apart at any moment. She could feel her hat slipping down over one eye, but she didn't dare let go of the handlebars to straighten it.

She tried to keep the Assistant Superintendent's broad backside in sight, while at the same time dodging the carts that seemed to swerve towards them out of nowhere. With everything else going on around her, it was impossible for Agnes to get her bearings. They seemed to be going south, but nowhere near the wide, busy thoroughfare lined with smart-looking shops that she had glimpsed from the taxi window. The streets Bess Bradshaw led her down were mean and dismal, with scruffy little corner shops on the end of each terrace. There was a poulterer's, a gentlemen's hair-dressers, a dusty-looking tailor's workshop, as well as a shop advertising 'Marine Goods' that seemed to be filled with nothing more than junk.

As the streets grew narrower, Agnes could feel her spirits starting to fail her. She followed Bess Bradshaw across Hope Street – a misnomer if ever Agnes had seen one – and plunged into a dark warren of alleyways and yards, the houses packed so closely together there was scarcely any daylight to be seen.

A group of women stood on the corner. They nodded briefly to Bess as she passed, then turned blank, hostile stares to Agnes. She could feel their eyes following her as she pedalled harder to catch up with the Assistant Superintendent.

'Where are we?' Agnes called out to her.

'Quarry Hill. It's one of the poorest areas of the city. The council keep trying to pull it down but the locals don't want to go.'

'Why on earth not?'

'Because it's their home.'

Bess turned sharply and led the way down a dirty, narrow alley. As they passed along, Agnes glimpsed various openings in the high wall, lead-ing to what seemed to be tiny yards, each crammed with a haphazard arrangement of ter-raced houses. The pungent smell of sewage mingled with dirt and stale sweat and factory smoke, which hung in the still warmth of the late-summer air.

Agnes shuddered. 'I don't know how they bear it,' she muttered. She risked lifting a hand to brush away a fly that buzzed around her face, then grabbed the handlebars again as the bicycle veered sideways into the wall.

Bess sent her a mocking look. 'Don't you have poor people in London?'

Agnes didn't reply. Of course she knew all about poverty. She had trained at the Nightingale Hospital in Bethnal Green, one of the poorest areas of the city. But by the time the local people were admitted to hospital, they had generally been scrubbed clean and deloused, their filthy clothes sent off to the incinerator. Agnes had never had to visit the patients in their homes or witness their poverty at such close quarters.

'You'll get used to it,' Bess said. 'Although I daresay some of the sights you'll see on your rounds will make your hair curl.'

Agnes pulled herself together. She knew she was making a bad impression, and she didn't want the Assistant Superintendent to think she couldn't manage.

'I'm sure it won't be that bad,' she said bracingly. 'Besides, I've been well trained. I think I can cope with anything.'

'You think so, do you?'

'Of course,' Agnes declared, then added, 'The Nightingale is one of the best teaching hospitals in the country.'

She hadn't meant to sound arrogant. But as soon as she saw Bess Bradshaw's frown she knew she'd said the wrong thing.

'Is that right? Happen you think you could teach us a thing or two, in that case?' she said, with a disparaging sniff.

'I didn't mean that,' Agnes murmured. But Bess had already cycled off ahead and she had no choice but to follow lamely behind. This wasn't what she'd been hoping for. District nursing was supposed to be a new start for her, and she had already managed to upset the Assistant Superintendent.

But deep down Agnes still had a sneaking feeling she probably could teach the other nurses a thing or two. After all, district nursing couldn't possibly be as difficult as working on a ward. Changing dressings and giving baths was the kind of work probationer nurses did at the Nightingale. It was hardly what Agnes would call proper nursing.

Although she was probably better off keeping those opinions to herself, she realised.

Bess took a sharp turn left into a yard. 'Right, here we are.' She swung herself off her bicycle and propped it against the whitewashed wall of an outside privy. 'We'll walk through from here.'

Agnes dismounted gingerly and stood for a moment, waiting to recover her balance. 'What shall I do with the bicycle?' she asked.

'Oh, we just leave them anywhere.'

'Will they be safe?'

Bess sent her an almost pitying look. 'Of course they'll be safe. No one round here would steal a district nurse's bicycle.' She retrieved her Gladstone bag from the front basket. 'Now come on.'

'Who are we going to see?' Agnes asked, following her through a tiny gap between two buildings.

'A lass called Maisie Warren. She's not been well all throughout her pregnancy, and since she's got no family around her, I've been calling in every week or so to keep an eye on her...'

Bess went on talking, but Agnes had ceased to listen. All she could hear was the blood thrumming in her ears.

Pregnant. Why did that have to be her first case?

She wanted to turn and run, but Bess had already ducked under a drooping line of grubby washing and was heading for a back door. The paint was peeling off it, exposing bare, rotten wood beneath. The sour odour of urine hung in the air from the outhouses across the yard.

A filthy-looking child sat on the doorstep, prodding at a crack in the concrete with a twig. She was no more than five years old, her feet bare and ingrained with dirt. From behind her, inside the house, came the sound of a baby screaming.

'Hello, pet,' Bess greeted her. 'I've come to see your mum.'

'She's asleep,' the girl replied, not looking up. 'Mrs Pilcher says she's poorly, and I'm not to bother her till she wakes up.'

'Mrs Pilcher?' Agnes saw Bess stiffen, her hand on the doorlatch. 'Has she been to see your mum, love?'

The girl nodded, still poking at the crack. Inside the house, the baby's cries grew more insistent. 'She told me to wait out here. But our Ronnie's been making such a racket.' She looked up for the first time, gazing at them with round, solemn eyes in a grimy face. She was the grubbiest child Agnes had ever seen. 'Shall I go and see to him? I didn't like to disturb Mum, not after Mrs Pilcher told me not to.'

'Why don't you let me see to him, love?' Bess

20

replied. Her voice was bright, but Agnes could see her smile was stretched a little too wide. 'You wait out here a bit longer, and I'll make sure your brother's all right.'

'What about Mum? Mrs Pilcher said—'

'Oh, I'm sure she won't mind. I'll be as quiet as a mouse. Now you be a good girl and wait out here.'

The little girl stuck out her chin. 'I *am* a good girl. Mrs Pilcher told me so. She gave me a toffee.'

'That's nice, love,' Bess replied absently, her hand already lifting the latch. The door stuck, and she leaned her shoulder against it to shift it open. 'Give us a hand' she hissed to Agnes, who quickly stepped forward to help. They pushed hard until the door finally gave.

Inside the cottage was in darkness, all the curtains pulled closed. Even though it was a warm September afternoon, a fire blazed in the grate. Agnes was nearly knocked sideways by the sweltering heat, as well as the sickening stench of decay, sour sweat and general filth. She put her hand over her mouth quickly as she felt the bile rising in her throat.

A screaming toddler waddled towards them out of the gloom, naked but for a grey, sodden nappy hanging low between his legs. He stretched out his arms imploringly to Agnes, his tearful face contorted.

'Well, don't just stand there. Can't you see the poor mite wants to be picked up?' Bess said.

Agnes reached down reluctantly and scooped him up, holding him at arm's length. The reek of ammonia from his urine-soaked nappy made her eyes water.

'What shall I do with him?' she asked through clenched lips.

'Use your common sense, girl,' Bess snapped, dumping her bag on the kitchen table. There was a strained edge to her voice that Agnes hadn't heard before. 'Now, let's get these curtains open, so we can see what we're doing.'

Bess pulled back the thin curtains, but scant light came through the grimy glass. 'Maisie?' she called out. 'Are you about, love?'

Agnes looked around. The single room seemed to be a kitchen and living room combined. A heavy black cooking range was built around the fire, with a stone sink on the opposite wall, under the window. A scrubbed table and chairs and a small, threadbare armchair filled the rest of the room. A door on the other side led to what Agnes guessed must be the bedroom.

'Who's Mrs Pilcher?' she asked.

'You don't want to know,' Bess said grimly. 'But if she's been sniffing around... Maisie?' she called out again. 'It's the district nurse, pet. Just come to make sure you're all right.'

She headed for the bedroom door, leaving Agnes still dangling the baby at arm's length. At least he'd stopped crying for the moment, and was staring at her with wide, wet eyes full of curiosity. Twin trickles of mucus ran from his tiny button nose.

She was looking around for somewhere to settle him when Bess reappeared, her face white.

'Miss Sheridan?' Agnes took one look at the

22

Assistant Superintendent's expression and quickly dumped the baby on the rag rug in front of the fire. Ignoring his screams of outrage, she hurried towards the bedroom.

'No, don't go in—' Bess tried to block her way but the metallic stench of blood had already filled Agnes' nose and throat. Over Bess' shoulder she saw a young woman lying on the bed, livid white against a tangle of blood-soaked sheets. Agnes reeled back, putting her hand up as if to ward off the dreadful sight.

'You asked about Mrs Pilcher.' Bess' voice was low and matter-of-fact. 'Well, this is her handiwork.'

'Is ... is she...?'

'She's dead, poor lass.' Bess shook her head. 'You'd best go and fetch the doctor,' she said. 'The surgery is on Vicar Lane, just down from the District House. Go by Templar Street, it'll be quicker... Miss Sheridan? Agnes? Are you listening?'

Bess' voice seemed to come from the end of a long tunnel. Tiny black dots danced before Agnes' eyes. She clutched at the doorframe for support as she felt her knees buckle beneath her. She closed her eyes, but all she could see was the woman's glazed, dead stare.

A pair of hands closed firmly on her shoulders, propelling her away from the scene. Agnes tried to take a step but her legs wouldn't hold her. The last thing she heard was Bess Bradshaw saying her name as she slithered gracefully to the floor.

She opened her eyes a moment later, to find herself slumped in the threadbare armchair with the Assistant Superintendent leaning over her, wafting a bottle of sal volatile under her nose. Bess Bradshaw's beady eyes were mocking.

'Do you still think you can cope with anything, Miss Sheridan?' she asked.

Chapter Two

'I'm sorry you had such an unsettling experience on your first day, Miss Sheridan.'

The Superintendent, Miss Gale, was at least more sympathetic than her assistant when Agnes met her on their return to the district nurses' house.

In fact, Susan Gale couldn't have been more different from Bess Bradshaw. She was in her fifties, and as delicate and fine-boned as the Assistant Superintendent was broad. She reminded Agnes of a little bird, perched behind her desk, with her bright dark eyes and beaked nose.

Agnes approved of her instantly. Miss Gale was neat and orderly, exactly the kind of nurse Agnes was used to, unlike rough and ready Bess.

Hot colour flooded Agnes' face at the memory of Bess waving a bottle of sal volatile under her nose.

'Call yourself a nurse?' she'd mocked. 'Much use you're going to be, if you keep fainting at the sight of blood!'

But Agnes couldn't help it. Even now, she could feel the oppressive heat of that room, and the smell so thick she could almost taste it on the back of her throat. And all the time the desperate, relentless wail of a motherless baby coming from the other room...

'Nevertheless,' Agnes snapped back to reality at the sound of Miss Gale's voice, 'this is the sort of thing you should expect as a district nurse. You must be prepared for anything.'

'Yes, Miss Gale,' Agnes murmured. 'I will be, I assure you.'

The Superintendent looked at her shrewdly from across the desk. 'We'll see,' she said. 'At any rate, you'll have a month to make up your mind whether or not you are suited to district nursing. You will be on an initial four weeks' probation period, during which time you will undertake a period of study, as well as accompanying one of our experienced district nurses on her rounds. Should you pass the probation period, you will spend a further five months going out on the district on your own, with only occasional supervision. Do you think you will be able to manage that?'

Agnes pressed her lips together. Of course she could manage! At the Nightingale, she had been trained to deal with all kinds of emergencies. Today had just been a shock to her, that was all.

But she was careful not to let her feelings show in front of the Superintendent. She had already offended Bess Bradshaw with one careless remark. 'I'm sure I'll learn a great deal, Miss Gale,' Agnes said humbly.

'That's the spirit!' The Superintendent smiled at her. 'Now, go up to your room and unpack.

I'm sure you'd like to refresh yourself after your long day. Tea is at five o'clock. We gather together in the dining room, so you'll be able to meet the other nurses then. Dottie?' she called out.

The door opened and there was the scrawny little maid who had given Agnes such a peculiar welcome earlier. Never had anyone lived up to their name so well, Agnes thought. She did look decidedly dotty, with her starched cap perched lopsided on her colourless flat hair. The apron she wore seemed to engulf her, skimming her ankles, the ties wrapped at least twice around her narrow waist.

'Ah, Dottie. This is Miss Sheridan, who will be joining us. She will be in room three, with Polly Malone. You remember, I asked you to put her suitcase up there earlier? Will you show her the way, please?'

Dottie kept shooting Agnes sideways glances as she led the way up the stairs. But Agnes was too busy listening to Bess Bradshaw's voice coming from the common room below her.

'Went as white as a sheet, she did,' she was saying. 'Honestly, you've never seen anything like it. Next thing she's fainted dead away.'

'You can't blame her,' another woman's voice said. 'I don't know how I would have managed if I'd been faced with something like that, especially on my first day. I hope you didn't frighten her off.'

'Happen I did,' Bess said.

'Oh, don't say that! We need more girls in district nursing. Miss Gale will have a fit if you scare this one away. Especially as her mother is a friend of hers.'

'I don't know if we need girls like her,' Bess Bradshaw said. 'Between you and me, I don't think she's got the heart for this kind of work. If I know anything, she'll be gone by the end of the month.'

That's where you're wrong, Agnes thought. She couldn't leave, no matter how much she might want to. She had nowhere else to go.

Dottie led her along the landing and opened the door to a bedroom. It was large and sunny, decorated with flower-sprigged wallpaper. The window had a view over a large back garden with a riot of shrubs, trees and slightly overgrown grass.

There were single beds on opposite sides of the room, one chest of drawers and two bedside cabinets.

'You'll sleep there.' Dottie pointed to the bed on the side farthest from the window. Having imparted this information, she turned and abruptly left, slamming the door behind her.

What an odd girl, Agnes thought as she listened to the maid thumping down the stairs.

But at least the room was pleasant, she thought as she lifted her suitcase on to the bed. Her bedroom at St Jude's in Manchester had been scarcely more than a cell, with a horsehair mattress, thin grey blankets, and walls decorated with a large wooden cross and framed Bible quotations worked in needlepoint, reminding them all that they were sinners in God's eyes.

She shuddered at the memory. She hadn't been sorry to leave that place, any more than Matron had been sorry to see her go.

Agnes set about unpacking her suitcase. It was

27

difficult to find space, since her roommate's belongings seemed to be everywhere. A silver-backed brush and mirror, hair curlers, a bottle of scent and various items of make-up littered the top of the chest of drawers, along with a couple of textbooks and a copy of *Picturegoer* magazine. There was a lipstick and a powder compact on the bedside cupboard, next to a framed photograph of a handsome, grinning young man.

It was lucky she hadn't brought much with her, Agnes thought as she cleared a small space in the wardrobe for her few items of clothing. She had left most of her belongings behind at St Jude's, along with her old life.

But she hadn't left her photographs behind, and she was thankful for that as she took out her favourite and gazed at it, losing herself for a moment in the warm memory.

It had been taken when she was ten years old. There were her parents, and her sister Vanessa, just fifteen and already blooming into a beautiful young woman. As usual, her sister was at their mother's side, both of them slim, fair and elegant, like two peas in a pod. Agnes was more like her father, with her chestnut hair and bright brown eyes. He stood with one arm around her shoulders, smiling into the camera. Dr Charles Sheridan, respected GP. Handsome and confident, he had always been Agnes' hero.

And there, in the middle of them all, was her darling brother Peter. Seventeen years old, posing with his cricket bat as if he didn't have a care in the world. Who could ever have imagined that two years later the Great War would take him away from them? Or that the same war would destroy her father's indomitable spirit, so that even now, seven years after the Armistice, he was still haunted by dreadful nightmares?

Poor Daddy, Agnes thought. She loved her father, doted on him as much as Vanessa did their mother. After Peter was killed, Agnes had done her best to make up for the loss of her brother. She had been son and daughter to her father. Always a tomboy, she had thrown herself into her brother's favourite pursuits, playing cricket and fishing in the lake for hours to keep her father company. She had even tried to fulfil his ambition for Peter by becoming a doctor. Her mother would never have allowed Agnes to study medicine, of course, but nursing was the next best thing.

Charles Sheridan had been so proud of her when she'd qualified. She could remember the day she'd collected her medal, seeing his beaming face in the crowd. He smiled so seldom, it had warmed her heart to see it. She was the best student in her year, and she'd done it for him, to make him proud.

Agnes put up her hand, as if she could feel his arm slipping from around her shoulders. She desperately wanted to grab it back, to feel the protective weight of it one last time, reassuring her that all would be well. But it was gone, and she knew it would be a long time before she felt that reassurance again.

She finished unpacking, and then quickly wrote a note to her mother, letting her know she had arrived safely. She wasn't sure if she would read it, but it comforted Agnes to write it anyway.

As she pulled the last envelope out of her note-case, another photograph fell out and fluttered to the ground. Agnes bent to pick it up without thinking, and a tremor of shock ran through her at the unexpected sight of herself holding hands with Daniel.

She must have taken it with her when she went to St Jude's, she thought. Or perhaps she had slipped it into her notecase the day she had written to him to end their engagement. It seemed strange to think that he had been with her for the past six months and she hadn't even known.

Perhaps it was better that way, she thought. Otherwise she might have weakened towards him. There were so many times over the past few months when she had longed to see his face and hear his voice again. It was difficult to stay strong when she was so dreadfully unhappy.

Agnes stuffed the photograph into her bedside drawer and slammed it shut. She knew she should throw it away, but even now she couldn't bring herself to do it.

She retrieved her toiletries bag, changed into her dressing gown and went off to the bathroom to wash off the stink of Quarry Hill, which still hung about her in a sour cloud. She would have to burn her clothes, she thought. She didn't think she could bear to wear them again, no matter how well they were washed.

The bathroom was large and she filled the tub up to the brim with water, adding a handful of Epsom salts she found on the shelf. Then she undressed and got into the bath, enjoying the luxurious feel of the warm water soothing her travel-weary limbs.

As she lay in there, in the distance she heard the front door opening and the sound of voices in the hall below. The first of the district nurses must be returning from their duties, she thought. Agnes wondered briefly about getting out of the bath and going downstairs, but couldn't bring herself to leave the warm, enveloping embrace of the water. She felt safe there. While she was lying there, with the water lapping around her chin and ears, no one could reach her or hurt her. She could put off facing the world. And besides, she was so tired, her heavy eyelids didn't seem to want to open...

A sharp knock on the door jolted her awake. On the other side of the door a cross voice said, 'I say, are you going to be all day?'

Agnes jerked upright, water splashing over the sides of the tub on to the linoleum floor. 'Hello?' she called out, startled.

'Are you coming out?' the cross voice demanded. 'Only it's nearly teatime and other people need to use the bathroom, you know.'

'Oh! I'm sorry.' Agnes quickly got out of the bath and pulled her dressing gown around herself. She opened the door, to be greeted by a young woman of about her own age. She was small and plain, with muddy brown hair and snapping grey eyes under heavy brows.

'I'm sorry' Agnes repeated, still fumbling with the ties of her dressing gown. 'I didn't realise I'd been in the bath so long. I – I must have fallen asleep...'

'I hope you haven't used all the hot water?' the

girl said, brushing past her. 'Oh, I see you have. And what's all this mess?' She looked accusingly at the puddles of water on the floor.

'I'll clean it up–' Agnes started to say, but the girl waved her away.

'I'll do it,' she said. 'Just go away, will you? I barely have enough time as it is.'

She slammed the door in Agnes' face, leaving her standing on the landing, staring in dismay.

Shaken, she returned to her room, and changed quickly into the uniform that had been provided for her. The plain blue dress was similar to the one she had worn at the Nightingale, but it had been so long since she'd worn it, everything seemed unfamiliar to her.

She was still fumbling with the studs on her starched collar when the door flew open and another young woman came in, pulling off her hat.

She stopped short when she saw Agnes. 'Oh, hello,' she greeted her. 'You must be my new roommate?'

Agnes nodded. 'I'm Agnes Sheridan.' She looked around. 'I hope you don't mind, I had to move a few of your things to make room for mine...'

'Oh, don't worry about it. I would have moved them myself if I'd known you were coming today.' The newcomer picked up an armful of belongings and tipped them into her bedside drawer. 'I'm afraid I'm not very tidy at the best of times, and I've got even worse since the last girl left.' She looked to be in her mid-twenties, perhaps a couple of years older than Agnes, tall and slender with fashionably shingled blonde hair framing a delicate, pretty face. Her accent was gentle, but unmistakably local. 'I'm Polly, by the way. Polly Malone. Have you been here long?'

'I arrived a couple of hours ago.'

'I suppose you'll just be getting used to the place, then. Don't worry, you'll settle in quickly.' Polly sat down on the bed and pulled off her shoes. 'Have you met Phil yet?'

'Phil?'

'Philippa Fletcher. Except everyone calls her Phil. She's the other trainee. About this height, brown hair, grey eyes. Usually in a bad temper about something.'

'Ah.' Agnes nodded. 'Yes, I think I have met her.'

Polly smiled. 'Oh dear! I can see you have. Don't worry, her bark is far worse than her bite. She's a sweetie once you get to know her.'

'We didn't get off to a very good start,' Agnes said ruefully. 'I stole all her bathwater.'

'No wonder she was cross, then. Phil and Miss Templeton cover one of the rural areas, out towards Wakefield,' Polly explained. 'They have to travel miles and miles on their bikes, and poor Phil so looks forward to her relaxing soak when she comes home. Don't look so stricken, you weren't to know!' She smiled at Agnes. 'You'll get used to everyone and their little ways soon, I'm sure.'

I wouldn't bet on it, Agnes thought, fiddling with her collar buttons. 'How long have you been here?' she asked.

'Just a month. I finished my probation last week, so I'm making calls on my own now.' Polly fluffed up her blonde hair and reached for her lipstick. 'Have they told you which nurse you'll be paired up with?' she asked, catching Agnes'

33

eye in the mirror.

'Not yet.'

'Oh, well, with any luck you'll get someone nice. Most of the district nurses here are delightful, with a couple of exceptions.' She grimaced at her reflection as she painted on a perfect pink Cupid's bow.

A picture of Bess Bradshaw came into Agnes' mind. If any of the district nurses were nice, she certainly hadn't met them yet.

A bell rang downstairs. 'Teatime,' Polly declared, pressing her lips together and putting the gold cap back on her lipstick 'Now you can meet everyone.'

The other nurses were already seated around the table, but the hum of conversation stopped the moment Agnes walked in. Her stomach sank at the sight of so many curious faces turned towards her.

'Ah, Miss Sheridan,' Miss Gale greeted her. She looked even tinier beside Bess Bradshaw, who sat next to her. 'Do come and join us. Everyone, this is our latest recruit, Agnes Sheridan.'

'But she doesn't like to be called Aggie,' Bess Bradshaw put in, a hint of mockery in her voice.

There was a low murmur of greetings around the table from the other women. Agnes tried to take in their names as Miss Gale introduced them all – Miss Templeton, Miss Goode, Miss Jarvis, Miss McLeod, Miss Hook – 'And of course, you already know Mrs Bradshaw,' Miss Gale finished, with a glance to the woman at her side.

'Oh yes, we know each other all right!' Bess said.

Agnes couldn't look at the other nurses as she

took her place at the table between Polly and Miss Hook. The women's expressions were bland, but she knew what they were really thinking behind those polite smiles. Bess Bradshaw would have told them all about their dismal visit to Quarry Hill, and how the new girl had made a fool of herself.

'And this is Miss Fletcher, one of your fellow trainees,' Miss Gale went on. 'I daresay she will help you to settle in.'

The cross-looking girl scowled back at her from the far end of the table. If their earlier encounter was anything to go by, Agnes didn't think Phil Fletcher was going to offer much help at all.

Dottie had set out a delicious-looking tea, with plates piled high with sandwiches, cakes and scones with jam. It was a long time since Agnes had seen such a spread. At St Jude's meals had been very Spartan affairs, eaten in silence at a long table in the chilly refectory, with the Matron watching over them all. Here, laughter and chatter flowed as plates were passed around the table, and cups filled with tea from the big brown china pot.

Of course, the nurses all wanted to know about Agnes. She braced herself against the barrage of questions. Where was she from? Did she have any family? What had made her decide on district nursing?

'I hear you trained in London?' Miss Goode spoke up. She was younger than most of the other nurses, in her late twenties, and looked as if she lived up to her name with her pleasant face, shiny pink cheeks, fluffy golden hair and wide blue eyes. Angelic goodness seemed to shine out of her.

Agnes nodded. 'At the Nightingale Hospital.'

'So you're a Nightingale girl, are you?' Miss MacLeod, a brisk Scot, nodded her approval. 'It's a very fine establishment, so I understand. We can expect great things of you, Miss Sheridan.'

Agnes heard Bess' muffled snort from the other side of the table and blushed furiously.

'I have a friend at the Nightingale,' Miss Goode said. 'Miriam Trott and I trained together, but she has just been appointed a ward sister there. You must know her?'

'I'm afraid I don't,' Agnes said quietly.

'But you must,' Miss Goode insisted. 'She has been there at least six months. She is on one of the female wards. Gynae, I think...'

'I left the Nightingale six months ago,' Agnes said.

'Oh? And where have you been since?' Miss McLeod wanted to know.

Agnes stared down at the crumbs on her plate. 'St Jude's,' she said in a low voice. She could feel her face flaming.

Miss McLeod frowned. 'I don't think I've heard of it.'

'It's a maternity home. In Manchester.'

'I suppose you went there to do your mid-wifery?' Polly said excitedly. 'Lucky you. I can't wait to do mine.'

Bess gave another derisive snort. 'You've got to finish your training here first,' she said, helping herself to a scone.

An uncomfortable silence followed. Agnes looked up, her own embarrassment forgotten.

There was something going on, but she wasn't quite sure what.

'And so she will, in a few months,' said Miss Jarvis, giving Polly an encouraging smile. She was in her forties, tall and angular. But her soft voice and warm smile transformed her gaunt features.

'I'll believe that when I see it,' Bess muttered. 'And I see you're wearing make-up again?' she added. 'How many times have you been told about that?'

Now it was Polly's turn to stare down at her plate. The poor girl looked crushed. 'I am off duty,' she murmured.

'You're still wearing your uniform.' Bess pointed the end of a butter knife towards her. 'I'm warning you, if I see you wearing it again I'll drag you to that bathroom and scrub it off your face myself!'

A slight frost seemed to descend over the tea table, and the conversation suddenly became stilted and self-conscious. Miss Hook lifted the mood slightly by reciting an amusing poem she intended to submit to the *Queen's Nurse* magazine. But as the other nurses listened, Agnes was still painfully aware of Polly sitting silently beside her.

Only Bess Bradshaw seemed unconcerned as she spooned jam on to another scone and stuffed it into her mouth. She really was an unpleasant woman, Agnes thought.

It was almost a relief when tea was over and they could all disperse. A couple of the nurses went off to the common room, while others returned to their rooms. Agnes approached Polly as she was heading towards the stairs.

'Are you all right?' she asked.

'Yes, I'm fine,' Polly replied, but her smile was brittle.

'Take no notice of Mrs Bradshaw. She's a horrible woman,' Agnes said.

Polly stopped on the stairs. 'What makes you say that?' she asked.

As they returned to their room, Agnes explained what had happened earlier that day. Polly listened sympathetically.

'Oh, you poor thing,' she said when Agnes had finished. 'What an awful thing to happen on your first day.'

'Mrs Bradshaw didn't make it any better,' Agnes said. '"Call yourself a nurse, Miss Sheridan?"' she mimicked the Assistant Superintendent's Yorkshire accent.

Polly smiled. 'That sounds just like her. And you're right, she can be very unkind sometimes.'

'Well, I've made up my mind I'm not going to pay any attention to her,' Agnes declared. 'And I don't think you should either.'

'That might be more difficult for me than it is for you.'

'Why?'

Polly's smile grew sad. 'Because she's my mother,' she said.

'You didn't have to humiliate poor Polly like that,' Ellen Jarvis said as they left the dining room together.

Bess had been expecting her to say something. Ellen was always sticking up for Polly. 'I were only speaking the truth,' she insisted. 'You know what she's like. Never sticks at owt.'

38

'That's not fair.'

'She didn't stick to her nurse's training first time round, did she?'

'Yes, but she went back to the hospital and got her qualification in the end. That can't have been easy for her. And she's doing very well with her district nursing.'

'She's only been training for a month! And you heard her, she's already going on about mid-wifery.' Bess shook her head. 'As I said, that girl never sticks at owt.'

'Well, I think she's showing a great deal of character, under the circumstances.'

Bess understood what she meant, but chose to ignore it. It was all very well for Ellen to lecture her, but she wasn't Polly's mother. She hadn't been through all the heartache that Bess had.

And even though they had been good friends for many years, sometimes Bess found Ellen Jarvis a bit too saintly.

'Time will tell,' she said. 'Anyway, I don't want to talk about my daughter. What do you make of the new lass?'

'Miss Sheridan? She seems all right to me. Very quiet, but I suppose she's just shy.'

'I think she's hiding summat.'

Ellen laughed. 'Oh, Bess! How can you say that? You hardly know the girl. Besides, Miss Gale has vouched for her. She and Miss Sheridan's mother were old school friends, I believe.'

'I know, but there's summat about her I can't put my finger on.'

'I might have known you'd be suspicious!'

'That's as may be,' Bess said. 'But I'm going to

ask Miss Gale if I can go on t'district with her.'

'Haven't you done enough? You've already frightened the girl out of her wits today. You don't want to scare her off completely.'

'She shouldn't be a district nurse in the first place if she's that easily scared. No, I'm going to find out exactly how well trained our hoity-toity Miss Sheridan really is.'

Ellen looked at her friend thoughtfully. 'You really have taken against her, haven't you?'

'As I said, there's summat about her I can't put my finger on,' Bess said. 'But if Agnes Sheridan has a secret then I mean to find out what it is!'

Chapter Three

'Butchered,' Lil Fairbrass said. 'That's what I heard, at any rate.'

Christine Fairbrass sat at the kitchen table, trying to fathom a difficult algebraic equation while her mother huddled on the other side of the room by the range, talking to their next-door neighbour Rene Wells in hushed whispers. Christine knew she wasn't supposed to be listening, least of all understanding what they were discussing, but it had been all over Quarry Hill by the time she got home from school. By teatime, everyone knew how poor Maisie Warren had been found dead by the district nurse, with her poor little bairns sobbing next to her.

Christine had come home to find that her

40

mother had taken in Maisie's two children. Now the eldest sat across the table, chewing on a crust of bread and dripping, while the youngest lay in Lil's arms sucking noisily on a bottle. Christine had to stop occasionally to brush away the crumbs the grubby little girl managed to scatter over the table.

'Look at him,' Lil sighed, hugging the baby closer. At least she'd changed his nappy so the house no longer reeked of pee. 'Poor little loves. They don't know what's going on, do they? Bless their hearts.'

'What will happen to them, do you reckon?' Rene asked.

Lil shook her head. 'I dunno. I suppose they'll have to go to the workhouse, since Maisie has no family to take 'em in. I'd have 'em myself, but what with Christine and the boys and my old dad just moved in, we can't afford any more mouths to feed.'

'And there's no sign of their father, I suppose?'

'That good-for-nothing!' Lil's lip curled. 'No one's seen anything of him since he cleared off last month.'

'And we all know why he went, don't we?' Rene lit a cigarette. 'Couldn't face up to his responsibilities. Left poor Maisie in the family way and with a load of debts to pay.' She drew on her cigarette and blew a plume of smoke out of the corner of her mouth. 'Poor lass, no wonder she were desperate. She were struggling to keep a roof over their heads as it was, without another baby to look after.'

'I'd wring Annie Pilcher's neck if I got hold of

her.' Christine's mother hissed the name, her voice full of venom. 'She's the one who did this to Maisie.'

Christine kept her eyes fixed on her school-work, but tilted her head so she could hear their whispered conversation.

Annie Pilcher lived on the other side of Quarry Hill, in a cottage even more rundown than the one where the Fairbrasses lived. She was a scrawny, grey-haired woman, so slightly built and unassuming that you could pass her on the street and never look twice at her. Christine couldn't imagine how she could have killed Maisie Warren. Maisie had been a big, tough woman, like Lil herself. She could have flattened Annie Pilcher in a minute.

'I heard Annie's gone off to visit her sister in Castleford for a couple of days,' Rene said.

Lil pursed her lips. 'Aye, and if she's got any sense, she'll stay there.'

Christine put down her pencil, curiosity getting the better of her. 'What did Annie Pilcher do, Mum?' she asked.

Rene and Lil exchanged wary looks.

'Never you mind,' Lil said.

'She just does – favours for women, that's all,' Rene explained to Christine.

'Favours!' her mother muttered, so low Christine could barely hear her. 'She didn't do poor Maisie any favours, did she?'

'All the same, there's plenty of women around here have reason to be grateful to her.'

'And a few more in their graves because of her, too! And I'll thank you not to go filling my Christine's head with any ideas about that woman, Rene

Wells.' Lil turned to Christine. 'You stay away from Annie Pilcher, d'you hear me? Don't even speak to her if you can help it.'

'Yes, Mum.' Christine went back to her work, feeling mystified. She knew her mother had a quick temper, but she couldn't imagine someone as inoffensive as Annie Pilcher ever upsetting her. She was like a little grey mouse, scurrying around the streets.

'I don't know why you don't tell your lass more about these things,' she heard Rene whisper. 'She ought to know.'

'The less she knows, the better it will be for her. She's far too young for all that.'

'Come off it, Lil. She's sixteen years old. She should know what's what by now.' Rene took another puff on her cigarette. 'Bloody hell, you weren't much older than her when you were expecting your Tony.'

'That doesn't mean I want my Christine to go the same way,' Lil said firmly. 'She's a good girl. She in't going to bother with men. She's going to make something of herself.'

Christine looked up and found the small girl staring at her across the table. She was wiping her nose on her sleeve, but her eyes were fixed on Christine, wide and reproachful. Almost as if she knew something...

Christine looked away sharply.

'She's still a lass, Lil,' Rene was laughing. 'Clever or not, one day she'll meet a young man who'll catch her eye, and the next thing you know...'

'Not my Christine. She's got a brain in her head, and I want her to use it. Why else do you think I work my fingers to the bone to pay for uniforms and books so she can go to that grammar school? It's so she won't spend the rest of her life in a dump like this.'

Christine stared down at the page in front of her, trying to concentrate. The numbers jumbled in front of her eyes.

She wished she could tell her mother the truth. Lil Fairbrass deserved that. She had been a good mother, looking after Christine and her five elder brothers single-handed since her husband died fifteen years earlier. There hadn't been a man in her life since. Lil lived for her kids, taking in washing and working night and day to keep a roof over their heads and food on the table.

Or perhaps she would understand. She loved Christine, and all she wanted was for her to be happy. To Lil, and to Christine's brothers, she was the baby of the family, the clever one, the little princess to be cherished and protected from harm.

But they couldn't baby her for ever. Rene was right. Christine was a young woman, not a little girl any more. She had grown up.

And she had fallen in love.

She caught her mother's gaze out of the corner of her eye. Lil was watching her, as she often did when she thought Christine wouldn't notice her. Love and pride shone out of her plain, worn face.

Tell her, urged a small voice inside Christine's head. She ought to know...

'D'you think Mum's awake yet?' the little girl piped up from across the table. 'Only I want to see her, and she'll be worried if me and Ronnie

44

in't there...'

'Oh, love.' Lil plonked the baby into Rene's lap and beckoned the little girl over. 'Come here a minute, pet. I've got summat to tell you.'

Christine watched her mother gather the child into her big, comforting arms, whispering quietly to her. Whether they could afford it or not, she already knew little Ronnie Warren and his sister wouldn't be turned away from Lil Fairbrass' house. She might have had a reputation in Quarry Hill for being tough, but Christine knew underneath it all her mother had a heart of gold.

She picked up her pencil and went back to her books. She knew Lil would have to know about Oliver one day. But not today.

Chapter Four

A box sat on the table in front of Polly, containing the needle and everything else she needed. Young Alec Jennings waited expectantly on the settee, sleeve rolled up, his mother perched anxiously at his side as usual. All Polly had to do was to give him the injection.

And yet somehow she couldn't make herself pick up the needle. Even looking at it made her scalp prickle with perspiration under her cap.

You've done this before, she told herself. Every morning for the past week she had come to give Alec his insulin before he had his breakfast. She had done it so many times she barely thought about it.

But not this morning. This morning Polly was a bag of nerves, because her mother was watching her.

Miss Jarvis had tried to protest when Bess announced she would be coming to assess Polly on her round.

'But she's only been on her own for a week,' Polly had heard Miss Jarvis saying in the district room the previous evening. 'Surely it wouldn't hurt to leave it for a few days, give her a chance to settle in?'

'No, it has to be tomorrow,' Bess replied. 'I'll be taking the new girl out on my rounds after that, so I won't have time to carry out any inspections.'

'Then can't you at least make it later in the day?' Miss Jarvis pleaded. 'You know what a difficult patient Alec Jennings can be. I find him and his mother trying enough, so it's hardly fair on Polly—'

'I suppose you'd rather I wasted my time watching her give someone a bed bath?' Bess had snapped. 'No, Ellen, it won't do any of us any good to give her an easy time.'

No one could ever accuse her mother of doing that, Polly thought as she read through the doctor's notes again. Her mother wanted her to fail, it was that simple. She had chosen to come and watch Polly give the Jennings boy his insulin injection because she knew that, he was bound make a fuss and then she could tell her daughter off for getting it wrong.

Polly could feel her palms growing clammy and wished she could rush off to the kitchen and wash her hands again. But Alec was already shifting impatiently in his seat. Another moment and he would start to cry, then all would be lost.

She carefully laid paper over the table and set out the contents of the box. She opened the jar containing the syringe. Mrs Jennings had already boiled some water, which Polly used to clean an egg cup before filling it with cooled boiled water from a bottle kept in the box.

All the time, she could feel her mother's gaze fixed on her, watching every move she made, ready to pounce on the slightest mistake. She could also feel Miss Jarvis watching her, willing her on. And then there was Mrs Jennings, her arm wrapped tightly around her son's shoulders, biting her lip and on the verge of tears in case Polly hurt her little boy.

As usual, Mrs Jennings' nerves were passed straight on to Alec. His round face was drained of colour, freckles standing out against his milk-white skin.

I know how he feels, Polly thought. It was all she could do to stop her hands from shaking as she swabbed the rubber cap of the insulin bottle, syringed boiled water through the sharper of the two needles, then laid it on a clean swab. Then she did the same with the blunter of the needles, and used it to draw up the required dose of the insulin.

Alec was already whimpering by the time she'd put on the other needle, in horrified anticipation of what she was about to do. He always made a fuss. His mother wasn't helping matters, clutching her son's other arm with a white-knuckled hand.

Polly glanced sideways. Her own mother was

leaning avidly forward, eyes fixed on Polly's hands, waiting for her to make a mistake. The moment Alec let out the slightest yelp, she would pounce and accuse her of being clumsy.

Polly looked back at the boy. He was watching her with a wide, fearful gaze, his copy of *Comic Cuts* abandoned on his lap. Suddenly inspiration struck Polly. She lowered the needle and said, 'Do you like comics, Alec?'

The question took him by surprise. He frowned at her, screwing up his freckled nose. 'What?'

'I prefer a longer read myself,' she said, quickly dabbing his arm with methylated spirit. 'Sexton Blake is my favourite.'

His eyes lit up. 'I like Sexton Blake too.'

'Have you read *Ill-Gotten Gains?*'

'Yes, but I preferred *The Yellow Tiger.* Wu Ling and Baron De Beauremon are better villains than Count Carlac and Professor Kew.'

'You're probably right.' Polly stepped back, the needle in her hand. 'There. All done.'

Alec stared at the pinprick in his arm, then up at her in astonishment. 'Have you done it?'

'Are you sure?' his mother said.

Polly nodded. 'And it didn't hurt at all, did it?'

Alec stared at her, mute with disappointment and betrayal that he'd missed his daily chance to make a fuss. Polly had a feeling she wouldn't be allowed to get away with the same trick twice. But it didn't matter. He could scream the house down tomorrow morning if he liked, as long as her mother wasn't there to see it.

Mrs Jennings was overcome with relief. 'That was wonderful!' she said. 'I've never known him to be so quiet. You're a marvel, nurse, you really are.'

Polly glanced at her mother. Typically, Bess had turned away and was busy scribbling notes in her book.

'He'll need something to eat soon,' was all she said.

'I've got some nice bacon and eggs for my brave little soldier.' Mrs Jennings pinched her son's cheek.

Her mother didn't speak again as Polly cleaned up, put everything away in the box, burned the swabs and wrote down the dosage carefully on the message paper for the doctor. As they left the Jenningses' house, Bess barely nodded at them before going off to collect her bicycle.

'Would it kill her to offer a word of praise, do you think?' Polly remarked when she'd gone.

'It's just her way. You mustn't take any notice,' Miss Jarvis said.

Polly watched her mother's broad figure trundling down the road in the direction of Steeple Street. She couldn't get away fast enough. 'I bet she would have had something to say, if I'd got anything wrong. She must be utterly furious that she doesn't have anything to complain about.'

'I'm sure that's not true.'

Polly turned on Miss Jarvis. 'Stop defending her. You know as well I do what Ma's like. She's much harder on me than she is on anyone else.'

'Perhaps she doesn't want to be seen to be giving you any special treatment, as you're her daughter?'

Polly laughed. 'Special treatment? I don't think anyone could accuse my mother of that!' She shook her head. 'She hates me, doesn't she? I don't think she's ever going to forgive me for what I did.'

'She will, pet. Give it time.'

'It's been two years now. How much longer is she going to go on punishing me? Doesn't she think I've suffered enough?' Her voice wobbled.

Miss Jarvis laid her hand on Polly's arm. 'She isn't trying to punish you. But she was very hurt by what happened...'

'*She* was hurt?' Polly echoed incredulously. 'What about what I went through?'

'I know,' Ellen Jarvis said soothingly. 'But you've got to try to see this from her point of view. She had such high hopes for you when you started your nursing...'

'That's it exactly!' Polly cried. 'It's always about her and what she wants, never about me. The only way I can ever win her approval is if I do exactly as she says.'

The one time in her life when Polly had felt even remotely close to her mother was when she had first applied to Leeds General Infirmary for her nursing training. She could remember her mother's excitement when the letter came, offering her a place. Bess had actually put her arms around Polly and hugged her, for the first time since she was a small child. It was a fleeting moment, but Polly still comforted herself with the memory.

Perhaps there might have been more moments like it, if Frank hadn't come along.

Time is a great healer,' Miss Jarvis said.

'I'm not bothered anyway,' Polly declared. 'If

50

that's the way my mother wants it to be, then I don't care.'

Miss Jarvis smiled. 'You don't mean that.'

'Yes, I do.'

'Then you're as stubborn as she is!' Miss Jarvis declared. 'Honestly, you're more alike than you think. And one day I'm going to bang your silly heads together and make you realise that!'

Ellen Jarvis might be a very kind woman and an excellent district nurse, but she had no idea what she was talking about, Polly thought later as she continued her rounds alone. She and her mother weren't at all alike, and never had been. If she resembled anyone, Polly was like her father. They even looked alike, both tall and fair-haired. They both liked to laugh, and they had both suffered from her mother's oppressive moods.

Polly had been a daddy's girl from the moment she was born. All her earliest and fondest memories were of her father. Albert Bradshaw was a giant of a man, physically as well as in character. He could fill a room just by walking into it. As a small child, Polly remembered climbing on to a chair every teatime to look out of the kitchen window for him coming home from work, her nose pressed up against the glass until she saw him walking down the road from the brickworks with the other men, swinging his snap tin. She could pick out Albert easily with his burnished gold hair and bushy whiskers, his towering height setting him above the crowd.

But more often than not she would hear him before she saw him. Albert loved life, and his bellowing laughter would ring down the street long before he strode into view. When she heard him, Polly would clap her hands with joy, while her mother would roll her eyes and mutter, 'I'm glad someone's got something to laugh about.'

Polly would clamber down from her chair so she could be waiting by the back door for her dad to walk in. The first thing he would do was to sweep her into his arms, high into the air while she screamed with excitement. And then her mother would ruin it all with a muttered, 'Put her down before you drop her.'

Her mother always spoiled their games with her stern voice and permanent scowl. Her father rarely laughed when Bess was around.

And then, when Polly was thirteen, Albert Bradshaw went off with his pals from the brickworks to join the war in France. Within three months he was dead, leaving Polly with a huge hole in her life and only her grim-faced mother to fill it.

The next few years had been dreadfully unhappy. Polly was desperate for comfort and reassurance, but her mother couldn't seem to give it. Polly understood she was preoccupied with trying to make ends meet, but couldn't help feeling that Bess' need to work was an excuse because she didn't know how to comfort her daughter.

And Polly was still looking for that comfort now.

She had lied to Miss Jarvis when she'd said she didn't care. That was why she had come back to train as a district nurse. Deep down, she still loved her mother and dearly wanted to be close to her.

And one day, Polly told herself, her mother might want to be close to her too.

52

Chapter Five

'The most important part of a district nurse's equipment is her bag. It must remain here, in the district room, at all times unless you are out on your rounds. It will be inspected regularly, so it must be kept clean and in good order...'

Agnes discreetly checked her watch as Bess Bradshaw droned on. It was already half-past nine, and according to the list they should have been on their way to see their first patient by now. All the other district nurses had long since gone, coming into the district room after breakfast to pack their bags before setting off on their rounds. A few of them had sent Agnes amused glances as she stood there, listening to the Assistant Superintendent's lecture and trying not to fall asleep on her feet.

They had already covered the contents of the store cupboard and shelves in minute detail, including the cleansing and proper storage of loan articles. Then Bess had proceeded to explain every scrap of paperwork, from the index cards and nurse's casebook to the daily visit book and the time book.

Agnes could barely suppress her impatience. But Bess seemed in no hurry as she talked on and on.

'As you can see, each bag has a removable linen lining, which must be changed every week. The lining must then be washed, boiled and ironed, ready for use again...'

It wasn't as if Agnes hadn't heard it before. Miss Gale had gone through exactly the same thing with her the day before. But that didn't seem to stop Bess Bradshaw.

'And then there is the separate pocket here, which is attached over the handle of the bag like so...' she demonstrated, hooking the handles of the pocket over. 'This should contain a nailbrush and scissors, soap and hand towel. It's most important that you wash your hands before removing any items from the bag...'

Agnes could feel a yawn coming, and tried to shield it with the back of her hand.

'I beg your pardon, Miss Sheridan. Am I boring you?' Bess snapped.

'Not at all, Mrs Bradshaw,' Agnes replied. 'But I can assure you, I already know all about the importance of hygiene and cleanliness from my work on the wards.'

'I see.' Bess stiffened, and once again Agnes knew she'd said the wrong thing. 'Well, you're very full of yourself, aren't you? I hope you'll be able to climb off your high horse long enough to learn something while you're with me.' She picked up her bag. 'Now, come on. We're already late as it is.'

Agnes followed her, still smarting from the Assistant Superintendent's criticism. Was she really full of herself? She didn't mean to be. But if she was going to get on here, she would have to learn to keep quiet, she decided. Especially when she was around Bess Bradshaw.

She remembered the warning Polly had given her as they prepared for bed the previous night.

'She's going to try to provoke you,' she'd said, as they brushed their teeth in the bathroom. 'Believe me, she'd like nothing more than to rush back to Miss Gale and report that you're rude, arrogant and impossible to work with. You must try very hard not to give her anything to complain about, no matter how hard she tries to get under your skin.'

'I won't,' Agnes promised.

Polly looked sceptical. 'Are you sure? She can be very difficult.'

'I can be very patient when I want to be.'

'Good.' Polly smiled at her. 'Because we've precious few nurses around here as it is, and I don't want to see you out on your ear.'

Agnes had studied her roommate's reflection in the mirror, still barely able to believe that she and Bess were related. They didn't even look alike. Polly was so tall and fair, while Bess was round, dark and solid.

And seeing them together... After just a couple of communal meals around the dining table, Agnes had come to realise that the awkwardness on that first evening wasn't unusual. Every day, Polly and her mother scarcely made it through breakfast or tea without sniping at each other. Polly generally tried to give as good as she got, but it was Bess who usually had the last word, putting her daughter in her place with a scathing comment that left them all feeling embarrassed for the poor student.

'Why don't you get on?' Agnes asked the question that had been troubling her since the day she'd arrived.

The toothbrush stilled in Polly's hand for a moment.

Then she said, 'I'm surprised no one has told you.'

'I haven't asked them. I don't like gossip.'

Polly didn't speak while she rinsed out her mouth. Then she said, 'I fell in love with the wrong person.'

'Really?' Agnes was intrigued. 'Who was he?'

'I thought you didn't like gossip?' Polly was smiling, but her face had taken on a closed look, and Agnes sensed this was something the other girl didn't like to talk about.

Agnes had all but forgotten their conversation by the following morning as she followed Bess to Quarry Hill by bicycle. It took all Agnes' concentration to stop herself from falling off. Overnight, one of the old bicycle's wheels had developed a worrying wobble, and wouldn't turn in the right direction unless Agnes leaned all her weight to one side and risked toppling over.

Bess, of course, was oblivious to her struggles as she cycled ahead, puffing like a steam train. She moved fast for a big woman, and it was all Agnes could do to keep up with her.

She tried to keep in mind everything Bess had told her about the way they ordered their calls. Diabetics requiring injections were first on the list, followed by complicated midwifery and maternity cases, then new patients, surgical cases requiring dressing changes, and finally the infectious patients. Chronics, casual calls and blanket baths were fitted in as convenient, late in the morning or in the early part of the evening round.

Their first call was to Mr Willis, who needed his leg ulcer dressed.

It's my first proper day on the district, Agnes thought, her legs pumping the pedals. This is where it all begins. But as they headed into Quarry Hill, and the streets began to narrow into the familiar rundown terraces and alleyways, she had a sudden, horrible vision of Maisie Warren's cottage and the grisly sight that had met them there two days earlier. She had barely slept for the past two nights for thinking about it. She only hoped there would be no more nasty surprises waiting for them in Quarry Hill.

The Willis family lived not far from where poor Maisie Warren had met her tragic end. Agnes kept her face averted as they passed the opening to the alley that led down to her cottage, hoping they wouldn't have to go down it. But fortunately Bess trundled past, then turned sharp right, through a narrow entrance and down another dark alley. There was a patch of daylight at the far end, which opened into a yard just like the one where Maisie had lived. This, too, was a small, cobbled area with a couple of brick-built outside privies. Flies buzzed around the overflowing dustbins, whose ripe stench filled the air.

Bess dismounted, propped her bicycle against a wall, then crossed the yard to one of the front doors, which stood half-open.

She knocked sharply. 'Hello? Mrs Willis? Are you in, love? It's the district nurse,' she called out.

'Can't we just walk in, as the door's open?' Agnes said.

Bess sent her a withering look. 'You're not in a

hospital ward now, Miss Sheridan. You can't stroll in and out as you please. This is someone's home, and we are guests. I don't know about where you come from, but up here we wait to be invited in where possible.'

Before Agnes could reply, a voice called out, 'Come in, nurse. I'm just in the scullery.'

They walked in and Agnes was stopped in her tracks by a strange, sickly odour. She put her hand over her nose. 'What is that awful smell?' she whispered.

'Bugs,' Bess said matter-of-factly, putting her bag down on the kitchen table. 'Don't worry, you'll get used to it. And mind you don't pull that face, it's very rude.'

The Assistant Superintendent took off her coat and Agnes did the same, still trying to hold her breath. Following Bess' lead, she rolled it up so the lining was tucked inside, then placed it on the scrubbed table beside her bag. She then unpinned her apron, which had been tucked up inside her coat.

By the time they had finished preparing themselves, Mrs Willis had emerged from the scullery, a baby propped on her hip. Three other small children clustered around her, peeping shyly past her skirt at the visitors. She was in her late twenties, only a few years older than Agnes, but the careworn expression on her thin face made her look much older.

'Sorry about that, nurse. I was just getting the pan ready for you–' She stopped speaking when she saw Agnes. 'Who's this, then?'

'This is Miss Sheridan, who is training to be a

58

district nurse. She will be with me for the next month, so I expect you'll get used to seeing her around and about. Miss Sheridan, this is Mrs Willis.'

'How do you do?' Agnes greeted her politely.

'Fair to middling, I s'pose.' Mrs Willis smoothed down her skirt with her free hand, then turned to Bess. 'I've got your tin out for you, nurse. It's on the dresser.'

'Thank you. Now, we'll just wash our hands and then we'll get started. Miss Sheridan?'

Agnes was so busy staring at the huge black patches of damp blossoming on the faded wallpaper, she didn't realise Bess had addressed her until she caught the older woman's eye.

'I'm sorry, were you speaking to me?'

'I was indeed, Miss Sheridan.' Bess' smile grew chilly. 'Fetch your things and we'll wash our hands.'

Agnes took her soap and towel from the outside pocket of her bag and followed Bess to the tiny scullery, where they stood side by side at the stone sink, washing their hands under the cold tap. But no matter how much she scrubbed with carbolic soap, Agnes wasn't sure she would ever feel clean. How could people live like this? she wondered. The mouldering brick walls of the scullery seemed to sweat filth and decay.

But Bess hardly seemed to notice as she finished washing her hands, dried them on her towel and then opened her bag and took out three sets of forceps ready for boiling in the pan Mrs Willis had provided.

'How is your husband today?' she asked the

59

young woman, who stood in the doorway watching them.

'Oh, you know my Norman, nurse. He's not one to say much about anything. But I reckon he's in a lot of pain.'

'Well, let's see if we can make him more comfortable, shall we? Now, you said you have the tin of dressings prepared?'

'I have, nurse. I put them in the oven last night, while I was cooking the tea–'

Before Mrs Willis could finish her sentence, a man's voice called out from beyond the scullery doorway.

'Is that t'nurse?'

'It is, Mr Willis,' Bess called back. 'I'm on my way. Just making sure everything is nice and clean for you.' She turned to Agnes. 'Finish boiling those forceps and then bring them in, please, Miss Sheridan. And I'll need another basin, some soap and a towel to wash the patient, if you could prepare them for me?'

She left the room, leaving Agnes in the tiny scullery with Mrs Willis and her assorted children.

Agnes could feel the woman's gaze on her as she set about filling the basin with water and preparing the wash things. The children were unnerving her too, staring up at her with their vacant eyes. Agnes braced herself, terrified that one of them might reach out and try to touch her with their filthy little hands.

'You're not from round here, are you?' Mrs Willis broke the tense silence.

'No,' Agnes said, folding the towel over her arm.

60

'I thought not. You speak proper posh. Where are you from, then?'

'London.'

'London, eh? You're a long way from home, in't you?'

Agnes looked around her, at the rough, damp-stained walls of the cottage. Further than you can ever imagine, she thought.

'I'll take these wash things through first, and come back for the instruments,' she said, before Mrs Willis could ask any more questions. 'Then the nurse can get started.'

She followed the sound of Bess' voice through the kitchen and up a darkened passageway. The Assistant Superintendent was in a room at the far end of the passage, talking to Mr Willis.

'Is this her, then?' he asked, nodding towards Agnes. He lay on the double bed in the front room, a wiry man in striped pyjamas. One trouser leg was rolled up to the knee, revealing a bandaged calf.

'Aye. This is her,' Bess said, not looking up as she laid out sheets of newspaper on the floor.

Agnes could only guess what Mrs Bradshaw had been telling him about her in the few minutes before she'd entered the room. But she was determined not to let it bother her. She smiled at Mr Willis, who glared back at her with the utmost suspicion.

'Well, don't just stand there, girl,' Bess interrupted. 'Put those things on the dresser.'

Agnes set the basin down as she was asked, and then went off to fetch the saucepan containing the boiled forceps. By the time she returned, Bess

61

had set out everything she needed and was removing Mr Willis' dressing.

'Is there anything else I can do?' Agnes asked.

'Not just now. Stand over there and watch what I'm doing. And try to keep out of the way.'

Agnes stood at the foot of the bed, fighting down her irritation. Why should she have to watch Bess Bradshaw change a dressing, for heaven's sake? She'd been doing them herself since she was a probationer. In fact, she reckoned she could probably do a better job than the district nurse herself.

But she had learned better than to question an order, so instead she stood quietly by, her attention drifting as Bess carefully cleaned Mr Willis' ulcerated wound. His leg was a terrible mess, Agnes noticed, criss-crossed with old scars.

She gazed around the room. It might once have been a parlour, judging by the ornate cast-iron fireplace, faded floral wallpaper and lace curtains. But now the whole room seemed to be made up of beds of one kind or another, filling the small space so it was difficult to pick a path between them. The room was dominated by the high iron bedstead on which Mr Willis lay. To one side of the bed was a cot, and under the window were two grubby-looking horsehair mattresses, made up with a thin blanket and some pillows.

Did the whole family sleep in here? Agnes wondered. She hadn't noticed a staircase, so she supposed they must. She couldn't imagine living in such grim, awful surroundings, packed into a couple of rooms together. How depressing it must be. No wonder the place was crawling with bugs...

She looked up and realised Mr Willis was watching her, eyes narrowed as if he could read her thoughts.

'Be it ever so humble, eh?' he said bitterly.

Agnes looked away, feeling hot colour flood her face.

Bess didn't seem to have noticed Mr Willis' comment as she briskly rolled up the dirty swabs in the newspaper and handed them to Agnes. 'Take these outside and ask Mrs Willis to burn them, will you, Miss Sheridan?'

Mrs Willis was waiting for them in the kitchen. She took the newspaper bundle from Agnes and said, 'I'll put them on the fire. And I've got a pan on the stove ready for the dirty instruments,' she added.

'Thank you,' Agnes said.

Not another word was spoken between them, and the silence stretched uncomfortably. It was almost a relief when Bess finally appeared. Agnes didn't think she would ever be pleased to see her, but even Mrs Willis seemed to be smiling again.

'You'll stop for a brew of tea, won't you, nurse?' she said. 'I've got the kettle on.'

Agnes glanced at Bess, expecting her to refuse. It was half-past ten already, and they had the rest of their list to finish before they returned to the district nurses' home for lunch at one. But to her dismay, Bess smiled and said, 'That would be very nice, thank you, love.'

It was all most uncomfortable. Agnes perched on the edge of a kitchen chair, hardly wanting to settle on it in case she caught something. All the while she was conscious of the children watching her curiously from the scullery doorway, as if she was some kind of sideshow exhibit.

'Are you sure we have time for tea?' she hissed to Bess.

'We always have time for tea,' Bess replied, smiling past her at Mrs Willis as she came in, bearing a tray.

Agnes stared at the teacups that Mrs Willis was setting out. They were aged china, veined with so many black cracks it was astonishing that they held together at all. The thought of drinking out of one of them made Agnes shudder. She would catch something for sure.

'No tea for me, thank you,' she said quickly, as Mrs Willis went to pour from the pot. She'd thought she was being polite, but Mrs Willis' face fell.

Bess stepped in quickly. 'Well, I certainly won't say no,' she said. 'Mrs Willis makes the best cup of tea in Quarry Hill.'

'If you say so,' Mrs Willis muttered, but there was a definite chill in her voice.

Agnes stared down at her hands folded in her lap and didn't meet anyone's eye. She didn't care, she told herself. She would rather offend Mrs Willis than end up in the sick bay with some dreadful infection.

Not that it seemed to worry Bess Bradshaw. She sipped her tea happily and discussed the worrying rash that Mrs Willis' youngest had developed.

'It sounds like ringworm to me,' Bess said. 'A touch of gentian violet should put it right. I'll bring some next time I come.'

'Thank you, nurse, I'd be much obliged.' Mrs Willis looked grateful.

Finally, after what seemed like a lifetime, Bess declined a third cup of tea and they were able to take their leave. It was a relief to step out of the cottage into the weak sunshine of the yard, where Agnes could finally breathe some slightly fresher air. She could taste the sickly odour of the cottage on the back of her throat.

No sooner had the front door closed on them than Bess turned on her.

'That was ruddy rude of you,' she said.

Agnes blinked at her. 'I beg your pardon?'

'Did you have to sit there like a sentry on guard duty? And why couldn't you have had a cup of tea?'

'It was all so dirty, I was afraid I might catch something.'

'Well, that much was obvious! Poor Mrs Willis was mortified, and so was I.'

'I'm sorry. I didn't mean to embarrass anyone...'

'Well, you did. Not everyone was born with your advantages, Miss Sheridan. Mr and Mrs Willis are trying to live a decent life and it isn't easy for them, especially since they don't have much money coming in. But they're doing their best, and the last thing they need is someone like you coming in and looking down her nose at them!'

'I – I wasn't–' Agnes tried to say, but Bess wasn't listening. She was marching ahead, wheeling her bicycle back down the alleyway that led to the main street.

'You're going to meet a lot of families like them, and you'd better get used to it,' she said to Agnes over her shoulder. 'Not only that, you will have to learn to care for them, and to take an interest in their welfare. You may even learn to like them, over time.'

'I – I'll do my best,' Agnes promised. But her heart was already sinking in her chest. She could never imagine learning to like the residents of Quarry Hill, with their dirty, bug-infested houses and their hordes of filthy children.

They turned the corner and headed further down the street. Somewhere in the distance, the sound of raised voices mingled with the steady clip-clop of dray horses from the brewery and the sound of a pot mender on his bicycle, calling out his wares.

'Now then,' Bess said. 'It's Lil Fairbrass' house we're visiting next. Her father's got another chest infection. And you'd better not go inspecting the cups there, if you know what's good for you.'

'Who's Lil Fairbrass?' Agnes asked.

They turned the corner and were greeted by a loud bellow of rage from the far end of the street.

'You're t'scum of the earth, Annie Pilcher! I've a good mind to knock your block off!'

Bess turned to Agnes, a mischievous smile on her broad face. 'That's her,' she said.

Chapter Six

The two women squared up to each other, almost nose to nose in the middle of the cobbled yard. One was small and scrawny, the other at least twice her size, her sleeves rolled up to reveal forearms as hefty as tree branches. But her intimidating stature didn't deter the smaller woman from standing her ground.

'I dunno what you're on about, Lil Fairbrass. I in't done nothing.'

'Tell that to Maisie Warren's kids. They in't got a mum now, thanks to you.'

Lil took a menacing step towards the smaller woman, who backed off.

'Like I said, I dunno what you're talking about. I in't been near nor by Quarry Hill for days now. Been visiting my sister in Castleford. You ask anyone.'

'You mean you ran off when you found out what you'd done! I dunno how you can live with yourself, Annie. I'd like to wring your bloody neck!'

'You come near me, and I'll–'

Annie didn't get to the end of her sentence before the big woman's fist came out, knocking her flat. The scrawny woman sprawled on the cobbles, her little stick-like legs in the air.

'I'll have you for that, Lil Fairbrass!' Annie scrambled to her feet and flew at her, clawed hands raised ready to strike. The next moment they were wrestling in the middle of the yard, while the neighbours hung out of windows and stood in doorways, egging them on.

'Here, hold this.' Bess thrust her bag into Agnes' hands and ploughed in to the fray.

'Leave it, Mrs Fairbrass,' she said, her arms wrapped around the bigger woman's waist, trying to pull her away. 'She isn't worth getting into trouble for.'

'She's right,' Annie Pilcher screeched, 'I'll have

the law on you.'

'Aye, bring 'em round!' Lil threw back at her. 'And I'll tell 'em what you did an' all!'

She took another swing at Annie. The blow connected and the smaller woman bounced off the privy wall. Agnes saw her staggering towards her, but was too slow to get out of the way. The next thing she knew, she was toppling backwards.

Annie managed to recover her balance just in time but Agnes landed with a crash among the dustbins, where she lay sprawled and winded in a stinking mulch of rotten rubbish. As she struggled to get up, her feet sliding away from her on the slimy cobbles, a sleek dark shape slithered past, inches from her hand.

Agnes let out a long, terrified scream that stopped Bess and the other two women in their tracks.

'What's up with her?' Lil demanded.

But Agnes could only point helplessly as the dark shape slid away into the shadows. 'It – it's a–'

'It's only a rat, what's the matter wi' you? The place is crawling wi' 'em.' Lil grabbed a broom and started poking around in the rubbish, looking for it. 'It'll be long gone, mind. You'll have frightened it off, bawling at the top of your voice like that.'

'Oh dear, Miss Sheridan.' Bess came over to where Agnes lay. Her face was a mask of sympathy, but Agnes could see the twinkle of laughter in her eyes. Her mouth definitely twitched as she put out a hand to haul Agnes to her feet.

By the time she was standing up, Annie Pilcher was nowhere in sight.

'Made herself scarce,' Lil said grimly, setting down her broom. 'Still, I daresay I'll catch up wi' her soon enough.' She regarded Agnes through narrowed eyes. 'By 'eck, lass, you look a right state. You'd best come inside and get yoursen cleaned up.'

Lil's cottage was just as small and drab as the Willises' home. The first thing Agnes noticed were the two small children playing on the rug. There was something oddly familiar about them.

'I see you've taken in Maisie Warren's kiddies?' Bess said.

'Aye, well, I couldn't let the poor bairns go to the workhouse, could I?' Lil muttered. She looked embarrassed by her own kindness.

Agnes stared at the children. They had been scrubbed so clean, she barely recognised the dirty urchins from a couple of days earlier.

She hobbled off to the scullery to wash her wounds. Her black woollen stockings were ripped into holes, exposing grazed skin and blossoming bruises. But her pride was hurt far more than her skinned shins.

And it didn't help that Bess Bradshaw was laughing at her. Agnes could hear her as she stood in the tiny scullery, washing the dirt out of her wounds.

'I don't think your friend found it funny,' Lil was saying.

'Yes, well, she doesn't have much of a sense of humour, I'm afraid,' Bess chuckled.

'She'll need one if she's going to fit in round here.'

'You're right about that,' Bess agreed. 'Between

you and me, I don't think she'll last long.'

Agnes finished cleaning her wounds and came back into the kitchen. Lil and Bess turned to greet her.

'Feeling better?' Bess asked, still with that maddening twinkle in her eye.

'Yes, thank you,' Agnes replied stiffly.

'You still whiff a bit,' Lil said, fanning her hand in front of her face.

'She's right,' Bess said. 'You'd best stay down here while I go up and see the patient. Here,' she reached into her bag and brought out cotton wool swabs and a bottle of antiseptic, 'better get some of this on.'

Bess went up the staircase leading from the kitchen, clutching her trusty bag, leaving Agnes to the tender mercies of Lil Fairbrass.

'You'll be wanting a brew, I suppose?' she said.

'I...' Agnes was about to refuse when she remembered Bess Bradshaw's warning. 'That would be very nice, thank you,' she said.

Agnes could feel Lil watching her from the scullery as she dabbed at her wounds with the antiseptic. The children were watching her too. Did everyone in Quarry Hill stare like that? she wondered. It was terribly off-putting.

She had just finished applying the antiseptic when the back door opened and a young girl walked in. At first Agnes thought she might be seeing things, the girl looked so out of place. She was dressed in a neat dark blue blazer and a straw boater, a shiny leather satchel slung over her shoulder. She was small and very pretty, with a delicate heart-shaped face dominated by a pair of

70

lustrous green eyes.

But before Agnes could speak, Lil came bustling out of the scullery, drying her hands on a tea towel.

'Christine? What are you doing home at this hour?' She looked up at the clock on the mantel-piece. 'It's not even dinnertime yet.'

'I wasn't feeling well, so they sent me home.' The girl pulled the satchel off her shoulder and put it down on the table.

'Not well? What's the matter with you, love?'

'I just felt a bit sick, that's all.' The girl took off her hat and a luxuriant mass of rich red curls tumbled over her shoulders. She sniffed the air. 'What's that horrible smell?'

'Oh, take no notice. It's just the nurse sitting there,' Lil dismissed. 'Sick? That's not like you. Have you got a temperature?' She went to put her hand on the girl's forehead, but Christine pushed her away.

'Stop fussing, Mum. I'm all right now, honestly. Just a bit tired, that's all.'

Mum? Agnes looked from one to the other in disbelief. She could scarcely believe that Lil Fair-brass could have given birth to such an exquisite-looking girl. Apart from the red hair, there was no family resemblance at all.

Feeling slightly at a loss, Agnes decided she might as well step in and try to make herself useful.

'I could take a look at her, if you like?' she offered.

'It's all right, we'll wait for t'nurse,' Lil said, still fussing over the girl.

71

Agnes pressed her lips together. 'I am a nurse,' she said tightly.

'You know what I mean. The proper nurse.'

Just as Agnes was opening her mouth to respond, Bess came down the stairs, the wooden steps creaking under her weight.

'His chest's a lot worse today, so I'm going to set up a steam tent–' she started to say, then she noticed the young girl standing there. 'Hello, Christine, love. No school today?'

'She's been sent home poorly,' Lil said. 'I wondered if you'd mind having a look at her? Only Vera Acaster's husband has just come down with scarlet fever, and I'm worried she might have it...'

'I did offer to examine her,' Agnes said, but neither of the women paid her any attention. Only the girl gave her an embarrassed smile, as if she understood her awkwardness.

'Let's have a look at you, then.' Bess reached into her bag for her thermometer and slipped it into the girl's mouth, then checked her over. 'Well, there's no sign of a rash that I can see.'

'It's not like her to be sick,' Lil said. 'Or to miss school.'

Bess took out the thermometer and examined it. 'There's no high temperature either,' she said, squinting at the numbers. 'It's all right, Mrs Fairbrass, I don't think she's got scarlet fever. Probably just a stomach chill, or she ate something that didn't agree with her.'

'Oh, thank the Lord!' Lil crossed herself. 'I don't think I could stand it if anything happened to my Christine.'

'If I were you, I'd put her to bed and let her get

some rest,' Bess advised. 'And nothing but weak tea and dry toast until the sickness passes.'

'You hear that?' Lil turned to her daughter. 'You get yourself off to bed. And no sitting up reading,' she warned. 'If I find you with those schoolbooks of yours, I'll tan your hide for you.'

'Yes, Mum,' the girl sighed. She smiled at Bess. 'Goodbye, Nurse Bradshaw. And goodbye – um–' She gave a shy little nod, then headed off. It suddenly occurred to Agnes that no one had bothered to introduce her.

Bess finished setting up the steam tent for Lil Fairbrass' father upstairs, by which time Lil had brewed a pot of tea. Agnes glanced at her watch as they all settled down for a cup. They had already missed lunch at the district nurses' home. At this rate, they wouldn't have any time at all before the afternoon round started.

But Bess seemed in no hurry to leave as she listened to Lil fretting about her daughter.

'Christine's always been delicate,' she declared. 'Her brothers are all as tough as old boots – well, you'll know that, nurse, you've looked after them often enough when they've broken bones and Lord knows what else. But our Christine's different. She's my baby.' Lil smiled, her hard-boned face suddenly suffused by love. 'And she works so hard. That's the trouble, I reckon. She's never away from those schoolbooks. But I suppose it's to be expected, seeing as how she wants to be a teacher.'

'She'll be all right, Mrs Fairbrass, I promise you.' Bess reached over and patted her hand. 'A couple of days' bed rest and she'll be up and about again.

73

I'll check on her when I come in tomorrow to see your father.'

'Would you? I'd be much obliged, nurse.'

When they finally left the Fairbrasses', Bess Bradshaw sent Agnes back to the district nurses' house to change.

'I can't have you trailing after me smelling like a rag and bone yard,' she said. 'You'll upset the patients.'

Despite her best efforts, Agnes managed to get herself lost in the warren of streets around Quarry Hill. By the time she found her way back to the district nurses' house, Dottie was clearing the dining room, and most of the nurses had retired to write up their notes from their morning rounds.

Agnes went upstairs to bathe and change, and found Polly already there. She was sitting at the mirror, brushing her hair.

'Hello,' she said. 'How did your first morning go?' Then she caught sight of Agnes' bedraggled reflection in the mirror. 'Oh dear,' she said. 'What happened to you?'

'Would you believe, I ended up in a fight?'

Agnes explained what had happened, and to her credit, Polly didn't laugh like her mother had.

'You poor love,' she sympathised. 'You're not having a great deal of luck in Quarry Hill, are you?'

'It was all horrible.' Agnes unfastened her starched collar and pulled it off. 'I hated every minute of it.'

'You'll get used to it,' Polly said soothingly.

'Will I? I don't think so.' Agnes sighed with frustration. 'It wouldn't be so bad if I'd actually done some proper nursing. But so far all I've done is watch Mrs Bradshaw drinking endless cups of tea!' Then she remembered who Polly was. 'I'm sorry.'

'It's all right,' Polly said. 'I know what my mother is like, remember? I told you she would try to provoke you, didn't I? She can probably tell it irritates you.' Polly turned back to her reflection and teased a strand of blonde hair into place.

It was then that Agnes noticed her roommate wasn't wearing her uniform, but a rather fetching pink dress. 'Aren't you back on duty this afternoon?' she asked.

Polly shook her head. 'It's my afternoon off.'

'You look very smart. Are you going somewhere nice?'

'I'm going to visit someone,' Polly said quietly.

'Oh yes? Anyone special?'

Polly paused for a moment. 'My husband,' she said.

Chapter Seven

The churchyard was deserted in the middle of the afternoon. Any funerals usually took place in the morning, and even though there were usually a couple of other mourners visiting their loved ones, this time the weather must have kept them away. Dark, threatening clouds, black as bruises, were rolling in, blocking out the sun and making the churchyard seem even more sombre.

Polly didn't mind the rain that started to spit as she passed through the lych gate and made her way up the path. She preferred the solitude the bad weather offered.

Yet she wasn't alone. As she drew closer to the church building, she noticed the lone figure of a gravedigger hard at work on the far side of the churchyard. Careless of the weather, he'd hung his jacket from one of the low branches of an overhanging tree while he worked. Even from the other side of the churchyard, Polly could see the rain had plastered his dark hair to his face. But the man barely seemed to notice as he dug into the ground, sending up spadefuls of earth on to a growing mound behind him.

Then, as if he sensed he was being watched, he suddenly stopped digging, straightened up and stared back at her.

Caught, Polly gave him a quick, embarrassed nod and hurried on, past the church and up the slight rise to the far end of the churchyard, where Frank rested close to the wall, under the shade of a yew tree.

Polly felt the familiar sense of panic and dread churning in her stomach as she approached his grave. Her knees went weak, her legs resisting her, so it was all she could do to force herself to walk the last few paces.

When she had first experienced the panic, going to visit Frank immediately after his funeral, to her shame she had given in to it and run away. But gradually she had forced herself to ignore the voice that cried out inside her, telling her to spare herself and turn back. Now, two years later, the pain and panic hadn't lessened, but she had learned to control them better.

It helped that over the years the grass had grown, softening what once had been a stark, raw mound of freshly dug earth. But the headstone was still as hard and uncompromising as it had been on the first day she saw it.

Polly kept her eyes averted from it as she kneeled down and replaced the faded flowers with the fresh carnations she had brought. Then, finally, when she couldn't avoid it any longer, she stood up, brushed the dirt from her knees, and forced herself to lift her gaze and look at his name.

Francis Patrick Malone
Born 18th September 1901
Died 22nd June 1922
Beloved son, brother and husband

Polly kept on staring at the letters, waiting for the pain to subside. But it only seemed to grow sharper, until the letters blurred as tears filled her eyes.

'"Jesus said unto her, I am the resurrection, and the life: he that believeth in me, though he die, yet shall he live."'

Polly swung round at the sound of the voice behind her. A smiling young man stood there, sheltering under an umbrella and leaning heavily on a walking stick. A starched dog collar was just visible under the mackintosh he wore.

'What did you say?' she blurted out.

His smile wavered. 'I'm sorry, I didn't mean to

intrude. I just happened to glance out of the vicarage window and saw you standing there. You looked so forlorn, I thought you might be in need of some consolation. You know – "blessed are those who mourn, for they will be comforted", that sort of thing?'

'What I'm in need of is to be left alone!' Polly snapped back, then regretted it immediately when she saw the young man's expression falter. A blush swept up from under his dog collar to flood his face.

'I do beg your pardon,' he murmured. 'You're quite right, I shouldn't have disturbed your privacy–'

He started to turn away, but Polly called out to him.

'No, wait! I'm the one who should apologise. I'm sorry for snapping. I know you were only trying to be nice.'

'I'm afraid the vicar is always taking me to task for my over-eagerness,' the young man said ruefully. '"Fools rush in where angels fear to tread" and all that.' He turned his gaze to Frank's grave. 'But I don't suppose there is any comfort I could offer someone who has lost a loved one so young.' He shook his head. 'Just twenty-one years old,' he murmured. 'Only five years younger than I am.' He looked up at Polly. His eyes were a gentle brown, the colour of hazelnuts. His hair was slightly lighter, curling slightly around his ears. 'Was he your brother?'

'My husband.'

'How tragic.' The young man fell silent for a long time, as if he couldn't find the right words.

The only sound was the steady rain pattering down on his umbrella. Polly tightened her mackintosh around her as water dripped off the brim of her hat. It would be a sodden mess by the time she got back to the district nurses' house, she thought.

'Oh, do excuse me. What on earth am I thinking?' As if he could read her mind, the young man suddenly hurried forward to cover her with his umbrella. 'Here, allow me.'

'It's all right,' Polly said. 'I'm going now anyway.'

'Then allow me to walk you back to the gate. You must think I have the most dreadful manners. We haven't even been introduced.' He juggled his walking stick and umbrella for a moment so he could offer her a free hand. 'I'm Matthew Elliott, the new curate. At least, I suppose I must still be new,' he mused. 'I've been here three months now, but that's how everyone still refers to me.'

Polly smiled. 'I'm Polly Malone.'

'Polly.' He repeated the name thoughtfully. 'I must admit, I've seen you a couple of times when you've been visiting. I had hoped you might come to church, so I could introduce myself properly.'

Polly looked down at the path, embarrassed. 'I'm afraid I don't attend as regularly as I should.'

'Oh, it's no matter,' he dismissed. 'Don't worry, I'm not going to tell you off about it. I leave all that sort of thing to Reverend Turner! No, I just noticed how sad you always looked.'

'Doesn't everyone look sad when they come to visit someone's grave?' Polly asked.

Matthew shook his head. 'Not always. I've seen people smiling like the Cheshire Cat. I suppose, to be charitable, it might be that they're relieved and happy that their loved ones are free from pain and have entered the Kingdom of Heaven. But sometimes I'm not so sure. Would you believe, I once saw a woman dancing on her husband's grave?'

'No!'

'It's quite true. They had barely finished burying him and she was doing a jig!'

Polly smiled in spite of herself. 'I suppose you must see some strange sights?'

'Some strange sights – and some very sad ones too. That was why I decided to brave the elements to see you today. I wanted to find out your story.'

'Well, now you know.'

'What do you mean? I hardly know anything about you. Where you live, for instance, and what kind of work you do. You do work, I suppose?'

But Polly wasn't listening. Her attention was fixed on a movement near the gate. A large dark shape was prowling along the wall, behind some overgrown shrubs. She could hear the rustling of the wet leaves as it moved slowly and carefully, just out of sight.

Then the bushes parted and a broad black head suddenly appeared, making her jump until she realised what it was.

'Look, it's a dog!' she cried.

Matthew looked in the direction she was pointing. 'So it is. What's that doing here, I wonder.' He turned and called out to the young man who was still digging a grave on the far side of the churchyard. 'I say – you there! Come and get rid of this thing, will you?'

The young man continued to dig, his spade

moving with a slow, steady rhythm.

Matthew tutted. 'I don't suppose he can hear me from so far away.'

Oh yes he can, Polly thought. She didn't know why, but somehow she knew the other man had heard every word. But for reasons best known to himself, he had chosen to ignore the curate.

She looked back at the dog. 'We should leave it,' she said. 'It isn't doing any harm. It will probably find its own way out of the gate in a minute.'

Matthew's smooth features twisted into a frown. 'We can't just leave stray dogs to wander around the churchyard. What if it attacked someone?'

'It seems harmless–' Polly started to say, but Matthew had already shoved his umbrella into her hand and was crashing into the undergrowth after the dog.

'Hey, you! Get away with you.' He advanced on the animal, his stick raised. The dog backed away, snarling, head lowered, hackles standing on end, its gaze fixed on the stick.

'You see? It's vicious,' the curate called back over his shoulder to Polly.

'Only because you've cornered it,' she called back. 'The poor thing is terrified. Just leave it, please.'

Matthew raised his stick again and the dog let loose a frenzy of barking. Its eyes rolled back in its head, revealing bloodshot whites.

'No!' Polly was about to rush at Matthew and stop him, but someone else beat her to it. The young gravedigger came out of nowhere, putting himself between Matthew and the cornered animal, brandishing his spade like a weapon. He

81

was still in his shirtsleeves and his damp shirt clung to him, revealing powerfully muscled arms.

'Don't you dare lay a finger on him,' he warned in a low voice that sounded even more ominous than the dog's deep-throated growl.

The curate froze for a moment, then slowly lowered his stick.

'It's a dangerous animal,' he muttered.

'It's just afeared, that's all. And waving a bloody stick at it won't make it any better.'

Matthew gasped. 'Watch your language! There is a lady present!'

The young man ignored him. He dropped his spade on the ground and turned away to crouch down in front of the dog.

'It's all right, lad,' he crooned softly. 'In't no one going to hurt you. Least not while I'm here.'

The dog seemed to sense what was being said. The tension went out of its emaciated body, although its brown, watchful gaze didn't leave his rescuer's face.

Polly watched as the young man ran his hands gently over the dog's flanks, checking it over. Even from a distance, she could make out the jutting bones of its ribs through the sleek black coat.

'He looks half starved, poor thing,' she said.

'Aye, he is. Nowt more than a bag o' bones. And there's a nasty wound on his neck too. Reckon that's what's putting him in a temper. In't that right, lad?'

'Let me see.' Polly went to approach, but Matthew grabbed her arm, holding her back.

'Have a care,' he said. 'You saw how it went for me.'

'I'm not afraid.' Polly removed her wrist from his grasp and walked over to where the young man still crouched in front of the dog. She took care to approach slowly, tiptoeing over the wet grass.

Even from a distance, she could see the raw wound all the way around the dog's throat. It was crusted with dried blood, but still oozing.

'It doesn't look too deep, but I think it's infected,' she said.

'Aye, that's what I thought.'

'Did he catch it on something, do you think?'

'More likely he's been tied up, and the rope's rubbed it raw.' The young man's face was grim. 'If I could catch the swine who did this to him, I'd string them up too,' he muttered.

'It will need to be cleaned up...' Without thinking, Polly reached forward. The dog whipped round and snapped at her. She snatched her hand back but the dog lunged forward and would have sunk its teeth into her if the young man hadn't managed to grab the scruff of its neck and pull it back. For all it was thin, it was still a powerful beast, but he held on to it fearlessly.

'It's all right, lad,' he murmured. 'She didn't mean you no harm. She were only trying to help you, just like me.' Somehow, miraculously, the dog calmed again, lulled by the low, soothing sound of his voice.

The young man looked up at Polly. 'Did it get you?' he asked.

'Not too badly.' Polly examined her hand where the dog's teeth had grazed her skin. If it hadn't been for the young man's quick actions, her injury might have been much worse. 'It was my own fault anyway.'

'I told you that thing was dangerous.' She had been so preoccupied, she hadn't realised Matthew Elliott was still there, standing behind them. Now the curate stepped in, trying to regain control of the situation. 'I want you to take it away and destroy it,' he ordered.

'No!' Polly cried.

The young man raised his gaze, slow and insulting, to stare at the curate. 'If you want it killed, you'll have to do it.'

They glared at each other for a moment, and Polly could feel the tension building between them. The gravedigger's eyes were as grey and threatening as the storm clouds overhead.

Matthew looked away first. 'Then get it out of here,' he muttered. 'Just get rid of it, before the vicar sees it.'

He turned to Polly, his smile back in place. 'I'll see you safely to the gate,' he offered.

She hesitated for a moment. She would have liked to stay, to see if she could help treat the animal's wound. But the other young man's expression was so forbidding, she didn't feel as if her assistance would be welcome.

She looked back over her shoulder at him as she and Matthew made their way down the path. The young man was still crouched down beside the dog, his arm around its neck, whispering to it. She knew the creature would come to no harm under his protection, whatever anyone else wanted.

'I must apologise for his appalling rudeness,' Matthew spoke up, breaking into her thoughts. 'Be assured I will be having a word with Reverend

Turner about that man.'

'Who is he?' Polly asked.

'The sexton's grandson, I believe. He's had some trouble at home, so the vicar has given permission for him to stay here with his grandfather for a while.'

'What kind of trouble?'

'I don't know. But looking at him, I wouldn't put anything past him.' Matthew shook his head. 'If it were up to me, I would have sent him packing a long time ago. But I'm afraid Reverend Turner is too soft-hearted for his own good.' He looked back at the young man, still cradling the dog. 'Look at them,' he sneered. 'Two strays together.'

They reached the gate and Polly tried to give Matthew his umbrella back, but he insisted she should take it.

'You can return it to the vicarage next time you come,' he said, then added with a smile, 'which means I'll have an excuse to see you again.'

'Thank you.' Polly glanced away past his shoulder, back to where the young man and the dog had been. They had both vanished into the rain.

Chapter Eight

It was a warm September day, and Miss Jennings' Upper Fifth history class was stiflingly hot and stuffy. Christine Fairbrass sat at her wooden desk, drowsy with the heat, watching the columns of swirling dust illuminated by the sun coming in through the tall windows and trying to listen to Miss Jennings' lecture on the Wars of the Roses. Christine loved history, but for once she could barely take in Miss Jennings' light, sing-song voice. It was all she could do to keep her eyes open.

It didn't help that behind her, Joan Cathcart and her cronies were growing restless in the heat.

'Ooh, it's so hot in here,' Betty Evans, one of the girls who vied to be Joan's best friend, was saying dramatically. 'I think I'm going to faint.'

'We need some air,' Sheila Dunbar, another of Joan's friends, joined in. 'There's a horrible smell in here, too. Can you smell it? Like overcooked cabbage.'

'It's probably Fairbrass,' Joan said, loud enough for everyone in the class to hear.

A titter rippled around the room. Christine sat perfectly still, her gaze still fixed on Miss Jennings' hand as it moved across the blackboard. She could feel the back of her neck burning with humiliation.

She lowered her head and sniffed surreptitiously under the arms of her blue cotton dress. It smelled of Sunlight soap and starch, the results of her mother's hard work. Lil Fairbrass took great pride in her daughter's appearance. Every Monday she would pummel Christine's school blouses in the dolly tub, hang them on the line in the shared back yard, starch the collars and cuffs, then lovingly iron them all.

'We might not have much money, but I won't have anyone looking down their nose at you, saying you're not as good as the rest of the girls,' she would say.

If only she knew, Christine thought.

'Is something amusing, girls?' Miss Jennings turned away from the blackboard, her keen gaze skimming across the room. She was a student teacher, barely five years older than the girls of the Upper Fifth. Christine adored her. She had already made up her mind that after her school certificate she would become a teacher just like Miss Jennings, and strut down the corridor with her arms full of books, admired and respected by everyone she met.

The room went quiet. Joan spoke up, her clear, well-spoken voice breaking the silence. 'Please, miss, may we open a window?' she said. 'Only there's an odd smell in here.'

Another snigger came from the back of the class. Christine felt perspiration running down between her shoulder blades that had nothing to do with the warmth of the September day.

Miss Jennings paused for a moment, as if summing up the situation. Her gaze settled briefly on Christine, as if she knew exactly what was going on. Christine felt the blood burn in her face. The last thing she wanted was the teacher's pity.

'Very well,' Miss Jennings said, turning back to the blackboard. 'Open the window, but hurry up about it.'

Joan strode to the front of the classroom, her blonde plait bobbing against her straight spine, and picked up the long wooden pole used to open the high window. In spite of what Miss Jennings had said, she took her time, fitting the metal hook into the fixing on the casement to push it open.

Finally, she finished her task. As she returned to

her desk, she deliberately brushed against Christine's arm with her hip, jogging her arm and making ink splatter across a page of notes.

'Oops! Sorry, Carrot Top!' she sneered.

Behind her, Sheila and Betty hooted with laughter. Miss Jennings swung round.

'What's the matter now?' she said.

'Please, miss, I think Christine Fairbrass has blotted her copybook,' Joan spoke up again.

Miss Jennings looked at Christine. 'How did that happen?'

She stared down at the pitted surface of her wooden desk. 'It was an accident, miss,' she mumbled.

Miss Jennings let out a long sigh. 'Well, clean it up, please. And try not to be so clumsy in future. Now, as I was saying, not everyone approved of Edward's marriage to Elizabeth Woodville...'

She turned away, the chalk squeaking as her hand flew across the blackboard. Christine picked up her blotting paper and tried to soak away the pool of ink that covered her carefully written script. She was determined not to give the other girls the satisfaction of showing how upset she was. But inside she burned with hatred for Joan Cathcart.

Joan was easily the worst of her tormentors. She thought she was better than everyone because her father was on the town council and owned a grocery shop. His delivery bikes, black with 'Cathcart's Fine Foods' written on them in curly gold script, could regularly be seen around the town, although never in Quarry Hill. No one ever had groceries delivered there.

Joan kept her special select group of friends around her. They walked with arms linked and noses in the air. They all lived in nice houses in Weetwood and Roundhay, and their fathers worked in banks and offices, and their mothers stayed at home and did charity work. Joan's father even owned a Ford Tudor Sedan, which she boasted about endlessly.

They had been friendly towards Christine at first. But when she had revealed that she was from Quarry Hill and had won a scholarship, they had quickly decided she wasn't one of them, and had shut her out ever since.

Worse than that, they seemed to resent her presence.

'It's not fair that she comes here free when our parents have to pay three guineas a term,' she had heard Joan saying loudly to Betty and the others just after they had started school.

Five years later, Christine's heart had hardened towards them. She had stopped trying to fit in and win them over. She didn't want to be like them anyway, she told herself.

'Now, who can tell me the name of the first battle of the Wars of the Roses?' Miss Jennings addressed the class.

St Albans. The name came into Christine's head straight away but she pressed her lips together to keep silent. She was fascinated by history and knew all about the various wars and battles, even remembered all the dates. But she didn't dare put up her hand and draw attention to herself.

'Come along, someone must be able to remember?' Miss Jennings' lively gaze roamed around the class. Christine looked down at her hands, her nails bitten down to the quick, and prayed the teacher wouldn't single her out.

'Christine Fairbrass.' Her heart sank at the sound of her own name. 'You must know the answer, surely?'

'St Albans, miss?' Christine whispered reluctantly, keeping her eyes lowered.

'Yes, that's right.' Miss Jennings' voice was warm with approval. 'I might have known you'd get it right. You are my best student.'

'Thank you, miss.'

'St Albans, miss. Thank you, miss,' Joan mimicked, as Miss Jennings turned back to the board. 'Teacher's pet!'

Christine shrank down in her seat in shame. She knew her mother would tell her not to stand for it. 'You're every bit as good as the rest of them,' Lil would say defiantly. 'You've got a scholarship. That means you had to work for your place, unlike them. You're a Fairbrass, girl. Don't you forget it.'

The Fairbrass family fought back. Christine's mother was forever rolling up her sleeves to sort out neighbours who lit fires when she'd put out her washing or occupied the shared privy for longer than they should. But Lil would never understand what it was like at school for Christine. The trouble she endured there was different. It wasn't the kind that could be sorted with a slanging match or setting about someone with a rolling pin. This was sly and subtle, like a thin blade straight to the heart, showing barely a wound but cutting deep all the same.

Christine was desperately lonely and miserable, but she knew she could never tell anyone, especially not her mother. It would break Lil's heart if she thought her daughter was unhappy. Sometimes Christine wished she'd never won that stupid scholarship, but she knew it had been the best moment of her mother's life. Lil Fairbrass had saved and taken in extra washing and mending to pay for the books and pens and stationery that her daughter needed. Christine's five elder brothers had contributed too, all so their little sister could have the chance that they'd never had.

Lil had gone all the way up to Matthias Robinson's on Briggate to buy the dark blue blazer and blouses and gymslips and the school hat with its coloured band, and she had paraded the bags in front of the neighbours when she came home, so everyone in Quarry Hill could see that the Fairbrass family was going up in the world.

Christine couldn't allow the likes of Joan Cathcart to spoil her mother's triumph.

Finally, the lesson was over, and they all surged out on to the school field for break time. The field was separated from the neighbouring boys' school by an invisible line down the middle. Prefects from both schools patrolled the centre, making sure each side kept themselves to themselves. Not that there was any need. The boys ran about like hooligans, shouting and letting off steam, while the girls played sedate skipping games or walked on the grass, arms linked.

Christine found a bench on the edge of the field and sat down quietly to read her book. She chose the bench deliberately because it was close to the

91

border with the boys' school, but not close enough to arouse suspicion.

She felt self-conscious as she took the book out of her bag, knowing he would be watching her. He would have been looking out for her to come, just as he always did. Christine took her time, opening the book and finding her place before she finally allowed her gaze to drift over the boys' half of the field to find him.

And there he was. He was a long way off, on the other side, so far away she couldn't make out his features. But she knew he would have seen her.

The thought made her smile to herself as she opened her book. Knowing he was there made up for a lot of the misery in her day.

'What are you smiling about, Carrot Top?' Joan's shrill voice dragged Christine out of her pleasant daydream. Her tormentor stood very close, flanked by Betty and Sheila, their arms firmly linked to make a barrier.

Normally Christine would have ignored them. But knowing he was watching made her bold.

'Wouldn't you like to know, Dung Cart?' she replied.

Joan's eyes widened as if she'd been slapped. Beside her, Betty fought to keep the smirk off her face. Christine had the feeling that even Joan's inner circle enjoyed seeing their leader's fine feathers ruffled sometimes.

'Come on,' Joan huffed, turning on her heel. 'We don't want to hang around here. Heaven knows what bugs we might catch!'

Christine smiled to herself as she watched her go. Joan Cathcart might have money and a posh car, but Christine had something much more special.

She had a secret love.

He followed her as she walked home from school that afternoon. They both knew better than to meet near the gates – if either of them was seen talking to the other, even out of school, they would be punished severely. But instead of going straight home to Quarry Hill, Christine walked north along Wade Lane, past the almshouses with their steeply gabled roofs, to the recreation ground where she knew he would catch up with her.

She had almost reached the bandstand before she heard his footsteps behind her, coming closer. She smiled to herself but didn't turn round.

Finally, when she couldn't wait any longer, she turned slowly to look at him, savouring the moment when their eyes met, not wanting to rush the pleasure. He was tall and dramatically attractive, with high, sharp cheekbones, olive skin, jet-black hair and eyes as dark as sloes. Even his name was exotic – Oliver Umansky.

He fell into step beside her as they walked for a while, neither of them speaking. Christine was always too tongue-tied to speak first. It was enough for her to have him there, at her side. Her heart skipped in her chest when he reached down and took her hand.

'I was watching you earlier,' he said.

'I know.'

'I saw those other girls talking to you. What were they saying?'

'Nothing.' Christine looked down at the cracked paving slabs beneath her feet. Her school shoes were showing signs of wear after three years, but she polished them every night to make them last.

She felt him send her a sideways look. 'They were being horrible to you again, weren't they? What did they say?'

'It doesn't matter.' Christine shrugged. And suddenly it didn't. Not when he was there by her side, holding her hand. She didn't want the happiest time of her day to be ruined by thoughts of Joan Cathcart. 'Anyway, I'm used to it.'

'They're only jealous, you know.'

'Jealous?' Christine was incredulous. 'Why would they be jealous of me?'

'Because you're pretty and clever, and all the things they'll never be.'

'Get away with you!'

'I mean it. You're a snowy dove trooping with crows.'

She laughed. 'A what?'

'It's from *Romeo and Juliet*. It means you stand out above all others. Christine "doth teach the torches to burn bright",' he quoted.

'I don't know about that,' she said, secretly pleased. Oliver was so clever, he was always saying such wonderful, romantic things to her.

She didn't know why he took such an interest in her. Compared to him, she was nothing special. He was so well-spoken, he obviously came from a good family. She was sure there were other girls who were far more suited to him than she was.

And yet he had chosen her. One day, out of the blue, when she had been sitting on her bench, trying not to cry because of some cruel remark

94

Joan Cathcart had made, she had suddenly heard a voice say: 'You remind me of Cathy Earnshaw.'

She looked up and there was Oliver, standing a few yards away on the other side of the line. He wasn't looking in her direction, but she knew he was speaking to her.

'I beg your pardon?' she'd said.

'I've been watching you for a few days now. You always wander around this field on your own like Cathy Earnshaw on the moors.' He glanced her way, his dark eyes meeting hers. 'You know? *Wuthering Heights?*'

'I've never read it.'

He shook his head. 'Gracious, what do they teach you girls?'

The following day, when she reached her bench, there was a battered copy of *Wuthering Heights* tucked underneath it.

He hadn't spoken to her again for some time, but Christine knew he was watching her from the other side of the field. And when no one else was watching, sometimes he would smile at her, or nod in her direction.

Then, one day when she was walking home from school, he'd followed her.

'I had to speak to you,' he'd told her breathlessly. 'I haven't been able to stop thinking about you.'

Christine was so shocked, it had taken a moment for her to speak. 'I – I've got your book,' she faltered. 'I finished it ages ago ... I didn't like to leave it on the bench...'

She had started to reach into her bag, but he'd stopped her. 'Never mind the book,' he had said.

'Just tell me your name before I go mad.'

And so it began. From then on, they met every day on the way home from school. She found out his name was Oliver, that he was twenty-one years old, and a student teacher at the boys' school. He came from a very old Russian family, and he and several of his relatives had fled the revolution in their homeland eight years earlier. He told her the most extraordinary stories, like something out of a novel. It all sounded dazzlingly exotic to Christine, compared to her humble background.

And yet he still seemed interested in her. He held her hand, recited love poetry to her, told her she was the most beautiful and fascinating girl he had ever met.

And then, one day, he had kissed her. It was a moment Christine knew she would never forget, the moment she fell dizzyingly in love with him.

She knew he loved her too. It was in his passionate kiss today as they sat on a bench by the empty bandstand, the way his tongue plundered her mouth and his hands roamed urgently over her body.

Christine sat up, pushing his hand away. 'Don't,' she said. 'Someone might see us.'

'You're right.' He pulled away from her, his high cheekbones flushed, his enlarged pupils darkening his eyes. 'But I can't help it. You're so beautiful, you make me want you so much.'

Christine leaned against him, enjoying the warm solidity of his body as she listened to him talk. It was a miracle to her that after six months he still loved and desired her.

'Can we meet tomorrow?' he pleaded huskily.

'The usual place?'

Christine hesitated. She looked down, kicking at a tuft of grass.

'I was thinking,' she said. 'Why don't we do something else for a change?'

'Like what?' His tone sharpened.

'I don't know... We could go to the pictures, or out for tea?'

Her eldest brother Tony was courting a girl from Fleet Lane. He was always taking her to the pictures, or she would come round to their house for tea.

'And what if someone saw us? You know I could get into trouble. I could lose my job.'

Is that the only reason? she wondered. 'Anyone would think you were ashamed to be seen with me,' she muttered.

He laughed. 'You know that's not true.'

'Isn't it?'

Oliver sighed. 'Look, it won't always be like this,' he said. 'When I've finished my training and you've left school, we can be together properly, I promise.'

'That's a long way off.'

'Well, you'll just have to be patient, won't you?' He kissed her forehead. 'I'll see you tomorrow, all right? After school?'

'I suppose so.'

'Good girl.' He kissed her again and then got to his feet, brushing the grass off his perfectly pressed trousers. 'Now, I have to go. "Good night, good night. Parting is such sweet sorrow that I shall say good night till it be morrow."'

He gave her an extravagant bow and then he

97

was gone. Christine watched him striding away, up the bank.

It was so romantic, she told herself. They were like Romeo and Juliet, kept apart by circumstances beyond their control.

And look what happened to them.

Christine pushed the thought from her mind. She and Oliver weren't doomed. One day they would be together, she was sure of it. All she had to do was trust, and be patient.

Chapter Nine

'Put the kettle on, Miss Sheridan!'

Bess Bradshaw sang out the now familiar words over her shoulder as she headed up the passageway where her patient, Mrs Gawtrey, was waiting to have her arthritic limbs massaged.

'Yes, Mrs Bradshaw.' Agnes gritted her teeth in frustration and went off to the kitchen. Typical, she thought. She had been accompanying Bess for over a week now, and so far hadn't been allowed to lay her hands on a single patient. She was little more than a glorified servant, carrying Bess' bag, preparing washbowls, or sterilising instruments if she was very lucky.

And sometimes, if the patient was bedbound, too poorly or had no obliging relative around, she had to make the tea.

Agnes was astonished at the quantity of tea Bess Bradshaw managed to get through in the course of a day. Every time they went to see a patient, the kettle would be on and the cups would be set out on the tray even before they'd managed to get their coats off.

Most of the time Agnes refused to join in, though she knew it irritated Bess to see her sitting there, empty hands folded in her lap, surreptitiously checking her watch every five minutes. But apart from thinking it was a complete waste of time, there was a practical reason for Agnes' refusal. She knew that if she drank the gallons of tea offered, sooner or later she would have to succumb to one of the disgusting outside privies. She had been forced by circumstance to use one on her second day, and she never, ever wanted to repeat the experience.

After a couple of days, she had ventured to suggest that they might get through their rounds quicker if they didn't stop for tea all the time, but Bess had been adamant.

'You may not think it, Miss Sheridan, but spending time with the patients, chatting to them and raising their spirits, is just as important as changing dressings and giving injections,' she had said. 'You'd be surprised what you get out of someone when you're sitting down with a brew together. They'll tell you all kinds of things they wouldn't bother the doctor about, things that can help their treatment. You want to be a bit less eager to pack up and get away all the time, then you might learn something.'

There's no chance of me learning anything at this rate, Agnes thought as she arranged the teacups on a tray and waited for the kettle to boil.

She felt like a maid of all work. If she went on like this for much longer, she would soon have forgotten all her nursing training.

Loud laughter was coming from Mrs Gawtrey's bedroom as Agnes carried the tray up the passageway. But it stopped as soon as she walked into the room. No need to ask what – or who – they were laughing about, she thought bitterly. Agnes had become the subject of much amusement among the patients, with Bess regaling them all with her funny stories. Her favourite was about the time when Agnes was knocked flying into the dustbins by Lil Fairbrass. It seemed to grow more colourful every time she told it.

Bess, of course, was completely unabashed, smiling blandly at Agnes as if butter wouldn't melt in her big mouth.

But for once Agnes forgot to be irritated as she was faced with the astonishing sight of Queenie Gawtrey's bedroom.

It was like stepping into a gypsy waggon, it was so crammed with colourful knick-knacks. Every surface seemed to be covered with brass oil lamps, copper milk churns, china ornaments and vases of coloured glass, and wooden panelling painted with birds, vines and fruit in bright shades of red, gold and green.

In the middle of it all sat Queenie herself. In spite of her great age – Bess reckoned she must be at least eighty, although no one was certain – her hair was the darkest jet black Agnes had ever seen, in stark contrast to her white powdered face and slash of crimson lipstick. Her eyebrows were two thin black arches drawn high on her forehead, giving her an oddly surprised look.

'You'll like Queenie Gawtrey,' Bess had told her that morning. 'She's quite a character.'

Agnes' heart had sunk. Over the past week, she had heard Bess Bradshaw say those words countless times, and on each occasion it had meant one thing – trouble. As it turned out, Quarry Hill was full of characters, most of them not particularly pleasant.

'Queenie was once a nurse herself, or so she likes to tell people,' Bess had informed Agnes as they'd cycled into Quarry Hill that morning. 'Not that she ever needed any kind of formal training. All her knowledge came from her mother and grandmother, who taught her all the old Romany ways of healing.'

'She's a gypsy?' Agnes asked.

'So she says. Although her travelling days are long behind her, thanks to her chronic arthritis. Well, it wouldn't do to be on the road at her age, I suppose.'

She might be infirm, but Queenie's wits seemed sharp enough as she greeted Agnes.

'So this is her, is it?' she said, her voice a low, throaty croak.

'This is Miss Sheridan,' Bess said.

'Miss, is it? In't you got another name?'

'Agnes.'

'But never Aggie, I'll bet?'

Bess laughed. 'How did you know that?'

'You'd be surprised what I know,' Queenie replied mysteriously. 'My eyes might be dim, but I've still got the sight.'

It was true, Agnes thought. The old woman's

101

eyes were opaque with age, but Agnes could still feel the sharpness behind her gaze.

'Only one person ever called you Aggie,' she said. 'And he's long gone, isn't he? Gone but not forgotten.'

An image of Daniel flashed into her mind. Agnes fought not to react, aware of Bess Bradshaw watching her. 'I don't know what you mean,' she managed to say.

Thankfully, Bess interrupted before Queenie could say any more. 'Right, let's get on,' she said. 'Fetch that blanket from in front of the fire, Miss Sheridan. Then you can pour the tea.'

Agnes handed it to her, still aware of Queenie's gaze fixed on her. The old woman unnerved her.

Fortunately, by the time she had finished pouring the tea, Queenie seemed to have lost interest in Agnes.

'Can't say as this massage lark is doing much good, to tell the truth,' the old woman grumbled, as Bess got to work. 'Now, my grandmother always used to swear by a liniment for arthritis. Made it herself, she did, out of Fuller's Earth and horse piss. It draws the pain out, you see,' she explained over Bess' shoulder to Agnes. 'It has to be fresh, mind. While it's still hot is best.'

'Yes, well, Miss Sheridan is not going out chasing horses and carts down the road, and no more am I. Not even for you, Queenie lass,' Bess said briskly.

'Ah, well, I s'pose I'll have to make do wi' another brew.' Queenie drained her teacup and peered into it. 'What's this?' she said. 'No leaves?'

'I used the strainer,' Agnes said.

'The strainer!' Queenie looked outraged. 'How am I supposed to read my fortune?'

Agnes glanced at Bess. 'I'm sorry; I didn't know—'

'Queenie fancies herself a bit of a fortune teller,' Bess explained.

'A bit of a fortune teller?' Queenie turned on her. 'I'll have you know they were queueing up on Bridlington seafront when I had my tent down there.' She looked meaningfully at Agnes. 'You'd like your leaves read, wouldn't you, lovey?'

Agnes shook her head. 'No, thank you.'

'Go on. I bet I could tell a lot about you from your leaves. I can already see you've suffered a great deal of sadness in your life. I'm right, aren't I?'

'Let's do the other leg, shall we?' Bess said briskly.

'I can tell what's in your future too,' Queenie went on, her gaze still fixed on Agnes.

'We know what's in our future, Queenie. Three sets of dressing changes, four bed baths and a bad case of measles!' Bess joked. But the old woman ignored her. As Agnes went to take the empty cup from her, she grabbed her other hand.

'I'll read your palm instead, shall I?'

'No!' Agnes tried to pull away but Queenie was surprisingly strong for an arthritic old lady.

'Ooh, I was right,' she said. 'You have had a lot of sadness in your life, haven't you?' She passed a gnarled finger over the softness of Agnes' palm. 'Yes, lots of troubles ... and they're not over yet, are they? There's something in your past that casts a shadow over your present...' She looked

103

up at Agnes, and the years seemed to fall away, leaving her gaze as sharp and dark as jagged jet. '"Wash me thoroughly from mine iniquity, and cleanse me from my sin,"' she quoted in a high, strange voice that didn't seem to belong to her.

Agnes snatched her hand away, hiding it in the folds of her blue dress. Her palm felt scalded. 'I – I don't know what you're talking about.'

'Come on, we've got work to do,' Bess interrupted sternly. 'We don't have time for fairground sideshows. Go and wash up those cups, Miss Sheridan, if you please.'

Agnes was silently thankful for Bess' intervention as she escaped. She stood in the tiny kitchen, trying to calm herself down.

Queenie couldn't know, she told herself. It was nothing more than a lucky guess.

But to say something like that... How could she possibly have picked that particular quotation out of nowhere?

Agnes thought about her cold, cheerless room at St Jude's, and the Bible quotation that hung on the wall in front of her bed, so it was the first thing she saw every morning, and the last thing every night.

Psalm 51, verse 2: 'Wash me thoroughly from mine iniquity, and cleanse me from my sin'.

Agnes scratched at her palm, as if she could somehow rub away the lines that had given her away.

Agnes was still trembling when they left Queenie's house. She tried to pretend she wasn't, but Bess had seen her hands shaking as she put her wash things away in her bag.

'What do you suppose Queenie meant just now?' Bess couldn't resist asking.

The young woman's face was carefully blank. 'I don't know what you mean.'

'When she was telling your fortune? She came out with something very strange, don't you think?'

'I have no idea.' Agnes' voice was dismissive, but Bess could hear the strain beneath.

'I think she was quoting from the Bible.'

'Was she? I wasn't really paying attention.'

Liar, Bess thought. She glanced at the girl's sharp profile. Her face seemed composed enough, but her lips were pressed tightly together, as if to stop herself from crying. The old lady had upset her far more than she was willing to let on.

For a moment, Bess felt sorry for her.

'You don't want to pay any attention to that daft old bat,' she said. 'She's always going on about something. It's all nonsense.'

'I know.' Agnes looked at her, and the mask was back in place, pointed chin lifted, ready to face the world. 'Shall we go?' she said, checking her watch. 'We don't want to be late, do we?'

Clock watching as usual, Bess thought, as the girl wheeled her bicycle out of the yard ahead of her. Or was it that she couldn't wait to put some distance between herself and Queenie Gawtrey?

Wash me thoroughly from mine iniquity, and cleanse me from my sin...

Bess couldn't help feeling the mystery of Agnes Sheridan had just deepened.

Chapter Ten

Matthew Elliott wasn't at the vicarage when Polly returned his umbrella. The vicar's house-keeper told her he was out visiting a new family in the parish.

'He'll be so sorry he missed you,' she added with a knowing smile. 'Between you and me, he's been waiting every day for you to arrive.'

Polly tried to smile back, but inside she felt relieved. She had been putting off coming back for nearly two weeks because she found Matthew's interest in her rather overwhelming. The last thing she wanted was to give him any encouragement.

After she'd left the vicarage, she followed the path to the churchyard. As she turned the corner around the church, her heart stopped in her chest at the sight of a tall, dark-haired figure standing over Frank's grave. It took a moment for her to recognise the sexton's grandson, hacking back the low branches of the yew tree that overhung the headstone. Once again, he had hung up his jacket and his shirtsleeves were rolled back to reveal sinewy forearms.

He stopped when he saw her approach, his expression wary.

'Sorry, miss,' he mumbled, lowering his knife. 'I can come back later...'

'It's all right,' Polly replied. 'I don't mind you being here, if you've got work to do.'

'Much obliged.' He touched the peak of his cap and went on with his work.

Polly had said she didn't mind, but she was painfully conscious of the young man close by as she laid her flowers on Frank's grave. This time she didn't force herself to look at the inscription. She didn't want anyone to witness her distress.

The young man kept his back turned, as if he didn't want to see it either.

Finally, she stood up and brushed the dirt from her dress. It was a warm day for early October, the sun high in the sky, and Polly had put on the cornflower-sprigged summer dress that Frank had always liked best.

She was going to walk away, but something stopped her. It was a question that had been troubling her ever since her last visit, and she knew she wouldn't be able to rest until she had an answer.

She cleared her throat. 'I wanted to ask you ... what happened to the dog?'

The young man didn't turn round, but she saw his broad shoulders stiffen. 'It's gone,' he muttered finally.

'Oh no!' Polly was filled with dismay. 'You didn't–'

'No, miss.' He shook his head. 'I wouldn't do anything like that.'

Polly let out a sigh of relief. 'I'm glad. Where has it gone, do you know?'

'No idea, miss.' The man went back to his work, ending the conversation. Polly watched him for a moment.

'It's such a shame,' she said. 'I wish it could have found a good home here. I don't like to think of it out there, fending for itself...'

The man turned slowly to look at her over his shoulder. He paused for a moment, as if weighing something up in his mind. Then he said, 'Can you keep a secret, miss?'

He said it in such a low voice, Polly wasn't sure she'd heard him at first. 'Of course,' she said. 'But what...'

He set down his shears on the grass. 'Come wi' me,' he said.

Polly followed him past the back of the church, through the churchyard, until they reached a narrow gate set in the wall. The young man shouldered it open and led the way into an untended area, a small patch of wasteland with a couple of low, tin-roofed outbuildings at the far end, screened by overgrown shrubs.

Polly picked her way through the long grass after him as he headed for the nearest shed. 'What–' she started to ask, but he put a finger to his lips to silence her.

'Don't make too much noise,' he warned. 'He's still a bit afeared around strangers.'

He gently lifted the latch on the shed door. 'It's all right, lad,' Polly heard him whisper. 'It's only me.'

He opened the door and Polly heard a rustle inside, followed by the scrabble of clawed feet moving across the wooden floor. She peered over his shoulder into the gloom and saw a dark shape trotting towards them.

Its hackles rose when it saw Polly. A low, warning growl came from its throat as a pair of brown eyes eyed her warily. Then, suddenly, it stopped growling and came to her.

Polly reached out and let it nuzzle her hand. 'Hello, you beautiful creature,' she said. 'My goodness, you look a lot better than the last time I saw you.'

In the shaft of sunlight flooding in through the open shed door, she could see the dog's skinny flanks had filled out, its ribs no longer jutting painfully through its now glossy black coat.

'That wound's healing up nicely,' she said. 'Someone's been looking after you very well.'

The young man coloured slightly. 'I've just been chucking him a few scraps now and then,' he muttered.

'You've been doing more than that, I can tell. Look at him. He seems so happy.' She could see the trust shining out of the dog's warm brown eyes. He looked as if he was smiling, his long pink tongue lolling from his mouth.

'All he needed was a bit of love and somewhere to call home.' There was something about the way he said it that made Polly turn to look at him in the gloom. His face was all hard planes and angles, his grey eyes too full of anger and resentment to be handsome. A faint scar ran down one cheek.

She dragged her gaze away. 'Are you going to keep him?' she asked.

'I reckon so. My granddad's said he won't have him in the cottage, but I don't reckon it will be long before he changes his mind about that. Eh, boy?' He bent down and fussed the dog. 'He says this fella's a mangy beast, but I've caught him feeding him a few scraps too, when he doesn't think I'm watching.' His mouth curved in a half smile.

'What does the vicar think about it?'

'I haven't spoken to him about it yet, but I reckon he'll be all right. He's a good man.' He looked at her warily. 'You won't tell your friend the curate, will you?'

Polly blushed. 'He's not my friend.'

She crouched down and stroked the dog, caressing his velvety ears. He responded by licking her hands.

The young man watched her. 'In't you scared to touch him, after he nearly took your hand off?'

'Why should I be? He only lashed out because he was afraid.'

'Aye, that's true enough. But I don't reckon I would have stood a chance of keeping him if you'd made trouble for him.'

'Why would I do that?'

'There's plenty who would.'

Their eyes met in the darkness of the shed, and Polly felt the sudden rush of an emotion she hadn't felt in a long time.

She turned away sharply, her attention back on the dog. 'Have you given him a name yet?'

'I've been calling him Job.'

'Job? That's an odd name for a dog.'

The young man scuffed the toe of his muddy boot on the bare boards. 'It seemed only right to give him a name from the Bible. Granddad says that Job had a lot of troubles, and I reckon this one's had more than his fair share of troubles too.

Eh, lad?'

Polly straightened up. 'I'm glad he's found a good home, at any rate.'

'Everyone deserves a second chance,' the young man muttered.

Polly glanced at him. There was something odd about the way he'd said it.

'I'd best go,' she said.

They slipped outside. As the young man lowered the latch, Polly heard a gentle whining from the other side of the door. She smiled.

'He wants you to stay with him.'

'It's you he wants,' the young man replied. 'He never cries when I leave him. Nor Granddad neither. I reckon he likes you.'

'I like him too,' Polly said.

As she started to walk away, the young man called out, 'Happen you could come and visit him again sometime?'

She turned to look over her shoulder at him. He was clutching his cap in both hands, a truculent expression on his face, as if he was angry with himself for asking.

Polly smiled. 'I'd like that,' she said.

Chapter Eleven

Agnes was about to be told off again.

After nearly three weeks of following Bess Bradshaw around, she had come to know when a reprimand was due. Bess wouldn't say anything in front of the patient, but her face would tighten, her brows would draw together in a stern line, and she would fold her mouth so that her lips disappeared. Then all Agnes could do was brace herself for the onslaught she knew was coming.

Sure enough, as they stepped out of Mrs Reed's cottage, Bess turned on her and said, 'And what was that all about, may I ask?'

'I don't know what you mean,' Agnes said, although she knew very well.

'Contradicting me in front of Mrs Reed like that. I wish you'd keep your opinions to yourself. It doesn't do for Queen's Nurses to be bickering in front of patients, you know.'

'I wasn't bickering,' Agnes replied calmly. 'And it wasn't simply an opinion. It's a medical fact that obesity puts unnecessary strain on the arthritic joints—'

'Don't you think I know that?' Bess snapped back. 'You're not the only one who's a trained nurse, you know, even though you seem to think you are!'

Then you should do something about it, Agnes said silently.

Winifred Reed was sixty years old, bedridden with arthritis, and easily one of the fattest women Agnes had ever seen. She lay marooned on her bed, her face lost in a sea of quivering chins, her flannel nightdress stretched over acres of blubbery flesh.

Agnes had been quite terrified every time the woman shifted on the bed. The springs groaned so painfully under her weight, at any moment she had expected the bedframe to splinter and crash

112

through the floor, taking Mrs Reed and them with it.

And yet the patient passed the time doing crosswords and eating cake. And Bess did nothing to stop her.

'All I suggested was that she should stop eating so much and try doing some exercise,' Agnes said.

'Yes, and I'm sure that did her a lot of good, listening to your lecture!' Bess retorted. 'You do realise you've just gone and undone weeks of work, don't you?'

'I don't understand.'

'Believe it or not, Miss Sheridan, I have been trying to educate Mrs Reed. But it's not an easy job, breaking the habits of a lifetime. And Mrs Reed is not an easy woman either. She's very sensitive when it comes to her weight. You have to approach these things slowly and carefully. Not like a bull in a ruddy china shop!'

'I'm sorry,' Agnes said quietly. 'I didn't know.'

'No, and you never bother to ask either. You just jump straight in, assuming you know every- thing.'

'Yes, but surely–'

'Really, Miss Sheridan, I do wish you'd stop offering your opinions all the time. You might know all there is to know about nursing, but you don't understand the first thing about people.' Bess shook her head. 'If you want to be a Queen's Nurse, you'll have to learn that not everything is as cut and dried as it is in your textbooks.'

'I don't know if I'll ever be a Queen's Nurse, since I'm never allowed to do anything!' Agnes muttered.

Bess Bradshaw stared at her. 'What are you on about? You're always doing something.'

'I make tea and wash instruments,' Agnes said.

'And you go to lectures.'

'What use are lectures, if I'm never allowed any practical experience?'

Bess sighed impatiently. 'As I've already explained several times, they're a funny lot in Quarry Hill. They don't take kindly to strangers. It takes a bit of time to win their trust.'

'How am I going to do that when all I ever do is put the kettle on? I am quite capable, you know,' Agnes said. 'I've worked in Theatre and assisted with complicated surgical procedures.'

She could have bitten her tongue the moment she said it. Bess' eyes lit up with that familiar mocking glint.

'Have you now?' Her mouth twitched, and Agnes knew she had amused her again. No doubt Bess would tease her mercilessly for it back at the district nurses' house.

But then the Assistant Superintendent surprised her by adding, 'I suppose you're right.'

Agnes stopped in her tracks. 'What?'

'It's about time you started taking on more nursing duties. And you can start by giving Mr Shapcott his bath this afternoon.'

Agnes stared at her. 'Do you mean it?'

'Of course. If you think you can manage it?'

Bess was teasing her, but Agnes didn't mind. She was too delighted at the thought of actually doing some real nursing. Even if it was the kind of nursing a probationer would usually do.

'Yes, I can,' she said.

'Good, that's settled, then.' Bess mounted her bicycle, and Agnes followed suit. She was so excited, she barely noticed when she pedalled through a puddle and soaked her stockings.

Just to make the day even better, they arrived back in Steeple Street before lunch was over, so Agnes was able to eat with the others for once. Afterwards, she went off to the district room to sterilise the instruments Bess had used that morning, ready for that afternoon's round.

Phil Fletcher came in as Agnes was loading up the temperamental old steriliser. The other student nurse was out of breath, still dressed in her coat, bag in her hand.

'I've missed lunch, haven't I?' she groaned. 'I knew it! I got a wretched puncture and had to wheel the bike all the way back from Otley.'

'You must be worn out,' Agnes said.

'I am.' Phil flopped down on the wooden chair. 'I'm almost too tired to go to the kitchen and beg Dottie to make me a sandwich.'

Agnes smiled sympathetically. She and Phil might not have got off to the best start, but over the past three weeks Agnes had learned that her fellow trainee's bark was much worse than her bite. Phil was a hardworking girl, fiercely bright, and most of her grumpiness stemmed from the fact that she and her mentor Miss Templeton covered a rural district nearly twenty miles away, and she had to cycle there and back every day on a worn-out old bicycle.

After seeing her coming home every evening in a state of exhaustion, Agnes had begun to understand why she looked forward to a relaxing soak in the bath.

'Would you like me to do your sterilising for you?' she offered.

Phil's eyes flickered open. 'Would you?'

'I'm just doing mine, so it'd be no trouble. Here, pass me your bag.'

'Thank you, you're an angel.' Phil handed it to her. 'Honestly, you don't know how lucky you are, working just round the corner in Quarry Hill.'

'I don't know about that,' Agnes said. 'It's rather grim.'

'Yes, but at least you don't have to cycle a hundred miles a day! Honestly, if the Association doesn't get me a motorcycle soon, I might just give up.' Phil ran her hand through her hair. 'Anyway, listen to me going on. How was your morning? Has Mrs Bradshaw let you anywhere near a patient yet, or is she still hogging them all to herself?'

'Actually, she's promised I can give a patient their bath this afternoon.'

'A bath, eh? Goodness, how daring. You'll be cutting their toenails next. How did that come about?'

'I had it out with her.'

Phil sat up straighter. 'You didn't?'

'I did.'

'Oh dear, I'm not sure that was wise,' Phil said.

'It worked, didn't it? I'm actually going to be doing some nursing at last. Well, after a fashion,' Agnes amended. 'Anyway, I think Mrs Bradshaw actually respected me for it,' she said. 'You know how fond of plain speaking she is, so I was just as plain with her.'

Agnes was very proud of herself, when she thought about it. She only wished she had thought of trying it sooner.

'If you say so, although I can't say I've ever heard of anyone getting the better of Bess Bradshaw.' Phil stifled a yawn with the back of her hand. 'So who is the lucky patient on the receiving end of your delicate ministrations?' she asked.

'Mr Shapcott.'

Phil's eyes widened. 'Isaiah Shapcott?'

'I think so. We haven't called on him before so I thought he must be a new patient. Why? Have you heard of him?'

'Oh, my dear, everyone in Steeple Street has heard of Isaiah Shapcott.' Phil grinned at her. 'And I hate to be the one to tell you this, but I think Bess might well have got her revenge on you after all!'

Chapter Twelve

Christine lay on her back, watching the cobwebs drifting in the breeze from the open window. Outside, she could hear the metallic clank of a tinker going past on his bicycle, plying his wares, and the rancid smell of yesterday's frying drifting up from the fish-and-chip shop next door.

Underneath her, the sheets felt threadbare and greasy. Christine shuddered to think how many people had lain on them before her.

'Penny for your thoughts?'

117

She turned to look at Oliver as he lay next to her, her head resting in the crook of his arm. His gaze was fixed on her, dark and intense, a slight smile on his soft lips. His olive skin still gleamed with perspiration from their love-making.

'I was just wondering how long it'd been since they washed these sheets,' she said.

Oliver laughed. 'How romantic! And there was I, expecting something truly profound.' He shook his head. 'You're a funny one, Christine Fairbrass.'

'I can't help it,' she said. 'I don't like this place. I swear something bit me last time I was here. It's–' She struggled to think of a word she'd read recently. 'Tawdry,' she said.

'Tawdry or not, it's all I can afford,' Oliver said. 'But if my princess is not happy with it, then I will try to find a heavenly bower more suited to her taste,' he replied with a touch of mockery.

'I don't know why we can't just go to your lodgings.' Christine spoke the words that had been on her mind for a while. 'You wouldn't have to pay anything then.'

He grinned. 'My landlady would love that! She runs a respectable boarding house. She will not put up with lady callers in the rooms!' he mimicked her high-pitched voice.

'But surely if we're courting...?'

'It wouldn't matter to her, she still wouldn't allow it.'

Christine swallowed down her disappointment. She was hoping Oliver would reassure her that they were indeed courting, because sometimes it didn't really feel as if they were. She understood why they had to be careful, but that didn't stop her feeling like a dirty little secret.

But she had to be content. Oliver might not be able to declare himself in public, but he certainly showed her in private how much he loved her, with his wonderful, romantic words and blissful love-making.

There were many girls who would give a lot for such an ardent lover, she told herself.

She sat up, pushing back the sheets and sliding her feet on to the bare wooden floor.

'Where are you going?' Oliver asked.

'I have to go home.'

'Surely not so soon? I'd hoped you might be able to stay a bit longer.'

'I can't,' she said, looking around for her clothes. 'My mum will be expecting me back.'

'Where does she think you are?'

Christine slid her gaze away. 'I told her I had to stay late at school for extra studies.'

'Well, I am teaching you a thing or two, I suppose!'

'Don't!' Christine turned on him. 'It doesn't feel right, lying to my mother. She doesn't deserve it.'

'Would you rather we stopped meeting?'

'No!' Christine replied, a shade too quickly. 'I just wish I could be honest with her, that's all. Couldn't you at least meet her?' she pleaded with him.

Oliver shook his head. 'And have your brothers tear me apart with their bare hands?'

'It wouldn't be like that,' Christine assured him quickly, although deep down she wasn't sure what her brothers would do, or her mother for that matter. 'Please, Oliver? You'll have to meet

119

her sometime, won't you?'

'Yes, but not just yet.'

'When?'

'Soon, I promise.'

She turned to face him. 'You do love me, don't you?'

'You know I do.'

'And you want to be with me?'

His mouth twisted. 'I'm here, aren't I?'

She blushed. 'I don't mean like that. I mean...' She paused, the words sticking in her throat.

Oliver reached for her hand, his expression mock-solemn. 'Christine Fairbrass, I love you. I adore you. I worship you. And one day, when the time is right, we will declare our love to the world and I will marry you.'

'Will you? Will you really?'

'I just told you so, didn't I? Now come back to bed.'

'I can't...' she started to say. But his fingers were trailing down the bare skin of her back, setting all her nerve endings on fire, and she knew she wouldn't be able to refuse him for long.

Who cared if they had to keep their romance a secret? she thought as she succumbed to Oliver's embrace. He loved her He wanted to marry her. And that made everything all right.

Isaiah Shapcott lived in an area of Quarry Hill Agnes had never seen before.

Bess led the way, pushing her bicycle down narrow alleyways and under low arches. It was a dull, drizzly day, and barely any daylight penetrated the gloomy, stinking warren. Agnes was used to the overcrowded yards, but here some of the houses had fallen into ruins, leaving mountains of cracked walls and crumbling rubble, over which children swarmed and played.

Finally, Bess stopped in a tiny, dark courtyard.

'Here we are,' she said. 'That's Mr Shapcott's cottage over there.' She pointed to a solitary door and two windows, one to the side and one above. The grimy glass on the lower window had been plastered over with yellowing newspaper.

Agnes looked at her. 'Aren't you coming with me?'

Bess shook her head. 'As you've said yourself, you're quite capable.' Her mouth twitched. 'Oh, don't look like that, Miss Sheridan. I'm sure giving someone a bath will present no difficulty for a nurse who's assisted with complicated surgical procedures!'

'Well, can you tell me something about the patient at least?' Agnes said as Bess turned her bicycle around.

'You'll find out for yourself soon enough!' And with that the Assistant Superintendent pedalled out the way they'd come, ducking under the low archway.

Agnes watched her go. I'll show you, she thought. She had no idea who or what lay in wait for her inside the cottage, but she was utterly determined to succeed in her task, if only to prove a point to Bess Bradshaw.

A group of children gathered in the entrance to the yard, watching her with interest. Agnes smiled at them as she propped her bicycle against the wall and knocked on Mr Shapcott's front door.

'Who is it?' came a muffled voice from inside.

'It's the district nurse, Mr Shapcott.'

'Bugger off.'

The children laughed. Agnes squared her shoulders.

'Open the door, please, Mr Shapcott.'

'No.'

More laughter from behind her. Agnes' face began to flame. 'You have to open the door.'

'Who says?'

She didn't have an answer to that, so she rattled the latch harder. 'Let me in,' she commanded, in her sharpest nurse's voice.

It seemed to work. There was a silence, then the muffled voice said, 'Wait there a minute.'

Agnes waited. She risked a glance over her shoulder. The children had gathered in a knot, watching with interest.

She heard the window opening above her and stepped back to look up – just in time to see a pair of bony hands emerging, holding a china chamber pot.

Agnes realised what was happening and threw herself out of the way a split second before the contents of the pot came down, splashing all over the cobbles.

The children fell about laughing.

'Oh, do shut up!' Agnes snapped at them as she examined the hem of her coat. Her shoes and stockings seemed to have got the worst of it. But it could have been a lot worse, she thought with a shudder.

'You know the door's open, don't you?' one of the boys called out from the archway. 'No one locks their doors round here, missus!'

One of the other children muttered something she couldn't catch, and they all laughed again.

Struggling to hold on to what was left of her dignity, Agnes stepped over the disgusting puddle, went back to the front door and tried the latch. Sure enough, the door swung open.

Inside the cottage was dark and stank of urine, stale grease and the tell-tale sweet odour of bugs. A meagre coal fire sputtered in the grate, surrounded by a clothes horse festooned with greying, stained long johns. From the sour odour they gave off, they hadn't been well washed.

Agnes searched around for somewhere clean to hang her coat and put down her bag. She finally found a stack of old copies of the *Sporting Life* by the fire and spread out a few pages on the kitchen table.

'Get out! Get out or I'll call t'police!' a thin, wavering voice called from upstairs as she washed her hands under the rusting tap.

'Not until I've given you your bath, Mr Shapcott.' Over the sound of running water she heard the creak of the stairs.

'I don't need one. I had one last week.'

Agnes turned round and started in shock at the sight of Mr Shapcott. He was scarcely bigger than a child, his threadbare clothes hanging off his slight frame. According to his notes he was thirty-seven, but it was difficult to tell his age because his face was so ingrained with dirt. His ashy brown hair stood up in filthy tufts around a blackened face.

Agnes looked him up and down. 'I can see

that's not true,' she said briskly. 'Now, where is your bath tub?'

'I in't telling you.'

Most of the residents of Quarry Hill kept their tin tubs hanging up in the yard. But it took at least two people to bring one in and, since Bess had abandoned her, Agnes didn't think she could manage it alone.

'Very well, we'll have to make do with a wash instead,' she said. 'I'll put the kettle on to boil.'

'You'll do no such thing!' Mr Shapcott stood in front of the range, blocking her path. As he spoke, his hands moved restlessly, scratching his chest through his filthy shirt. Agnes shuddered to imagine what nastiness she would find under there. 'You just go away and mind your own business, missus.'

If only I could, Agnes thought. She could feel her own skin crawling at the thought of touching him, but it had to be done. 'I'm afraid I can't leave until I've made you clean and presentable.'

'You'll wait a long time, then!'

'Don't be like that, Mr Shapcott. I'm sure you'll feel better once you–' She turned round, the kettle in her hand. 'Mr Shapcott?' she called out. But he had vanished.

Agnes set the kettle down on the draining board. 'Mr Shapcott, where are you?'

'I daresay he's locked himself in the cupboard. That's his usual hiding place.'

She swung round to see Bess Bradshaw standing in the doorway.

'I came to see how you were getting on,' she said.

Agnes pushed a stray wisp of hair off her face. 'Very well, thank you,' she replied, with all the dignity she could muster.

'Except you've managed to lose your patient.'

'I...'

Without waiting for an answer, Bess pushed past her and crossed the room to a tiny broom cupboard under the stairs. She rapped smartly on the door.

'Mr Shapcott? Are you in there?'

'And you can bugger off an' all!'

Bess sighed. 'Very well, Mr Shapcott, we'll go,' she said. 'But you know this can't go on for ever. We'll have to give you a bath one of these days.'

A muffled oath came from behind the door, making Agnes blush.

'Come on,' Bess said, 'let's leave him to it.'

Agnes looked back at the cupboard door, unwilling to accept defeat. 'I'm sure I could persuade him to come out.'

'Not in a month of Sundays,' Bess said. 'No one's managed it yet, in all the years I've been here.'

'Then why did you tell me to give him a bath?' Agnes asked as she followed her outside.

Bess sent her a teasing look. 'I wanted to see how long it would take for him to run rings around you. Oh, don't look at me like that, lass. I were only having a bit of fun with you.'

'A bit of fun?' Agnes echoed in disbelief. 'But he – he tried to empty a chamber pot over me!'

'He didn't?' Bess hooted with laughter. 'Oh, that's a new one! Wait till I tell the others about that!'

Agnes was so full of rage she couldn't trust herself to speak. All she'd wanted to do was to prove herself, and Bess Bradshaw had made a fool of her again.

And then she noticed something else.

'Where's my bicycle?'

Bess frowned. 'I don't know, do I? Where did you leave it?'

'Just here.' Agnes stood in front of the blank space and looked around. The yard was suspiciously empty. The children had all disappeared, like rats down a hole.

'Someone must have pinched it,' Bess voiced the thought that was going through Agnes' head.

'I thought you said people here wouldn't touch a district nurse's bicycle?'

'Happen they know you're not really a district nurse,' Bess said with a touch of spite.

Agnes watched her helplessly as she retrieved her own bicycle from the other side of the yard and mounted it. 'But what shall I do?'

'Reckon you'll have to start walking, won't you?' Bess gave her a wink then cycled off, leaving Agnes standing in the yard.

It took her a long time to find her way out of the warren of Quarry Hill on foot. All the time, she kept looking around for any sign of the children who might have stolen her bicycle. But they were nowhere to be seen.

Finally, she reached a street she recognised, which opened up into a wider road, and she could breathe again. The rain had started to fall steadily and she pulled her coat tightly around her. She bit her lip, determined not to cry.

Bess' cruel remark had stung.

Happen they know you're not really a district nurse.

Agnes was doing her best. She studied hard, and did everything she was supposed to. It wasn't her fault that things seemed to keep going wrong for her, or that she couldn't get any of the patients to like her.

She kicked at a wall in frustration. I don't care, she told herself. I hate district nursing, I hate Quarry Hill, and most of all I hate Bess Bradshaw. The Assistant Superintendent was probably already back in Steeple Street, having a good laugh with the other nurses about Agnes' latest misadventure.

She dashed away an angry tear with the back of her hand. She wouldn't give Bess the satisfaction of seeing her cry, at any rate. It was just what she wanted.

Agnes so wished she were back in the Nightingale, looking after the patients in a nice clean ward where she knew exactly what she was doing.

But even as she wished it, she knew it could never happen. Those days were long gone.

Within a moment, she realised she was lost again. Somewhere she had taken another wrong turning and ended up in a part of the city she didn't recognise. There were some shops, and a pub, and a rundown bed and breakfast.

Agnes paused on the corner to get her bearings, when her attention was briefly caught by a couple caught in a passionate embrace just inside the doorway of the bed and breakfast.

Embarrassed, she started to avert her gaze, but as the girl pulled away a bright flash of copper hair caught the corner of Agnes' eye. She looked round and found herself staring into the face of Christine Fairbrass.

She didn't know which of them was more shocked and embarrassed. Christine grabbed the young man's arm and pulled him away hurriedly down the street. A moment later, they were gone.

Chapter Thirteen

'Here she is again.'

Henry Slater nodded his grizzled head towards the lych gate. The two men were making the most of the Indian summer to cut back the overgrown shrubs at the far end of the churchyard, but Henry kept having to stop because he couldn't catch his breath. Job lay a short distance away, enjoying the October sunshine, watching them from between his outstretched paws.

'Who?' Finn didn't look up. He didn't need his grandfather to tell him Polly was there. He could sense her presence, like a prickle at the back of his neck.

'Your young lady.'

'She in't my young lady,' Finn muttered, hacking at a thick branch.

'You always seem to be with her these days. Sneaking off when you think I aren't looking.'

Finn felt an uncomfortable flush rising in his face. 'I pass the time of day with her sometimes, that's all.'

'Is that right? I've never known you say more than two words to anyone before.'

'I'm just being polite. Nowt wrong with that, is there?'

'Nay, don't look at me like that, lad. I'm pleased for you. She seems like a nice lass.'

His words hung heavily between them.

'Too nice for me,' Finn said bitterly.

Henry sighed. 'Don't be so hard on yourself.'

'I'm only speaking the truth.'

His grandfather said nothing. He didn't try to contradict him, Finn noticed. Because deep down Henry Slater knew it was the truth. No girl as nice as Polly Malone would or should ever go near Finn.

And yet... Finn struck at another branch with his blade. He thought he had taught himself to stop dreaming, to stop hoping that something good might happen in his life. But Polly had made him forget himself. She had made him wish for more than he had.

And that was a dangerous thing.

He hadn't meant to get to know her. As his grandfather had observed, he usually made a point of trying to avoid the people who visited the churchyard, preferring to stay in the shadows. But then all that business with Job had happened, and Polly had been so good, standing up to that stuffed shirt curate and helping Finn to protect the dog.

He glanced down at Job, stretched out on the grass. This is all your fault, Finn chided him silently. Job gazed back at him with wise brown eyes. He liked Polly too. Finn knew nothing of the dog's history, but he sensed that, like him, his experiences of life had made him wary and ready to attack. And yet somehow Polly Malone had managed to worm her way through both their defences.

It was all right for Job, but Finn had been careless. He shouldn't have let it happen.

He allowed himself to glance over his shoulder, while pretending to stretch his stiff muscles. He saw her straight away, her pretty summer dress bright in the sunlit churchyard, her burnished gold hair lit by the sun. She was walking up the path to her husband's grave, a wicker basket of flowers over her arm. But she was looking around, searching for something – or someone.

'I reckon she's looking for you.' His grandfather spoke the thought that went through Finn's mind. 'Happen you should go and have a word?'

Finn turned back to his work, keeping his head down. 'I'm busy,' he muttered.

He was at the other side of the churchyard, half hidden by overhanging branches. Polly saw his tall, broad-shouldered figure, bent over his work, his powerful arms hacking away at the branches, and felt a treacherous lift of her heart at the sight of him.

He would be waiting for her. He would keep a respectful distance while she spent time at Frank's grave, but all the while she would know he was there, watching her. Then, when the time was right, she would hear his footsteps on the path behind her. She would turn, and there he'd be with Job. The dog would rush to greet her, and she would pet him and ask Finn about him, and then he would walk down to the gate with her and they would talk.

It was only ever small talk, about the dog, the weather, the various plants that were blooming in the churchyard. Or sometimes they would stroll in silence, watching the bees and butterflies fluttering between the flowers. It was nothing, just the briefest of shared moments, but Polly had begun to look forward to them.

She saw him looking at her, and raised her hand in greeting. Finn paused for a moment, then went back to his work. Polly frowned. He must have seen her, surely.

Job certainly saw her. He jumped eagerly to his feet and started trotting towards her, but Finn gave a sharp whistle, calling the dog back to his side.

Polly stared at them, disappointed and confused. Had she done something to offend Finn? she wondered.

'Hello, again.'

She started at the sound of a man's voice behind her. She turned, trying to give herself time to paste on a smile before she faced Matthew Elliott. 'Oh, hello.'

'I haven't seen you in a while. I hope you haven't been avoiding me?' he said teasingly.

'Of course not. Why should I?'

'No reason, I suppose.' His confident smile didn't waver. He reminded her of a schoolboy, his bright, freshly scrubbed face shining, surrounded by a halo of wispy light brown curls.

She hitched her basket higher on her arm and

started up the path to Frank's grave. Matthew followed her. She could feel him hovering behind her as she kneeled down to arrange her flowers. Someone – Finn, she supposed – had scrubbed the headstone to get rid of the dirt and moss, so it gleamed in the sunlight.

She took her time, hoping Matthew might take the hint and leave. But when she finally straightened up, brushing the grass off her knees, he was still there, his head bowed in prayer.

Finally, he murmured an 'Amen' and looked up at her. 'I hope you don't mind my saying a prayer for your husband?'

'Not at all. Thank you.' Polly smiled back, touched. Matthew meant well, she thought. Although she couldn't imagine what Frank would have made of a curate praying over him. He was never one for going to church and the like.

'May I walk you back to the gate?' Matthew asked.

'I–' Polly cast a quick glance about her, looking for Finn. There was no sign of him. Either he hadn't followed her, or he was staying away because of the curate.

She would have made an excuse to linger and wait for him, but she had the feeling Matthew wouldn't leave her alone.

'If you like,' she said, with as much enthusiasm as she could muster.

They made their way down the path together, and Matthew insisted on carrying her empty basket for her.

'I was very much hoping to see you again,' he said. Polly didn't reply. 'I wanted to ask your advice,' he went on.

'Oh yes?'

'The church committee has been trying to think of ways to raise funds for the new roof. I've suggested we might have a dance in the church hall. But the vicar isn't sure it's a good idea. What do you think?'

Polly frowned. 'I'm not sure why you're asking me.'

'I'd value your opinion.' His earnest gaze held hers.

'I'm sure it would do very well,' she said.

'So am I.' Matthew's smile widened. 'So you'd come, then?'

'Yes, I suppose so.' Polly looked away, her attention caught by the sound of excited barking from the other side of the churchyard. Job had spotted her again, and this time he was determined to greet her. He reared up, his front legs pawing uselessly at the air, while Finn held him back by his collar.

Matthew tutted. 'Wretched beast! I can't think why the vicar has allowed it to stay,' he muttered.

'He's harmless.'

'That's what Reverend Turner says. But I'm not so sure.' Matthew lowered his voice. 'To be honest, if it were up to me I'd get rid of the dog and his master.'

Polly turned to him in surprise. 'Why do you say that?'

'I don't know,' Matthew replied. 'There's just something about that man, the insolent way he has about him... He's trouble, I know it.' He put his hand on her arm, guiding her in the opposite direction. 'I'd stay away from him, if I were you.'

Polly glanced back over her shoulder. Finn caught her eye for a moment, then looked away sharply.

'It doesn't seem as if I have much choice,' she murmured.

Henry Slater pushed back his cap to scratch his balding head. 'Well, you've done it now,' he said.

'I dunno what you're on about,' Finn muttered, going back to his work.

'You could at least have spoken to the lass. She'll be wondering what she's done to offend you.'

'She probably won't give me a second thought.' Not when she had Matthew Elliott dancing attendance on her, Finn thought. The idiot curate was probably working his charm on her already. Finn took a savage swipe at a branch, bring down half the bush with it.

'Steady on,' his grandfather said, ducking out of the way. 'It's not that poor shrub's fault you're a fool, is it?'

'I'm no fool,' Finn growled.

'You're letting a lass like her slip through your fingers. I'd say that makes you a right fool. And there's no need to look at me like that,' he added, as Finn scowled at him. 'You don't frighten me, lad.'

Even in his late sixties, Henry Slater was still a burly man, more than capable of giving Finn a hiding if he needed one. But Finn knew Henry would never do it, which was why he respected his grandfather so much. Henry would never give up on him, not like the rest of Finn's family. 'I'm

134

just saying, she seems like a nice girl,' Henry went on, going back to his work.

'I told you, she's too nice for me.'

'You in't such a bad lad.'

'No? There's some folk around here as would say different.'

'You can't let one mistake ruin your whole life.'

'A mistake! Is that what you'd call it?'

Once again, his grandfather couldn't meet Finn's eye. 'As I said, you can't let it ruin your whole life.'

Finn managed a rueful smile. 'Bit too late for that, don't you reckon?'

Chapter Fourteen

Cedar House
Steeple Street
Leeds
15th October 1925

Dear Mother
How are you? I haven't heard from you since I arrived here, so I am hoping this finds you well. I think about you and Father all the time. I would love to hear your news. I miss you all.

Things are working out well for me here in Leeds. Very well, in fact. You'll be pleased to hear I have passed my first month's probation, so I will be going out on the district by myself from tomorrow. I must say, I'm looking forward to it. Up until now it has been rather frustrating, having to do things the way my supervisor Mrs Bradshaw has always done them. I'm already thinking about the changes I would like to make. There is a great deal of work to do, but I really feel as if I can make a difference.

But I would still dearly love to come home and be with you all again. I just wanted you to know that I am doing all I can to fit in and to make the best of my situation, as you said I should.

I am trying so hard, Mother. I know I have made mistakes and disappointed you and Father, and I long to make it up to you, and for you to be proud of me again. I promise you, I am trying very hard.

When do you think I might come back to London? It would be wonderful to see you all again. I am especially looking forward to meeting my new niece!

Please write back to me as soon as you can. I am longing to hear all your news.

Your loving daughter,
Agnes

Agnes read the letter through to herself again. She had written and rewritten it several times, but no matter how hard she tried, she could still hear the wheedling tone of her own voice coming through the lines.

Perhaps she shouldn't send it at all, she thought. Her mother disliked self-pity, and the last thing Agnes wanted was to antagonise her further.

Or perhaps she simply wouldn't read it. The thought lingered in Agnes' mind, tormenting her. Elizabeth Sheridan hadn't replied to a single letter from Agnes since she'd left St Jude's. It was

136

as if she had ceased to exist for her.

Agnes tried to tell herself her mother wasn't a reliable correspondent at the best of times; she had only written a handful of letters during the six months Agnes was in Manchester. But it was unlike her not to write at all.

'Miss Sheridan, are you about?'

The sound of Bess Bradshaw's voice booming from downstairs startled Agnes out of her gloom. She hastily stuffed the letter in an envelope and dropped it in her apron pocket before she had a chance to change her mind.

Bess was waiting for her at the foot of the stairs.

'There you are,' she said. 'Come on, we need to be off.'

Usually, the sight of the Assistant Superintendent's truculent face was enough to plunge Agnes into despair for the rest of the day. But today even Bess Bradshaw couldn't dampen her spirits.

'Yes, Mrs Bradshaw.' Agnes beamed at her.

Bess' beady eyes narrowed. 'Someone's in a good mood,' she commented.

'This is my last day on probation.' It was all Agnes could do not to skip over to fetch her coat from the peg.

'Surely it should be me who's smiling, in that case, since I won't have to put up with you any more.'

And I won't have to put up with you either, Agnes thought. 'Then we both have reason to celebrate, don't we?' she said sweetly.

Agnes still couldn't get over her surprise that she had survived her probation period. Not because she wasn't capable, but because Bess Bradshaw had seemed determined to trip her up at every opportunity.

Bess had never allowed her to relax for a moment. As Polly had predicted, she was always watching her, waiting for her to make a mistake so she could pounce on her.

Agnes had returned to the district nurses' home exhausted and close to tears nearly every evening, but she was determined not to allow Bess to get the better of her. She had applied herself to her books, and if there was something she didn't know she would make a point of swotting up on it so she could do better the next day.

Not that she ever received a word of praise or encouragement from the Assistant Superintendent, of course. The only time she heard anything was when she made a mistake.

But in spite of her efforts, she still expected Bess to try and trip her up. So Agnes could hardly believe it when Miss Gale had summoned her after breakfast that morning and informed her that she had passed.

Agnes couldn't wait. She was already thinking about what she was going to do when she had her own rounds. There would be no more pandering to patients, or wasting time. There would be no more endless cups of tea, or idle chatter. She would bring some efficiency to her district.

'We've still got one more day together though,' Bess' voice broke into her thoughts ominously. 'Let's see if we can both manage to get through it, shall we?'

That morning they had been invited by the headmistress of the local grammar school to give a talk on health and hygiene to the third-year girls.

'I expect you'll enjoy it since they're all posh like you,' Bess said, as they left the house.

Agnes smiled back beatifically. The Assistant Superintendent was trying so desperately to provoke an argument, it was almost amusing. 'I'm sure it will be very interesting,' she replied evenly.

'I thought you'd like it,' Bess said. 'Seeing as how you enjoy telling people what to do.'

I'd like to tell *you* what to do! Agnes thought 'Will I be giving the talk too?' she asked.

'Gracious, no! You just stay in the medical room and keep out of trouble,' Bess said. 'Think you can manage that?'

'I'll certainly do my best,' Agnes replied sweetly.

She waited for Bess to fetch her bicycle from the back of the house as usual. Her own bicycle had still not turned up, so Bess insisted Agnes had to walk everywhere while she cycled ahead. It caused a great deal of amusement for their patients and also Bess herself.

But to her surprise, Bess headed straight down the path.

'Aren't you cycling to the school?' Agnes asked.

Bess shook her head. 'It's a fine day and not too far to walk. I thought you'd like the company, since we're not going to be seeing much of each other after today.'

Agnes gritted her teeth. 'How thoughtful of you.'

Even on foot, Bess moved surprisingly fast, and it was all Agnes could do to keep up with her.

'I suppose the Association will have to give me

a new bicycle now?' she panted, as she trotted at Bess' heels.

'Whatever makes you think that?'

'Well, surely they won't expect me to walk, now I've got my own rounds to do?'

'You'll only be helping me out in Quarry Hill. You managed that perfectly well on foot before.'

'Yes, but–'

'The Association doesn't have money to waste on replacing bicycles, Miss Sheridan. Not when you were careless enough to lose yours in the first place.'

Bess marched on, leaving Agnes indignant in her wake.

As they passed a pillar box, she slid the letter she had written out of her pocket. She had hoped to post it quickly, but of course nothing escaped Bess Bradshaw's notice. Even walking ahead, she still managed to see Agnes slip the letter into the slot.

'What's that?' she demanded.

Agnes fought the urge to tell her to mind her own business. 'Just a letter to my mother.'

Bess' brows lifted. 'Do you write to her often?'

'Quite often.'

'You never talk about your family,' Bess observed. 'Do you have any brothers and sisters?'

'I have one sister, Vanessa. My brother was killed in the war.'

Bess paused. 'Is your sister older or younger than you?'

'Older.'

'Is she married?'

Agnes nodded.

'And what about your father? What does he do?' Bess asked.

'He's a GP.'

'Ah,' Bess said, as if that explained everything. 'And I suppose you wanted to follow in his footsteps?'

'I suppose so.'

Bess looked at her curiously. 'You don't like talking about your family, do you?'

Agnes forced herself to meet Bess' eye. 'Do you like talking about yours?'

She felt a brief flare of satisfaction as Bess' mouth tightened with anger. It made a change for her to score a point over the Assistant Superintendent.

Serves you right, she thought.

'"He who would valiant be, 'gainst all disaster ..."'

It was morning assembly, and Christine stood at the back of the hall with the other upper-school girls. The high rafters rang with the sound of three hundred girls' voices joined in song, but Christine kept her mouth tightly closed, afraid to open it in case she was sick.

It was stiflingly hot in the hall, and she could feel perspiration trickling down inside her shirt. When she put up her hand to wipe her brow, her skin felt damp and clammy.

She glanced to one side, where the row of teachers stood, and caught Miss Jennings' sharply disapproving look. Christine stared down at the hymn book in her hands, but the tiny print blurred in front of her eyes.

She tried to focus instead on the headmistress,

141

Miss Marchmane, who stood on a dais at the front of the hall. A beam of sunlight shone through the window, illuminating her as if God Himself were shining a spotlight on her.

'"Who so beset him round, with dismal stories..."' The sound rose up, engulfing her. Sweat was running down Christine's face. At the other end of the hall, Miss Marchmane seemed to be receding into the distance, as if Christine were watching her through the wrong end of a telescope. She blinked hard, but somehow she couldn't make the picture right again.

'Christine Fairbrass?' She heard her name, pronounced quietly but insistently. She turned her head to see Miss Jennings standing beside her. She looked more worried than stern now. Christine stared at the faint smattering of freckles over her tiny turned-up nose. The teacher had never been close enough for her to notice them before. 'Are you quite all right?' Miss Jennings enquired.

Christine shook her head, still not trusting herself to speak. All around, girls were beginning to look at her, shifting to get a better view.

'You look rather unwell. Perhaps you should go outside for a breath of fresh air?'

She did her best to get out, sidling past the other girls, but failed to reach the end of the row before the sickness that had been roiling inside her rose up without warning and burst out in a vile torrent, splattering Miss Jennings' shoes.

Suddenly there was panic, with girls squealing and shoving to get away.

'What is it? What is going on back there?' The piano music died away and Miss Marchmane's

142

voice rang out from the front of the hall. Christine found herself standing in the middle of a small, empty circle, surrounded by a ring of appalled-looking faces.

It was the last thing she saw before her knees buckled and she slid to the floor.

Bess Bradshaw had gone off to the science room to prepare for her talk to the third years. Agnes was alone in the sick bay, trying to make herself useful by checking the contents of the medical cupboard, when there was a knock on the door and a prefect entered, hauling a limp Christine Fairbrass by the arm.

'Please, miss, this girl fainted in the middle of assembly,' the prefect announced. 'And she was sick,' she added, her nose wrinkling in disgust.

Agnes looked at the girl. 'Christine?'

She looked dreadful. Her coppery hair was drawn back in a tight ponytail, revealing red-rimmed eyes in a ghastly greenish face.

Agnes gathered herself together. 'Get her on to the bed,' she ordered the other girl, while she herself hurried to the cupboard to fetch a receiving dish, which she placed next to Christine.

The prefect looked uneasy. 'Do you think she's going to be sick again?'

'I don't know. But it's better to be safe than sorry, isn't it?' Agnes replied briskly as she loosened Christine's tie and unfastened the top button of her blouse.

'Should I fetch Nurse Bradshaw?' The prefect fixed her gaze uncertainly on Christine.

Agnes bristled. 'I can manage perfectly well,'

she said. 'You may go back to your classroom.'

'I'm all right, really,' Christine whispered when they were alone.

'Girls don't collapse for no reason,' Agnes replied. She checked Christine's pulse and her temperature. 'Now, do you have a headache?'

'No, miss.'

'Any visual disturbance? Blurred vision, spots before the eyes, anything like that?' Christine shook her head. 'And you haven't had a bump to your head?'

'No, miss.'

'When was the last time you had anything to eat?'

Her words seemed to trigger a strange response in Christine. Her face puckered and Agnes managed to grab the receiving dish seconds before her patient was sick again.

Agnes pushed a stray red curl back from the girl's face. A feeling of unease began to stir in the back of her mind.

'Have you felt like this for long?' she asked when Christine had finally finished retching.

She wiped her mouth with the damp cloth Agnes had handed to her. 'I really couldn't say, miss.'

'But I recall you were sent home from school last month?'

Christine lowered her gaze. 'I've been sick a few times. But I've had a lot of schoolwork to do,' she added.

Schoolwork doesn't make you sick, Agnes thought. She looked down at the girl on the bed, trying to choose her words carefully.

In the end she knew she had no choice but to

say it outright. 'Christine, do you think you might be pregnant?'

Her mouth fell open. 'No, miss!'

'Are you sure?' Agnes spoke gently. 'Be honest now.'

Christine's gaze dropped, her face flooding with mottled colour. 'No, miss,' she repeated.

'When did you last have your monthlies?'

The girl frowned. 'I don't understand—'

But before Agnes could reply, the door swung open and Bess Bradshaw bustled in.

'What's going on?' she demanded, looking from one to the other.

Agnes straightened her shoulders. 'Christine fainted and was sick during assembly,' she said.

'I know that! I've just spoken to the head-mistress. What I want to know is why you didn't send for me straight away?'

'I felt I could manage by myself.'

Bess frowned at her. 'That's as may be, but I am the Queen's Nurse, not you. I am responsible for this school and the wellbeing of its pupils.' She crossed the room, almost elbowing Agnes out of the way. 'Now, let's have a look at you, lass,' she said to Christine.

'I've already checked her pulse and tempera-ture,' Agnes muttered.

'I'll just check it again, to be sure.'

Agnes burned with humiliation as she watched Bess examine the girl. All the while Christine watched her warily over the Assistant Super-intendent's shoulder, eyes huge and terrified in her pale face.

'Yes, well, that all seems to be in order,' Bess said

145

finally. 'Let me look at your tongue.' Christine opened her mouth obediently. 'It's probably just another infection you've picked up. Nothing to worry about.'

'Actually–' Agnes started to speak, but Bess held up her hand.

'I'm not interested in hearing one of your interesting new medical theories,' she declared.

'But–'

Bess ignored her, turning back to face Christine. 'Now, lass, I want you to rest here until you feel better, then get yourself home,' she said.

Christine's pale face filled with dismay. 'But we've got an important arithmetic test today!'

'Not another one arguing with me?' Bess shot Agnes an accusing look. 'I don't want to hear it, young lady. I'm a nurse and I know what I'm talking about. Now, I'll have a word with the headmistress and let her know what's going on.'

'Shall I stay with her?' Agnes asked. She was hoping she might have another chance to talk to Christine.

But Bess seemed to sense her eagerness, and shook her head. 'No, you can come with me while I give my talk,' she declared. 'I want you where I can keep an eye on you. If I turn my back, you'll probably be writing out a prescription for her or some such daftness!'

Agnes looked back at Christine as she followed Bess out of the room. There was no prescription that could help the girl now, if Agnes' suspicions were correct.

Chapter Fifteen

There was a new name on Polly's list of calls that morning.

'Dr Marsh telephoned about him first thing this morning,' Miss Jarvis explained as they went through the coming morning's list together. 'He collapsed yesterday. He has a history of heart and lung problems, but he's refused to go to hospital. The doctor has done everything he can, but he'd like us to keep an eye on him every morning. I get the impression he's a rather stubborn old man,' she said, smiling.

It must run in the family, then, Polly thought, staring down at the piece of paper in her hand. She didn't want to react, but all her senses were on the alert.

'I can understand if you don't want to go?' Polly looked up sharply as Miss Jarvis seemed to read her thoughts. 'It's where Frank is buried, isn't it?' the district nurse said kindly. 'If you feel it might be too much for you...'

'Not at all,' Polly said, slipping the list into the outside pocket of her bag. She was dismayed to realise that Frank hadn't been in her thoughts at all. 'I'll go first thing as the doctor is concerned.'

It had been nearly two weeks since Polly had last been to the church. She was annoyed with herself for staying away so long. No matter how humiliated she felt, she shouldn't let the likes of Finn

Slater keep her from doing her duty to Frank.

But all the same, her stomach lurched as she parked her bicycle just inside the lych gate. She couldn't forget how offhand Finn had been the last time she'd visited. Their fledgling friendship had obviously meant more to her than it did to him, and this was his not-so-subtle way of keeping her at arm's length.

Job saw her first, as he lolled against the front step of the sexton's cottage. He lifted his big black head at the sound of Polly's approach, then jumped to his feet and let out a joyful volley of deep barking at the sight of her.

A second later the front door flew open and Finn stood there.

'Quiet, Job! You don't want to bring–' He saw her and stopped dead. 'You!' he said. He looked her up and down, registering her uniform. 'I didn't know...'

Her first thought was how tired he looked. His jaw was shadowed with stubble, and there were deep shadows under his stormy grey eyes.

Polly gripped the smooth leather handle of her bag tightly, determined not to give away her raging nerves. 'I've come to see your grandfather,' she said.

Finn recovered himself. 'Yes, of course. You'd best come in.' He stood aside to let her enter.

Inside the cottage was small, but neat and well kept. Polly looked around, taking it all in. Finn seemed to fill the cramped space, so she couldn't help but be aware of him as he led the way down a narrow passageway to a bedroom.

Henry Slater was propped up against his pillow.

He looked ashen, not at all like the robust man she was used to seeing up and about. But he managed a smile when he saw Polly.

'Hello, love,' he greeted her. 'Well, this is a turn up for the books. What a bit o' luck, eh, Finn lad?'

Finn said nothing. He lingered sullenly in the doorway, arms folded across his chest, Job sitting at his feet.

'Good morning, Mr Slater,' Polly greeted the old man. 'How are you feeling today?'

'Like a fool, nurse. I shouldn't be lying here in my bed when there's so much work to be done. We've got two funerals tomorrow, and no one's going to be buried if I don't fettle it.'

'I told you I'd do them,' Finn muttered.

'And there's the fence to be mended.'

'I've already done it. I did it first thing this morning. So you've no need to worry.'

The old man looked disgruntled. 'All the same, I'd rather be up and about.'

'You should be in hospital,' Finn said.

Henry shook his head. 'I aren't going to no hospital.'

'You heard what the doctor said.'

'I told you, I aren't going! Now stop your mithering, lad, and go and do summat useful.'

Finn mumbled a curse under his breath and stomped off, Job at his heels. A moment later they heard the front door slam. Polly flinched, but Henry just gave her a toothless grin.

'He'll be back when he's had a chance to calm down.'

Polly read the message paper from Dr Marsh. Auricular fibrillation, possibly due to congestive

149

heart failure. No medication prescribed as yet, but he had left instructions that the patient was to be kept in bed, propped up, TPRs to be checked twice daily. Also Polly had to telephone the doctor every evening to report on Henry's symptoms.

'Not bad news, I hope?' She looked down to see Henry gazing up at her. A smile was still fixed to his grizzled old face, but she could see the anxiety behind it.

'You're in good hands, Mr Slater,' she replied, putting the paper aside. 'Now, I'll just go and wash my hands, then I'll make a start.'

Polly took the old man's temperature and pulse, and asked him various questions about his symptoms. Had he eaten? Had he been to the toilet? While she was talking to him, she was aware of the front door opening and closing again. Finn had come back.

'Told you!' Henry Slater cackled. 'He just needed some time to clear his head, that's all.'

'He's worried for you,' Polly said.

'I know. He thinks I'm all he's got.'

'Is he right?'

Henry paused. 'Well, I suppose so,' he said. 'God knows his own family don't want to know him, not after–' He broke off.

'Not after what?'

Henry looked down at his callused old hands, resting on the coverlet. 'It in't my business to say,' he muttered. 'He just had a few troubles, that's all. But Finn's a good lad,' he added quickly. 'He tries to hide it, but there's a heart in there. Trouble is, I reckon it's more broken than mine,' he added with a grim smile.

Polly would have liked to ask him what he meant, but she knew he wouldn't tell her. Henry Slater was a closed book, just like his grandson.

She finished examining him and fetched some extra pillows to prop him up, then stood back.

'Right,' she said. 'Now, would you like me to help you wash?'

Henry's whiskery face coloured. 'No, thank you, nurse,' he mumbled.

'Are you sure? You might feel better if you freshen up a bit.'

'I'm much obliged, nurse, but Finn can do all that for me, if you don't mind?'

Polly looked at the old man's anxious expression and understood. 'Of course,' she said. 'I'll leave you to sort it out between you, then.'

'Thank you, nurse.' Henry looked relieved.

'But you said you hadn't eaten. Would you like me to make you something?'

'Oh no, I wouldn't want to put you to all that trouble.'

'It would be no trouble to make you some tea and toast. Besides, it's my job to make sure you're well nourished.'

'I'm sure Finn could manage...'

From the look of him, Finn hadn't eaten either, Polly thought 'All the same, I might as well do it, while I'm here.'

She packed up her bag, told Henry she would be back that evening to check on him, and then went into the kitchen. Finn was there, leaning against the sink, moodily watching Job gnawing on a bone. He looked up sharply when Polly walked in.

'How is he?'

151

Polly drew a deep breath. 'As well as can be expected,' she said, setting her bag down on the table. 'He's quite comfortable at the moment, but time will tell–'

'Tell me the truth!' Finn cut her off harshly.

Polly turned on him, ready to bite back at him, until she saw the desperate look on his face. 'That is the truth,' she replied quietly.

Finn's gaze dropped. 'I'm sorry,' he muttered. 'I didn't mean to be so abrupt. I'm just worried.'

He suddenly looked so vulnerable, like a lost little boy, all she wanted to do was to put her arms around him and console him. But she held herself rigid.

'To be honest, your grandfather would be better off in hospital,' she replied. Then, seeing Finn's expression, she added, 'but trying to force him there will do more harm than good. He's all right where he is for now, with us keeping an eye on him. If the doctor thinks it's necessary, he will make him go to hospital.'

'You're sure about that?' His eyes were fixed on her.

'I'm quite sure.'

Finn's tense features relaxed slightly. 'I didn't know what to do,' he said. 'The old man's had attacks before, but never like that. I really thought...'

Once again, Polly felt the urge to reach out and comfort him.

She covered it up, hiding behind her brisk, professional exterior as she went to fill the kettle. 'I'm making him some tea and toast,' she said. 'Can I make you something too?'

Finn shook his head. 'I'm not hungry.'

'But you need to eat.'

He stared down at his boots. 'Don't you worry about me.'

'I am worried about you.'

He looked up sharply and their eyes met. The room suddenly seemed to crackle with electricity.

'You need to keep up your strength,' Polly went on, so flustered she could barely get the words out. 'To look after your grandfather, I mean. We don't want you getting ill too, do we?'

Silence stretched between them, and for a moment Polly thought she caught a glimpse of vulnerability in his eyes.

Then Job let out a loud bark, breaking the spell. He abandoned his bone and rushed to the door, pawing at the wood.

'What's wrong with him?' Polly asked.

'That'll be your friend t'curate.' Finn went to the window and twitched aside the lace curtain to look out. 'Aye, there is he, lurking about. Job doesn't care for him. Reckon he hasn't forgotten the way he tried to go for him with that stick.' He turned to her. 'I daresay you'll be wanting to go and see him,' he said shortly. 'Don't bother about the tea and toast, I can make it mysen.'

'Certainly not.' Polly moved away from the window and set the kettle down on the stove. 'And I'll thank you to lower that curtain, I don't want him to see me. Now, where do you keep the bread?'

'I'll fetch it.' Finn let the curtain drop and went to the larder. 'What's wrong? Have you had a lovers' tiff?'

'A what?'

'You heard.' Finn put the loaf down. 'You two

153

are courting, aren't you?'

Polly turned to face him, a box of matches in her hand. 'Whatever gave you that idea?'

He lowered his gaze. 'I saw you ... talking together the other day.'

'You were watching, were you? I thought you were ignoring me.'

He made a great show of rifling in the drawer, clattering noisily in search of a knife. 'He likes you,' he said. 'I can tell.'

'Perhaps he does,' Polly said. 'But for your information, I have no interest in Matthew Elliott.'

Finn shrugged. 'It in't my business if you do or if you don't.'

'Isn't it? Polly looked at his profile. She was sure she saw the faintest hint of a smile curving his lips.

'Oh! Has she gone?' Henry looked disappointed when Finn took his breakfast in to him.

'Aye, she has. She's got other folk to see, y'know. Can't be fussing round you all day.' He set the tray down in front of his grandfather. 'You're stuck wi' me, I'm afraid.'

Henry looked at him. 'I dunno about me, but I reckon seeing her has made *you* feel better. Put a right smile on your face.'

Finn let his features drop into his usual scowl, embarrassed that he'd allowed the mask to slip.

'Nay, lad, you can't fool me that easily,' his grandfather chuckled. 'Anyone can see you're fond of the lass. And I reckon she likes you too.'

Finn moved away from the bed to open the window, not wanting his grandfather to see his face. He'd already given away far too much about how he felt.

He scarcely dared to allow himself to think it, but he suspected his grandfather was right. There had been something between them. He'd sensed it as they worked together in the kitchen, making breakfast.

Finn thought about what she had said about the curate, and his smile broadened. That alone had been enough to make his day.

But then his grandfather ruined it all by saying, 'Have you told her anything?'

Finn stiffened, instantly wary. 'What about?'

'You know.'

He went on staring out of the window. 'I've told her nothing,' he muttered.

'Don't you think you should?'

The hope and happiness that had briefly warmed him faded away, leaving him feeling cold and empty again. 'I thought this was meant to be a fresh start for me, coming here?'

'It is, lad. But I reckon it's only fair she knows what she's taking on.'

Finn flinched. He knew his grandfather meant well, but he made him sound like an unwelcome burden.

But then, wasn't that exactly what he was?

'You should be straight with her,' his grandfather carried on. 'Better she hears it from you than someone else.'

'And who'd tell her? There's no one round here knows, except you and me.'

'And Reverend Turner. I had to tell him, don't forget.'

Finn tensed. 'You don't think he'd say any-thing–'

His grandfather shook his head. 'Nay lad, he'll not go out of his way to make trouble for you, any more than I would. But all the same, it wouldn't take much for someone to remember your name, or your face.' He paused. 'I reckon you should speak to her. For your own sake.'

Finn stared out of the window again, his gaze fixed on nothing. Of course he'd thought about telling Polly. He'd tried to imagine talking to her, opening his heart and letting all his secrets spill out.

But then he imagined the look of dawning horror on her face, the light fading from her eyes. And he couldn't bear that. Finn would rather lose her completely than have to endure that.

'Better she never has to know at all,' he mur-mured.

Chapter Sixteen

Christine perched on the bed, her hands laced tightly in her lap, staring at the grubby net cur-tains. Beyond, the window looked out on to the gable end of the shop opposite, a high brick wall covered in a weather-worn advertisement for Bovril. Christine had never noticed it before. But then, she had always been too wrapped up in Oliver to notice anything.

She wished they could have met somewhere

else. The grim little room in the bed and break-fast hardly seemed right for what she had to say, especially when they had spent so many happy times there together. But they couldn't be seen in public, and Oliver wouldn't hear of her visiting his lodgings, so here it had to be.

But perhaps that would all change, she thought. Everything would change after today, one way or another.

'On your own?' The landlady had looked her up and down as she handed over the room key.

'My – er – husband will be coming later.'

'Of course. I'll send him up, shall I?' The woman gave her a shrewd little smile. It was the first time Christine had noticed the contempt in her eyes. How did she ever think they had fooled the landlady with their false name in the register and the curtain ring on Christine's left hand?

She was so nervous, she could feel the perspira-tion gathering under her arms. Her hands were slippery with it, and yet her throat was as dry as sand.

Christine, do you think you might be pregnant?

The nurse's words had been spoken so calmly, and yet they had blown Christine's world apart. Up until that moment, it had never occurred to her that she might be in trouble. It was true, she couldn't remember the last time her monthlies had come. But she hadn't given it a second thought. It certainly hadn't occurred to her that it had anything to do with having a baby, until the nurse mentioned it. Then Christine had gone to the library and consulted one of the dusty old medical books in the reference section, and discovered the awful truth.

Up until then, she had only had the vaguest of notions about where babies came from. It was difficult not to pick up ideas in a place like Quarry Hill, where the women gathered to gossip on every doorstep, and people lived so crammed in together that the messy details of everyone's lives couldn't help but be shared. But somehow her mother had managed to shield her from the facts of how they came to be made.

'All in good time,' was all she'd say, whenever Christine asked a question. 'You'll know all about that once you're married.'

And so Christine had remained blissfully ignorant, convinced that somehow only married women could ever conceive a baby. She was aware that what she and Oliver did in this very bedroom was somehow wrong and forbidden, but she had never imagined that it would result in her falling pregnant.

Now she felt ashamed and foolish. She was Christine Fairbrass, the scholarship girl. She should have asked questions, known better.

And now look at her.

But it would be all right, she told herself. She had Oliver. He loved her, and she could trust him to make everything all right. That was how she had comforted herself during the past two weeks of sleepless nights, while she'd listened to her mother snoring beside her and tried to still her own rising panic.

Sometimes Christine had been so desperate, she'd almost woken her mother up to tell her, just to get it over with. She knew Lil would be angry and upset. But surely she wouldn't mind so much once she found out Christine was engaged, and everything was respectable. And to a teacher, no less. Christine might have to say goodbye to her own dreams, but wasn't being the wife of a teacher nearly as good? It would still give Lil a chance to hold up her head among her neighbours in Quarry Hill, at least.

Christine heard Oliver's footsteps coming up the stairs and shot to her feet. She smoothed down her skirt and fussed with her hair, tucking it behind her ears as the door opened.

Her treacherous heart lifted at the sight of him, so dark and handsome. He smiled when he saw her, and Christine felt sick, knowing what she had to say to him.

'Hello, there. The landlady said you'd already arrived. Am I late?'

'No, I – I'm early.'

'I'm glad. It will give us even more time together.'

He came towards her, his arms held out, but she side-stepped his embrace.

'No,' she said. 'I can't.'

He frowned. 'What is it, my love?'

His gentle concern, mingled with her own overwhelming anxiety, was too much for Christine, and she burst into tears. All her carefully planned words were swept away in a tidal wave of sobbing.

'Oh, my love!' Oliver gathered her into his arms, comforting her. 'There, don't cry,' he crooned softly, his lips buried in her hair. He smelled of clean, lemony cologne. 'Whatever it is, it can't be that bad. Has something happened?'

'Oh, Oliver.' She pressed her face against his chest, muffling her words. She wished she could stay there for ever, in the comforting circle of his arms. Being there would make everything all right.

'What is it? Tell me.' He took a deep breath. 'Oh God, don't say your mother's found out about us?'

Christine shook her head. She could hear the steady beat of his heart. 'Do you love me?' she asked.

'Of course I love you, you silly goose.' He pulled away from her and took her face in both his hands, tilting her chin up to look down at her. His eyes were the deepest brown, so warm and gentle. 'Now tell me what's wrong,' he said.

Christine lowered her gaze. If she looked at him, she was afraid she wouldn't be able to say the words.

'I ... I think I'm pregnant,' she whispered.

She heard his sharp intake of breath and felt him freeze, his fingers stiffening on her face. She didn't dare look up, afraid of what she might see in his eyes.

'No.'

He released her abruptly and turned away. He started to pace the room, as restless as a caged beast, running his hands through his dark hair.

'No,' he muttered again, under his breath. 'No, no, no!'

Christine held herself rigid. He was just in shock, she told herself. In a moment he would calm down and tell her what to do, and everything would be all right again...

'Oliver?' she said. He didn't hear her. He was lost in a world of his own, pacing the room, his face buried in his hands.

This wasn't right. She had wanted him to be the one to take her in his arms and reassure her that all would be well. She needed his comfort, not the other way round.

'Oliver, please–' She went to put her hand on his arm, but he flinched from her touch.

'How could you?' he snapped. 'How could you let it happen?'

She felt his anger like a blow, and it took her a moment to steady herself.

'Me?' she echoed faintly.

He turned away from her and fixed his gaze on the faded wallpaper, as if it would somehow tell him what to do.

'Are you sure?' he said.

'I – I think so.'

'You think so?' he swung round to face her. 'You mean you're not certain?'

'I...' She fumbled desperately for the right words. No, I'm not sure, she wanted to shout. I've never been in this position before and I don't know what's happening to me. She wanted to take back what she'd said, just so he wouldn't turn away from her again. But she couldn't turn back the clock, no matter how much she wanted to.

She remembered flicking through the whispering pages of the medical book in the library, reading the words written there, her desperation spiralling. 'Yes,' she said quietly. 'Yes, I am certain.'

He turned away again and Christine stared at the space between his shoulder blades.

Why wasn't he helping her? Why wasn't he making this better? He was losing control, letting his emotions get the better of him, when he should have been looking after her.

She wanted to rage at him, but she knew she had to stay calm. She wrapped her arms around her body, trying to comfort herself.

'I know it's a shock,' she said quietly. 'But it isn't as bad as it seems, honestly.'

He gave a derisive snort, but Christine ignored him. 'It just means we'll have to bring our plans forward, that's all,' she continued.

He looked over his shoulder at her, his face blank. 'Plans? What plans?'

'We're going to get married, aren't we?'

'Married?' There was something in the cold way he said it that made her uneasy. Up until that moment she had never doubted him. She knew he would be shocked, angry even. But it had never occurred to her that Oliver wouldn't take care of her.

'You do want to marry me, don't you?' she said in a small voice.

He didn't reply, but he didn't have to. One look at his blank expression and Christine knew he had been lying to her. All those fine words, those flowery declarations of love, but he'd only been telling her what she wanted to hear.

And, like a fool, she'd believed him.

She felt tears pricking the back of her eyes again. Now she really was frightened, because she realised she was utterly alone.

'Look, don't cry.' His voice was gentle when he spoke again, more like the Oliver she knew. He took her hands in his, thumbs circling her knuckles, coaxing the warmth back into them. She hadn't realised how cold she was until he held her. 'I meant it when I said I loved you. But I can't marry you, you must see that?'

'Why not?' Her voice was thick, blurred with tears. 'Why can't you marry me?'

'It would be the end of everything for me – for us. Who would ever employ me once word of this got out? My career would be over before it started. I could never support you, or the...' His gaze dropped to her belly, still quite flat beneath her loose dress.

'Then you could find other work.' Surely the only thing that mattered was that they were together.

'I don't want another job.' His jaw tensed obstinately. 'I've worked hard for this. I'm not going to throw it all away because of one silly mistake I ... I.'

Too late he realised what he'd said, and his mouth slammed shut.

Christine stared at him. 'Is that all I am to you? A mistake?'

Oliver released her hands and stepped away from her, putting distance between them again. 'My family would be furious,' he muttered.

'My mother will be furious too,' Christine pointed out.

'It's hardly the same thing.'

His dismissive tone needled her. 'Why isn't it the same?' she asked. But she already knew the answer. She wasn't good enough for him. And no matter how many scholarships she won, she would never be good enough for him because of who she was and where she came from.

'I don't know why you bothered with me in the first place,' she said. But she knew the answer to that, too. He had taken advantage of her because she was lonely and vulnerable. And she had fallen for it.

She started to cry again. Oliver sighed impatiently. 'Look, don't get upset,' he said. 'I'm sure we can think of something. I'm not going to leave you in the lurch, don't worry about that.' A spark of hope lit up inside her, only to be dashed when he went on. 'I can give you money.'

'Money?' She looked at him blankly. 'Why would I want your money?'

'To ... you know...' he nodded towards her belly.

Christine stared at him. 'I don't understand... What do you want me to do?'

'Oh, come on, Christine! You know exactly what I mean. You must know someone who could – help you.'

She had a sudden mental image of Annie Pilcher, skulking around the streets, never meeting anyone's eyes.

She does favours for women. Wasn't that what Rene Wells had said?

Christine thought about poor dead Maisie Warren. 'I can't do that,' she murmured.

'You must,' Oliver urged her. 'It's the only way. Look, I don't mind paying,' he said. 'I have some savings, although I don't know how much these things cost...'

'I don't want your money,' Christine said.

'But I want to help. I'm only thinking of you.'

She would have laughed if she hadn't been so terrified. 'No, you're not. You're thinking of yourself.'

'That's not true. I'm just trying to be practical, that's all. You don't want to end up burdened with a child, do you? You said yourself, you want to make something of your life.' Oliver took a step towards her. 'Just think,' he said, 'once this is all over, you could finish your education, become a teacher yourself... You could have a future.'

His voice was soft as a caress, insinuating its way into her thoughts. He had always had a way of charming her, bending her to his will with his words.

But now she could see those words for what they were – empty.

'Are you sure it's not *your* future you're worried about?' she said to him.

He blanched. 'What do you mean?'

'You said yourself, no one would employ you if word of this got out. I could go to the boys' school, tell them what you'd done.'

'You wouldn't!'

'Why not? I've nothing to lose, have I? It's not as if I've a good name like yours!' she threw back at him.

His chin lifted, but she could see the fear in his eyes. 'If you did that then we would both be in a mess and I wouldn't be able to help you.'

Christine laughed harshly. 'Help? So far all you've done is offer me money.'

'And that's all I have to offer.'

'We'll see about that.' She barely knew what she was saying. All she wanted to do was to lash out, to hurt him as he'd hurt her. 'What if I went to your family and told them? They'd make you marry me...'

Oliver's mouth twisted. 'Is that what you really think? I'm sorry, my dear, but you're quite wrong. I daresay they'd be utterly furious, but the last thing they'd want me to do is marry someone like you.' He shook his head pityingly. 'Look, if you think you can make trouble for me, then you are welcome to try. But I'm warning you, I will deny everything. And who do you think people will believe?'

Christine reeled away from the look of utter contempt in his face. It was the same look Joan Cathcart gave her, the look that said she would never be rich or important enough to matter to anyone.

How had she not seen it before? she wondered. Had she really been so blinded by love she hadn't seen him for what he was?

Oliver picked up his hat, ready to leave. 'My offer still stands,' he told her coldly. 'The money is there if you want it. But I'm warning you, if I find out you've tried to make trouble for me, then you're on your own.'

'Oliver—' she started to say, but he'd already slammed out of the room. Christine listened to his footsteps hurrying down the stairs, as if he couldn't put enough distance between them.

She curled up on the bed, where they'd made love and he'd whispered sweet words to her, and they'd talked about their future so many times.

He was wrong, she thought. She was already on her own.

Chapter Seventeen

'What happened to the real nurse?'

Agnes pressed her lips together and said nothing as she undid her bag and took out the massage lotion. After nearly three weeks of doing rounds on her own, she was getting heartily sick of hearing those words.

'I am a real nurse, Mrs Gawtrey,' she said through a tight smile. 'Now, let's have a look at your legs, shall we?'

Queenie looked dubious as Agnes rolled down her stockings and started the massage. She kept up a steady pace, kneading and rolling the flesh between her fingers, feeling the shapeless lumps of arthritic bone underneath.

'Steady on!' Queenie protested. 'I in't made of bread dough, y'know!'

'I have to use a lot of friction or you won't feel the benefit.'

'I think I preferred t'other one,' the old woman grumbled. 'You're a bit rough. And your hands are cold.'

'Sorry.' Agnes rubbed her hands together to warm them. She wished Bess had kept Queenie on as one of her patients. Agnes had been wary of her ever since the old woman had tried to tell her fortune.

She hadn't mentioned that day since, and Agnes hoped she might have forgotten about it.

But as she continued to massage, she could feel Queenie watching her closely, her rheumy eyes narrowed.

'I remember you,' she said at last. 'You came here before.'

'I've been here a few times, Mrs Gawtrey,' Agnes replied lightly.

'Aye, I know that, lass. But it's just come back to me. I read your palm, didn't I?'

'Did you? I can't remember,' Agnes said. Then, as Queenie opened her mouth to speak, she said, 'Could you please not talk while I'm doing this? It interferes with my concentration.'

'Concentration be blowed!' Queenie muttered. 'T'other one never had to concentrate. She could chat all day long, whatever she were doing. Mind you, she were a real nurse,' she added with a sniff.

Agnes sat back on her heels and rubbed her hands on a cloth. 'There. All done.'

Queenie's baggy face settled into an expression of dissatisfaction. 'That was quick. Are you sure you've done it proper?'

'Quite sure.' Agnes had already rolled the old woman's stockings back into place and was on her feet, packing up her bag.

'You'll stop for a brew of tea?' Queenie said.

'I'm afraid I can't.' Agnes did her best to sound regretful. 'I don't have time. I have a lot of patients to see this morning.'

'The real nurse always had time for a brew.'

'Perhaps next time?' Agnes said.

'Happen I won't offer next time,' Queenie muttered.

I should be so lucky, Agnes thought, as she let

168

herself out of the house. She was terrified that Queenie might try to read her tealeaves again.

Agnes looked back at the cottage. She felt slightly guilty that she hadn't offered to make the old lady a pot of tea before she left. She knew Queenie found it difficult to get about.

But then she reminded herself it wasn't her job. Agnes was there to massage her patient's legs and provide general nursing care, not to run around after her. If she started making tea for everyone, before long she would end up cleaning or running errands for them too, and then she would have made a rod for her own back.

Agnes checked her watch and was pleased to see that it was only eleven o'clock and she had already almost finished her list of calls. That's what a bit of efficiency does, she thought.

Of course, not all the patients had taken to her new way of doing things, any more than they'd taken to the idea of Agnes replacing Bess. But she had stood firm. There was to be no more drinking endless cups of tea or wasting time with idle chit-chat. She timed herself to make sure she didn't dawdle too long, and if a patient needed extra care, would note it carefully in her book so she could call in a bit earlier the following day.

It was all a matter of teaching them what to expect, Agnes told herself. Bess Bradshaw had spoiled them, and now Agnes had to show them she was a nurse, not a companion or a maid of all work.

She finished her rounds and hurried back to Steeple Street. Dottie looked most put out to see her.

'You're not due back while twelve,' she said accusingly.

'Yes, I'm a little earlier than I expected.' Agnes consulted her watch. Perhaps she could have spent a bit more time on Mr Fentiman's bunions, but no matter. The old boy had seemed happy enough.

'Dinner in't on the table while one,' Dottie told her.

'I know,' Agnes agreed equably. 'But I'd love a cup of tea.'

Dottie stared at her, then rushed off. Agnes sighed. After more than six weeks, she still couldn't get the girl to say more than a few words to her.

She checked the pigeon holes. There was still no letter from her mother. It had been so long since she'd had any news, Agnes had ceased to feel disappointed.

She went into the district room to write up her notes. As time passed and midday drew nearer, the other district nurses began to arrive home. One by one they came into the district room to unpack their bags, sterilise their instruments/ write up their notes and make telephone calls.

Agnes finished her notes just as the clock struck one. She joined the others around the dining table. The only one missing was Bess Bradshaw.

She came rushing in ten minutes later. They heard her before they saw her, puffing and panting and muttering under her breath as she hurried to wash her hands. Finally she appeared, red-faced and flustered.

'Sorry I'm late,' she muttered. 'Nasty case of croup.'

'Really, Bess, you should take a leaf out of your protégée's book,' Miss Goode remarked, helping herself to a spoonful of mashed potato. 'Miss Sheridan had finished her round and was back before the rest of us.'

Agnes shot her a quick glance. Miss Goode might look angelic, but Agnes had quickly learned that she was a great mischief-maker, always looking to stir up trouble wherever she could.

'Was she now?' Bess muttered, pulling out her chair and plonking herself down in it.

'And all on foot too,' Miss Goode added. 'Poor Miss Sheridan. When are you going to sort out a new bicycle for her?'

'I've already told her, she shouldn't have been so careless with the last one,' Bess muttered. She was in a foul mood, Agnes could tell. And Miss Goode wasn't making it any better.

'I'm sure I can wait until Miss Gale can arrange another one,' Agnes said quietly.

'You'll wait a long time then,' Phil Fletcher put in from the other end of the table. 'The Association have to find the funds for a motorcycle for Miss Templeton and me first. Our need is greater than yours.'

Fortunately the conversation turned to the subject of motorcycles, and whether it would be safe for elderly Miss Templeton to go careering around the country lanes on one. It wasn't until after lunch that Agnes had to face Bess' interrogation of her.

'Why did you finish your round so early?' she said.

Because I'm more efficient than you are, Agnes

171

thought, but said nothing.

'Are you sure you saw everyone?' Bess looked suspicious.

'Indeed I did.'

It was too much to hope she might be praised for her hard work, of course. Bess was determined to find fault. Her square chin jutted, a sure sign she was looking for trouble.

'You changed Mr Marsh's dressing? And you checked the wound as I asked you?' Agnes nodded. 'And you didn't rush Queenie Gawtrey's massage? She doesn't like it when you're rough, you know.'

'All done.'

'Did any of them ask for me?'

'No,' Agnes lied. 'They all seemed perfectly satisfied.'

'Hmm.' Bess sniffed. She looked most put out, Agnes decided. 'Well, I've got your calls for this afternoon.' She handed over the list. 'It's all quite straightforward. A couple of baths, a message and the rest general nursing care. Oh, and then there's this one.' She pointed to a name at the bottom of the list. 'New patient. Well, new to you anyway. She's well known to the rest of us, unfortunately.'

Agnes read the name on the list. 'Sarah Franklin. Gastric influenza.'

'That's what she says, anyway.' Bess grimaced. 'She's over the worst, and the doctor's advised plenty of rest and fluids until she can face food again. But don't spend too much time on her.'

Agnes looked up from her list in surprise. She'd never heard Bess say that before. 'Why?' she asked.

'Because she's been on and off our list for years. Always something wrong with her. If it's not headaches, it's stomach pains or something else. If you ask me, she just enjoys the attention. Anyway, I daresay she'll try to get you running round her like all the others, so don't give in to her,' Bess warned. 'And make sure you leave her till last, otherwise you'll get nowt else done.'

The idea of someone who could waste even Bess Bradshaw's time intrigued Agnes all afternoon, and she couldn't wait for her last visit of the day. The address on the list was a grocer's shop on the corner of Regent Street and Myrtle Street. 'H. Franklin & Son' was written in faded gold lettering above the door.

As Agnes approached, she saw the shop door was open, and she could hear voices coming from inside.

'I'm sorry, love. I can't do it,' a man was saying.

'Please, Mr Franklin?' The woman's voice was familiar. 'I wouldn't ask if I wasn't desperate. I'll pay you back, I swear.'

'I know, and I wish I could help you. But I've already given you more credit than I should. I can't give you any more.'

Agnes stepped quietly into the shop and realised where she'd heard the woman's voice. Mrs Willis was standing at the counter, a small child clinging to each of her hands.

'But what am I going to do? We haven't got a penny coming in now Norman's lost his job again. How am I going to feed the kids?'

'Like I said, I wish I could help you.'

The distress in Mrs Willis' voice was so painful,

Agnes couldn't bear to witness it. She was about to turn and leave the shop when the shopkeeper suddenly said, 'All right, nurse? I'll be with you in a minute.'

Mrs Willis swung round, colour rushing into her face. Her expression hardened when she saw Agnes.

'It's all right, I'll not keep you,' she muttered, and fled the shop, pushing past in her haste to get away.

The shopkeeper shrugged apologetically to Agnes. 'Poor woman,' he said. 'I've lost count of the number of times her husband's been out of work It's the war injuries, y'see. Can't keep a job for long, poor soul.'

Agnes thought of the terrible scars on Mr Willis' legs and body. There was barely, a man walking who hadn't experienced horror in the trenches. 'Anyway,' the shopkeeper went on, brightening, 'you're here to see my Sarah, aren't you? You'd best come this way.' He lifted the flap on the counter to let Agnes through.

Sarah Franklin was propped up in bed. She greeted Agnes with a wan smile.

'Oh, hello,' she said. 'You're new, aren't you?'

'That's right. I'm Miss Sheridan.'

Agnes braced herself, waiting to be asked where the 'real' nurse was, but all she did was nod and say, 'I'm Sarah Franklin. I daresay the other nurse has told you about me? I'm afraid I'm rather a regular patient of hers.' She looked like the tragic heroine of a pre-Raphaelite painting, her dark hair spread over the pillow around her long, pale face. Her eyes were wide and filled with sadness, and

Agnes had to remind herself that she was probably quite adept at playing the suffering martyr.

'Let's see what we can do for you today, shall we?' She consulted the message paper the doctor had left for her. As Bess had said, Mrs Franklin had recently suffered a bout of stomach flu. The nausea and sickness had gone, but it had left her feeling very tired and listless.

'How are you feeling today?' Agnes asked her.

'Still very weak, I'm afraid, nurse.'

'Any pain?'

'A little.' She ran a thin white hand over her abdomen.

'She's being brave,' her husband joined in from the doorway. 'She was wretched with it last night. Up half the night, she was.'

Sarah gave him a tremulous smile. 'Shouldn't you go and mind the shop, Harry? I'm sure the nurse can manage without you.' She waited until the door had closed, then said, 'Poor lamb, he does fuss so.'

And I bet you enjoy every minute, Agnes thought. 'Have you eaten anything?'

'Harry made me something last night, but it made me feel so ill...'

'You were sick again?'

'No, just pain. The most awful pain you could imagine.'

'Are you still in pain now?'

'A bit.'

'I'll make you a hot water bottle. That might help.'

'Thank you, nurse. You're very kind.'

Agnes prepared the hot water bottle and

175

wrapped it in a towel. But as she put it near her patient, Sarah yelped in pain.

Agnes frowned. 'Does it hurt when I touch it?' Sarah nodded. 'Where does it hurt?' She laid her hand on her stomach, close to her heart. 'Here?' Sarah shook her head. 'What about here...?' Agnes moved her hand to the epigastrium and pressed lightly. Sarah hissed, catching her lip between her teeth to stop herself from crying out.

Agnes took her hand away. Odd, she thought. Gastric influenza didn't usually cause so much pain.

Sarah must have noticed her puzzled expression because her eyes widened. 'What is it, nurse?' she whispered. 'What's wrong with me? Is it serious?'

Agnes came to, remembering Bess' warning. 'Oh no,' she assured her briskly. 'Nothing to worry about. I'll give you an aspirin for the pain, shall I? That should help you get some rest.'

'Thank you, nurse.' Sarah smiled up at her. 'You know, I'm so glad you came instead of Mrs Bradshaw. I really don't feel she ever listens to me.'

The shop was empty, and Mr Franklin was cleaning down the bacon slicer when Agnes left. He looked up from his work and said, 'How is she, nurse? Is she getting any better, do you think?'

'I'm sure she's almost over her gastric flu,' Agnes replied.

'Are you?' Mr Franklin frowned. 'She were proper bad last night. In agony, she was. Mind, I blame myself,' he said. 'It were me that made her eat something. I didn't think it would do any harm,' he said. 'Just a bit of salad. That in't going

176

to do anyone any harm, is it, nurse?'

'No,' Agnes said. 'No, I daresay not.' But her thoughts were already elsewhere, trying to recall something. Something she had once been told, or that she had seen written down...

No, it was gone. It crept in the shadows on the edge of her memory, refusing to show itself no matter how hard she tried to bring it into the light.

'Something wrong, nurse?' Mr Franklin frowned at her.

'No, not at all.' Agnes managed a smile, but the elusive memory bothered her.

It was still troubling her when she returned to Steeple Street that evening. For once, Bess had returned before her and was waiting in the district room.

'You took your time,' she said with great satisfaction. 'Yes, well, it took a long while for me to walk back,' Agnes replied pointedly.

'I thought Mrs Franklin might have kept you with her list of symptoms. How did you get on with her anyway?' she asked.

'She did seem very unwell.'

'You see what I mean? Always after attention.'

'I'm not sure if she was. She was in a great deal of pain. And she should have recovered from her gastric influenza by now.'

'Oh, she'll probably spin it out for as long as she can, if I know her,' Bess dismissed. 'She loves to have everyone fussing around her, like that besotted wretch of a husband of hers.'

'All the same, I think I'd like to go and see her again.'

Bess shook her head. 'There's no need. You'll only encourage her.'

'But I think there might be something genuinely wrong with her.'

Bess laughed. 'I can see she's already got you twisted round her little finger!'

'It's nothing like that. I just–' But Bess cut her off.

'I won't hear of it, Miss Sheridan,' she said, wagging a warning finger. 'I forbid you to go again. Do you understand?

Chapter Eighteen

October was proving to be a wet and turbulent month. The month that had come in with such a glorious Indian summer went out with grey skies and thunderstorms. Stormy gusts of wind shook the last of the leaves from the trees and rain fell steadily, churning the grass in the churchyard to a soggy quagmire.

Polly paused on the front step of Henry Slater's cottage, carefully scraping the mud off her shoes as she waited for someone to answer the door. Chilly raindrops dripped from her cap and ran down inside the collar of her coat.

There was no reply. No sound of approaching footsteps, or Job's eager barking as he threw himself at the door.

She lifted the latch and let herself into the cottage, looking round. The kitchen was empty, the range cold. Finn must be out, Polly thought, fighting down her disappointment. She hadn't realised how much she'd looked forward to seeing him until he wasn't there.

She reminded herself she was here to see Henry, not his grandson. But over the past few days she had been calling, her friendship with Finn had started to blossom again. He still barely spoke to her, but Polly sensed things were more relaxed between them.

'Mr Slater?' she called out, as she unfastened her coat and hung it carefully on the back of the door.

There was no reply although she thought she could hear the low murmur of voices coming from the old man's bedroom at the end of the passageway.

Polly set her bag down on the table. Finn had spread newspaper out for her, even though the table was spotlessly clean as usual. She smiled to herself. He might not make a fuss about it, but he was always so thoughtful.

'Mr Slater?' she called out again, as she stepped into the passageway. Again, there was no reply but for the low hum of voices.

Polly followed the sound to the old man's bedroom. Henry was sitting up in bed, with Matthew Elliott at his bedside, head bowed, hands clasped, lips moving in prayer.

She started to creep away, just as Matthew looked up.

'It's quite all right, nurse,' he said. 'We've finished now.' He smiled up at her. 'I just popped round to see how Mr Slater was getting on, and to say a prayer for his safe recovery.'

That explained Finn's absence, Polly thought. He would have made himself scarce if he knew the curate was visiting.

'I'm sure it's a great comfort to him,' she said.

'The sooner he recovers the better. We can't do without our faithful sexton.' Matthew smiled down at Henry.

'Oh, I don't know about that,' he said quietly. 'Finn does most of the heavy lifting work these days.'

Matthew's smile slipped slightly. 'Yes, but it's hardly the same as seeing your friendly face around the church, Mr Slater.'

No one could accuse Finn Slater of being friendly, Polly thought. 'I'll just go and wash my hands,' she said.

Matthew followed her into the kitchen. 'I'm glad to see you,' he said. 'I wanted a word with you.'

'Oh yes?'

'That dance I mentioned, to raise funds for the new roof? Well, it's this Friday,' he said. 'So – I wondered if you'd like to come?'

'Well, I–'

'Oh do say you will. It will be such fun.'

Matthew's gaze was so earnest, it made Polly's heart sink. She knew he was interested in her, and didn't want to raise his hopes.

'I will come,' she said. 'And I'll bring some of the other district nurses too,' she added. 'The more the merrier, don't you think?'

Matthew's face fell. 'Oh, er – yes, of course. Absolutely.'

Polly looked at his crestfallen expression and

felt a twinge of guilt. Matthew had only ever been charming to her; she didn't know why she found it so hard to like him.

She went to the sink. She could feel him standing behind her, watching her.

'Was there something else?' she asked over her shoulder.

'I – um – I just wondered how Mr Slater is doing. Has he shown any improvement?'

'He's doing as well as can be expected,' Polly gave the automatic reply. If Matthew wanted to know any more, he would have to talk to Henry himself. It wasn't her place to discuss patients' progress with anyone but their family.

'I do feel for the poor man. He really should be in hospital. I keep telling the vicar he should try to persuade him, but he says Mr Slater feels better at home.'

'And so he does,' Polly said.

'Yes, but it can't be very good for him, being at the mercy of that grandson of his...'

'Actually, Finn cares for his grandfather very well.' She looked around the kitchen. 'You only have to look at this place to see that.'

'Hmm.' Matthew didn't sound convinced. 'All the same, I'm not surprised the poor old fellow collapsed. It must be a terrible strain, living under the same roof as someone like that.'

Polly pressed her lips together and went on soaping her hands. She could tell the curate had more to say, but she had no wish to hear it.

'Actually, I'm surprised your Superintendent allows you to visit by yourself,' Matthew went on. 'I must say, I'm not happy about you being alone

181

with someone like him.'

Polly couldn't ignore him any longer. 'What on earth do you mean?'

'You mean you don't know?'

An unpleasant sensation crept up her spine. 'Know what?'

'Finn Slater has been in prison. He stabbed a man.'

The soap slipped from her hand and splashed into the bowl. She fished around for it, her hands shaking. All the time she could feel the rapid drum of her pulse crashing in her ears.

You're lying, she wanted to scream. You must be lying.

'Cornered him in a dark alley and stuck a knife in his ribs.' Matthew went on, his tone casual and unconcerned, as if he weren't delivering the most dreadful and shocking news imaginable. 'It was a local mill owner, so I suppose it must have been a robbery. Anyway, the vicar told me that's why Slater was sent here, because his family in Huddersfield wanted nothing to do with him after he came out of prison. 'And I really can't say I blame them,' he added. 'I'm only sorry we appear to be stuck with him now.'

Polly gripped the edge of the stone sink. 'Did the man die?' she heard herself murmur.

'No, by some miracle he survived, otherwise Slater would have been hanged. As it was he got seven years' hard labour. Although I don't know why they didn't hang him anyway, since he obviously intended to murder the poor soul.' Matthew peered at her closely. 'Now do you see why I'm so concerned about you?'

Polly pulled herself together enough to turn and face him. His pious expression made her want to scream.

'I'm sure I have nothing to fear,' she answered stiffly. 'Now, if you'll excuse me, I have a patient who needs my attention.'

She started to usher the curate towards the door, but he stood his ground. 'Just be careful, won't you?' he said. 'I would never be able to forgive myself if anything bad happened to you.'

'As I said, I have nothing to fear.' Polly held herself rigid until she had closed the door behind him. Only then did she allow herself to collapse against it, the strength leaving her body until it was all she could do to hold herself upright.

It took her a while to gather herself together enough to face Henry Slater. By the time she entered his room, she had splashed her face with cold water and managed to paste on the semblance of a smile.

Henry was sitting up in bed, doing the newspaper crossword. 'Has Mr Elliott gone?' he asked.

'Yes.'

'Good thing too. I know he thinks he's doing me a kindness, coming up here to say prayers and the like, but I can't help feeling as if I'm already dead and he's practising my funeral service!' Henry looked up at her. 'Here, are you all right, lass? You look proper pale.'

'I'm fine.' Polly picked up the doctor's notes to read them, then put them down again when her hands wouldn't stop shaking. The GP had prescribed digitalis for Henry, which meant she would have to pay particular attention to his

183

pulse rate.

It took her a while to count the beats as her concentration kept slipping away, back to what the curate had said. It couldn't be true. It couldn't.

'Finn will be sorry to have missed you,' Henry said, as she slipped the thermometer out of his mouth. 'He's out digging a grave. In this weather, I ask you!' He rolled his eyes. 'I told him it in't needed till Thursday, but he would insist. Between you and me, I don't think he's that keen on the curate,' he confided.

Polly tried to smile, but her mouth felt tight.

Henry frowned. 'Are you sure you're all right, lass? You seem all of a fluster.'

'Yes, of course.' She held up the thermometer to check the reading, but it slipped through her fingers. She scrabbled around to pick it up. 'I'm just in a bit of a hurry today, that's all.'

'Then you won't wait for Finn?'

'I – I can't.' She couldn't look at Henry as she said it.

'Just as you like. I'll see you later on, shall I?'

'Yes.' But she had already made up her mind that she would ask Miss Jarvis to take over the old man's care. She couldn't do it any more, not after this.

She'd reached the door when Henry said, 'You know, don't you?'

She froze. She couldn't think of anything to say, but she knew her silence gave her away.

'It was him, wasn't it? That ruddy curate!' Henry's voice was gruff with anger. 'I wish the vicar hadn't said anything to him, but I suppose he felt he had to be told.' He shook his head. 'I might have known he'd try to cause trouble. He's got it in for Finn, interfering little beggar!' He paused, and Polly could hear him fighting for breath.

'You mustn't upset yourself,' she said quietly.

'I told the lad he should say something,' Henry went on. 'I warned him this would happen, but would he listen?'

He drew in a deep breath. Polly turned to face him. 'Please, Mr Slater, try not to upset yourself,' she said.

She tried to settle him but he fought against her, brushing off her hands, determined to be heard.

'It in't what it seems,' he said. 'Finn's not a bad lad, truly he's not.'

But he stabbed a man. Polly pressed her lips together to hold on to the words. Henry was already getting himself in a state, and she didn't want to upset him further.

'It's none of my business,' she said quietly.

'Of course it's your business!' Henry retorted. 'The lad needs a friend, and he ... trusts you. I know he might not show it,' he let out a wheezing breath, 'but that's just Finn's way. He's had that many doors slammed in his face, he doesn't ... know how to show his feelings any more.'

Polly reached across, plumping up his pillows and helping him to sit upright to save herself having to reply. But when she'd finished, the old man grabbed her hand, his gnarled fingers closing around hers, trapping her.

'Talk to him, please,' he begged. 'Let him tell you his side of the story, then make up your mind.'

'And if he doesn't want to tell me?'

A look of defeat came into the old man's eyes. 'Then Finn's an even bigger fool than I think he is,' he said wearily.

Chapter Nineteen

Finn braced his boots in the mud and thrust his spade into the sodden earth. He had been digging for the past hour, and every muscle in his body ached. What made it worse was that the pouring rain was already causing the mud to slide back into the hole. Tomorrow he would have to come out and do it all again.

Job sat shivering on the rim of the grave, looking down at him with reproachful brown eyes. The dog's black coat was slick with rain.

Finn sighed. 'You're right,' he said, putting down his spade. 'It's time we were heading back.' He squinted up at the clock on the church tower. It was nearly ten. That wretched curate was bound to have gone by now.

And perhaps Polly would still be there. Finn found himself smiling at the thought as he placed his hands square on the muddy ground above him and levered himself up and out of the hole. He was wiping the mud off his hands with his handkerchief when he saw her come out of the cottage.

He lowered his gaze and told himself he wasn't looking at her, but he couldn't stop himself watching her as she picked her way gracefully down the path, her slender figure wrapped in her navy blue uniform coat, cap perched on her blonde hair.

He was trying to work himself up to give her a casual wave when Job sat up, his tail thumping on the ground. Finn tensed, suddenly aware of footsteps coming across the wet ground towards him. And then she was there, close behind him, and he could smell her light flowery perfume. His heart drummed in his chest.

But then another thought struck him. There could be only one reason why she would seek him out...

He swung round, forgetting his shyness in his sudden panic. 'Granddad...' Finn glanced past her towards the house, muscles taut, ready to run. 'Is he–'

'Your grandfather is quite well,' Polly said.

He felt some of the tension leave him, but still couldn't tear his gaze from the cottage. Mostly because it stopped him from having to look at her.

Job brushed past Finn to approach her, and Polly put her hand down to pat him. But she didn't smile at the dog as she usually did, or dig in her pocket for some treat to give him. She looked tense, her face pale. If Finn didn't know better, he would say she looked almost afraid...

She knows.

It was like a bolt of lightning in his brain, illuminating everything in a sudden, blinding flash. He didn't even pause to question how she knew. He just understood that she did.

He was surprised by how calm he felt. It was as if he had been waiting for the axe to fall, and now it had and he had nothing left to lose.

187

For a moment they stood looking at each other, the rain streaming down their faces. It was as if they were speaking without words.

Then Polly said, 'Your grandfather said you'd explain everything.'

Finn turned away. 'There's nothing to tell,' he said brusquely. 'I stabbed a man, I went to prison for it. I took my punishment, and here I am.'

'There must be more to it than that.'

'There isn't.' He wanted her to go away. He wanted her to hate him and shun the way everyone else did, because then it would be easier.

He bent down to retrieve his spade from the hole, but she didn't move. He didn't turn round but he knew she was still standing there, not moving. She must be soaked to the skin, he thought.

'You'll catch pneumonia,' he muttered.

'I don't care.'

He shot her a sideways glance. 'You're very stubborn.'

'That makes two of us, doesn't it?' Polly tilted her head to one side. She didn't look angry, or frightened. Her lovely face was calm and composed, her gaze fixed on his. 'Well?' she, said. 'Are you going to tell me or not?'

He paused for a moment. He wanted to deny everything, to run, to hide, to do anything but allow her to see what was in his heart. But then he looked into her face, saw the raindrops sparkling on her lashes, and he knew he couldn't lie to her.

'Come with me,' he said.

He led her to a distant corner of the churchyard, a place she had never been before. There was a grave there, with a small headstone.

'Granddad insisted they buried her here,' Finn said. 'He said he wanted to look after her. God knows my parents never did,' he muttered bitterly.

Polly peered at the name on the inscription. Amy Ann Slater. According to the dates below it, she was fifteen when she died, six years previously.

'Your sister?' she said. He nodded. 'How did she...?'

'She drowned.' Finn's voice was flat, devoid of emotion. But she could see a muscle working angrily in his jaw. 'Suicide, or so they said.'

Polly swung round to face him. 'But you don't believe that?'

'Oh, I believe she took her own life all right. But he drove her to it.'

'You mean the man you—'

'The man I stabbed.' Finn's voice was low. 'He killed her, as surely as if he'd pushed her into that river himself.'

Polly stared into Finn's hard, angry face. Slowly, very slowly, things were beginning to fall into place.

'What did he do to her?' she asked, although she was sure she already knew the answer.

Finn didn't reply, and she knew he couldn't. Even now, years later, he couldn't seem to find the words.

'Ruined her,' he said finally. His voice was faint, as if it was coming from a long-distant memory. 'Amy was just a little girl, playing out with her mates after dark. She was on her way home when he grabbed her and dragged her down an alley-way.' Finn took a deep, ragged breath, and his

189

hands balled into fists. Polly looked down at them, and thought about the damage they could do. Even Job whimpered in the face of his master's raw anger.

And yet he'd chosen a knife.

'I was out all night, looking for her,' he went on. 'It wasn't like Amy not to come home. She was such a good girl...' He swallowed, and Polly could see him fighting for control. 'I was the one who found her, left like a sack of old rubbish in that alleyway. I hardly recognised her, she'd been so badly beaten. And her clothes were all torn...' He braced himself. 'I'm glad I was the one who found her,' he said in a hollow voice. 'I wouldn't have wanted a stranger to see her like that.'

Polly clutched her hands together to stop herself from reaching out to him. 'What happened then?' she whispered.

'I carried her home in my arms, and my mam washed her and put her to bed.' His voice was flat again, all emotion gone. 'She wanted that to be the end of it. All washed away.'

'But why?'

'Because she didn't want any trouble, and neither did my dad.' He flicked a look at Polly. 'The man who did this – we all knew him, you see. He owned the mill in town. The mill where my dad and all my uncles worked. No one wanted to cause trouble, not for him.'

'But surely the police...?'

Finn gave a derisive snort. 'Didn't you hear what I just said? They didn't want to go to the police. My dad made out it was for Amy's own good. He said if it all went to court, she'd be dragged up as a witness and publicly shamed. It would be her word against the boss', Dad said, and he didn't want our family to be disgraced, and everyone to know what had happened to Amy.' Finn's face was a mask of contempt. 'Dad said he was doing it for her, but really he was doing it for himself. He betrayed his own daughter because he didn't want to make trouble. Perhaps if they'd stood up for her, she wouldn't have been so ashamed. Then she wouldn't have done what she did.'

'So you took matters into your own hands?' Polly said.

'I couldn't let that man get away with it. I didn't care what my parents said, I wanted to make him pay. So one night I stole a knife out of the kitchen and went looking for him.'

'You meant to kill him?'

'I was nineteen years old, I didn't know what I was doing. But I knew I had to do something – for Amy. He couldn't be allowed to get away with it, not after what he'd done to her.'

'What did you do?'

'I tracked him down to one of his drinking places, then followed him home.' Finn's voice was devoid of emotion, as if he was telling a story about someone else. 'I waited for him in a dark alley. I wanted him to feel the same fear my sister had.'

'But you didn't kill him?'

'Only by sheer luck. It was dark, I didn't know what I was doing. All I know is there was a lot of blood.'

'And then what happened?'

'I stood over him until the police came.'

Polly jerked back as if he'd slapped her. 'Why didn't you run away?'

'Because I wanted everyone to know what I'd done.' Finn lifted his chin. 'I wasn't a coward like him, attacking little girls in the dark and then hiding. I wanted him to look me in the eye and remember my face for ever. And I wanted people to know the truth about him.'

'And did they?'

'What do you think?' Finn shook his head. 'No charges were brought against him, because no one would come forward with any evidence.'

'Not even your parents?'

'Not even them.' His face was bitter. 'They would rather have saved face than stand up for their own children.'

Polly stared at him. What he had done was truly terrible, but she couldn't comprehend the thought of his own family not standing up for him, especially under the circumstances. 'So he got away with it?' she murmured.

'As far as I know, he's still running the mill. And my father and uncles are still bowing and scraping to him. But I couldn't have gone back there. Even if my mother and father had wanted me to, I couldn't have walked the same streets as him, knowing what he'd done. And neither could poor Amy. After I'd been sent to prison she did away with herself.' Finn gazed down at the grave, lost in thought for a moment, then turned to face Polly. 'So now you know the whole story,' he said. 'Now you know the kind of man I really am.'

'Yes,' she said. 'Yes, I think I do.'

'I suppose you'll want to walk away from me

while you've still got the chance?'

She looked at him. His eyes glinted with the light of challenge, but there was something else there too. A spark of vulnerability. He was waiting for her to reject him, to turn her back on him the way everyone else, including his own parents, had.

And if she was wise, perhaps she should. She thought briefly about her mother. Bess had loathed Frank, believing he had ruined Polly's life by marrying her and putting paid to her nursing career. What she would make of Finn Polly could only imagine.

She had worked so hard for the past two years to win back her mother's respect. Did she really want to throw it all away again?

'Why would I want to walk away?' said Polly.

That surprised Finn. His brows drew together over stormy grey eyes. 'I don't understand,' he murmured.

'I've seen the way you are with your grand-father, and even with Job here.' She patted the dog's damp head. 'I know you pretend you don't have a heart, but I've seen it. And what you did … I can't say I approve, but I understand why you did it, and that's something. And I don't believe you set out to kill that man, no matter what you say.'

His eyes narrowed. 'What makes you believe that?'

'Because if you'd really meant to kill him, you would have had plenty of chance to finish the job while you were waiting for the police.' Polly shook her head. 'You're no murderer, Finn Slater.'

He stared at her, eyes fixed on hers, so hard she

thought for a moment she might have read it all wrong.

Then she saw a tiny spark of warmth light up the darkness of his eyes, kindling into the faintest of smiles around the corners of his mouth.

'Aye,' he muttered. 'Happen you're right about that.'

Chapter Twenty

'Please come out, Mr Shapcott.'

'Bugger off!'

Agnes suppressed a sigh of irritation and looked at her watch. He had been shut in the cupboard for nearly half an hour now, and she was running late. But she was determined that today would be the day Isaiah Shapcott had his bath.

She had enlisted the help of a neighbour to drag in the old tin tub from the yard, even though the man had laughed and said, 'Tha'll niver get him in that, nurse!'

'We'll see,' Agnes had replied grimly, taking off her cuffs and rolling up her sleeves.

It had taken endless boiling of kettles to fill the tub. She had added a generous splash of Lysol, and warmed the towels by the fire. Everything was in place, and now all she needed was someone to wash.

But Mr Shapcott wasn't coming out.

She pressed her ear up against the door. She could hear him shuffling about in there, so at least

194

he was still alive. Agnes could only imagine Bess Bradshaw's face if she'd returned to Steeple Street with the news that she'd accidentally managed to suffocate a patient while trying to give them a bath.

'You can't stay in there for ever, Mr Shapcott,' Agnes pleaded with him. 'It can't be very comfortable for you.'

'I'm all right,' a muffled voice insisted stubbornly from the other side of the door.

'Why won't you just have a bath? I'm sure you'd enjoy it.' There was no reply. Agnes sighed. 'All right,' she said. 'Have it your own way, I won't waste any more time on you.'

She stepped away from the door and made a great show of getting her things ready. 'Can you hear me, Mr Shapcott? I'm leaving now. You can come out. I'll see you next week.'

'Not if I see thee first!'

Mr Shapcott wasn't a trusting soul, and it was a full two minutes before Agnes finally heard the cupboard door creak open. She lurked in the shadows, ready to pounce.

By the time he spotted her bag sitting on the table it was too late for him. Agnes jumped out from behind him, wrapping her arms around him and trapping him.

He was so small she could almost pick him up, but he fought like a demon, kicking and twisting in her arms.

'Help! Help!' he shrieked. 'Someone help me, I'm having a heart attack!'

'No, you're not,' Agnes said, hanging on grimly, 'you're having a bath.'

She hauled him across the room, a tangle of flailing limbs. Close to, the stench of stale urine, sweat and filth coming off him made her feel sick She managed to wrestle him over to the fireside, and dumped him in a chair.

'There,' she said. 'Now sit down.'

He tried made to make a run for it, but Agnes stood over him. 'Don't you dare,' she warned. 'You're not moving until I've had a good look at you.'

To her amazement, he complied, sitting still and quiet, his hands gripping the sides of the chair. Agnes could see his bright eyes darting as she inspected his hair.

'Just as I thought,' she said. 'You're crawling with lice. I'll have to shave your head.'

'Nay!' he protested. 'Tha'll not scalp me. Tha'll not! And tha'll not bath me neither. I won't have it!'

'Oh, come on, Mr Shapcott, it's only a bath. And you'll feel so much better afterwards. Come on, let's get this shirt off.'

She made a move towards him and he suddenly went hysterical. 'Nay, nay!' he screamed, flailing his arms. Agnes tried to dodge out of the way but he caught her with one hand, his long, thick yellow nails clawing the side of her face.

'Ow!' Agnes jumped back, her hand to her cheek.

She expected Mr Shapcott to make another run for it, but he sat rigid in his chair, staring at the floor.

'You can blame yoursen,' he muttered under his breath. 'I told thee I didn't want no bath.'

196

Agnes' ears were ringing. She forgot her own rules about avoiding contact with the furniture, and sank down into an armchair.

Mr Shapcott was looking at her out of the corner of his eye. 'What's up wi' thee?' he asked.

'I'm all right. I just need to sit down for a moment.' She took her hand away from her face. Her palm was sticky with blood.

She heard footsteps scuttling across the stone-flagged floor. Mr Shapcott was going to his hiding place again, but this time she really didn't care. If he disliked baths as much as that, she wasn't going to risk life and limb giving him one.

But then her nostrils were filled with the overpowering stench of Isaiah Shapcott, and she knew he was standing over her. She felt the cool of a damp cloth being pressed to her temple.

'For t'bleeding,' he mumbled.

'Thank you.' She took the cloth away from her face and inspected it. It was a filthy dishcloth, but at least the thought was there.

'I never meant to hurt thee,' he mumbled. 'I just didn't want a bath, that's all. I swore no one was ever going to do it to me again, not after last time–'

Agnes looked up at him. 'Last time?'

His mouth shut like a trap, his eyes lowered, and she knew he wouldn't say any more.

He jumped back as Agnes rose to her feet, but she stepped past him and went to her bag for some antiseptic and a swab. She could feel him watching her with interest as she carefully cleaned her wound in the spotted scrap of mirror hanging over the kitchen sink.

'It in't my fault,' Isaiah muttered, over and over again. 'I told thee I didn't want no bath, I told thee.'

'Yes, you did, Mr Shapcott,' Agnes sighed. She wrapped the swab in newspaper and went to throw it on the fire. 'Well, I wouldn't worry about it. No one is going to try and force you to have one again. Well, not me, at any rate.'

'Tha'll not?' His voice sounded wavering, uncertain.

'I'll not,' Agnes said firmly. 'I can't say they won't send another nurse, but I won't be coming again.'

Bess Bradshaw could howl about it all she liked. It might seem like a cruelty to leave Mr Shapcott in his filth, but it was an even bigger cruelty to put him through this terror.

And it really was terror. For some reason Agnes couldn't fathom, Isaiah Shapcott was petrified of having a bath.

She lifted her gaze and noticed for the first time a solitary photograph on the mantelpiece of a smiling young man sitting astride a chestnut horse. It faced the camera boldly, nostrils flaring, proud head tossed, showing off the powerfully muscled neck.

Without thinking, she said, 'What a beautiful creature. Racehorse, isn't it?'

'That's right, missus. That's Jackotino. By Roustabout out of Sweet Susanne. Won five of his twelve starts over seven furlongs, and was placed in four more. One of the toughest beasts I ever met.' Isaiah squinted up at her. His voice had lost its tremor, she noticed. 'Know much about 'orses, do you?'

198

'I used to ride, when I was a child.'

'Did you have an 'orse?'

Agnes nodded. 'A pony, Daffodil.'

He leaned forward eagerly. 'What were it like?'

'She was dapple grey, an Arab, fourteen hands high. She was very good-natured, but she hated going out in the rain.' Agnes smiled to herself at the memory. It was all so long ago, she felt as if she were describing someone else's life. 'She belonged to my sister really, but Vanessa never liked riding so she passed Daffodil on to me.'

'There were nothing good-natured about Jackotino.' Isaiah Shapcott sidled over and took the photograph from the mantelpiece. 'He had a temper on him all right. And if he had a mind not to do summat...' Isaiah shook his head. 'None of the other lads understood him like I did. I used to tell 'em: he'll come round in his own time, you can't rush him.'

'You were a stable lad?'

'Not just a stable lad, missus. I worked at Paddy O'Neill's yard, out in Middleham. Tha's heard of it, I suppose?' Agnes hadn't, but she nodded anyway. 'Aye, he trained some champions there.' Isaiah's chin tilted up with pride. 'I were going to be a jockey.'

'You've certainly got the build for it.'

He smiled sheepishly. 'Aye, the Superintendent at the workhouse said it were all I were good for. That or going up chimneys!'

'You were brought up in a workhouse?'

She knew at once it was the wrong thing to say. The shutters came down and he seemed to shrink in on himself, his shoulders hunched, his mouth pressed tight closed.

Agnes quickly changed the subject. 'Tell me more about Jackotino.'

Isaiah looked down at the photograph in his hand, tracing the horse's profile with the tip of one finger. 'We were going to Royal Ascot together, him and me. Might have even won, too. Except I had my accident before we could go.' His face was bleak. 'I broke my hip and hit my head, knocked myself out cold for a week, so they told me. Not much good for racing after that,' he said, his mouth twisting. 'Could barely even sweep the yard, let alone anything else. I got laid off, and Jackie boy was sold not long after. Not that it were his fault,' Isaiah went on hastily. 'I in't blaming the horse. It were me that let him have his head.'

'What a shame,' Agnes said.

'Aye, that's what it was.' He propped the photograph back on the mantelpiece. 'Happen you could bring round a picture of your pony next time you come, if you've got one? I'd like to see it.'

'Oh, but I thought you didn't want me to—' Agnes started to say, then changed her mind. 'I will,' she promised.

She moved away from him and had started to pack up her bag when Isaiah said quietly, 'I'll have that bath now, if you like?'

Agnes looked over her shoulder at him. Isaiah was like Jackotino, she thought. He needed to come round in his own time.

'If you like,' she said, trying to keep her voice casual.

'But I'll do it myself. I don't want you coming

near me.' He eyed her warily.

'I'll tell you what. Why don't we make a screen out of the clothes horse and a couple of blankets? Then you'll be nice and private.'

He nodded. 'Good idea, missus.'

Agnes found a couple of blankets in the cupboard. They were none too clean, but they were the best he had.

As he undressed behind them, Isaiah said, 'Tell me more about your pony. Did you go riding much?'

'All the time, when I was a child. My brother Peter and I–' She took a deep breath, her voice faltering at his name. 'My brother and I used to go off hacking in the woods,' she finished. 'We'd lose all track of time and come back late and filthy, and of course my mother would be furious.'

'What was your brother's horse called?'

'Prince, I think. Or was it Storm? I can barely remember.' As Agnes struggled to recall the name of Peter's pony, she heard a splash. Isaiah Shapcott was in the bath.

'What colour was it? How big? Was it an Arab?' he bombarded her with questions.

'Goodness, I don't know. I can scarcely remember the poor beast's name, so how am I supposed to recall anything else? It was a bay, I think. Yes, definitely chestnut bay. And bigger than Daffodil, so I suppose it must have been about fifteen–' Agnes stopped dead. She had been pacing the room as she talked, trying to remember the answers to Isaiah's questions. But without thinking, she'd looked up and caught his reflection in the mirror over the mantelpiece.

She wanted to look away, but she couldn't. Her gaze was drawn and repelled at the same time by the silvery, withered flesh that covered his back. It spread across his skinny shoulders and down his arms.

She had only seen a scar like that once before, during a stint on the Children's ward at the Nightingale. A little girl had tipped a pan of boiling water from the stove all over herself...

Isaiah glanced up and Agnes caught his gaze, sharp and accusing in the mirror.

'Workhouse,' he said in a low voice, his voice thick with shame. 'Didn't want a bath so they said they'd make me.'

Their eyes met, and Agnes understood.

'No one will ever make you do it again, Mr Shapcott,' she said quietly. 'I promise you that.'

Once she'd finished her rounds for the day, Agnes made sure her route home took her past the Franklins' shop on the corner of Myrtle Street. She had waited two whole days since her last visit, which was longer than she would have liked. Besides, she wasn't really defying Bess Bradshaw if she had to walk past anyway, she reasoned.

She had spent most of the previous two evenings reading through her old study notes from her training days at the Nightingale, searching for the piece of the puzzle she knew was missing.

And she thought she might have found it.

Mr Franklin had just finished serving a customer when Agnes walked into the shop.

'Hello, nurse,' he greeted her in surprise. 'I didn't expect to see you today.'

'I was just passing, so I thought I'd drop in,' she said. 'How is your wife today?'

Mr Franklin's smile faded. 'Not good,' he said heavily. 'No better than t'other day, at any rate.'

'Is the pain still bad?'

'It comes and goes, nurse. I've been giving her hot water bottles, but she's still having a tough time of it.'

'Has she eaten anything else?'

'Not since the other night.'

'And you say it was a salad she ate?'

He nodded. 'That's right, nurse.' Then his expression changed. 'You don't think I made her ill, do you? Oh, don't say that, I'd never forgive myself...'

'It's all right, Mr Franklin, I don't think you've hurt her,' Agnes assured him. 'If my suspicions are right, you might even have helped get to the bottom of what's troubling her.'

'You think there's something wrong with her, then? Not just the gastric business?'

Agnes took a deep breath. 'I'd like to have another look at her, if that's all right?' she said. 'And then we'll see, shall we?'

Chapter Twenty-One

'You did what?'

Bess Bradshaw could scarcely contain herself the following morning. Her lips were white with fury.

Agnes straightened her shoulders, determined

203

to defend herself. 'I telephoned for the doctor,' she repeated.

Bess let out a long, angry breath. 'I can't believe it,' she muttered. 'It's bad enough that you defied my instructions and went to see Mrs Franklin again, but to call the doctor out–'

'I had reason to believe she was very ill. I thought it was better to be safe than sorry.'

'You're the one who should be sorry!' Bess turned on her, tiny eyes glittering with fury. 'I've told you before, Miss Sheridan, no one is interested in your opinion. You're to do as you're told!'

'But–'

'Be quiet! You never know when to stop, that's your trouble.' Bess shook her head. 'Well, you've done it now,' she said. 'You've not only wasted your own time, you've wasted Dr Branning's too. He'll be utterly furious. I wouldn't be at all surprised if he reported you to Miss Gale...'

'Did someone say my name?' The Superintendent stood in the doorway to the district room behind them. Agnes hadn't heard her come in, and from the look on her face neither had Bess. 'What on earth is going on in here?' said Miss Gale. 'Mrs Bradshaw, you were making such a racket I could hear you all the way from my office.'

'I'll tell you what's going on, Miss Gale. This girl' – Bess jabbed a furious finger in Agnes' direction – 'has taken it upon herself to summon the doctor without asking my permission.'

'I see.' Miss Gale turned to Agnes. 'Is this true, Miss Sheridan?'

Agnes nodded. 'But it was an emergency,' she said. Bess snorted.

'And I take it you don't agree, Mrs Bradshaw?' Miss Gale responded calmly.

'Indeed I don't, Miss Gale!'

'Well, if Miss Sheridan was acting on the basis of her nursing instinct, then I suppose we have to trust her judgement.'

Bess' mouth fell open. 'But...' she started to splutter, but Miss Gale held up her hand.

'We can argue the point later, Mrs Bradshaw,' she said. 'But now it's nearly nine, and there are patients to see.'

'Yes, Miss Gale.' Agnes hardly dared look at Bess as she slipped past her out of the district room. She could only imagine the Assistant Superintendent's fury.

Agnes' first call of the morning was to Mr Willis. After their brief meeting in Mr Franklin's shop a couple of days earlier, Agnes wasn't looking forward to seeing his wife again.

Mrs Willis looked just as uncomfortable when she opened the door.

'Oh, it's you,' she said, and stood aside reluctantly to let her in. Agnes could feel the woman's suspicious gaze on her as she washed her hands at the sink, along with the equally suspicious gazes of the children.

'How is your husband today?' Agnes did her best to make conversation.

'You tell me. You're t'nurse,' Mrs Willis replied rudely.

Agnes forced her lips into a smile as she reached for her towel. 'I'd best go and see then, hadn't I?'

No sooner had Mr Willis recovered from his last leg ulcer than another had developed, even worse than the last. It had taken longer to heal, and Agnes braced herself for the worst as she removed the old dressing.

But to her relief, the wound was fairly clean, and granulation had started to form around the edges.

'That looks as if it's mending nicely,' she said.

'About time something started going my way,' Mr Willis grumbled.

'I heard about you losing your job,' Agnes said, as she dabbed the wound with antiseptic. 'I'm so sorry.'

She'd made the remark without thinking, and regretted it instantly as she felt Mr Willis' limbs stiffen.

'Who told you?' he hissed.

Agnes blushed. 'I – er – heard your wife talking to Mr Franklin,' she admitted, conscious that every word she said landed her deeper in trouble.

'Aye, well, I daresay it'll be all over Quarry Hill by now. Norman Willis, the man who can't support his own family!'

'I'm sure no one is saying that.'

'Then you don't know the folk round here, do you?' he spat. 'Why do you think I never go out? Because I don't like the way they talk about me. I can hear 'em whispering when I walk down the street.' He jabbed a warning finger at her. 'I don't want to hear you've been spreading gossip neither!' he snarled.

Agnes flinched away. 'I can assure you I won't!'

'You see you don't.' He stuck out his leg. 'Now just get on with what you're here to do.'

Agnes kept her head down and quietly set about

dressing the wound. His leg was a mass of old scars and wasted muscle. No wonder it ulcerated so much, she thought. Exercise would have helped, but she decided not to suggest it. She could already feel Mr Willis' resentment vibrating through him.

Instead, she asked quietly, 'How did your leg get so badly damaged?'

'How d'you think?' he snapped back.

Agnes looked at him. According to his notes he was thirty years old, roughly the same age Peter would have been, had he lived. 'The war?'

'Ypres. A German shell caught me when I was face down in the middle of no-man's-land. Left me for dead in the mud.'

'Lucky you survived.'

'Lucky? Is that what you think?' His bitterness shocked her.

'How did you get back to safety?' she asked.

'A couple of medics found me and dragged me back to the trenches. Bloody fools!' His mouth twisted. 'They could have been killed themselves, with all those shells around waiting to explode.'

'My father was a doctor at Ypres,' Agnes said quietly.

Norman Willis lifted his head sharply, and looked as if he might say something, but Mrs Willis appeared in the doorway.

'That's enough war talk,' she said shortly. 'You know I don't like hearing it in this house. It's bad enough you had to go through it.' Her mouth was set in a tight line. 'It's all over and done with now.'

'Aye, you're right. It's all over and done with, thank God,' Mr Willis muttered. He was smiling,

207

but when Agnes glanced at him, she could see the pain in his eyes. It was the same hollow despair she had seen on her father's face whenever he thought no one was watching.

The war would never be over and done with for either of them, thought Agnes.

It was a long, exhausting day. By the time Agnes returned to the district nurses' house, every muscle in her body was aching from endlessly lifting patients in and out of beds and baths, bending to dress wounds and give injections. All she longed for was a long, hot soak.

She certainly wasn't in the mood to go dancing. But tonight there was the dance at the church hall, and she and Phil had promised Polly they would go with her.

Agnes was trying to think up all kinds of excuses why she couldn't go as she walked up the steps to the house. Before she had a chance to put her hand on the door latch, it swung open and Dottie greeted her. Agnes suspected the maid had been lurking behind the door, looking through the frosted glass for her to arrive.

'There you are,' she said. 'Miss Gale wants you in her office. And she's got the doctor with her,' Dottie added ominously.

The first thing Agnes saw when she walked in was Bess standing in a corner of the room with a face like thunder. Beside Miss Gale at her desk was an elderly man Agnes took to be Dr Branning. He reminded her of her father, with his shock of silvery hair and warm, twinkling brown eyes.

'Ah, Miss Sheridan,' Miss Gale greeted her.

'We've been waiting for you. Dr Branning has dropped in especially to see you.' She made it sound as if it were a great honour.

Agnes flashed a glance at Bess. She must be enjoying every minute of this. If Dr Branning had come to give Agnes a dressing down in person, he must be very angry indeed.

Dr Branning rose to his feet to greet her. 'So this is the young lady we need to thank, is it?' he said.

Agnes looked up sharply, 'Thank, sir?'

'I went to see Mrs Franklin this morning. You were quite right, nurse. She had a very nasty duodenal ulcer.'

Agnes was so taken aback, she forgot her nerves. 'How is she, sir?'

'She is in hospital, and doing very well now she's getting the treatment she needs. Poor woman, who knows how long she has been going on with it.' He shook his head. 'I must say, the diagnosis hadn't occurred to me in all the times I'd seen her.' He pursed his mouth. 'You might have gathered, Miss Sheridan, that our Mrs Franklin has something of a reputation around here.'

'The boy who cried wolf,' Miss Gale put in.

'Indeed, Miss Gale. Although this is a salutary lesson for us all never to ignore a patient's symptoms, no matter how often they complain about them.'

Agnes risked another glance at Bess Bradshaw. She was staring at the wall, her expression fixed.

'Poor Mrs Franklin might have had to endure a great deal more pain, if you hadn't spotted her symptoms,' Dr Branning went on. 'Tell me, my dear, what made you think it might be an ulcer?'

'It was just something I recalled from my nursing training, doctor. Unlike gastric ulcers, ulcers in the duodenum don't cause pain until several hours after a meal, and then often in the early hours of the morning. Raw fruit and salads also aggravate them. And then there was considerable pain in the epigastrium–'

'All right, all right,' Bess muttered, unable to contain herself any longer. 'We don't need you showing off.'

'Well, I for one am most impressed,' Dr Branning declared, ignoring Bess. 'Where did you train, Miss Sheridan?'

'The Nightingale Hospital in London, sir.' Out of the corner of her eye, Agnes saw Bess rolling her eyes.

'Indeed? I've heard of it. Well, Miss Sheridan, your superior training has really proved its worth today.'

'Thank you, sir.'

'Then I'm glad the matter has reached a satisfactory conclusion,' Miss Gale said. 'Now, Miss Sheridan, you'll want to be excused. I understand you're going to a dance with the other students this evening?'

'Yes, Miss Gale.'

'Have a nice time, but don't be too late. Dottie locks the doors promptly at ten o'clock.'

'Yes, Miss Gale.' As she passed her, Agnes couldn't help smiling to see Bess' sulky expression.

Suddenly she thought she might be in the mood for dancing after all.

Chapter Twenty-Two

Polly was at the mirror, sorting out Phil's hair for the dance, when Agnes came in, grinning from ear to ear. It made a startling change from her roommate's usual beaten-down expression after the latest disagreement with her mother.

'Someone's in a good mood,' Phil observed. 'Don't tell me they've found your bicycle?'

Agnes shook her head. 'Better than that.'

'They've bought you a new one!' Phil looked outraged. 'I knew it! I don't suppose I'll ever get my motorcycle now—'

'Stay still!' Polly tapped her on the shoulder with the hairbrush. It was difficult enough to untangle Phil's thick thatch of brown hair without her wriggling about all the time.

'It's nothing to do with my bicycle.' Agnes sat down on the bed. 'I've just had a visit from Dr Branning.'

'Why? Are you ill?' Phil asked.

'No!' Agnes looked pleased with herself. 'He came to thank me for my work.'

As she changed out of her uniform she told them the whole story. How Bess Bradshaw had forbidden her to go and visit a patient, but she'd gone anyway and somehow ended up saving their life.

All the while she was talking, Polly could feel a chill of foreboding uncurling in the pit of her stomach.

211

'And you say Dr Branning came all this way just to thank you?' Phil Fletcher said. Her voice was light, but Polly could see the set of her jaw. Phil had been used to getting all the praise until Agnes Sheridan came along. She was a nice girl but fiercely competitive, and Polly knew it wouldn't sit well with her to have her position usurped.

'I must say, I was surprised myself,' Agnes said. 'After the way Mrs Bradshaw went on about it, I was sure I was going to get into trouble.'

'I'll bet she was furious,' Polly said quietly, her hands busy plaiting Phil's hair.

'She was completely beside herself,' Agnes confirmed. 'And she looked as if she was about to explode when Dr Branning complimented me.'

Polly caught Phil's eye in the mirror and knew they were both thinking the same thing.

Agnes caught it too. 'What?' she said. 'Why are you looking at each other like that?'

Polly paused for a moment, choosing her words carefully. 'It doesn't do to antagonise my mother, you know. She has a way of getting her revenge.'

Agnes rolled her eyes. 'Don't I know it! But I didn't set out to antagonise her.'

'All the same, you should watch your step.'

Agnes tilted her head arrogantly. 'Bess Bradshaw can do her worst. I'm sure I'll be able to cope with it.'

Polly opened her mouth to reply, but Phil said, 'Oh, just let her enjoy her moment of triumph. Lord knows we students don't get many of them. Have you finished?'

'Nearly.' Polly jammed the last pin in place. 'There, all done.'

'You've worked a miracle, my dear.' But Phil hardly bothered to check her reflection. She was the least vain girl Polly had ever met, at least as far as her appearance went.

Phil stood up. 'Now it's your turn to be transformed,' she said to Agnes.

Agnes shook her head. 'There's no need–' she started to say, but Phil interrupted her.

'Oh, go on. I had to endure it, and so should you.'

'Charming!' Polly said. 'And after all my hard work too.' She turned to Agnes. 'Come on, it'll only take a minute,' she coaxed. 'I'll just brush it out for you.'

Agnes slid into the chair reluctantly, and Polly got to work with her brush. Released from the pins that held it in place, Agnes' hair flowed over her shoulders in glossy waves. It was a rich chestnut colour and felt like silk rippling through Polly's fingers, especially after Phil's coarse brown curls.

'You have the most beautiful hair,' she said.

'Thank you.' Agnes lowered her eyes, blushing at the compliment. She was a lovely-looking girl, Polly thought, but like Phil she was careless about her appearance. Polly was certain they didn't own a lipstick or a bottle of scent between them.

'So what's this dance you're dragging us to?' Phil asked.

'It's a fund-raiser for the church. I just thought it might be fun.' Polly didn't add that she needed them there with her to keep Matthew Elliott at bay.

'I can't say I feel much like dancing,' Phil said. 'A pig stood on my foot today.'

213

Polly caught Agnes' eye and laughed. 'And we thought we had it tough!'

'Don't!' Phil grimaced, massaging her bruised toes. 'It's too much, what with the perils of the farmyard and all that walking and cycling too. If the Association doesn't give me a motorcycle soon, I think I might give up the job completely.'

Polly smiled at Agnes. Phil must have said those words at least twice a day.

'I couldn't imagine Miss Templeton on a motorcycle,' Agnes said.

'Oh, I've told her she can ride in the sidecar,' Phil replied carelessly. 'She's quite happy about it.'

She went off to her room to change and returned less than a minute later, wearing a dowdy-looking dress at least two sizes too big for her and in an unflattering shade of green.

Polly eyed it dubiously. 'Is that what you're wearing?'

'Yes, why? What's wrong with it?'

'It's...' Polly opened her mouth, then closed it again. Phil clearly didn't think there was anything wrong with the way she looked, and Polly didn't want to offend her. 'It's very nice,' she said finally.

'So will your young man be at the dance?' Phil asked.

Polly froze for a second as a sudden vision of Finn Slater flashed into her mind. Then she carried on brushing. 'I don't know what you mean,' she mumbled.

'Oh, come on! You can't fool us. We've seen you going out all dressed up on your afternoons off!'

Polly kept her head down. 'I always dress up to

214

go and visit my husband's grave,' she said, but she could feel herself blushing.

'Yes, but you've been even more dressed up than usual recently.' Phil smiled archly. 'I'm right, aren't I? It's written all over your face.'

'There isn't anyone, honestly.' Polly turned her worried gaze towards the door as she said it. She wouldn't put it past her mother to lurk on the landing, listening to their conversation.

'Don't worry, your secret is safe with us,' Phil whispered conspiratorially. 'Although really, I do think it's too bad that you're not even allowed to have an admirer at your age. Is your mother worried you're going to elope again?'

Agnes looked up, startled. 'You eloped?'

'You mean you've been sharing a room all these weeks and you haven't told her?' Phil stared at Polly accusingly.

'She hasn't asked,' Polly replied quietly. She was grateful that Agnes Sheridan kept herself to herself and didn't pry. She wasn't sure she could have put up with a gossipy chatterbox.

'Oh, but you must tell her now!' Phil insisted.

Polly felt her blush deepening. 'I'm sure Agnes doesn't want to hear about–'

'I'm sure she does,' Phil said. 'You want to hear it, don't you?'

Agnes caught her eye in the mirror, her expression sympathetic. 'Not if Polly doesn't want to tell me...'

'You see? She's all ears. Go on, Polly.'

Polly took a deep breath. She knew Phil would only keep going on about it until she told her story.

'I met Frank when I was working at the Infirmary,' she began the story slowly. 'I was training on the Orthopaedic ward, and he'd fallen off a roof and broken his leg.'

Typical Frank, she thought, always getting into scrapes, daring to do what no one else would. The ward sister used to shake her head and say there was never a dull moment with Mr Malone around, and she was right. His devil-may-care attitude was part of the attraction for Polly, that and his fair good looks. He reminded her of her father, with his lively sense of humour and ready laugh that seemed to echo down the ward. No wonder she fell for him so quickly. By the time Frank was discharged three months later, they were deeply in love and planning to marry.

'But your mother didn't approve?' Agnes guessed.

Polly shook her head. 'She didn't think he was good enough for me. I knew she'd be disappointed that I wanted to give up my studies and get married, but I hoped in the end she'd understand and be happy for me. I couldn't have been more wrong,' she said bitterly.

She remembered the argument vividly. Frank Malone was a bad lot, her mother had said. He would break her heart and ruin her life.

'But you don't know him!' Polly had protested.

'I know his type,' Bess had replied grimly. 'You mark my words, my girl. He'll bring you nothing but misery.'

'But–'

'Do as you're told, lass. Stick to your studies and get that qualification under your belt. And

we'll have no more nonsense about marriage,'
Bess had declared firmly.

It was typical of her, Polly had decided mutinously. Her mother had to have the last word on everything. She had done it to Polly's father, and she was doing it again to her.

'So you decided to elope,' Phil jumped in.

'I had no choice. I wasn't going to let her ruin my life the way she'd–' The way she'd ruined my father's, Polly was going to say, but stopped herself. There were some things no one else needed to know.

Agnes shuddered. 'I can't imagine how terrifying it must have been for you, having to come back and tell her you'd married in secret. I'm scared enough telling her when I've broken a thermometer!'

'It was terrifying,' Polly agreed. 'It was one of the hardest things I've ever had to do.'

But not just because she feared her mother's wrath. Bess might not have been the most loving mother in the world, but she had been the guiding light in Polly's life since her father died. Polly couldn't stop thinking about how hard her mother had worked, and all the sacrifices she'd made. Running away and getting married against her wishes felt like a terrible betrayal.

Polly didn't think she would ever forget the look of utter devastation on Bess' face.

'What did she say?' Agnes asked.

'"God help you."' Polly remembered her mother's words as clearly as if they'd been spoken yesterday. 'That was the last thing she said to me for two years.'

Frank had been confident that Bess would come round in the end, but Polly knew her mother better than that.

They moved into rented rooms. Polly was happy being a bride, but she missed her old life too. She missed the hospital, and the friends she'd made there.

Most of all she missed her mother. As luck would have it, Bess was the district nurse for the Bank, the area where they lived, and most days Polly would stand at the window with her nose pressed to the glass, watching out for her the way she had watched out for her father when she was a small child.

Sometimes she would see Bess cycling down the street with her Gladstone bag in the front basket. Whenever she saw her, Polly would hold her breath and hope that Bess might come through the yard or at least glance her daughter's way, but she never did.

Once Polly had even plucked up the courage to go to Steeple Street and visit her mother, in an effort to make the peace. Bess was out on an emergency call, but Miss Jarvis had invited her in for a cup of tea. They had talked, and Miss Jarvis had promised to get her mother to call, but Bess never did.

'When was the next time you spoke to her?' Agnes asked. 'Not until after my husband's funeral.'

'How did he die?'

'Influenza. There was an epidemic in the city that winter, almost as bad as the Spanish Flu after the war. It nearly took me too.'

218

Not that Polly would have cared. She'd wanted to die, to be with Frank. They had been married barely a year, but she couldn't imagine going on without him. She had curled up in bed, under the old patchwork quilt she had shared with Frank, and prayed for death to come for her.

But death didn't come. Her mother did.

Polly had thought she was dreaming when she saw Bess at her bedside in her dark blue uniform. It must be the fever, she'd decided. She couldn't imagine her mother nursing her so tenderly, sponging her forehead with cool, damp cloths, making her sip liquids to soothe her parched throat, waiting and waiting beside her bed.

By the time Polly was well again, Ellen Jarvis had taken over her care and Bess was nowhere to be seen. It was Miss Jarvis who helped Polly recover emotionally too. She was sympathetic and caring, and she listened to Polly in a way her brisk mother never would.

'Was it she who suggested you should go back to nursing?' Agnes asked.

Polly nodded. 'I had to do something to earn a living, and nursing was the only thing I knew. I wasn't sure how to go about it, but Miss Jarvis helped me write a letter to the Matron of the Leeds General Infirmary, where I'd started my training, and she was kind enough to allow me to go back.'

And it was Miss Jarvis who had sat at her side when she'd told her mother. Polly had hoped Bess might be pleased at the news, but all she'd got was a very dismissive, 'And how long are you going to stick at it this time? I wonder.'

Her mother's words haunted her once she had resumed her training. Even though Polly was grateful to be offered a second chance, it was still humiliating to walk back through the hospital doors and become a student again. Most of the set she'd started training with were now staff nurses, and Polly found herself in the difficult position of taking orders from her old friends.

But even when she felt like giving up, she still persevered, her mother's words ringing in her ears.

'Is that why you became a district nurse? To prove her wrong?' Phil asked.

'Or to redeem yourself,' Agnes spoke up suddenly. Polly met her eyes in the mirror and a look of mute understanding passed between them. How did she know that? she wondered.

'Yes,' she said. 'Yes, that's exactly it.'

She'd wanted Bess to notice her, to respect her. Polly knew it shouldn't matter, but still she longed for her mother's approval. Wanted to show that even after all the mistakes she'd made, she could still be worthy of her mother's love.

Chapter Twenty-Three

'Well, don't you look nice?'

Miss Jarvis beamed at them as they came downstairs. 'Don't they look lovely, Miss Goode?'

'I hardly recognised them,' the other nurse said dryly as she rearranged her hat in front of the hall mirror.

'You should come with us,' Polly said to Miss Jarvis.

'Oh no, I'm far too old for all that,' she laughed. 'My dancing days are over, I'm afraid.'

'And I already have plans to go out,' Miss Goode put in, even though none of them had asked her.

'Besides, I'm on emergency call this evening,' Miss Jarvis went on. 'I'm just on my way out, actually. One of my old chaps has had a fall.'

At that moment, Bess appeared from the Superintendent's office. She stopped in her tracks when she saw them.

'I was just saying how beautiful they all look, Bess,' Ellen Jarvis prompted her. 'Quite a picture, wouldn't you say?'

Polly held her breath, waiting for her mother's approval. But before Bess could say anything, the telephone rang, loud and shrill.

'Saved by the bell,' Phil murmured, as Bess bustled up the passage to answer it.

'So where is this dance?' Miss Jarvis asked.

'At the church hall.'

'St Martin's?'

'That's right.' But all the while she was talking, Polly was listening to her mother speaking on the telephone. As she listened, she could feel the chill foreboding uncurling itself inside her again. Something was going to happen; she could feel it like a cold breath on her skin.

Bess put the telephone down and returned to them. 'Mrs Wendle has gone into labour,' she announced. 'Acorn Street.'

Polly recognised the name straight away. 'She's

221

one of ours,' she said. 'But she isn't due for another couple of weeks, surely?'

'Well, I don't suppose anyone's thought to tell the bairn that,' Bess snapped. 'Her husband reckons it's on its way now.'

'That's rather a nuisance,' Miss Jarvis sighed. 'She'll have to hang on while I attend to Mr Fitch.'

'I'll go,' Bess said. 'From the way her old man was talking, I don't think she can hang on that long.' She turned to Polly. 'You'll have to come with me.'

Polly heard the other girls gasp, but she wasn't surprised. She had known from the moment her mother picked up the telephone that something would happen to spoil tonight.

'But she can't!' Miss Jarvis protested. 'It's her night off.'

'Night off or not, I'll need her. Mrs Wendle knows her, and that'll be a comfort.'

'She knows me too,' Miss Jarvis said firmly. 'Why don't you go and see to Mr Fitch while I attend to Mrs Wendle?'

Bess didn't reply, her beady gaze still fixed on Polly. 'I thought you were keen to learn midwifery?' she said.

Polly read the mute challenge in her mother's eyes. Prove yourself, her look said.

'I'll get changed,' she said quietly.

She turned to Phil and Agnes. 'You two go without me,' she said. 'I'll try and come along later, if I can.'

'But–' Phil started to protest, but Agnes took her arm.

'Come on,' she said. 'No point in everyone's evening being ruined, is there?' She glared at Bess when she said it. As Polly went upstairs, she could hear Miss Jarvis still arguing with her mother.

'Honestly, Bess,' she was saying. 'Can't you allow the girl to enjoy herself for once?'

'She's here to learn.' Her mother's voice was implacable.

'Good Lord, it's not as if she'll never have another chance to see a baby being born!' Miss Jarvis sounded exasperated. 'They arrive more often than buses around here, as you well know.'

Polly closed the door to her room, shutting out her mother's reply. She didn't need to hear what Bess had to say.

She paused in front of the mirror, taking a moment to admire her own reflection. She was wearing her favourite dress, in a silky eau de Nil fabric. It was the latest fashion, falling in a straight line from her shoulders, skimming over her slender hips to just above her ankles. Polly had made a band from matching ribbon to put around her hair, and stuck a brooch just above her ear. It was only paste, but it caught the light beautifully, illuminating her face. She looked just like a flapper from a fashion magazine.

It was a shame no one would see it, she thought sadly, as the dress slid into a silky pool around her feet.

But then, perhaps it was for the best. She shouldn't really be going to the dance at all because she knew there was a chance she might see Finn there.

Not that he was the type for dancing, as he'd

already told her. But she'd had the feeling she would see him anyway. The attraction between them was so strong, they had a way of finding each other, like magnets pulled from opposite ends of the earth.

So far Polly had managed to resist it. Much as she was drawn to him, to the point where she couldn't think of anything else when she was with him, the fear of not pleasing her mother was even stronger. Polly couldn't disappoint her again, because she knew there would be no going back this time if she did.

Bess was already waiting by the door when Polly returned downstairs. She had swapped her leather Gladstone bag for the metal midwifery case that was always used for deliveries.

'Come on,' she said. 'She'll have had it by the time we get there.'

They cycled to Burmantofts in the east of the city in silence. As they passed the church, Polly gave it a sideways glance. The dance was in full swing. The church hall was lit up, and the sounds of music and laughter drifted through the open doors.

It was for the best, she told herself. She could feel her mother's questioning gaze on her and looked away, afraid her longing was written all over her face.

Mr Wendle was pacing up and down the street waiting for them as they turned the corner from Great Garden Street. It was a wild, windy night, but he was in his shirtsleeves.

He saw them and rushed over. He barely gave Bess a chance to get off her bicycle before he

224

seized her hands, half dragging her towards the house.

'Oh, thank God!' he kept saying. 'Thank God you're here, nurse. She's having a terrible time of it. Joyce, the midwife's here!' he shouted.

'About bloody time!' came the answering scream.

'Sorry about that.' Mr Wendle blushed. 'My Joyce in't usually one for cursing.'

'She's having a baby, love,' Bess said grimly. 'That would make a saint curse.'

By the time they'd scrubbed their hands, changed into clean caps and aprons and put the instruments on to boil, they found Joyce Wendle on her hands and knees amid a tangle of sheets, hanging on to the bedpost for dear life.

'I want to puuush!' she screeched.

'Nonsense, lass, I expect you've got ages yet,' Bess said briskly, taking charge of the situation. She turned to Polly. 'Now, I want you to put some paper down on this floor, while I get a mackintosh and a clean draw sheet on the bed...'

'Never mind the sodding sheets!' Mrs Wendle stared at them through a tangle of sweat-dampened hair. 'I – noooo!' Her final words were lost in a drawn out wail of agony.

Mr Wendle hovered in the doorway, wringing his hands.

'Is there anything I can do?' he asked, looking fearful.

'Bugger off, you've done enough!' his wife screamed.

Bess sighed. 'My goodness, what a fuss,' she tutted. 'Come on, then, let's have a look at you.

But I daresay you've got a way to go before–' She stopped talking.

'What is it?' Polly looked up from laying out the sheets of newspaper.

'What is it?' Mr Wendle echoed from the doorway.

Bess straightened her shoulders. 'Better go and fetch those instruments,' she said to Polly. 'I can see the head!'

After half an hour of pushing, screaming, encouragement, and whimpering from Mr Wendle, the baby slithered into the world, puce-faced and screaming in outrage.

'It's a boy,' Bess said. Polly watched her mother as she deftly cut the cord, then wrapped the infant up and plonked him on the scales. 'Six pounds three ounces.'

'A boy!' Mr Wendle whispered from the doorway, his voice full of wonder. 'Our Archibald.'

Archibald! Polly almost laughed out loud. And it seemed her mother was just as amused, judging from the twinkle in her eyes.

'Archibald, is it?' Bess' brows rose above her mask. 'That's a big name for a tiny lad.' She turned to Polly. 'Keep mother nice and warm and well covered, and let me know when the placenta is coming. I'm going to give little – Archibald – a wash.'

'It still hurts,' Mrs Wendle complained when Bess had gone. She shifted restlessly against the pillows, her face screwed up in pain.

'I suppose that's to be expected,' Polly replied, trying to comfort her. 'You've just given birth to a baby, and it's bound to–'

226

'Nay, nurse, tha doesn't understand – I want to push again!'

Polly shot to her feet. 'Ma?' she called out, without thinking. 'Ma, I think the placenta's coming!' She turned back to Mrs Wendle, who was thrashing around, trying to scramble back on to her hands and knees. 'Try to lie still,' pleaded Polly.

'Lie still, be buggered!' Joyce Wendle shot back. 'Bloody hell, I didn't think it was supposed to hurt like this!'

'It isn't.' Polly looked around for her mother, but Bess had gone downstairs with Mr Wendle. She lifted the sheet gingerly and peered into the gloom.

'Can tha see owt?' Mrs Wendle panted. 'Is the afterbirth coming?'

'No,' Polly murmured. 'But something else is.'

'What?'

'Mrs Wendle, I think you're having twins!'

'Twins! Oh, f–' Thankfully Mrs Wendle never finished her sentence before another contraction seized her. Polly caught a glimpse of a small, blood-smeared pink dome appearing between the woman's legs.

'Ma!' she yelled out, her scream almost matching Mrs Wendle's. A moment later she heard her mother's footsteps thudding up the stairs, but it was already too late. By the time Bess had burst into the room, another baby had slithered into the world.

Polly held it in her hands, feeling dazed. 'Another boy,' she whispered.

'Well, I never!' Bess shook her head. 'Two for the price of one, eh?'

It was another hour before they left the Wendles' house.

'Well, you don't see that every day,' Bess said as they stepped out into the damp November night.

'They seemed very happy,' Polly said. They had left both parents cradling a child in their arms, looking at each other in happy bewilderment.

'Aye, they did. Once they'd got over the shock!' Bess shook her head. 'When I think of poor Mr Wendle's face as he came in, holding his son, and found he had another one waiting for him. Talk about surprised!'

'Not half as surprised as you were!' Polly reminded her.

'Aye, that's true. It caught me out, all right,' Bess chuckled. It was a strange sound, one Polly wasn't used to hearing. 'And their names!'

'Archibald – and Joe. I feel a bit sorry for poor little Joe, don't you? His name is a bit of an afterthought.'

'I feel more sorry for poor Archibald!' Bess replied. They both laughed, and then stopped abruptly as they realised what was happening.

'You did a good job,' Bess said quietly.

It was so unexpected, it took Polly a moment to speak. 'Thank you,' she whispered. 'I wouldn't have missed it for the world.'

There was a long pause. Then Bess said, 'Why don't you get off to your dance?'

Polly shook her head. 'It's too late.'

'It's not nine o'clock yet. You've still got a while. I'll tell Dottie not to lock the door while half-past ten,' Bess added conspiratorially.

Polly stared at her. Was this really her mother

speaking? 'I can't,' she said. 'I'm hardly dressed for it.'

'You look fine,' Bess said.

It wasn't much of a compliment, but Polly was so used to being criticised she hardly knew what to do with herself.

'Go on,' Bess said. 'I reckon you've earned an hour off.'

Suddenly Polly understood. This evening had been another test, to find out if she was as committed as she claimed to be.

And she had passed. The thought filled her with relief, but also annoyance. Would her mother ever trust her? Polly wondered.

Chapter Twenty-Four

The dance was still in full swing at the church hall when Polly arrived. Some couples were whirling around the floor in each other's arms while others attempted a very daring Charleston, waving their hands and kicking their legs about in time to the music.

Polly pushed her way through the throng, looking for Agnes and Phil, and found them lingering beside the punch bowl.

Phil laughed when she saw her. 'Good heavens, look at the state of you! Cinderella has decided to come to the ball without the help of her Fairy Godmother, I see!'

'How did it go?' Agnes asked. 'Did the baby

arrive safely?'

'Babies,' Polly said. 'Twin boys.'

'Twins!' Phil laughed. 'Imagine that.'

'Are they all right?' Agnes asked. 'They're both well?'

'Very well,' Polly said, looking over her shoulder. She knew Finn wouldn't be in the hall, but at the same time she couldn't help hoping to see him.

As if she could read her thoughts, Phil said, 'There was someone looking for you earlier.'

Polly's heart jolted. 'Oh yes?'

'He's been badgering us all evening, asking where you were. He seemed quite disconsolate when we said you might not come. And you tried to tell us you didn't have an admirer!'

Polly smiled archly. 'I–'

'Oh, here he is now,' Phil nodded in the direction of the dance floor before Polly could reply.

She turned to find herself staring into the blandly handsome face of Matthew Elliott.

'Hello,' he greeted her. 'I didn't think you were coming.'

'I nearly didn't.' Polly forced herself to smile back, ignoring the surge of disappointment she felt. 'I'm afraid I'm hardly dressed for the occasion!' she said ruefully.

'You look beautiful to me.'

Polly glanced around for Phil and Agnes, but they had melted into the crowd.

'Would you like to dance?' Matthew asked. 'I'm afraid I'm not really one for this modern lark, since the old war injury.' He indicated his stick. 'But I'm sure if we hang on to each other in the old-fashioned way, I could just about manage a

230

turn around the floor...'

'Thank you, but I'm rather tired. It's been a long evening.'

'In that case, can I get you a drink? Or perhaps something to eat? There was a good spread earlier, but I'm not sure how much is left.'

He was being so kind, Polly thought. Almost too kind. She could feel his eagerness pressing on her, stifling her.

'Thank you, but I really think I should go and find my friends. I don't want them to think I've abandoned them,' she said.

Matthew's smile dropped a fraction. 'Of course,' he said. 'Perhaps we could meet up later?'

'I'll come and find you,' she promised, but she knew she wouldn't.

Agnes and Phil had both found partners and were on the dance floor, so Polly slipped past them and out into the cold night air.

The events of the evening were finally beginning to catch up with her, overwhelming her. Her muscles ached with weariness, and all she really wanted to do was go home.

No, that wasn't quite true. All she really wanted to do was to see Finn Slater.

She passed around the back of the church hall and looked over in the direction of the sexton's cottage. There was a light burning in the window. Polly fought the overwhelming urge to go up and knock on the door. She was desperate to see him, but nervous of what might happen if she did.

Instead, she followed the path down to the gate, picking her way carefully between the headstones by the cold, silvery light of the moon. The cold wind whipped around her, moaning through the bare trees. It didn't occur to her to be afraid. She had spent so long here at Frank's grave, it felt almost like home.

And then a sound in the bushes behind her made her tense with fear. Something was out there...

She swung round, just as a large, dark shape emerged from the undergrowth. Polly felt weak with relief as she found herself looking at a pair of bright eyes and a happily lolling tongue.

'Job!' Her voice sounded loud in the darkness. 'Goodness, you gave me a scare!' She put out her hand to him. 'What are you doing out here on your own?'

'Looking for rabbits, if I know him.'

Polly looked up sharply as Finn strode towards her. She could scarcely make out his tall, broad-shouldered outline in the moonlight.

He clicked his fingers and Job trotted to his side. 'He got out while I wasn't looking,' he said. 'You're a terror, in't you, lad? One of these days that curate's going to catch you wandering about on your own, and then there'll be no helping you.'

Polly stared at Finn, suddenly tongue-tied with nerves. He was standing a distance away, not even looking at her, and yet her skin tingled with awareness of him.

He raised his gaze to meet hers. 'You didn't go dancing, then?'

She shook her head. 'I had an emergency call.'

'That's a shame.'

She shrugged. 'I'm sure there will be other dances.' She gazed at him in the darkness. 'How about you? Didn't you want to go?'

His mouth twisted. 'Me? Go dancing?'

'Why not?'

Finn shook his head. 'I wasn't really one for dancing, even before–' he broke off. 'Besides, I don't think your friend the curate would care for my company.'

No, but I would. The words hovered, unspoken, on the tip of her tongue. Polly knew that if she admitted her feelings she would be unleashing something she wouldn't be able to control. 'I – I'd better go,' she murmured instead.

She started down the path, but Finn called after her, 'I thought you wanted to dance, Polly Malone?'

She stopped and turned to face him. 'Dance?' she echoed. 'What you mean – now? Out here?'

'Why not?' There was a glint of daring in his eyes.

She held back. 'I thought you weren't one for dancing?'

'Depends on the partner, doesn't it?' he said softly.

He held out his arms to her.

Polly took a step towards him and hesitated. 'We haven't got any music.'

'Who needs music?' He caught her hand and pulled her into his arms. Pressed against the warmth of his body, her ribcage felt suddenly too tight, making it hard for her to breathe. She could hear the insistent drumbeat of Finn's heart, smell the male scent of him. His face was only inches above hers. If she just looked up for a moment

She pulled away, turning her back on him. 'I

233

can't,' she whispered.

'Why? Don't you like me?'

The notion was so absurd, she couldn't help smiling in the darkness. 'You know I do,' she said. 'But I made a promise...'

'To Frank?'

She shook her head. 'To my mother.'

'Your mother?' She heard the disbelief in Finn's voice.

'I told you how things were with her when I went off with Frank.' She and Finn had shared so many stories about their pasts over the last few days. Since Polly now knew his secrets, she'd felt it only right that he should know hers. 'I'm only just starting to make things right with her again.' She thought of this evening and the way they had laughed together, both caught off guard. It was only a tiny step, but at least it was a start. 'It's taken me so long to win her trust, I daren't make another mistake.'

'Is that what I am to you? A mistake?' Finn's voice was cold.

She swung round to face him at last. He towered over her in the darkness, tall and powerful, the silvery moonlight casting shadows over the planes and angles of his face. He looked like a statue carved in silver.

No, she wanted to say. No, you're not a mistake. You must never, ever think of yourself that way.

But when she looked at him, saw the dark glitter of desire in his eyes, he seemed like the devil himself, leading her into temptation.

She was on the brink of a precipice, about to step over the edge. One step, one kiss, and she could lose everything she had worked so hard to achieve.

She knew she should walk away, step back from the edge of the abyss, follow the path she had made for herself, back to her mother. But still she couldn't drag her gaze away from his face, his eyes, the shadows falling on the hollows of his cheeks, the shape of his mouth...

Anticipation sizzled through her like a hot wire, right to the core of her being.

'Yes,' whispered Polly. 'You're a very big mistake.'

And then he smiled, and bent his head, and the next moment Finn was kissing her. His mouth was gentle at first, his lips brushing hers, but then harder, more insistent. His strong hands closed on her shoulders, forcing her gently backwards until she felt the roughness of a tree trunk pressing into her back. Her arms went up, twining around his neck as she felt herself tumbling down into the abyss...

Job's loud bark startled them and they broke apart. Finn was instantly tense, looking over his shoulder into the darkness.

'Quiet, lad!' he said. But Job let out a low growl, his head lowered. In the moonlight Polly could see the menacing glint of his bared teeth.

'I think he's seen something,' she whispered.

Finn moved away from her, stepping fearlessly into the darkness. 'Who is it?' he called out. 'Who's there? Show yourself!' His words echoed around the silent churchyard.

'Perhaps he found a rabbit after all?' Polly said.

Matthew Elliott watched from the shadows, bitterness running like acid through his veins. He could feel his temples throbbing and his hand tightened into a fist on his stick.

How could she? How could Polly choose that low beast over him? He'd warned her. He'd told her what a monster Finn Slater was, and yet there she was, kissing him.

It disgusted him to watch them, pawing at each other like animals. But at the same time he couldn't seem to tear his gaze away.

It should have been him, he thought. He'd planned all this so carefully. This dance had all been for Polly's benefit. It had taken a long time to persuade the vicar that it would be a good idea. Matthew had said it was to raise funds for the church roof, but really he had done it all for her.

And yet she could hardly bring herself to look at him.

Matthew was sweating in spite of the chill of the night. He wanted to take his stick and beat Finn with it until he was lying on the ground, broken and bloodied. He ground his teeth together at the thought of it, the satisfaction of hearing his rival beg for mercy...

He could do it too. People might look at him now and see a mild-mannered clergyman, but before he'd joined the church he had been just like Finn, every bit as capable of inflicting harm on another man. Hadn't he fought for his country while Finn Slater was languishing in jail? And he had the scars to prove it.

And now Finn had taken Polly from him. It wasn't her fault, Matthew knew that. She was innocent in all this, led astray by that devil.

She had to be protected. This couldn't be allowed to happen. Matthew would look after her.

Chapter Twenty-Five

Cedar House
Steeple Street
Leeds
10th November 1925

Dear Mother,
How are you? It's been such a long time since I've heard from you. I wonder if you've received my last four letters?

Things are still going well for me here at the district nurses' home. As I already told you, I have my own set of patients now to visit on a regular basis. I'm still getting used to the various backstreets of Quarry Hill, and some of the people I meet are most peculiar (I really don't know what you'd make of them!), but I think we're beginning to understand each other.

One of my patients, Mrs Franklin, was recently admitted to hospital with a duodenal ulcer. I happened to see her husband yesterday morning as I was passing his corner shop. He came out to wish me good morning and to tell me his wife was recovering well. He was so overcome with gratitude, poor man, he made me a promise that if there was anything he could do for me, then I had only to ask.

And then I had an idea. One of my other patients,

Mr Willis, lost his job recently, and his family is struggling to cope. So I suggested to Mr Franklin that, as a favour to me, he might think about cancelling the debt Mrs Willis has run up in his shop. And he agreed! Quite readily, in fact. Between you and me, I think he has been worrying about them too, and looking for a way to help them.

Anyway, I can't wait for Mrs Willis to hear the good news. I imagine it will be quite a weight off her mind. I'm so pleased I've been able to help her, even in a small way.

I think you and Father would be very proud of what I'm doing here. I really am trying to fit in and to make the best of my situation, as you suggested I should.

Have you thought any more about me coming to visit you? I would dearly love to see you all again, and spend time with you, and meet my new niece (I'm sorry, I don't even know her name yet!). Please write back to me as soon as you can. I am longing to hear all your news.

Your loving daughter,
Agnes

She scanned the letter, trying to imagine how her mother might feel when she read it.

If she read it. Her mother had still not replied to any of the previous letters, not even a note to tell her to stop writing. Agnes had a picture lurking in the back of her mind of her mother throwing the unopened letters on to the fire, jabbing at them with a poker to make sure the flames consumed every last scrap...

She pushed the thought away. Of course her

238

mother would read her letters. And hopefully she would be proud that Agnes was doing so well. Elizabeth Sheridan had always taken such pleasure in her daughter's achievements in the past.

Agnes read through the letter again. She hoped she didn't sound like she was showing off, talking about what she had done for the Willis family. She hadn't meant it that way, but she was pleased to be able to help.

And now she was hoping to help another of her patients, though the thought of it filled her with trepidation.

Agnes couldn't stop thinking about Christine Fairbrass. It had been nearly a month since she'd last seen the girl, but the image of her shocked face that day in the school medical room still haunted Agnes. If she was right about Christine's condition then the poor girl must be beside herself with terror.

Agnes hadn't had the chance to talk to Christine again, as Lil and her family were still on Bess Bradshaw's list. But today Miss Gale was meeting the District Association and her assistant had to deputise for her at the Miners' Welfare meeting. So Agnes had to add Bess' list of calls to her own.

And as fate would have it, Lil Fairbrass' father was on her list for that afternoon.

It was a cold, windy Monday afternoon, and Lil was hanging out bed sheets on the line strung across the yard when Agnes arrived. They flapped about wetly, like giant sails, and it was all Lil could do to fight them into place.

She barely nodded at Agnes when she arrived.

'Where's t'nurse?' she asked, through a

mouthful of clothes pegs.

Agnes pasted a smile on her face. 'Mrs Bradshaw is away today, so I've come in her place,' she explained as patiently as she could manage.

Lil eyed her dubiously. 'Are you sure you know what you're doing?'

'I'm quite sure, Mrs Fairbrass.' Agnes gripped the handle of her bag to stop herself from swinging it in rage.

'Aye, well, I s'pose t'nurse wouldn't send you otherwise.' Lil jerked her head in the direction of the cottage. 'You'd best go in and see the old man.'

'Is he upstairs?' Agnes asked.

'He's where t'nurse left him last time she came. In't been out of bed except to use the pot!'

Lil's father Wally Hollins was an ex-miner in his late sixties. A lifetime spent working as a miner had all but destroyed his lungs, leaving him with bronchiectasis. His face was drawn, his body wasted due to the absorption of toxins into his system. But considering how gravely ill he was, he had a strangely cheerful nature. He made no bones about the fact he didn't have long to live.

'Hello, nurse,' he greeted Agnes. 'Has that lass of mine been giving you an 'ard time? Take no notice of her, love. She takes after her mother, God rest her soul. She were always looking for a fight an' all.'

'How are you feeling, Mr Hollins?' Agnes asked, scanning the notes the doctor had left.

'Oh, champion, thank you. T'other nurse has had me hanging upside down like a bat!' He looked pleased with himself.

Agnes smiled. 'It's called postural drainage, Mr

Hollins. To help clear your lungs.'

'Oh, aye, it's done that, all right. Been coughing up some right muck, I have. I had Lil keep it in that mug over there to show you.'

'Thank you, that's very – helpful.' Agnes eyed the mug on the mantelpiece dubiously.

'Will I be hanging upside down again today?' Wally asked hopefully.

'I'm afraid not. But the doctor has left instructions for you to have a creosote inhalation instead. That will be all right, won't it?'

'Aye, you carry on, love. I know nothing you do will make a blind bit of difference to me living longer, but it'll help pass the time, won't it?' He grinned at her, showing off a mouth full of broken teeth.

He chatted happily while Agnes set up the steam tent around his bed using two large sheets and a clothes horse, pausing only when he was seized by one of his lengthy coughing fits.

'The way I see it is once your time's up, it's up,' he said. 'And if you ask me, my time will be up sooner rather than later. Not that I mind, I've had a right good innings. Even if I did have to spend most of it stuck under the ground. Mind you,' he added, 'at least I'll feel at home when they put me back there!' He laughed, which then turned into another paroxysm of coughing.

While he was inside the steam tent, Agnes stood at the window, looking down at the yard below. Lil was still hanging out her washing, but as Agnes watched, Christine came into the yard, carrying a satchel over her shoulder. She wore a heavy coat over her school uniform, so it was impossible to

241

make out her shape. But as she stopped to talk to her mother, the wind suddenly snatched at her coat, blowing it aside and flattening her pinafore against her, and even from above, Agnes could make out the definite curve of her belly.

So I was right, she thought grimly. The thought gave her no pleasure.

By the time her mother turned to her, Christine had pulled her coat back round herself, hiding her body. But she couldn't hide it for ever, Agnes thought.

How could her mother not see it? wondered the nurse. Perhaps it was because Lil wasn't looking. If she believed her daughter was a good girl, devoted to her studies, then it probably wouldn't occur to her to look for tell-tale signs.

But even good girls could make a mistake.

'Excuse me, nurse?' Wally Hollins croaked from behind the makeshift curtain. 'I reckon I'm just about cooked now, if you don't mind?'

Agnes checked her watch and was shocked to find she had been standing at the window, deep in thought, for far longer than she'd meant to be. 'Yes, of course, Mr Hollins. Let me get you out of there.'

'Thank you, nurse. I thought for a minute you'd left me to steam in here like a suet puddin'!' He smiled gratefully up at her as she unpinned the sheet curtain and dismantled the apparatus.

Lil was at the stove in the kitchen by the time Agnes came downstairs.

'All finished?' she grunted over her shoulder.

'Yes, thank you.' There was an awkward silence as they stood shoulder to shoulder so Agnes could

242

wash her hands at the sink. 'He seems in very high spirits,' she commented.

'Aye, he always is, the cheerful old bugger. Right gets on my nerves sometimes.' Lil shook her head. 'You'll be wanting your money,' she said. 'It's there, on the mantelpiece.'

'Thank you.' Agnes dried her hands on her towel, then slipped it back into the pocket of her bag.

As she collected the coins and made a note of them in her payment book, she said, 'Where's Christine?'

'Gone to the library. Why?'

'I just wanted to see her, that's all. I've been wondering about her, since she was taken ill at school that day.'

Lil paused, frowning. 'That were a long time ago. I wonder you remember it.'

'How has she been since?'

Lil shrugged. 'Right as ninepence, I'd say. She was poorly for a while, but it's passed now. I put it down to all that studying,' she said.

'Do you?'

Lil must have noticed the tone of her voice, because she turned to face Agnes, her eyes narrowing. 'Why? What else could it be?'

Agnes hesitated. She remembered one of Bess' very first warnings to her.

You don't want to get on the wrong side of Lil Fairbrass.

But surely she wasn't doing anything wrong? All she was doing was telling a mother what was going on. She would want to know...

Lil was staring at her. 'Well?' she said. 'Spit it

243

out, if you've got summat to say.'

Agnes slipped the payment book back into her bag and took a deep breath.

'Mrs Fairbrass,' she said. 'I think there's something you should know...'

Chapter Twenty-Six

Oliver lived in Headingley, a long way from Quarry Hill to the north of the city. He always made his lodging sound very basic, but the broad, tree-lined streets were nicer than anything Christine had ever seen, full of well-proportioned houses with bay windows and neat front gardens. There were cars too, not like the plodding horses and carts that plied their trade in Quarry Hill. Christine had to keep looking over her shoulder to stop herself from being run down.

It was a cold, windy November afternoon but she was sweating inside her thick coat. Her arms ached from carrying the heavy books she had pretended she needed to take back to the library. At least her mother wouldn't be expecting her back for a while, she thought. She understood that Christine could lose herself for hours in the library, surrounded by books.

It was the excuse she'd often used when she went off to meet Oliver.

She stopped on the corner, her heart bumping in her chest. The conviction that had carried her on to the tram and brought her all the way to the other side of the city suddenly failed Christine as she stood within sight of his lodgings.

She felt the now familiar stirring in her belly and put her hand over it. It had taken her by surprise when it first happened. It had felt out of place, like the fluttering of butterflies trapped low down inside her. She'd had no idea what it was, until it dawned on her that it was her baby starting to move.

Her baby... Her mind still rejected the idea every time she thought about it.

She still wasn't showing too much, which was a blessing. Christine had no idea how far along she was, or how many weeks or months it might be before the baby arrived. She had tried to work out how many monthlies she'd missed, but once she'd reached six she was so panic-stricken she couldn't count any more. Instead she would lie awake at night, feeling it shifting inside her, too terrified to sleep in case she woke up and found herself in labour.

She knew it would hurt, when it happened. Her mother was always whispering to the neighbours about what a terrible time this woman or that had had, giving birth to their latest. They would all shake their heads and agree that no woman should have to go through such agony.

How bad was it? Christine would have liked to ask. And where exactly did the baby come from? She had tentatively examined herself under the covers, but couldn't find a place big enough for a baby to pass through.

She had so many questions, but no one to ask. She couldn't even look it up in the medical book from the library, because the librarian had started to watch her and she was afraid she would soon start to ask questions.

Her mother would know, of course. Lil Fairbrass had brought six babies into the world: childbirth held no mysteries for her. She would be able to advise Christine, tell her what to do.

Or perhaps that young nurse? She'd seemed kindly enough, that day at the school. Surely she would understand.

But then, Miss Sheridan was so prim and proper, she would probably look down her nose at Christine. And she didn't think she could bear that.

Besides, she didn't want to ask anyone's advice, because then it would all be real, and Christine didn't want it to be real. As long as she didn't allow herself to think about it, she could pretend it wasn't happening.

But she didn't know how much longer she could go on ignoring it. Now the baby was moving, making its presence felt, and Christine had to accept it was a living thing, with arms and legs that shifted around restlessly inside her.

And all too soon it would want to come out. Which was why she needed Oliver.

He was the only one who could truly share her predicament, the only one who could help her. At first, Christine had been too proud and angry to contact him, but as time passed and her fear grew, she knew she had to seek him out.

It had been over two weeks since she'd seen him. She had started to look for him in the school field, but he was never there. Which was why she'd taken the drastic step of coming to visit him at his home. She knew he would be angry, but he had left her no choice.

The wind tugged at the scrap of paper on which she'd written his address, nearly tearing it out of her hand, as Christine walked down the road where he lived. Her footsteps slowed as she approached the tall Victorian house and she had to force herself up the short flight of stone steps to the front door.

She knocked and waited, hands thrust into the pockets of her coat to stop them from trembling. It was all she could do not to turn and flee.

The door opened and a well-dressed woman stood before her, her arms folded across her chest.

'Yes?' she said, looking Christine up and down haughtily. 'What do you want?'

Christine lifted her chin, determined not to be cowed. 'I've come to see Mr Umansky.'

'He isn't here.'

She had been building up to this moment, nerves thrumming with anticipation. Now she didn't know what to do.

Christine cleared her throat. 'Do you know when you're expecting him back? Only I have some books to return to him...' She held up the library books she had carried all the way from Quarry Hill.

'I'm not expecting him back. He's gone.'

'Gone?' Christine stared at her.

'That's right. Settled his rent and cleared off. Over a week ago now.'

'Do you know where he went?'

'Back home, I think. That's what he said anyway. Didn't leave a forwarding address. Not that it's any of my business anyway.'

Christine stayed rooted to the spot. She had played out all kinds of imaginary scenes in her head on the long tram journey, but this wasn't one of them.

The woman looked down her long nose at her. 'Was there something else you wanted?' she asked. 'Only I can't stand here freezing all night.'

'No,' Christine said heavily. 'No, there's nothing else. Thank you for—'

But the door had already closed in her face.

The journey back to Quarry Hill was long, but Christine hardly noticed as she sat huddled on the tram, her coat pulled around her, lost in a turmoil of thoughts.

Her last shred of hope had gone. Somewhere in the back of her mind, she had been clinging to the idea that Oliver might relent and want to marry her after all. Or at any rate, that he would look after her. But instead he'd run away, abandoned her to her fate.

And now she was completely alone.

She felt the stirring in her belly. No, not completely alone.

The tram dropped her off in Vicar Lane and she made her way past the shops and factories of Lady Lane. The sweet aromas of chocolate, toffee and ginger scented the air around Henry Thorne & Co., the cocoa manufacturer, mingling with the stench of fish from Kirkgate Market.

By the time she reached Quarry Hill, Christine had made up her mind. She had no choice but to throw herself on her mother's mercy. She could only hope that she would forgive her, that she would understand at least...

She could hear the shouting as she walked into the yard.

'I won't have her in my house again!' her mother was shrieking. 'Do you hear me? She in't setting foot over that step again!'

Rene Wells was in the yard, taking in the washing. She seemed unperturbed by the commotion coming from inside the Fairbrasses' house. Like all the other neighbours, she knew Lil was always angry with someone.

'Sounds like your ma's had another set-to!' she chuckled. 'I wonder who's upset her this time.' Rene thrust the sheets into Christine's arms. 'Here,' she said. 'I thought I'd best take these in, since it's set to rain. Get them aired round the fire, there's a good lass.' She gave her a wink.

'Thank you.' Christine could feel Rene watching her as she struggled to lift the latch on the front door with her free hand and let herself in, staggering under the weight of the armful of damp washing.

There was a shocking scene going on inside the kitchen. Two of her brothers, Eric and Alfie, had her mother pinned to a kitchen chair. But even the two of them struggled to hold her down, such was Lil's angry strength. Christine's eldest brother Tony was pacing around. He was still in his work clothes, his overalls dusted a rusty orange from the brickworks.

'Calm down, Ma,' he was saying. 'You'll not sort anything out in that state.'

249

'Calm down? I'll give you calm down! You let me go!' Lil tussled to free herself, her eyes wild. 'I'm going to belt the life out of her, so I am! Pregnant! I'll give her bloody pregnant!'

The strength ebbed from Christine's arms and the washing slid to the stone-flagged floor. She wanted to run but her legs wouldn't move.

'Christine!' She jumped at the sound of her name. Tony was standing over her.

'What do you think you're doing?' he hissed. 'Get that washing picked up before Ma sees. She's beside herself as it is.'

Christine bent to scoop up the sheets. Her mother hadn't noticed her yet. But it was only a matter of time before she did, and then the washing would be the least of her concerns.

'I'm going down there,' Lil was saying. 'I'm going to go down to that nurses' home and complain. I'm not having her coming to this house, making all kinds of accusations about my girl!'

There was a buzzing in Christine's ears, a high-pitched hum, as if a bee were trapped inside her head. She shuffled towards the fire, still holding the washing, but the movement caught Lil's attention.

'There you are!' she said. 'Where have you been?'

'I told you, I had to go to the library.' Christine didn't meet her mother's eye as she forced herself to fold the sheets calmly.

'The library! You see?' her mother addressed the others. 'Now does that sound like the kind of girl who'd go and get herself in the family way? Does it?'

Every muscle and sinew in Christine's body stiffened. 'What's been going on?' Her voice sounded high and strange.

'Oh, you missed a right show,' Tony told her. 'Ma attacked the district nurse!'

'She was asking for it!' A vein pulsed in her mother's temple. 'You should have heard her, sitting there all prim and proper, telling me all kinds of lies!'

Christine draped the sheet over the clothes horse and tried to appear unconcerned. 'What did she say?'

'I'll tell you what she said.' Lil pointed a shaking finger towards her son. 'She were stood there, right where our Tony is standing now, and she says to me, "Did you know your daughter was pregnant, Mrs Fairbrass?" Can you believe it? You, lass! An innocent bairn.'

'We came in and found Ma dragging the poor girl across the kitchen,' Eric added cheerfully.

'I was throwing her out,' Lil muttered.

'You would have half killed her if we hadn't come home when we did!' Alfie put in.

'Aye, and I still would!' Lil's jaw was clenched. 'She'd better make sure she never crosses my path again. Hoity-toity little madam, coming here with her airs and graces, spreading vicious gossip and upsetting decent people!'

'I don't reckon she'll want to come back, don't you worry!' Eric said. 'She couldn't get out of here fast enough.'

Christine finished hanging the sheets over the clothes horse. 'I'll go and make us all a brew,' she said.

251

She stood in the scullery, staring at the kettle as she waited for it to boil. What was she going to do now? Agnes Sheridan had ruined everything, jumping in like that. If she'd had time, Christine could have talked to her mother in the right way, explained everything. But now Miss Sheridan had decided to make it her business, she'd taken away the only chance Christine had to break the truth to Lil gently.

'Chrissie?' She swung round. Tony stood in the doorway, watching her. 'That's going to boil dry in a minute.' He nodded towards the kettle, which was filling the scullery with billowing steam.

'Oh. Sorry' Christine went to grab the handle, then snatched her hand back as the hot metal burned her skin. She reached for the pot cloth instead.

'Reckon we might need a nip of brandy in that tea,' Tony commented.

'Is Ma still in a state then?'

'Not for her. For you. You're as white as one of those sheets round the fire.' He tilted his head to one side. 'Are you all right, love?'

'Yes, I'm fine. Just a bit of a shock, that's all.' She forced a smile in Tony's direction.

'Aye, it's a rum thing.' He paused then said, 'Dunno what that nurse was thinking of, do you? Where do you suppose she came up with an idea like that?'

Christine didn't like the long, considering look he was giving her. 'I don't know,' she shrugged.

'I mean, she must have got the notion from somewhere. It's not the sort of thing you'd make up, is it?'

'I suppose not.' Christine concentrated on stirring the tea in the pot.

'So why do you think she said it?'

'I don't know.'

'Are you sure?'

Christine glanced at him out of the corner of her eye. His face was full of kindness and sympathy. He would help her, she thought. Tony was the eldest, the man of the house. He would make things right with her mother.

But she still couldn't bring herself to say the words.

'Perhaps she got me mixed up with someone else?'

His face cleared. 'Yes, I daresay that's it,' he said. 'I mean, imagine you, being daft enough to get caught like that. Our little Christine. The brains of the family. It's daft when you think about it, isn't it?'

'Yes,' Christine agreed heavily. 'Yes, it is, isn't it?'

Chapter Twenty-Seven

'We've had a complaint, Miss Sheridan.'

Agnes stood before Miss Gale's desk, her hands locked behind her back. Bess Bradshaw stood by the door, as stiff as a sentry.

'Mrs Fairbrass has been to see us,' Miss Gale went on. 'She claims you have slandered her daughter.'

'I only spoke the truth,' Agnes said. 'And if anything, I should be the one complaining about her!' A day later, her scalp was still sore from where Lil had dragged her across the kitchen by her hair.

'Nevertheless, she says you barged your way into her house and made spurious claims that her daughter was pregnant.'

'She *is* pregnant.'

'Not according to Mrs Fairbrass.'

'What does she know about it?' Agnes dismissed. 'She's too blind or too stupid to see the truth in front of her eyes.'

She heard Bess' sharp intake of breath. 'The girl herself denies it,' Miss Gale said. 'And she should know, don't you think?'

Agnes looked down at the ground. 'Perhaps she just isn't ready to admit it to herself?' she said quietly.

'Perhaps,' Miss Gale conceded. 'But the fact remains that you had no right to say such things.'

'I was only trying to help.'

'Oh yes, that really helped, didn't it?' Bess muttered, tight-lipped.

Agnes swung round to face her. 'What was I supposed to do, say nothing?'

'There's a first-time for everything,' Bess shot back.

'Please, Mrs Bradshaw, this is not getting us anywhere.' Miss Gale turned back to Agnes. 'I want you to write a letter to Mrs Fairbrass, apologising for your actions.'

'But that's—' Agnes started to protest, but Miss Gale held up her hand.

'That is my final word on the matter, Miss

Sheridan, and I don't want to hear any further argument. Is that understood?'

'Yes, Miss Gale. Will that be all?' Agnes muttered through tight lips. She needed to escape. She wasn't sure how long she could hold on to her simmering rage.

'For now. But I hope we won't have any cause to reprimand you again.'

'No, Miss Gale.'

The Superintendent looked at her over the rim of her spectacles. 'You're a very hard-working nurse, Miss Sheridan. And extremely bright, too. But you need to consider the consequences of your actions.'

'Yes, Miss Gale.'

Agnes escaped to the district room. The morning's calls were over, and Polly and Phil were busy loading the steriliser ready for the afternoon.

'What did Miss Gale want?' Polly asked.

'To tell me off.' Agnes was so angry she could barely speak. 'Mrs Fairbrass has complained about what happened yesterday.'

'Well, I can't say I'm surprised,' Phil said, closing the lid of the steriliser.

'But I only told her what she needed to hear!' Agnes protested.

'I still can't believe you actually confronted her,' Polly said. 'You were very brave.'

'Foolish, more like,' Phil muttered.

Agnes glared at her. 'I've a good mind to go to the police and charge her with assault!' she said.

'Oh, don't do that!' Polly looked dismayed. 'You don't want to make matters worse, do you?'

Phil laughed unkindly. 'I would have loved to

have been there last night and seen her dragging you round the kitchen by your hair.'

'It's not funny,' snapped Agnes, massaging her tender scalp. She hadn't been able to brush her hair properly that morning, it had hurt so badly. 'I truly thought she was going to kill me. She might have done too, if her sons hadn't come in when they did.'

'Still,' Polly said, 'at least you've escaped with only a reprimand. You could have been dismissed.'

'Not quite,' Agnes said. 'I have to write a letter of apology to the awful woman. Although I don't know why I should bother, since the ignorant creature probably can't read anyway!'

'Agnes!' Polly looked shocked. 'You shouldn't make assumptions about people. Just because they're poor, it doesn't mean they're any less than you.'

Her reproach stung. Agnes pressed her lips together, ashamed of her outburst. But before she had chance to reply, Dottie rang the bell for dinner.

The other nurses were already gathered around the dining table. The conversation ceased and all eyes fell on Agnes when she walked in, flanked by Polly and Phil.

But nothing was said as Dottie went around them all, dishing up steaming platefuls of stew and dumplings. Gradually the hum of voices lifted again, but Agnes still kept her gaze fixed on her plate, afraid to meet anyone's eye.

Then the conversation turned to Miss Gale's meeting with the District Association the previous day.

'I don't suppose the Association said anything about giving Miss Fletcher and me our motorcycles?' Miss Templeton asked hopefully.

'I'm afraid not,' Miss Gale said. 'Or rather, they did mention it but not in the way we might have hoped. Apparently there are insufficient funds available at present.'

Phil groaned loudly. 'I knew it!'

'Miss Templeton, you should go and address the Association yourself, tell them the trials you and Miss Fletcher have to face every day,' Miss McLeod said.

'Or better yet, send Miss Sheridan,' Miss Goode put in mischievously. 'She likes a good row!'

Everyone laughed. 'Nurses, please!' Miss Gale admonished them mildly, but even she was smiling when she spoke.

Agnes did her best to ignore them, but humiliation washed over her in a scalding wave.

'I think Miss Hook should write another poem for the *Queen's Nurse* magazine, all about your exploits,' Miss Goode continued, warming to her theme. 'What do you say, Miss Hook?'

'I beg your pardon?' The elderly nurse looked up vaguely from her meal. 'What's that?'

'I said you should write a poem about our Miss Sheridan.' Miss Goode grinned. 'Now, how would it go? "There was a young student called Aggie..."'

Luckily Agnes was spared the next line by a sharp rap on the front door. It was so loud, Dottie nearly dropped the tray of cups and saucers she was carrying.

Miss Gale looked up. 'Who on earth could that be? Go and answer it, please, Dottie.'

The maid dumped the tray on the sideboard and scuttled off. All around the table the nurses fell silent, listening. There was the sound of Dottie's footsteps pattering on the tiled floor, then the creak of the front door, followed a second later by a bellow of rage.

'Where is she?'

Agnes recognised the voice straight away. Her heart sank.

'Where's that stuck-up, interfering cow? You send her out here now! Send her out and let her face me!'

'Good heavens!' Miss Gale went to stand up, but Bess was already on her feet.

'I'll go,' she said. 'I know her. It's Mrs Willis, from Quarry Hill.'

Bess left, and all eyes turned once again to Agnes. 'That's your area, isn't it, Miss Sheridan?' Miss Goode spoke the words they were all thinking.

'Let's get on with our meal, shall we?' Miss Gale said. 'I'm sure Mrs Bradshaw has the matter in hand.'

They all picked up their knives and forks as Bess' coaxing voice drifted in from the hallway.

'Now then, Nettie lass, calm down and tell me what's going on. You're not making sense.'

There was more indignant squawking, which no one could make out. Agnes sat very still as the other nurses stirred around her, trying to work out what was going on.

Polly leaned across. 'Do you know anything about this?' she whispered.

Agnes opened her mouth to speak, but then

258

Bess appeared in the doorway.

'Miss Sheridan, could you come with me?' she said. Agnes was aware of everyone watching her as she got to her feet.

'Not again!' Miss Goode murmured, clearly enjoying every minute. 'What's she done this time?'

Miss Gale said nothing, but her eyes were full of reproach.

Nettie Willis was in the hallway, clutching a scrap of paper in her hand. She seemed calm, but when Agnes appeared she flew at her like a snarling tiger. Agnes shrank back as Bess put herself between them, blocking the woman's path.

'Calm down, love. Remember what I said?' she warned quietly. 'You'll get nowhere by shouting and carrying on.'

But Nettie didn't seem to be in the mood to listen.

'Did you do this?' She waved the piece of paper at Agnes over Bess' shoulder. 'Is this right, that you've been going round the place, settling our bills for us?'

'I–' Agnes lost her voice, helpless in the face of Nettie's anger.

'Well?' Bess said. 'Is it true or isn't it?'

Agnes rallied, pulling herself together. 'I was only trying to help,' she said. 'Mr Franklin wanted to thank me for helping his wife, and I thought it would be a good idea–'

'Oh, you did, did you?' Nettie's face was mottled with rage. 'You thought you'd throw a few scraps my way, like I was some beggar?'

Agnes stared at her. 'But I don't understand. I

259

thought you'd be pleased...'

'Pleased? Pleased?' Nettie's voice was shrill with outrage. 'I in't a charity case, you know. We pay our bills. I was going to pay this one, until you decided to take matters into your own hands!'

'The lass never meant any harm by it, Nettie.' Surprisingly, it was Bess who stepped in to defend her. 'She doesn't understand the way we go about things around here, that's all.'

'Nay, she doesn't.' Nettie glared at Agnes. 'She thinks she's above the rest of us, that's her trouble. But you listen here, madam. I might not speak posh like you or have your education, but there's no reason to treat me like I in't good enough to clean your boots!'

'But I didn't...'

'All right, Nettie, you've said your piece.' Bess was already ushering her towards the door. 'You've told the lass what you think, and we'll leave it at that, shall we?'

'Oh, I haven't even started to tell her what I think!' Nettie flared back. 'She don't belong here, nurse, I could see that the minute I set eyes on her. And the sooner she goes back where she came from, the better!'

'Aye, well, you might be right about that.' Bess glanced at Agnes. 'Wait in the district room,' she ordered Agnes. 'I'll be with you presently.'

Agnes closed the door to the district room and leaned against it, weak with relief. Outside, she could see Bess guiding Nettie down the front path, patting her arm and talking quietly to her. By the time they'd reached the front gate, Nettie Willis was calm again, and even managed a smile for Bess as she left. She had never done anything but scowl at Agnes.

She braced herself as the door to the district room opened and Bess walked in.

'Well,' she said. 'You've managed to upset two people in one day. Who else will be knocking on our door, I wonder.'

'I was only trying to help,' Agnes pleaded.

'You don't understand, do you? Help is the last thing Nettie Willis needs. Not your kind of help anyway. All the poor woman had left was her pride, and now you've taken even that away from her.'

'I – I didn't know.'

'No, you didn't,' Bess said. 'That's the trouble with you. You don't understand anything about the people around here, or how they live.'

'I'm trying to.'

'Are you? I haven't seen it. From what I've seen, Mrs Willis is right. You swan in like Lady Bountiful and act as if you're doing them a favour by being there.'

Agnes opened her mouth to argue, then closed it again. There was no point, she thought. Trying to fight her corner would only land her in more trouble. Better to humbly accept her fate.

'I'm sorry,' she said. 'I'll make more of an effort, I promise.'

'You can make all the effort you like, but I don't believe you'll ever understand the people of Quarry Hill,' Bess said shortly. 'Because to be honest, Miss Sheridan, you don't belong here.'

Agnes felt tears sting the back of her eyes. 'That's not true!'

261

'Your place is back in your fancy London hospital, not here. I wonder if it's even worth finishing your training.'

Agnes stared at Bess. 'I want to finish,' she insisted quietly. I have no choice, a small voice added.

'Very well,' Bess sighed. 'But from now on, I'll be coming out on your rounds with you again.'

'But–'

'No arguments, Miss Sheridan. You clearly can't be trusted on your own. We don't want a riot on our hands, do we?'

Agnes stared down at the toes of her shoes. Bess must be enjoying this, she thought. The Assistant Superintendent had been looking for a reason to humiliate her, and now Agnes had given it to her.

And all she could do was accept the consequences. 'No, Mrs Bradshaw,' she said quietly.

'We'll start this afternoon. And you can be sure I will be watching you very carefully, Miss Sheridan. Very carefully indeed.'

Chapter Twenty-Eight

Agnes woke up with a start from a nightmare. She had dreamed that she was in a courtroom, standing in the dock. The jury was made up of Lil Fairbrass, Nettie Willis and some of her other patients from Quarry Hill, and Bess Bradshaw was the prosecuting counsel. She strode around the court in her wig and gown, jabbing her finger at

Agnes and telling everyone what an utter failure she was, while Miss Gale looked on solemnly from the judge's seat, nodding along to every word.

Agnes fumbled for her alarm clock. It was just after four in the morning. She was about to turn over and pull the covers back over her when Bess Bradshaw's voice pierced her consciousness, jolting her awake.

'Miss Sheridan? Get up, we've got a call to make.'

Agnes sat upright, not sure for a moment whether or not she was still dreaming. But there was Bess, solid and all too real, standing at the foot of her bed.

Agnes pushed back the covers and swung her legs out of bed. The floorboards felt chilly under her bare feet. She was so befuddled with sleep, it didn't even occur to her to wonder why Bess was summoning her.

'We don't have time to waste,' she said, as Agnes rubbed sleep out of her eyes. 'We're needed at Mrs Rankin's. Her mother's just called to say she's gone into labour.'

That was enough to shock Agnes awake. She remembered Maggie Rankin's name from her list, but she had never met her. According to her records, Mrs Rankin already had six children, and was expecting the seventh. Agnes was guiltily aware she should have visited her before the birth, but she had never managed to make the time.

Bess was waiting for Agnes in the hall when she came downstairs, still pinning up her hair. 'Come on, you can borrow one of the other nurses' bicycles. I daresay we'll be back by the time they need it.'

Agnes felt as if she were still in a terrible dream as she followed Bess through the darkened streets. Fear wrapped itself around her ribcage like a snake, making it hard for her to breathe.

'It should be a fairly straightforward birth,' Bess said over her shoulder as they pedalled along. 'Mrs Rankin's in good health, and she's never had any trouble before. But I daresay you'll know that already, won't you?'

Agnes looked down, grateful that the darkness hid her blushing face.

It will be all right, she told herself over and over again, her thoughts chiming with the rhythmic circling of the pedals. This time it will be all right.

The Rankins' house was blazing with light. They were met by a cheerful middle-aged woman in a pinny.

''Ello, nurses. Thank you for coming out so early,' she greeted them with a broad smile.

'Not at all, Mrs Irvine.' Bess turned to Agnes. 'This is Mrs Rankin's mother,' she explained.

'It's a good thing I only live next door,' Mrs Irvine chuckled. 'Maggie sent one of the bairns to wake me up about an hour since. Their dad's on the night shift, y'see. He won't be home while six. He's going to get a surprise, in't he?' She patted Agnes' arm. 'Eeh, you're all of a tremble, lass. Is it your first time?' She looked sympathetic.

'I should think not,' Bess said. 'Miss Sheridan worked in a maternity home before she came to us.'

'It's just the cold,' Agnes said, her teeth clenched.

'It is a bit nithering, in't it? Let's get indoors before you freeze. I shouldn't keep you chatting anyway, or my Maggie will have had the baby before you get up the stairs!'

Maggie Rankin was sitting up in bed, knitting. She looked surprisingly composed for a woman in the throes of labour, with her fair hair neatly combed over the shoulders of her lacy bed jacket. She had the same sort of bright, pleasant face as her mother, her cheeks pink and glowing.

'Excuse my knitting,' she said, her needles clicking busily. 'I was hoping to get this matinee jacket finished before the baby arrived. I didn't think it would be while next week.'

'I've put clean sheets on and laid newspaper and got everything ready for you, just how you like it,' Mrs Irvine said to Bess.

'So you have.' Bess smiled. 'Thank you, Mrs Irvine, you've saved Miss Sheridan here a job. In't that right, Miss Sheridan?'

'What? Sorry.' Agnes started at the sound of her name. She had been leaning in the doorway, fighting the feeling of faintness that washed over her.

'Don't drift off to sleep, Miss Sheridan. I'll have need of you later on!' Bess' voice was light, but there was a warning look in her eyes. 'Now, let's get changed and see what's to do, shall we?'

'My waters broke at teatime,' Mrs Rankin told them matter-of-factly, as Agnes finished washing and shaving her. 'But I wasn't in any pain, so I didn't see the point in troubling you and spoiling your evening. I wouldn't have asked Mum to fetch you now, but I've had a few twinges.'

'Let's have a look, shall we? Do you want to do the examination, Miss Sheridan?' Bess asked.

'No! No, you can do it,' Agnes said quickly. Too quickly, judging by the questioning look Bess shot her.

'Right, where are we?' Bess examined Mrs Rankin in silence for a moment, then stepped back. 'Well, I dunno what you'd call a little twinge, lass, but I reckon you're just about ready to push!' she grinned.

'I thought so,' Mrs Rankin said. 'I'll just finish this row and we'll get started, shall we?'

'I've never known anyone give birth so easily,' Mrs Irvine told Agnes proudly. 'Honest to God, it's like shelling peas. I s'pose it must run in the family. I've had seven kids myself, and none of them gave me any trouble.'

Agnes smiled weakly. In the back of her mind she still hoped she was asleep and that at any moment she would wake up and find herself back in her room, with Polly groping for the alarm clock.

As Bess opened her bag and set out her forceps and catheters and receiving dishes, Agnes shrank into the corner. She shouldn't be here. The heat of the room, the smell of disinfectant, the sight of that neat line of implements gleaming … it was all too much for her.

She drew in a deep breath, forcing herself to calm down. It would be all right, she told herself. All would be well. Mrs Rankin gave birth like shelling peas, her mother had said so. There was no oppressive shadow of fear hanging over the room, just a happy feeling of anticipation as the mother-to-be looked forward to welcoming her new baby into the world.

This time all would be well, and the light would at last blot out all those dark memories of the last time Agnes had been in a birthing room...

'You're doing very well,' Bess said, and for a moment Agnes thought the remark was meant for her, until she realised Bess was encouraging Mrs Rankin.

Not that she needed much encouragement. In what seemed like no time at all, the baby's head crowned, then a shoulder, and the infant slithered easily into the world.

'Is it a girl?' Mrs Rankin craned forward to look. 'I'd love another little girl.'

'Yes, it's a girl. Well done, lass.'

'Told you it was like shelling peas, didn't I?' Mrs Irvine said triumphantly.

Bess clamped and cut the cord. But as she gathered the baby in the warmed towel Mrs Irvine had prepared, Agnes noticed something that made her scalp prickle with fear.

'She's quiet, in't she?' Mrs Rankin voiced the thought that ran through Agnes' mind.

'It takes a moment for babies to catch their breath sometimes,' Bess said. But Agnes saw the rigid look on her face as she rubbed briskly at the baby's tiny chest.

Luckily Mrs Rankin hadn't noticed anything amiss. 'That makes a change!' she laughed. 'All my others have been screaming from the moment they arrived. Eh, Mum?'

'Aye, love, so they have.' Mrs Irvine was sharper than her daughter. She looked from Agnes to Bess and back again. 'Is summat wrong?' she asked.

'Baby's taking a bit longer to get her breath back.' Bess' smile was strained. 'I'll just sit with her for a minute, see if I can't give her a bit of help.' She turned to Agnes, gesturing with a slight lift of the chin for her to follow.

They retreated to the warmth of the kitchen and Agnes closed the door behind her. 'What is it?' she asked. 'What's wrong?'

'She isn't breathing,' Bess said in a low voice.

Agnes jerked her gaze away, towards the fire. Her knees weakened under her and suddenly she wanted to fall down and curl up into a ball on the rug.

Not again. She couldn't go through it a second time...

'She – she's not–'

Bess shook her head. 'No, her heart's still beating, but she's gone into shock. It's called white asphyxia. You must have come across it during your midwifery training?'

'I–'

'We've got to try and revive her,' Bess went on before Agnes could reply. 'Miss Sheridan? Agnes? Are you listening to me?'

'I – I can't...' The words came out as a low moan from deep in her throat.

'Of course you can. You must. Now pull yourself together!'

The sharp words were like a slap in the face, bringing Agnes back to her senses. She turned slowly towards Bess, eyes fixed on her face. She didn't dare look at the baby in her arms. 'What – do you want me to do?'

'Lay the baby down by the fire and hold on to her by the ankles while I try to open up her chest. Keep her covered up with that blanket, mind, we don't want her to get cold.'

The sound of laughter drifted from the other room. Mrs Rankin was chatting happily to her mother, oblivious to the drama going on.

The infant's feet were so tiny, they fitted easily into Agnes' palm. They looked as if they belonged to a doll, so tiny and white and perfect, with their toenails like little pink shells.

Opposite her, Bess was holding the baby's arms between her thumb and forefinger, slowly and gently circling them upwards and outwards. Her face was perspiring from the heat of the fire. A stray lock of greying hair had escaped from its pins and hung limply in front of her face.

'Come on, little lass,' she whispered. 'Come on – breathe!'

As soon as she said it, Agnes noticed the slightest rise and fall of the blanket that covered the baby's body. 'She did!' she cried. 'She breathed, I saw it!'

Bess stopped her circling and bent down to check the baby's breathing. Agnes held her own breath until Bess looked up and she saw the light of hope fade from her face.

'Nothing,' said Bess. 'There's no heartbeat now, either.'

Agnes fought against the raw despair that clutched at her. 'But I saw it,' she insisted. 'She was breathing, I swear it. Please, let's try again,' she begged.

Bess shook her head. 'She's gone.'

Agnes gathered up the baby in her arms. She

felt limp and lifeless, like a rag doll.

'Isn't there something else we could do?' she pleaded. 'Perhaps if we gave her a warm bath, that might–'

'She's gone, lass. Don't make it worse than it is.' Bess clambered to her feet. 'I'd best go and tell her mother,' she said quietly.

Alone, Agnes tucked the blanket tighter around the baby, wrapping her up carefully as if she could warm life into her tiny limbs.

But in her heart she knew she was dead, as dead as her own baby boy she had once held in her arms.

Agnes would never forget the ice in the midwife's voice as she'd wrenched him away. 'Stop crying, you silly girl,' she'd snapped. 'No one cares about your tears.'

She could feel them falling again, but this time she didn't try to stop them.

Chapter Twenty-Nine

'Really, Mrs Bradshaw. Was there any need to take the poor girl out in the middle of the night?'

Miss Gale was unimpressed when they returned to the nurses' home just after eight o'clock and she saw the state Agnes Sheridan was in. Even Bess had to admit the girl looked dreadful. Her skin had a greyish pallor, and she couldn't stop shivering.

Miss Gale, had sent her straight to bed and

summoned Dr Branning.

'She's probably taken a chill,' she said.

'Chill, my eye!' Bess snorted. 'It wasn't even that cold last night.'

'Then what do you think is wrong with her?'

Bess was silent. She didn't want to tell the Superintendent what she'd witnessed earlier that morning. 'I don't know,' she said quietly.

'At any rate, we can't send her out to care for patients until we can be sure she isn't infectious,' Miss Gale went on. 'As if we weren't short-handed enough.'

'I'm already visiting her patients with her anyway, so she'll not be missed,' Bess said dismissively. 'It'll probably be easier without her, to be honest.'

Miss Gale gave her a look of reproach. 'Don't you think you're being a little unfair on her?'

'Hardly! Have you forgotten all the trouble she's caused lately? We've had patients lining up to complain about her.'

'I know,' Miss Gale sighed. 'But the girl tries hard, and she's very keen to make amends for her mistakes.'

A fleeting vision came into Bess' mind. The loss of a baby was always sad for a nurse, but she had never seen anyone shed tears like Agnes Sheridan had done. It had shocked Bess to see Agnes kneeling there on the rug, silhouetted against the firelight, sobbing helplessly over the infant's lifeless form. Not even a mother could mourn like she had. The girl had seemed utterly heartbroken.

It made Bess wonder what had happened to her during her training to make her react in such a

271

way. Now she came to think of it, Agnes had seemed scared to death throughout the birth.

As Bess turned to go, she asked, 'Did she have a reference?'

Miss Gale didn't look up, already absorbed in some paperwork. 'Hmm?'

'Miss Sheridan. I wondered if she had a reference from that maternity home – St Jude's, wasn't it?'

Miss Gale thought for a moment. 'No,' she said finally. 'As I recall, her reference was written by the Matron of the Nightingale Hospital. And very good it was too.'

'Don't you think it's odd that St Jude's didn't supply one? After all, you'd think–'

Miss Gale sighed. 'Really, Mrs Bradshaw, I'm beginning to think you have some kind of grudge against the girl.'

'That's not true!'

'Isn't it?' Her superior sent her a long, steady look. They had been working together for a long time, but she still had the power to make Bess blush. 'Since it clearly troubles you so much, I'll just remind you that Agnes Sheridan is the daughter of an old school friend of mine. She wrote to me, saying that her daughter had expressed an interest in district nursing, and wondering if I might take her under my wing, so to speak. Having met the girl, and seen her excellent reference from her training hospital, I decided to give her a chance. I hope that satisfies you, Mrs Bradshaw?'

Miss Gale's steely gaze spoke volumes.

'I'll go and see about Miss Sheridan's list of patients,' Bess muttered.

Fortunately the list wasn't too long or trouble-some, and Bess was glad to reacquaint herself with some of her former patients that Agnes Sheridan had been attending.

She had half expected to find discontent among them, but she was surprised to find that most of them had come to accept the new nurse. Some even had a good word to say for her.

'Although she in't like you, nurse,' Mrs Wilson was quick to reassure Bess. 'And I do miss having a gossip sometimes.'

And then, at the end of the list, came Isaiah Shapcott.

This was an old patient Bess wasn't so pleased to be meeting again. It had been such a relief to pass him over to Miss Sheridan after so many years of frustration and failure. Not to mention all the things she'd had thrown at her.

Bess braced herself as she knocked, peering up at the window above to make sure no nasty sur-prises landed on her head. She would give it five minutes, she decided, before she gave it up as a bad job.

No sooner had she knocked than the front door swung open. But there was no sign of Isaiah Shapcott.

The dapper little man who stood on the thres-hold bore a passing resemblance to Mr Shapcott, with the same slight build and narrow, foxy face. But there any similiarity ended. Because this man had a shining pink face and closely cropped hair. His shirt and waistcoat were slightly shabby, but at least they didn't reek of stale sweat.

'Mr Shapcott?' If it was indeed him, he had

273

undergone a miraculous transformation.

He looked just as puzzled to see her. 'What do you want?' he demanded.

'I'm Mrs Bradshaw, the district nurse. You remember me, don't you?'

His frown deepened. 'Aye, I remember you all right.' He leaned out of the doorway to look up and down the street. 'What happened to t'other one? The real nurse?'

Bess fought down a stab of annoyance. 'Miss Sheridan is unwell, so I've come in her place. Do you mind if I come in?'

Isaiah looked dubious. 'Depends,' he said.

'On what?'

'You won't try to give me a bath, will you?' He screwed up his face. 'Only t'nurse said no one was going to make me, ever again.'

'You look quite clean to me,' Bess said.

'Oh, I am,' he said proudly. 'I have a bath every week. I quite like it, as it turns out. It in't that I ever minded having one before,' he told her. 'Only I prefer to do it by myself.'

'Well, if you're managing by yourself you won't need my help, will you? But I'd like to come in for a minute, just to check everything's in order.'

He stood aside to let her in, but Bess could sense his wariness. Inside the house had undergone a similar transformation. The thick layers of dust had been swept away, the floor had been scrubbed, newspaper had been taken away from the windows and the glass cleaned, to let the sunshine stream in.

'I've got the bath all ready.' Isaiah led her over to the fireside. 'I brought the tub in and filled it

274

with water and everything.'

Bess stepped behind the makeshift clothes-horse screen and bent down to test the water with her hand. She was conscious of Isaiah watching her attentively, waiting for her approval. 'It all seems to be in order,' she said.

His skinny shoulders relaxed, his smile broadening. 'I like to do it, to save t'nurse the trouble,' he said. 'It's not fair to make her lift and carry heavy things around, little scrap like her.' He looked Bess up and down, then added, 'Mind, if I'd known you were coming I would have let you bring it in by yoursen!'

Bess ignored his comment. 'Well, it all seems to be in order,' she said, looking around her. 'I see you've cleaned the house up too.'

'Aye. T'nurse helped me get it straight.'

'Miss Sheridan helped you?'

'She did. She said I'd feel better if I kept it all tidy, like. And she were right an' all.' He looked around his home, glowing with pride.

Bess frowned, trying to picture prim Miss Sheridan on her hands and knees, scrubbing floors. Her imagination failed her.

'I don't s'pose you've brought t'paper with you?' asked Isaiah.

His voice brought Bess back to the present. 'Paper?' she said blankly. 'What paper?'

'T'real nurse always brings me the *Sporting Life*. She sits and reads it to me while I'm having me bath. I'm teaching her about the horses, you see. All the bloodlines and suchlike. She says I must know everything there is to know,' he said proudly.

'I'm sure you do, Mr Shapcott.'

275

'I don't suppose you're interested in bloodlines, are you, missus?'

'I don't know much about them,' Bess admitted.

He looked her up and down again. 'I daresay you've never been on a horse in your life neither. T'real nurse can ride. She used to have a pony called Daffodil.'

'Did she indeed?'

'I'll have me bath now, if you don't mind. Before t'water gets cold.'

Isaiah disappeared behind the screen to get undressed. 'You can busy yoursen for a while, can't you, missus?' he said.

'Oh, aye. I've got plenty I can be getting on with.' Bess settled herself down at the table to catch up with her notes while Isaiah splashed happily on the other side of the screen, every so often stopping to make conversation.

He was full of glowing praise for the 'real' nurse. 'I know all about her,' he told Bess. 'She don't come from round here, her dad's a doctor and her brother was killed in t'war. Oh, and she's got a sister too, who's married. She's just had a baby. But I s'pose you'll know that already, seeing as how you work together.'

'No,' Bess said. 'No, I didn't.' There was a great deal about Agnes Sheridan she didn't know, she reflected.

Isaiah finally emerged from his bath, clean and pink and dressed in a fresh shirt.

'T'real nurse got it for me from a jumble sale,' he told Bess. 'Imagine, folk throwing out good clothes like these. Anyway, she reckons I can wear one while I wash the other. Clever, in't it?' He beamed at her.

'Very clever, Mr Shapcott.'

'Aye, well, I won't keep you.' He was already ushering her to the door. 'Will t'real nurse be back next week, d'you reckon?'

Bess looked at his shining, hopeful face.

'I expect so,' she said.

She returned to the district nurses' house to find Agnes Sheridan was still confined to bed.

'She's running a slight fever, according to Dr Branning,' Miss Gale said. Bess ignored the Superintendent's look of reproach.

The truth was, she did feel slightly guilty. Seeing how the patients had taken to Miss Sheridan, and particularly how she had transformed the life of Isaiah Shapcott, had made Bess see the student nurse in a new light.

But there was still something about Agnes Sheridan that didn't sit right with her. And Bess needed to get to the bottom of it.

She was in the common room, finishing off a letter to the Matron of St Jude's, when there was a knock on the door and Dottie appeared.

'There's a vicar wanting to see you,' she announced.

'A vicar? What on earth would a vicar want with me?' Bess saw Dottie's blank face and knew there was no point in asking her. It would have taken her all her mental capacity just to open the door. 'Best show him in, lass,' she said.

He seemed too young to be a vicar. He was thirty years old at the most, his square-jawed face softened by a frame of light brown curls.

'Mrs Bradshaw?' He stepped towards her, holding out his hand to shake hers. 'I'm Matthew Elliott, the curate of St Martin's.'

'Oh, aye?' Bess looked up at him. 'Well, I'm afraid if you're collecting for anything, you should see the Superintendent, Miss Gale. But I warn you, we're as poor as church mice ourselves here...'

'Oh no, it's not your money I'm after.' He shook his head. 'I'm here about your daughter. I am right in thinking Polly Malone is your daughter, isn't she? That's what the vicar told me.'

Bess stiffened. 'What about her?'

Matthew Elliott looked grave. 'May I sit down?' he asked. 'I have a story to tell you, and it may take some time.'

Chapter Thirty

Polly felt for Henry Slater's pulse under his papery skin, and counted the slow, steady beats under her fingers. Fifteen ... sixteen... She looked at her watch, willing them on.

Her frowning face must have given her away because Henry grinned and said, 'Has it stopped, nurse?'

Polly managed a smile. 'No, Mr Slater, you'll be pleased to know your heart's still beating.'

'Well, that's a relief!'

'Isn't it?' She let go of his wrist and busied herself plumping his pillows. 'Now, can I get you something to eat?'

'That's kind of you, nurse, but you don't need to bother. Finn made me a bit of toast earlier on.'

'That was good of him.'

'Oh, aye, he's a decent lad when he wants to be. Or else summat's put him in a good mood.' Henry winked at her.

Polly glanced at Finn, who was staring out of the window, feigning unconcern as usual. His face was turned away, but she could see the tide of colour sweeping up his throat.

'I'll see about making you a cup of tea, at any rate,' she said.

She left the room and Finn followed close at her heels.

'What's wrong?' he asked.

'Nothing.' She went to the sink to wash her hands.

'Don't give me that. You might be able to fool the old man, but you can't fool me. I saw your face when you took his pulse.' Finn's frown deepened. 'He's getting worse, in't he?'

Polly looked over her shoulder at him. She should have known Finn would notice. His eyes were so sharp, they missed nothing.

'Your grandfather's pulse is a little slower than usual,' she admitted.

Finn's face clouded. 'What does that mean? Is he all right?'

'I'm sure he is, but I'll need to speak to the doctor before I give him his medication.'

She saw Finn tense, and fought the urge to put her arms around him. She badly wanted to comfort him, but she knew it wouldn't be professional.

279

She always made sure she kept her distance when she was tending to his grandfather. While Polly was working, Finn was nothing more to her than the relative of a patient.

It was only when they were alone together that she could give in to her true feelings.

'Are you sure I shouldn't call for an ambulance?' he asked.

'No, I'll walk up to the telephone box.'

She went to fetch her coat from the peg by the door. Finn watched her.

'Is there anything I can do?'

'Just sit with him until I get back. He'll be all right, honestly.' Finn looked so lost that she reached for his hand without thinking. His fingers immediately curled around hers. He lifted her hand to his mouth and planted the lightest of kisses on her palm. His lips barely brushed her skin, yet it was enough to send shockwaves pulsing through her.

Polly pulled away, before her impulse could take over.

'I'll be back as soon as I can,' she promised.

She could have called at the vicarage and asked to use their telephone, but she didn't want to run the risk of meeting Matthew Elliott. So instead she hurried down the path through the churchyard towards the lych gate. It was a bright, cold day, and the wintry sun was shining through the bare branches of the trees, laying stripes of light across her path.

Everything seemed to be bathed in sunshine, and she was happy. It bubbled up inside her, making her want to laugh out loud. It was as if she'd thrown off a heavy mantle that had been weighing her down, so suddenly she could step lightly, her head held high.

What would your mother say if she could see you now? The fear crept in, irritating her.

Polly pushed it aside determinedly. She refused to listen to the inner voice that told her she was letting her mother down, heading for disaster.

Polly knew there could be no future for her and Finn. She told herself time and time again that she wouldn't allow her feelings for him to escalate, not the way they had with Frank. She had too much to lose.

But that didn't mean she couldn't enjoy what they had now. Surely it wouldn't do any harm to bask in a little happiness, even if it was only for a short time? They weren't hurting anyone. No one need ever know...

She was fooling herself, and she knew it. Already, her feelings were beginning to overtake her. When she tried to picture a future without Finn in it, she felt desperately miserable.

Which was why she tried not to think about it. For now, she lived in a little bubble of joy, telling herself that the future would take care of itself.

She telephoned the doctor, just as morning surgery was coming to an end.

'You're lucky,' the cheerful woman on the other end of the line said. 'Dr Marsh hasn't started on his rounds yet. I'll make sure he calls in to you first.'

Polly thanked her and hurried back to the church. As she entered through the lych gate, she caught a glimpse of Matthew, deep in conversation with Reverend Turner. She quickly swerved off the path but not before the curate turned around and saw her. He lifted his hand in a wave, and Polly waved back half-heartedly. She couldn't ever look at him without feeling a twinge of guilt. She didn't know why, since she'd never set out to encourage him.

But today he looked happy, his smile broader than she'd seen it in a long time. Perhaps he'd finally got over his unrequited feelings for her, she thought.

The cottage door was half open, so Polly hurried inside.

'I've spoken to the doctor, and he says he'll be here within an hour so...' She glanced around the empty kitchen. 'Finn?'

She heard his footsteps coming down the passageway from his grandfather's room. A moment later he appeared in the doorway, a strange, frozen expression on his face.

Polly frowned. 'Finn? What is it? What's wrong?'

And then a second figure appeared, just behind his shoulder, and she realised why he looked so stricken.

'Now then,' said her mother, looking from one to the other of them. 'What's to do here?'

Polly stared at Finn in horror, but his rigid expression gave nothing away.

Bess didn't seem to notice the tension between them. 'Mr Slater tells me you've telephoned the doctor?'

Polly nodded, still shocked and baffled by her mother's presence. 'Mr Slater's pulse was slow this morning.'

'You didn't give him the digitalis?'

'No, I thought it best to wait.' All the time, Polly's mind was racing. Had she given herself away? she wondered.

If she had, her mother gave no sign of it. 'Good idea,' she said. 'We'll wait and see what the doctor says, just to be on the safe side. Mr Slater seems comfortable enough anyway. Has he eaten?'

'I gave him his breakfast this morning.' Finn's voice sounded gruff. His eyes were fixed on Polly.

'And his appetite was all right?'

'I think so. He ate what I gave him, at any rate.'

'Well, that's something. I'll go and check his pulse again, just to make sure.' Bess turned and bustled off down the passageway to Henry's room, and at last Polly could let out the breath she'd been holding.

'What's *she* doing here?' she hissed to Finn.

'I don't know, she knocked on the door a couple of minutes ago. I thought it was you come back,' he said. 'You weren't expecting her, were you?'

'No!'

'Then why has she come?'

'I don't know.' And that was what was worrying her.

'Perhaps the doctor told her to come?'

Polly shook her head. 'I've only just spoken to him. Besides, she would have said—'

Then Bess reappeared and they stood away from each other guiltily.

'And you say Dr Marsh is on his way?' said Bess, checking her watch. Polly nodded. 'Very well, you get off and I'll wait for him.'

'But Mr Slater is my patient!' Polly protested.

'And you have others waiting who need you just as much as he does,' Bess reminded her.

'No, I'll wait and talk to the doctor myself.' Polly had caught Finn's look of dismay. 'You don't know the case as well as I do.'

'I know heart disease when I see it!' Bess scoffed. 'Now do as you're told, lass. I'll see you back at the nurses' house later. Don't look so worried,' she added. 'I'm sure I can manage here just as well as you can. Unless there's something you're not telling me?' she added, her brows rising.

Polly looked at her mother's questioning face. She couldn't know, she thought. Polly had been so careful not to give herself away. She was just being silly, reading too much into things.

'No,' she said. 'There's nothing to tell.'

'She lied to me,' Bess said. 'You should have seen her, Ellen. She looked right into my face and lied to me without turning a hair.'

'How do you know Polly was lying?' Ellen Jarvis said. 'She might have been telling the truth for all you know.'

Bess shook her head. 'I could see it in her eyes. As soon as she walked in, before she knew I was there. It was the way she looked at him...' Bess stopped, too furious to carry on. That look had stopped her in her tracks. As soon as she'd seen it, she had known Polly was lost to her again.

Bess hadn't taken to that curate either. He was far too pleased with himself for her liking. The way he'd sat there, on the same couch where Ellen was sitting now, looking so self-righteous.

'This gives me no pleasure, believe me, but I thought you ought to know... I'm very concerned...'

Concerned, my backside! Bess had thought. He'd come to make trouble, it was plain to see. And as for it giving him no pleasure – well, she could see that sneaky little twist to his lips that he tried so hard to hide.

Bess might have sent him packing there and then, if he hadn't touched a core of fear deep inside her.

She had wondered about it. Polly seemed so content these days, Bess had dared to think that all her restless grieving of the past two years was finally over, that she was beginning to settle down. Bess had even allowed herself to reach out to her daughter, albeit cautiously.

And then that wretched Mr Elliott had shown up at the door with a terrible tale to tell of how Polly had gone and got herself infatuated with a dangerous criminal.

Bess hadn't wanted to believe it. But then when she'd seen the two of them together, she'd known.

It was all starting again. She was going to lose her daughter once more.

'Well, what's the harm in it?' Ellen was saying. 'Polly's a young woman. It's only natural that she should fall in love. I'm glad for her,' she declared.

Bess glared at her. She and Ellen Jarvis had known each other for a long time, but her friend's habit of always trying to see the good in everything and everyone got on Bess' nerves. Ellen had never married, and all her knowledge of love came from the romance novels she devoured from the lending library. No wonder she had such rose-tinted ideas.

'Haven't you heard a word I've said? The man's been to prison.'

'Perhaps he's a reformed character?'

Bess snorted. Finn Slater didn't seem like a reformed character to her, with his gruff manner and glowering expression.

'Once a bad 'un, always a bad 'un,' she muttered. 'And I know a bad 'un when I see one.'

'Do you? I wonder,' Ellen said.

'What's that supposed to mean?'

'You don't really know him at all, do you? You've only met him once. And yet you've already made up your mind about him, just like you did about poor Frank.'

'Frank!' Bess stiffened at the sound of his name. She might have known Ellen would bring him into it.

'You never took the time to get to know him either,' Ellen said.

'I knew enough.'

'No, you didn't. You're too quick to judge, that's your trouble. You took against him, and that was that.'

'He ruined my daughter's life!' Bess flared back. 'Polly had a bright future ahead of her, until he came along. He dragged her down to his level, took away all her chances, made her live in a hovel. Do you think I wanted that for her?'

'It was what Polly wanted, and that was what mattered.'

'Polly doesn't know her own mind.'

'Yes, she does, Bess. She loved Frank. And he

286

loved her too. They were happy together.'

'For how long? Love doesn't last. Within a couple of years she would have been wretched...'

'You don't know that. Not everyone is like you and Albert, you know.'

Bess glared at her. 'This has got nothing to do with me or Albert. This is to do with Polly. She's been given a second chance and now she's going to ruin it again.'

Ellen sent her a wise look. 'Perhaps it's because it's not what she wants?'

'Why did she come back to nursing, in that case?'

'Oh, Bess.' Ellen sounded almost pitying. 'You'll never see it, will you? Polly didn't come back to nursing. She came back to you.'

Bess stared at her. It was the first time she'd heard such a thing, and her mind instantly rejected it. 'Don't be daft!'

'It's true. Everything she does, the fact that she's here now, putting up with all your nonsense, is because she wants to please you. Can't you see the poor girl's desperate for your approval?'

Bess frowned, trying to take it in. It wasn't right, any of it. Polly was a daddy's girl, and always had been. There had never been any room in her life for Bess. How often had she sat and watched the two of them laughing together, and wished she could be as close as that to her little girl? But Polly never seemed to welcome her mother's attention. It broke Bess' heart when she looked at her with the same indifferent gaze as her husband did.

There had been a time, after Albert's death, when she'd had her daughter to herself and then she'd thought that perhaps they might be able to build the bond that had been missing all those years. But then Frank had come between them and ruined everything.

And now another man was going to do the same thing.

'If Polly cared that much, she wouldn't be doing this,' muttered Bess.

'If you cared, you wouldn't make her choose,' Ellen replied.

'What am I supposed to do? Stand by and watch her throw her life away again? It's all very well for you to sit there and give advice. You don't have a daughter, you don't know what it's like.'

Bess saw her friend wince, and regretted her sharp words straight away.

'You're right,' Ellen agreed. 'I don't know what it is to be a mother, and perhaps that is why I can see the situation more clearly than you can. And I can see you'd be doing the wrong thing if you interfered.' She leaned forward, her expression serious. 'I mean it, Bess. You drove Polly away once. Don't make the same mistake again.'

Chapter Thirty-One

By the end of the week her fever had abated and Agnes was back on her feet and ready to start on her rounds again. Dr Branning had put her illness down to a winter chill, and she saw no reason to argue otherwise.

But at least now Bess had abandoned the idea of following her on her rounds, checking up on her. Instead, she seemed preoccupied with making her daughter's life a misery again.

Agnes was mystified that morning when Polly told her Bess was accompanying her to visit a patient.

'Why doesn't she ask Miss Jarvis to supervise you?' Agnes asked. 'She's the district nurse for your area after all.'

'She doesn't trust Miss Jarvis to keep a close enough eye on me,' Polly said. She sat at the mirror, pinning her cap in place on her fair hair.

'Good heavens, does she think you're that bad?'

'I don't think it's anything to do with my work.' Polly paused for a minute, then said, 'Can you keep a secret?'

Agnes resisted the urge to smile. If anyone could keep a secret, she could. 'Yes, I can. What is it?'

'I – I think I've fallen in love.'

'Really? Who is it? Do I know him?' Agnes hoped it wasn't the curate they'd met at the church hall dance. Phil had been very taken with him, but there was something about him Agnes didn't like.

'No, he's called Finn Slater.' Polly blushed lightly as she said his name. 'He's the grandson of a patient I've been visiting.'

'And you think your mother has found out about him?' Agnes guessed.

Polly nodded. 'I'm afraid so. Mr Slater ... his grandfather ... is the only patient she insists on visiting with me, and there's something about the way she watches me when I'm there... She knows, I'm sure of it. And she's very cold towards

Finn, too.'

'For goodness' sake, why shouldn't you fall in love if you want to?' Agnes said impatiently. 'It's nothing to do with your mother, is it?'

'But that's just it,' Polly said. 'I've spent so long trying to prove to her that I'm serious about nursing, and as soon as I start to think I'm getting somewhere, this happens! She's bound to think history is repeating itself.'

'And is it? Are you planning to run off with him to Gretna Green?'

'No!' Polly said through a mouthful of pins. 'I would never do that again. But my mother won't believe it. She'll just think I'm being silly again, letting my heart rule my head.'

'What's more important?' Agnes asked. 'Proving yourself to your mother or being with the man you love?'

Polly sighed. 'Put like that, I suppose... Oh, I don't know! I really want to be with Finn, but I don't want to let my mother down again.' She looked at Agnes, her mouth twisting. 'What must you think of me? You're so sensible. You probably think I'm quite mad to worry so much about what my mother thinks!'

'No,' Agnes said quietly. 'No, not at all.'

'Anyway,' Polly said, rising to her feet, 'I'd better go or I'll be late. And then my mother will have something else to scold me about!' She gave Agnes a cheery little wave. 'Wish me luck, won't you?'

'Good luck,' Agnes called after her, then turned back to her own reflection in the mirror. After a week, she was filled with apprehension at the thought of seeing her patients again. Even her blue uniform looked oddly unfamiliar on her.

Polly wasn't the only one who would need some luck, she thought.

Thankfully, most of Agnes' calls weren't too difficult, and she was gratified that a couple of her patients even seemed pleased to see her.

Until she reached the last call on her list.

She hadn't seen Mrs Willis since their encounter at the district nurses' house. But from the frosty expression on her face when she opened the door, she still hadn't forgiven Agnes.

'You're back, are you?' she muttered.

'Good afternoon, Mrs Willis.' Agnes pasted on her brightest smile, determined to make peace with her. 'How are you today?'

'If I say, will you go running off to tell the world?' Mrs Willis snapped back.

'Now then, Nettie, leave the lass alone. She were only trying to help.'

Agnes was surprised to see Mr Willis in the doorway, leaning heavily on his stick. She was even more surprised that he was defending her.

'We don't need any help from the likes of her!' Mrs Willis grunted, turning back to the vegetables she was peeling. Her movements were quick and agitated.

Mr Willis shook his head. 'Come through, nurse,' he said.

Agnes followed him into the bedroom, picking her way carefully between the grubby mattresses strewn over the floor. 'I see from your notes that your stomach is playing up today?' she said.

'Aye, that's right, nurse. Been having terrible pains. Can't keep anything down either.' He

291

grimaced, running his hand over his abdomen. 'No sooner has one thing got sorted than another starts up, eh?'

'You certainly don't seem to be having a lot of luck, Mr Willis, that's for sure.' Agnes glanced through the message paper the doctor had left for her. As well as all his other problems, Mr Willis also suffered from chronic gastritis. The doctor had prescribed bed rest, with an aperient for the sickness, and hot fomentations and aspirin for the pain.

'Luck!' said Mr Willis bitterly. 'I dunno if I know what that is any more.'

'Well, let's get you into bed anyway,' Agnes said bracingly. 'The doctor said you have to rest.'

'That's about all I seem to do these days!'

There was a hostile silence from the kitchen as Agnes set about making the hot fomentation for Mr Willis' painful stomach. Mrs Willis made a point of fussing over her children and ignoring her.

Mr Willis looked amused when Agnes returned. 'I'm sorry about the wife,' he said.

'I have upset her, haven't I?' Agnes looked rueful.

'She in't usually like that. She's just got a lot on her mind, that's all, what with making ends meet – and before you say owt, we don't want any more charity,' he warned.

'I wouldn't dream of it, Mr Willis,' Agnes said. 'Believe me, I learned my lesson after last time.'

Mr Willis' expression softened. 'As I said to Nettie, I know you were only trying to help,' he said. 'But she's proud, that's her trouble.'

It's all she's got left. Bess' wise words ran through Agnes' mind.

'I dunno why,' Mr Willis continued. 'God knows I've not given the poor lass much to be proud about.'

'You mustn't think like that.'

'Why not? It's the truth. I can see it on her face, even though she tries to hide it. She must wonder what she ever did to deserve a man like me.' He shook his head. 'I can't keep a job, can barely keep a roof over our heads or put food on the table. My own wife has to go out scrubbing floors to pay the rent. And all because I'm not man enough to take care of my own family.'

His voice was heavy, weighed down by sadness. His head was bowed, and wretchedness seemed to ooze out of him, deadening the room around them. Agnes floundered for a moment, at a loss for what to say.

'But surely there must be some kind of work you can do, even with your injuries?' she ventured cautiously.

She knew she'd said the wrong thing as his head snapped up, his eyes meeting hers angrily. 'Don't you think I've tried?' he said. 'I'm always at the labour exchange or round the factory gates, looking for work. But as soon as I find summat, my wretched useless body lets me down again, and I'm back where I started.' His face was bitter. 'I tell you what, nurse. It might have been better for everybody if I'd been left to die in no-man's-land,' he muttered.

Agnes kept her head down, trying to concentre on the fomentation she kept pressed against his

293

abdomen. She thought of Peter, her beloved brother. She didn't know how he'd died because no one would ever tell her. But she was haunted by the idea that perhaps he'd lain injured too, in the cold mud, waiting for death. But unlike Norman Willis, no help had ever come for him.

'You mustn't say that,' she murmured.

'Why not? Nettie would have been free. Then she might have found a better man to look after her.'

'She wouldn't have wanted that, I'm sure.'

'You don't know that. You don't have to look into her eyes like I do.' He shook his head. 'She hates the war for taking away the man she fell in love with, that's why she never talks about it. She sent a man off to fight and all that came back was this.' He gestured at his wasted body in disgust. 'No, it would have been better for everyone if I'd been left face down in the mud where I lay after that German shell got me...'

His self-pitying whine pierced Agnes like a red-hot needle. The fomentation fell from her hand as she straightened up to face him.

'How dare you!' she hissed. 'How dare you sit there and wish your life away!'

Shock registered on his face. 'Who are you to tell me what I can or can't say?'

'My brother died in that war, Mr Willis. He was nineteen when he went off to fight, just like you. But he was killed at Cambrai. You complain about the state you've been in since you came back home. But at least you *did* come home!'

His face paled. 'I – I didn't realise.'

'No, because you're too deep in self-pity to

294

worry about anyone else. You want to know why your wife won't talk about the war? It's because she wants you to get better. She wants you to leave it all behind and start afresh, but you won't. You keep clinging on to it, growing more and more angry and bitter.' She saw his face tighten but she was too furious to stop. 'My brother would have given anything to come home from that war like you, injuries and all. And I would have given anything to have him home, too, because I loved him. So don't you dare say your wife would have been better off either, because I'm telling you now ... she wouldn't!'

A shocked silence followed her outburst. Agnes reached for the fomentation, but her fingers were trembling so much she could hardly hold it still.

'I – I'm sorry,' Mr Willis said quietly. 'I had no idea.'

Agnes didn't reply. Now her anger had abated, she felt thoroughly ashamed of herself. She should never have lost her temper with a patient, especially not one as frail and damaged as Norman Willis. It was so unlike her. She prided herself on being self-possessed. But Mr Willis had touched a very raw nerve.

She was going to get into deep trouble for this, she thought. No doubt Nettie Willis would be banging down the door of the district nurses' house before the day was out.

'He was killed at Cambrai, you say?' Mr Willis sounded tentative, humble.

Agnes nodded. 'He was twenty-three.'

Willis was silent for a while, then he said, 'My brother was killed too. Right by my side. One minute he was there, and the next–' He squeezed his eyes shut. 'I don't think I'll ever forgive myself.'

'What for?'

'For it not being me.' He opened his eyes and looked at her. 'My brother was the clever one, the one with all the prospects. He should have been the one who lived.'

Agnes paused. 'I told you my father was a medic, didn't I? Well, he was in the same regiment as my brother. Except he was on leave when Peter died. I don't think he's ever forgiven himself for that either. Wondering if he could have saved him, if he'd been there...' She saw Mr Willis' face change, go blank with shock at her revelation 'But it wasn't his fault my brother died, any more than it was your fault that yours did. It was just – something that happened.'

She finished his treatment. It wasn't until she was collecting everything together afterwards that he said, 'Nurse?'

'Yes?'

'How does he live with summat like that? Your dad, I mean.'

Agnes thought about his nightmares, the agonised screams that rang through the house.

'I don't know,' she said. 'I suppose you just have to, don't you? Either that or let it eat you up until there's nothing left inside. But I think you owe it to the dead to make the most of your life.'

She returned to the nurses' home, exhausted. The emotionally draining experience of talking to Mr Willis, added to all the back-breaking physical work she'd done that day and the long haul back to Steeple Street from Quarry Hill, was almost too much for her. She could feel a dull, insistent pain in her temples and wondered if perhaps she had returned to work too early after her fever.

She let herself in. As she wiped her feet on the mat, her eyes flicked automatically to her pigeon hole. It was empty as usual.

She should stop looking, she thought. She shouldn't allow herself to be so disappointed.

Dottie was listlessly dusting in the hall, flicking the dirt from one spot to another.

'You've had a visitor,' she said.

Agnes' heart sank. Please, Lord, not another complaint!

Nettie Willis had probably already come to report Agnes for upsetting her husband. 'Who was it?' she sighed.

Dottie made a half-hearted attempt to rub away a spot on the banisters then gave up.

'She reckoned she was your sister.'

Chapter Thirty-Two

Agnes felt the blood draining to her feet, leaving her lightheaded. 'Vanessa was here?' She looked around, half expecting to see her sister appear from the sitting room. 'Where is she now?'

'Gone. But she left you this note.'

Dottie scrabbled in the depths of her apron pocket for what seemed like an agonisingly long time. It was all Agnes could do not to shake the

297

girl until the note fell out.

Finally she retrieved it and handed it over. 'Your sister's very posh, isn't she?'

'I suppose so.' Agnes' fingers were trembling so much she could hardly unfold the paper.

'And she doesn't look much like you either. She's tall and blonde and you're...' Dottie stopped for a moment, lost for a description. 'You in't,' she said finally.

Agnes tuned out the girl's voice as she scanned the note. Vanessa was staying in Leeds, at the Queen's Hotel close to the station. She was catching the train back to London in the morning and was anxious to see Agnes before she left.

Agnes folded the note carefully to give herself time to think. If Vanessa was here, it must be because their mother had sent her. And that must surely be a good sign, after all this time.

She stuffed the note into her pocket and started for the stairs. 'I have to go,' she said. 'Could you let Miss Gale know where I've gone?'

'I s'pose you'll not be back for your tea then?' Dottie called after her.

Agnes smiled to herself. If everything went as well as she hoped, she might not be back at all.

Half an hour later, Agnes sat in the lounge of the Queen's Hotel, watching the people go by and scanning their faces for her sister.

She tugged nervously at the hem of her skirt, smoothing it over her knees. She wished she'd taken the time to choose her outfit more carefully. Vanessa was bound to see the darn in her stockings, and that her blouse needed ironing. She was like their mother; she noticed these things.

Agnes was sure her parents must have sent Vanessa. There was no other reason her sister would have made the long journey to Leeds if not at their mother's bidding. They were very close. If anyone knew what Elizabeth Sheridan was thinking, it was Vanessa. With any luck, she would have come to tell her that she could go home at last.

Agnes turned her gaze towards the window. It was nearly six o'clock and the darkened streets were filled with people heading to and from the station. She had done her best to make a life for herself in Leeds, but it wasn't for her. She had grown used to the place, and to some of the people. But Bess Bradshaw was right, she didn't fit in here.

Agnes' mouth felt dry with anticipation, and she was about to ask the waiter for a glass of water when she saw Vanessa coming towards her. She recognised her sister straight away, tall and straight-backed and elegant as ever in a deep pink two-piece, a stylish cloche hat pulled low over her head.

Agnes felt an immediate rush of affection for her. She and Vanessa had never been close, but she forgot all their differences in the excitement of seeing a familiar face after being among nothing but strangers for so long.

'Nessa!' She shot to her feet, waving excitedly. Her sister turned and Agnes caught her slight frown. Straight away she knew she'd already made her first mistake.

Vanessa's cool smile was back in place by the time she had come over. She looked like an ice queen, with her pale blue eyes and silvery-blonde hair.

'Really, darling, I see you still haven't learned how to conduct yourself in public!' she chided her gently.

Agnes lowered her gaze, feeling at once like a misbehaving child. 'I was just pleased to see you, that's all,' she murmured.

'Likewise, I'm sure.' Vanessa presented the side of her face for Agnes to kiss; Guerlain perfume wafted from her. Agnes couldn't remember the last time she'd smelled anything so expensive.

They sat down. Agnes pressed her lips together, trying to hold back the torrent of words that threatened to burst from her. She didn't want to do or say anything that might offend or alarm her sister, or give her another bad impression.

'I'm pleased you could come all this way,' Agnes said finally.

'Yes, well, I had to, didn't I?' Vanessa said quietly, pulling off her gloves and arranging them neatly in her lap. 'Would you like some tea?' Without waiting for a reply, she summoned the waiter and ordered.

'You look very well,' Agnes remarked, then added, 'How is the baby?'

Vanessa paused for a moment, still fussing with her gloves. 'She's very well,' she said finally.

'What did you call her?'

'Grace Elizabeth.'

Agnes smiled. 'Such pretty names. Mother must be pleased?'

'Yes. Yes, she is.'

'I wish you could have brought her with you,'

she said.

'All the way up here? I hardly think so!' Vanessa looked horrified. 'I don't think the air would have been good for her at all. Besides, she's only four months old. Far too young to travel.'

'I suppose you're right. But I'm looking forward to meeting her soon.'

Vanessa didn't reply. 'Where on earth is that waiter with the tea?' she said, looking around. 'One could die of thirst.'

'Is she a good baby?' Agnes asked.

'Of course.' Vanessa looked slightly puzzled, as if there could be no question of any offspring of hers being anything less than perfect. 'She's very content. And she's growing up so fast. She's already trying to make sounds, and she loves nursery rhymes—'

She stopped, her lips tightening, as if she had suddenly remembered what she was saying. Agnes understood her reticence. She leaned forward and patted her sister's hand reassuringly. 'I'm so pleased for you, Nessa,' she said. 'Motherhood suits you.'

It was true. Vanessa's face softened when she talked about her daughter. Agnes had never thought of her sister as maternal, but it seemed the baby had melted her heart.

Vanessa stared down at Agnes' hand covering hers, and a deep blush rose in her face. 'Yes, well—' she started to say, but before she could add anything else their tea arrived. Vanessa drew her hand away and busied herself examining the cups.

'They're rather stained, but at least there are no

cracks,' she pronounced. Her mask of composure was back in place and suddenly she resembled their mother again, cool and critical.

Agnes smiled to herself. If she thought these cups were bad, she was glad her sister would never lay eyes on Nettie Willis' best china.

As Vanessa poured the tea, Agnes changed the subject and asked after their father.

'Oh, you know Father.' Vanessa shook her head. 'He's still busy with his practice, but might have to retire soon if his health doesn't recover.'

'Poor Father,' Agnes said. 'His patients will miss him.'

'Goodness, you sound just like him!' Vanessa snapped. 'He has to think of himself, not his patients!'

'Of course,' Agnes agreed, taken aback by her sister's outburst. Then she added, 'And how is Mother?'

Vanessa's face clouded. 'As well as can be expected, considering everything she's had to go through over the past few months.' She sent her sister a meaningful look.

'Does she ever talk about me?'

'She says you've written to her.'

'So she's read my letters?'

Vanessa didn't reply. Instead, she held the sugar tongs to the light. 'Oh, look, these haven't been polished properly. That simply won't do.' She summoned the waiter with an imperious wave of her hand.

Agnes watched in frustration, fighting the urge to snatch the wretched tongs out of her sister's grasp and fling them across the room. It seemed like an age before Vanessa had finished fussing about the cutlery and was finally satisfied.

'What has she said about me?' Agnes wanted to know, as soon as the waiter had gone.

Vanessa considered the question carefully. 'She is pleased you seem to be doing so well,' she said at last.

'Is she? Is she really?'

'Of course,' Vanessa said, then added, 'She only wants the best for you, Agnes. We all do.' Agnes caught the note of reproof in her voice. 'Anyway,' Vanessa went on, 'you seem to be settling in here very nicely. We're all very relieved you've found a place that suits you.'

If only you knew, Agnes wanted to shout. It was her own fault for trying to present such a positive view of her life. She clenched her hands tightly in her lap, trying to stay calm. 'But I would rather come home,' she said quietly.

'Would you?' Vanessa looked mildly startled. 'But you sound happy enough in your letters. Don't you want to stay here and finish your training?'

The thought of enduring Bess Bradshaw for another three months was almost too much for her. But Agnes was determined not to be difficult.

'Perhaps,' she agreed carefully. 'But what about after that? I'd like to come home then. Perhaps I could transfer to another area ... somewhere closer to home?'

Vanessa looked pained. 'We were rather under the impression that you would settle here,' she said, toying with her teaspoon.

Panic started to rise inside Agnes. 'But why

would I want to settle here? I want to come home,' she repeated. 'I've been away for so long. Surely I've been punished long enough?'

'No one is trying to punish you,' Vanessa said.

'Aren't they? That's what it feels like. I was sent away, no one has replied to my letters... I feel as if you've all forgotten about me!'

'For heaven's sake, calm down!' Vanessa hissed, casting a wary look over her shoulder. 'Why do you always have to make such a display of yourself, Agnes?'

'I can't help it. I'm trying to make you understand that I want to come home, and you don't seem to want to listen!'

Vanessa sighed. 'I don't think your coming home would be a very good idea,' she said.

'Why not?'

'You know very well why not. Surely I don't have to explain?' She sent Agnes a scathing look.

Agnes tried to collect herself. She didn't want Vanessa reporting back to their mother that she was as stubborn or difficult as ever.

'But I don't understand,' she said. 'I've done everything Mother asked of me.'

'Mother didn't send you away to punish you,' Vanessa said. 'She sent you away because she thought it would be best for you to make a new start. And it has worked out for the best, hasn't it? You've settled in here—'

'I wish you'd stop saying that!' Agnes cut her off angrily. 'I don't want a new start, or a new life. I want my old one back!'

'Yes, well, you should have thought of that before you caused so much trouble, shouldn't you?'

'It wasn't my fault,' Agnes muttered.

'Then whose fault was it? You did it, Agnes. You were the one who brought disgrace on the family. And you're the one who has to pay the price.' Vanessa sent her a look that was almost pitying. 'You didn't really think this was going to be temporary, did you?'

Agnes stared at her tea, cooling untouched in her cup. Her throat was closed so tightly she didn't think she would be able to swallow a drop.

Yes, of course she had thought it was going to be a temporary exile. She truly believed she had been sent away only until she had found a way to redeem herself for her past mistakes, and her family had found it in their hearts to forgive her. If she'd known it would be for ever she would never have agreed to it.

'Could I come home for a visit, at least?' she pleaded. 'I miss everyone so much.'

'I don't think that would be a good idea.'

Why did she have to keep saying that? It was all right for Vanessa, she wasn't the one stuck up here, so far from home. 'Why?' she demanded. 'Why wouldn't it be a good idea?'

'Because everything is settled now, and no one wants you stirring it up again.'

'I wouldn't–'

'Yes, you would. You know how it would be. Your presence alone would stir things up.'

Her heart felt like a stone inside her chest. 'So I'm never to see my family again, is that it?'

Vanessa sighed. 'Why do you always have to be so dramatic? Perhaps you could come home – in a while,' she conceded.

'How long?'

Her sister gave a careless shrug. 'I don't know,' she said. 'A few months, I suppose.'

'A few months!' Agnes looked across the table at her sister and it suddenly dawned on her that Vanessa was enjoying this. 'I suppose my banishment must suit you down to the ground?' she said bitterly.

Vanessa paused, her cup halfway to her lips. 'And what's that supposed to mean?'

'There's just you now, isn't there? The precious only child.'

'Don't be absurd!'

'It's true, isn't it? You've always resented having to share Mother and Father with me. Now you have their undivided attention. No wonder you don't want me to come back!'

'You're the one who tore this family apart, not me!' Vanessa blurted out angrily. 'Do you think I enjoy having to deal with Mother when she's so upset? I didn't make this mess, Agnes. You did. I'm just trying to pick up the pieces and keep the peace.'

'I know,' Agnes said quickly, desperate to appease her. She shouldn't have lost her temper. She knew a good word from Vanessa could change her future for ever. If only she and her sister had been closer, perhaps none of this would be happening now. 'I know how hard it must have been for you, Nessa. And I want to help. I'm sure if I could just come home and see Mother, talk to her–'

'Don't you understand? She doesn't want you!'

Vanessa's words hung in the air between them.

Agnes stared at her, shocked. Suddenly the hum of the busy lounge seemed to fall silent, and all Agnes could see was her sister's beautiful face, tense with impatience.

'Do you want to know why I'm really here?' Vanessa said. 'Mother didn't send me. She doesn't care about you. To be frank, she would rather she never saw you again.'

Blood sang in Agnes' ears. 'That's not true!'

Vanessa pulled a handful of letters out of her bag and slapped them down on the table. Agnes recognised her own handwriting on the unopened envelopes.

'Mother refuses to read them. She doesn't want to hear from you, or anything about you. She finds it all too upsetting.' Vanessa kept her voice low, leaning across the table. 'You really hurt her, Agnes. All that business with Daniel, and breaking off your engagement, and then St Jude's... It made her terribly ill. Father and I didn't think she would ever recover.' Vanessa sat back, sighing. 'I didn't want to have to tell you because, in spite of whatever you believe, I care about you. I was trying to let you down gently and not make it too hard for you. But, typically, you had to push me into a corner and force the issue.'

Agnes was too numb with shock to react. All she could do was look at the letters lying on the table between them.

'Mother hasn't read them,' she murmured.

'No,' Vanessa said. 'I told you, she doesn't want to hear from you again. As far as she's concerned, you are dead to her.'

Her words were like a stinging blow. Agnes

reeled back, too numb with shock to react for a moment.

'What about Father?' she found her voice at last. 'Surely he must want to see me...'

Vanessa stared down at her hands in her lap. 'He doesn't want to see Mother put through any more agony,' she said. 'He agrees with her, it would be best for everyone if you stayed away.'

Agnes stared at her sister. She could see Vanessa's mouth moving, but she couldn't hear the words for the thrum of blood in her head.

Her father, her beloved father didn't want to see her again. Knowing he had turned his back on her was far, far worse than her sister's spite or her mother's silence. Throughout everything, Agnes had always told herself that she still had her father's love, even if he couldn't show it. And now this...

Hot tears sprang to her eyes, blurring her vision. She didn't want to cry in front of her sister, but she couldn't help it.

'Oh, for goodness' sake!' Vanessa was impatient. 'Why do you have to make such a spectacle of yourself all the time?' She fished in her bag for a lace-edged handkerchief and pressed it into Agnes' hand. 'You never think of other people, only about yourself. That's what caused all this trouble in the first place.' She sighed. 'Well, I can't feel sorry for you, because you brought it on yourself. You were always the clever one, the one with the bright future. Wonderful Agnes, who was going to save lives just like Father.' There was an edge of bitterness in Vanessa's voice. 'Then you ruined it all, didn't you?

And now you've only yourself to blame.'

Agnes barely heard what her sister was saying. Even now, her mind was scrambling to find a way out. 'Couldn't you talk to them?' she pleaded.

'I've tried, but Mother won't listen.' Vanessa didn't meet her sister's eye when she spoke. 'Honestly, I've done everything I could.'

She must have seen Agnes' utter wretchedness because she seemed to soften.

'None of this needed to happen,' she said. 'You could have married Daniel, and everything would have been all right. But, no. You had to go your own way. Why couldn't you just have done as you were told for once?' She sounded more exasperated than angry

'I couldn't. It wouldn't have been right,' Agnes murmured.

'And this is?' Vanessa gestured around her. 'My God, Agnes. When you make a mess of things, you don't do it by halves!'

She signalled to the waiter to bring the bill. Agnes stared at her in panic. 'You're not leaving?'

'I really don't think we have much more to say to each other, do you?'

'But I thought we could spend longer together.' She and Vanessa might not have much in common, but she was the only link Agnes had to her family and her old life, and she was desperate to cling on to her. 'I haven't seen you in so long. I don't have to be back at the nurses' home until ten.'

'I can't stay, I'm far too tired,' Vanessa said, putting on her gloves.

'But what about supper? You have to eat.'

'I'll have something in my room. Although I shudder to think what kind of meal this place would offer, considering they can't even serve a decent cup of tea!' Vanessa shuddered delicately.

She leaned forward and gave Agnes a light peck on the cheek. 'Look after yourself,' she said.

'Will you write to me?' Agnes pleaded.

'I'll try.'

'At least send me a photograph of the baby...'

But her sister was already walking away.

Chapter Thirty-Three

'I'll be coming to call on Mr Slater with you this morning.'

'Again?' Polly could have bitten her tongue as soon as she'd uttered the word. But her mother had taken her by surprise, coming into the district room as Polly was packing her bag for the morning round.

She turned away so that Bess wouldn't see her blushing. 'There's no need for you to come, you know,' she said, more calmly. 'I can manage perfectly well on my own now the doctor is happy that Mr Slater's condition has stabilised.'

'Yes, but I wanted to check on him. Besides, I've got rather a soft spot for the old man. There isn't a problem, is there?' Bess' face was blandly enquiring.

'Not at all,' Polly lied.

'That's settled then.'

There was no point in arguing with her, Polly reflected as she trailed miserably after her mother on her bicycle. Once Bess' mind was set on something, it was as good as done.

And besides, Polly didn't want to arouse her mother's suspicions even further.

Finn was waiting for them as usual. Polly saw his face fall when he noticed Bess, but her mother seemed oblivious.

'Good morning, Mr Slater,' she said, breezing past him. 'How is your grandfather today?'

'Better, thank you.' Finn stared at Polly as he said it. She managed a slight, helpless shrug in reply.

'Well, we won't keep you,' Bess said briskly, dumping her bag on the table. 'I'm sure you must have plenty to be getting on with, especially with your grandfather laid up.'

'But I usually wait with him while the nurse—'

'We can manage perfectly well on our own, thank you,' Bess cut him off. 'We have done this before, you know.' Her smile was cheery, but there was an underlying note of steel in her voice.

Finn glanced at Polly. She looked back at him, silently pleading with him not to argue.

Thankfully, he seemed to get the message. 'I'll finish the washing-up and be off then,' he muttered.

They left him in the kitchen and went in to see old Henry. He was sitting up in bed waiting for them.

'What's this?' He beamed with delight. 'Two nurses again? Either I'm the luckiest man in Leeds or I'm at death's door!'

'Neither, Mr Slater.' Bess smiled back at him. 'I've just come to lend a hand, that's all.'

'Well, that'll be nice for you, won't it?' Henry said to Polly. 'It's good to have your family around you, for a bit of company, like.' He looked beyond them. 'Speaking of which, where's Finn?'

'I sent him off to make himself useful,' Bess said.

Henry chuckled. 'I'll bet he loved that! Finn's not one for taking orders.'

Just at that moment the back door slammed. 'See what I mean?' Henry turned to Polly. 'All the same, he'll be sorry, not to see you, lass,' he said with a wink.

Polly felt her face flood with fiery colour and shot a quick glance at her mother, but Bess was reading the doctor's message paper and thankfully didn't seem to notice the old man's remark.

Polly washed her hands and went to fetch the thermometer from the jar of disinfectant, ready to take Henry's temperature, but Bess snatched it out of her fingers. 'I'll do his TPR,' she said.

Polly held on to her temper. 'What shall I do?' she asked, through clenched teeth.

'Why don't you go and make Mr Slater a nice cup of tea? You'd like that, wouldn't you, love?'

'I wouldn't say no,' Henry said.

'Nor would I. Off you go, Polly, and put the kettle on.'

'Polly put the kettle on!' Henry laughed. 'That's a good one.'

But Polly wasn't laughing as she went into the kitchen. She was beginning to understand how poor Agnes must have felt, never being allowed to do anything but make the tea.

She had just picked up the kettle from the stove when a voice behind her said, 'What's she doing back here?'

Polly dropped the kettle with a clatter and swung round as a figure separated itself from the shadows behind her.

'Finn? What are you doing here? I thought you'd gone out.'

'Your mother might be able to tell you what to do, but she doesn't give me orders!' His face was grim. 'How long is she going to keep coming here?'

'I don't know.' Polly picked up the kettle again and went to fill it at the big stone sink.

'Do you think she knows about us?'

'I don't think so or I would have heard about it by now.'

He moved towards her and the next moment she felt his hand gently caressing the back of her neck. She flinched away.

Finn let out a sigh of annoyance. 'I don't know how much longer I can stand this,' he muttered. 'Not being able to touch you, or even talk to you...'

'It won't be for much longer, I promise.'

'Won't it?' There was a tinge of bitterness in his voice. 'Nothing's ever going to change, is it? You're never going to tell your mother about us. I'm always going to be your shameful secret.'

'Finn, that's not true.'

Polly was about to reach for him but then she heard her mother's heavy footsteps coming down the hall, and snatched her hand away just as Bess

313

appeared in the doorway.

'Has that kettle boiled yet? I need some hot water for–' She stopped when she saw Finn standing there. 'Oh, hello. I thought you'd gone out.'

'Yes, well, I came back in.'

'What for?'

'Because it's my house and I can do as I please.' He faced Bess insolently. Polly caught her mother's darkening expression and jumped in quickly.

'I'll bring the hot water in, shall I?' she offered.

'No,' Bess said, her stony gaze still fixed on Finn. 'You go and do Mr Slater's teeth for him. I'll wait for the kettle to boil.'

Polly sent a last helpless glance at Firm and went off. Something must have gone on between him and her mother because a moment later she heard the door slam again.

'Sounds like they've had a falling-out,' Henry said.

I hope not, Polly prayed silently. Finn wasn't doing either of them any favours by trying to get the better of her mother.

She didn't see him again. But as they retrieved their bicycles from around the side of the cottage, her mother suddenly said, 'You needn't visit Mr Slater again. I'll be taking over his care from now on.'

All kinds of thoughts ran through Polly's mind. She kept her lips pressed close together to stop herself from blurting out the wrong thing. 'What about Miss Jarvis?' she managed finally. 'This is her area, and she's supposed to be supervising me, not–'

'I'll speak to her about it,' Bess cut her off.

Polly looked at her mother and saw the mute challenge in her eyes. This was another test, to goad Polly into saying something she shouldn't.

'If that's what you want,' she said, and had the scant satisfaction of seeing her mother's thwarted anger written all over her face.

That afternoon was Polly's half-day holiday so she hurried back to the church to see Finn.

She found him at the far end of the churchyard, cutting back the overhanging skirt of a yew tree, with Job lying on the ground close by as usual.

Job's head shot up out of the tall grass at the sound of her approaching footsteps. He scrambled to his feet and galloped to greet her, but still Finn didn't acknowledge her as he hacked away at the branches.

Folly's heart sank, sensing his dark mood. But she pressed on up the path towards him.

'I see Job's not off after rabbits today?' she commented.

'Happen he's already caught his fair share.'

Finn's broad back was turned to her. Polly took a step towards him and put out her hand to touch his shoulder, feeling the warmth of his body and hard play of muscle beneath his shirt.

'Aren't you afraid someone will see you?' His voice sounded bitter.

'I don't care if they do.'

'That's not how it seemed earlier.' He moved away from her to reach for another branch, shrugging her off.

Polly sighed. 'I'm sorry, I didn't mean to hurt you. It's just my mother–'

315

'You don't have to tell me what she's like,' Finn muttered.

Polly scratched Job's head. He looked up at her with trusting brown eyes. 'Then surely you can see why it's so difficult?'

'Oh, I can see that all right. Too difficult, I reckon.'

Polly looked up at him. 'What do you mean?'

'The way I see it, I don't think there's much point in us carrying on.'

Panic fluttered in her chest. 'Don't say that!'

Finn dropped his blade and turned to face her. 'Look, I don't want to hurt you,' he said softly. 'But I don't want to be your secret either.'

'You're not.'

'I am, Polly. And that's all I'll ever be. But that's not what I want. I love you, and I want the whole world to know it.'

Polly stopped dead in her tracks. 'You – love me?'

Now it was Finn's turn to freeze. 'I didn't mean to come out with it like that,' he murmured, turning away from her

Polly found herself staring at his back again. He loved her. It didn't matter how he'd said it, the words were out there.

'I love you too,' she said. He didn't turn round, but she saw the muscles in his broad shoulders stiffen.

She took a deep breath. 'I'll talk to my mother,' she promised.

'You don't have to.' His voice was gruff.

'I do,' she insisted. 'You're right, you deserve to be more than a secret. She needs to know.'

'Do you want me with you? I don't like to think of you being by yourself...'

Polly had a sudden vision of Frank. 'No,' she said quietly. 'This is something I need to do alone.'

But telling her mother proved harder than Polly had thought. She returned to Steeple Street to find that Bess had been called out to attend a birth. When her mother came home in the middle of the evening, she promptly disappeared to the district room to catch up on her notes from the day.

When Polly asked if she could talk to her, she was dismissed with a brisk 'Can't it wait until tomorrow? I've spent the last six hours delivering a baby, and now I'm up to my eyeballs in paperwork. I'm in no mood to chat.'

Polly went to bed that night in despair. If she didn't know better, she could have sworn her mother was avoiding her on purpose.

But that couldn't be right, she thought. Bess Bradshaw never ran away from an argument. Especially not one with her daughter.

Polly lay in the darkness, tossing and turning, her body weary but her mind too wide awake for sleep. On the other side of the room, she could hear Agnes' soft breathing. She was awake too, but Polly sensed she wouldn't want to talk. Agnes had been quiet for a few days now, lost in her own thoughts. But when Polly had tried to speak to her, her roommate had forced a smile and insisted that all was well.

Eventually, even Agnes fell into a fitful sleep. But

317

Polly was still restless, staring at the hands of her alarm clock in the moonlit darkness as they crept towards midnight. She had promised Finn she would talk to her mother before the day was out, and she was determined to keep her promise.

She was fully prepared to wake her mother up, but when she crept out on to the landing, she saw a crack of light under Bess' door. So she hadn't been able to sleep either. Polly couldn't imagine her mother being kept awake by doubts and fears. She was far too sure of herself for that.

She tapped softly on the door, and heard the sound of footsteps padding across the floorboards. A moment later Bess opened the door, pulling her old dressing gown around her. She looked much softer without the armour of her nurse's uniform, her greying hair in loose wisps around her face. Softer, but also older and more tired.

'Yes?' she said. 'What is it, lass? Are you ill?'

Polly shook her head. 'No, but I need to speak to you.'

'Can't it wait until morning?'

Any other time and she might have been put off by her mother's irritable tone. But Polly had made a promise.

'No, it can't,' she said, calm in spite of the drumming of her heart against her ribs.

'You'd best come in then.' Bess stood aside to let her in.

Polly had rarely entered her mother's room, and was surprised by how sparsely furnished it was. Just a single bed covered in a worn pink quilt, a small sink in one corner and a few pieces of dark wood furniture. Bess' uniform hung from the wardrobe door, grey and formidable. There were no pictures on the walls or knick-knacks on the dresser, save for a small brown pot with ugly yellow squiggles on it that held a handful of hair-pins.

A book lay open on the bed. Polly picked it up. 'What's this?'

'Oh, just some nonsense Ellen Jarvis lent me,' Bess dismissed it.

'*Close to My Heart?*' Polly read the title aloud. The cover depicted a woman in a revealing off-the-shoulder dress, apparently being ravished by a pirate. 'I didn't know you like romances?'

'I don't.' Bess plucked the book out of her hands and threw it on to the bedside table. 'As I said, it was just something Ellen Jarvis lent me. I wouldn't have bothered with it, but I couldn't sleep so...' She glared at the lurid book cover. 'It's a lot of old nonsense.'

That was her mother's attitude to romance generally, Polly thought. She remembered whenever her father had tried to kiss or cuddle her, Bess had always shrugged him off. What must it have been like, Polly wondered, being married to someone so cold and unloving?

'Well?' her mother said, sitting down on the bed. 'What did you want to talk to me about?'

Polly hesitated. Now she was here, her words were trapped in her throat.

She fixed her gaze on the ugly brown pot. It looked oddly familiar, but she couldn't recall where she might have seen it before.

'I suppose you're going to tell me about the Slater boy?' Bess interrupted her thoughts.

Polly looked up sharply. 'How did you...'

Bess' mouth twisted. 'Did you really think I wouldn't notice the way the two of you carry on? Making eyes at each other, whispering behind my back. I'm not daft y'know.' She sent Polly a steady look 'So how long has it been going on?'

'Not long,' Polly said cautiously.

'And did you know he'd been in prison?'

She felt as if she'd been slapped. 'How did you know that?' Polly gasped.

'Oh, I know everything about young Mr Slater. Your friend the curate came to see me. He couldn't wait to tell me how worried he was that my daughter had taken up with a criminal.'

'I'll bet,' Polly muttered. She could just imagine Matthew Elliott telling her mother the whole tale, pretending to be so terribly concerned, when all he really wanted to do was make trouble.

'And I had to sit there and listen to him,' Bess went on bitterly. 'Of course, I told him he must have got it wrong. My lass would never been daft enough to do something like that. She's got more sense, I said. But then I realised you don't, do you?'

Polly ignored her mother's insult. She was under no illusions about what Bess thought of her. But that didn't matter now. All that mattered was that Polly make her understand.

'You don't know Finn,' she said. 'You don't know what he's like.'

'I know he tried to kill a man,' Bess said flatly.

'But it wasn't like that. He was only defending someone else.'

'I don't care why he did it. All I know is that he

320

has it in him to go after someone and put a knife into them. He's dangerous, Polly. He has a violent streak. Who's to say he wouldn't do the same to you?'

The idea was so ridiculous Polly almost laughed. 'He wouldn't.'

'You don't know that. You can't know what he's like. You've not known him that long. When someone's got that kind of violence in their heart, you truly don't know what they might do.'

'You're wrong,' Polly insisted. 'Finn would never hurt me. He loves me.'

'Love!' Bess rolled her eyes. 'I might have known you'd say summat like that. You sound like one of t'lasses in that silly book, thinking love will conquer all.' Her lip curled. 'You say he loves you. How many girls have said the same thing as you, d'you reckon? How many poor lasses do you see around here, nursing black eyes and broken ribs and still insisting their husband loves them? Love is just a word, Polly. It means nowt.' Bess jabbed an accusing finger at Polly. 'I'm disappointed in you, I really am. I thought you'd learned your lesson after last time. I really believed you were going to buckle down and make something of yourself.'

'I am,' Polly said. 'I want to finish my qualifications.'

'Why? So you can throw it all away again? Why waste your time, lass? You might as well just go off and abandon it all.' Bess stood up and crossed to the window, pulling her dressing gown tighter around her. 'Anyway, I'm surprised you're even telling me,' she said, staring out of the window at the night sky. 'I dunno why you haven't just run off with him, like you did the last time.'

Bess was angry, but Polly could still hear the edge of hurt in her mother's voice.

'I know what I did was wrong,' she said quietly. 'That's why I wanted to tell you now. I – we – want your blessing.'

'My blessing?' Bess snorted. 'Well, you're not going to get it. I'm sorry to disappoint you, lass, but I'm not going to let you throw your life away on another wastrel!'

Polly flinched. 'Finn isn't a wastrel, and neither was Frank,' she said. 'And I'm sorry you feel like that about it, but there isn't much you can do to stop us. I'm over twenty-one and I can do as I please.'

'No, you're right,' Bess agreed heavily, her back still turned. 'But I don't have to stand by and watch you make another mistake.'

'What do you mean?'

Bess turned slowly to face her. 'I mean, if you're set on going off with this – man, then you'll have to leave this place.'

'No!' Polly gaped at her. 'That's not fair! You can't do that–'

'Can't I?' Bess' face was implacable. 'I'm sure Miss Gale can find you somewhere else to finish your training – if that's what you really want.' Her mouth twisted. 'But I'm warning you, there'll be no going back. No more second chances. Not this time.'

'You're making me choose between Finn and my job here?' Polly said, appalled.

Bess' heavy jaw lifted. 'That's right,' she said.

'But that's not fair! Why are you being like this?'

'Because I want you to see sense. I want you to think with your head for once, and not your heart.'

'At least I've got a heart!' Any trepidation Polly might have felt about facing her mother had been replaced by cold anger, as hard as a diamond. She had no right to do this to her, to try to ruin her life. 'You want to control everything, don't you? Everything has to be done your way, and even then you're never satisfied.' Her breathing was fast and shallow, but she couldn't control it. It was as if a dam had broken inside her, releasing a torrent of pent-up emotion. 'Do you know how hard I've worked, to try to please you? But I've never had a good word out of you. You're a beast, that's what you are. A hard, heartless monster!'

Polly stopped talking, fighting for breath. Bess stared at her. There was no trace of emotion in her face.

'Then I suppose you've made your choice, haven't you?' she said stonily.

Chapter Thirty-Four

'I think I've got dry rot.'

Agnes looked up absently into the face of Queenie Gawtrey. 'Hmm? I'm sorry, what did you say?'

'I said, I think I've got dry rot. In my legs. You

323

see how they've swelled up? Same thing happened to the roof joists last winter. Landlord reckoned there was nothing to be done about it. I daresay it's the same for my legs,' she said mournfully.

'Yes,' Agnes replied, continuing with her massage.

'What do you reckon, then? Will it spread all over, like?'

'Hmm?'

Agnes jerked back as Queenie kicked out sharply, knocking her off balance. 'What's the matter with you, lass? I don't think you've listened to a word I've said since you got here. Fine nurse you are!'

'I'm sorry,' Agnes said, pulling herself together.

Queenie sent her a shrewd look. 'You've got troubles, haven't you? I can tell.'

Agnes smiled. 'I forgot you had the gift.'

'Gift be buggered!' Queenie chuckled. 'You don't need second sight to see what's going on in your head, love. You only have to look at your face. It's as long as a fiddle.' She settled back in her chair, looking speculatively at Agnes. 'Go on, then. What's troubling you?'

Agnes shook her head. Even if she wanted to tell Queenie what was on her mind, she wouldn't know where to start. Ever since Vanessa's visit Agnes' thoughts had been all over the place.

Was Vanessa lying to her, or was she telling the truth when she said their mother never wanted to see her again? Every time Agnes tried to comfort herself with the notion that her sister was acting out of spite and jealousy, she would see those unopened letters lying on the table and her heart would sink.

She kept trying to tell herself nothing had changed, that she was no better or worse off than she had been before Vanessa came to visit. Life still went on at Steeple Street, a simple steady routine of breakfast, rounds, dinner, writing up notes, then more rounds before returning for tea.

But it was different now. Vanessa's visit had changed everything. When she'd left, she had taken Agnes' hope with her. Before her sister came, Agnes had gone through each day with a sense of purpose. She'd truly believed that if she worked hard enough, did well enough, one day she would be able to go home.

But now that sense of purpose was gone. Vanessa had made it very clear that no matter what she did, Agnes would never be able to redeem herself in her mother's eyes.

As far as she is concerned, you are dead to her.

Her sister's words rang in her ears, keeping her awake long into the night. What was the point in trying any more, if she was never going to get anywhere?

'Do you want me to read your tealeaves for you?'

Agnes came back to the present to find Queenie looking at her, her eyes shrewd in her wrinkled face. She asked the same question every time. It was her answer to everything. No matter what problems life presented, the answer always lay in the tealeaves.

'The leaves don't lie,' she would say.

Agnes smiled and was about to refuse as usual. Then a mad impulse struck her and she heard herself saying, 'Why not?'

It wasn't what Queenie had been expecting to hear either. 'Truly? You want me to do a reading for you?'

'If you like.' Agnes had nothing to lose any more. She sat back on her heels and reached for a cloth to wipe the lotion off her hands. 'How do we start?'

Queenie rolled her eyes. 'Why, you have to go and make a brew o' tea first! Can't read tealeaves without the tea, can we? Besides, I'm parched,' she added.

Agnes went off to wash her hands. After she'd cleaned all her equipment and packed it away in her bag, she made the tea as Queenie instructed.

'I hope you've made it strong enough?' the old woman said when Agnes brought it in.

'I'm not sure.' She peered anxiously into the pot. 'Does it need to be strong for you to do a reading?'

Queenie sent her an old-fashioned look. 'No, I just can't be doing with weak tea. It makes me bilious.'

She had Agnes pour the tea and then they had to sit and drink it. 'Hold the cup in your left hand, since you're right-handed,' Queenie instructed. As she carefully sipped the hot brew, Agnes could feel the old lady watching her eagerly over the rim of her cup. Agnes could tell what she was thinking. For the past few weeks Queenie had been plaguing her to have her fortune told. Now she must be wondering how dire Agnes' life had become for her actually to give in.

Agnes herself didn't even know why she was

doing it, but she was desperate enough to try anything.

Queenie drained her cup and smacked her lips. 'Finished? Good. Make sure you leave a bit of tea at the bottom of the cup. Now swill it round three times and turn it upside down in the saucer, then pass the cup to me.' She held out a clawed hand.

Agnes watched the old lady peering into the depths of the cup and began to feel rather foolish. How could she possibly think anyone could see her future in the bottom of an old teacup? A none too clean one at that...

Suddenly Queenie said, 'I see a jealous person in your life. Someone close to you, who doesn't want you to succeed.'

Agnes instantly thought of Bess Bradshaw. She certainly didn't want Agnes to succeed. But then Queenie said, 'I see a broken necklace. That means there's a bond that needs to be mended.'

Agnes sat up straighter. 'Go on,' she said.

'You'll need to be the one to mend it,' Queenie said, turning the teacup slowly in her hands. 'The other person won't come to you. If you want to sort it out, you need to be the one to do it.'

She turned the cup again, holding it at arm's length. 'I see a pair of scissors as well,' she said. 'That means you might have to remove yourself from a situation, cut all ties...'

Agnes frowned. 'So which am I supposed to do, mend the bond or cut all ties?'

'I don't know, do I?' Queenie snapped back irritably. 'Happen it means you have to do one or the other.'

Agnes thought about it. Perhaps she needed to

cut all ties with district nursing and go home to mend the bond with her family? That would make sense.

Or perhaps it was all nonsense, a small voice in her head said.

'Hang on a sec, I've been looking at it the wrong way round. It's not scissors, it's a letter V ... or happen it's a letter L. It's someone who means you harm, at any rate.'

The hairs on the back of Agnes' neck prickled, as if a sudden draught had come from nowhere.

'And there's a baby,' Queenie said.

'My sister has just had a baby,' Agnes said.

Queenie looked up at her with eyes that had taken on a strange, opaque look. 'Oh no,' she said. 'The baby is in your arms.' She shook her head sadly. 'It didn't cry, did it? But it's crying now...'

'That's enough!' Agnes snatched the cup out of the old woman's hands.

'But I haven't finished!'

'I'm sorry, Mrs Gawtrey, but I don't have time.' Agnes was already scrambling to her feet, brushing down her skirt. 'Thank you, that was very — entertaining.'

As she went to leave, Queenie cleared her throat and said, 'Haven't you forgotten something?'

Agnes frowned. 'What?'

'It's customary to cross a gypsy's palm with silver.' She held out her bony hand expectantly.

Agnes burrowed in her pocket and dug out a farthing. 'Here, will this do?'

'I s'pose it'll have to.' Queenie gazed at the coin in her palm mournfully. 'Anyway, I hope you've got the answers you were looking for?'

Agnes smiled politely. But in truth, the only conclusion she had come to was that she was utterly foolish for agreeing to it in the first place.

It was a lot of superstitious nonsense, she told herself. But at the same time she couldn't get Queenie's words out of her mind.

A broken necklace... Someone who meant her harm. The initial V – or L...

Agnes kept telling herself it was all nonsense. But it still haunted her all through the day as she went through her routine of changing dressings, giving injections and hauling patients in and out of beds and baths.

If you want to mend it, you'll have to do it yourself.

Vanessa had certainly made that much clear when she came to Leeds. Agnes needn't expect any further visits from her or the rest of the family. If Agnes wanted to see them again, she would have to go back to London herself.

The idea filled her with apprehension. And yet...

She was so preoccupied that she barely noticed Mr Willis sitting on an old orange box outside his cottage. She would have walked straight past him if he hadn't called out to her.

'Looking for me, nurse?'

Agnes swung round. 'Mr Willis! What are you doing out of bed?'

'Thought I'd get a bit of fresh air, since the weather's turned fine.' He winked at her. 'Surprised to see me up and about, I'll bet?'

'I am.' Agnes stepped across the cobbles towards him. 'What are you doing?'

'Just straightening this out.' He held up a buckled bicycle wheel. 'I've been doing a bit of fixing and mending lately. Odd jobs, like. Mr Gardner down at the bicycle shop on Vicar Lane's been kind enough to pass a bit of work my way too.'

'Kind my foot! You're doing him a favour.' Nettie's voice came from the doorway. 'He reckons you've got a real talent for it.'

Mr Willis smiled shyly. 'I dunno about that. But it pays a few bob.'

Quiet pride shone out of him. Being able to contribute to the household expenses, feeling needed and valued, had worked far better than any amount of dressings and medication she could have given him. It had given him the confidence he needed to face the world.

'I'm very happy for you,' Agnes said.

'Well, as a wise woman once said to me, you owe it to the dead to make the most of your life. In't that right, nurse?' Norman Willis winked at her.

Agnes felt herself blushing. 'I'd hardly call myself wise,' she said.

'Oh, you are, nurse. You've certainly talked some sense into me, stopped me lying about feeling sorry for myself. Where there's life, there's hope, eh?'

Hope. The word struck a chord with her, touching at the sadness she carried deep inside. People could get through anything, endure anything, if they had some hope in their heart that one day things would be better. But Agnes' sister had cruelly taken all her hope away, and left her with nothing.

But she wouldn't accept that, she thought. She wouldn't lie down meekly. Like poor Mr Willis,

330

she had to get up, dust herself off and fight back.

And she would start by going to see her family. *If you want to mend it, you'll have to do it yourself.*

Once the idea had taken root it blossomed in Agnes' mind. She couldn't stop thinking about it as she examined Mr Willis in the bedroom later. She would catch a train down to London and visit them. She was sure Miss Gale would allow her the time off, especially as Christmas was coming, and Agnes hadn't taken a holiday since she arrived in Steeple Street.

And her mother wouldn't turn her away, she was sure of it.

'Everything all right, nurse?' She looked round, distracted, to see Mr Willis buttoning up his shirt. She had been so preoccupied, she scarcely remembered taking his TPR.

'Yes. Yes, everything's fine.' She smiled brightly at him, her mind still in a whirl.

As she was packing her bag, he said, 'I wonder if I might trouble you about something else?'

'What's that, Mr Willis?'

'It's John, our eldest. He's been right poorly this past couple of days.'

'What are his symptoms?'

'He's not been himself. He doesn't want to run about and play. He's got a sore throat, too. It's probably just a chill, but I wondered if you could have a look at him?'

'Of course.'

He led Agnes back to the kitchen where Nettie Willis was drying pots at the sink. She stood aside to let Agnes wash her hands.

'I've told t'nurse about our John,' Mr Willis said.

Nettie glared at him. 'What about him?'

Agnes joined in. 'I hear he's not feeling well. I wondered if I could have a look at him?'

Nettie stared at the stone-flagged floor. 'Nay, there's no need,' she mumbled.

'But your husband said–'

'John's just got a bit of a cold, that's all. I've some medicine from the chemist. That should do him.'

'All the same, I might as well check on him, since I'm here.'

'I don't want you to!' Nettie looked up at her, eyes flaring with anger.

'Nettie!'

Mrs Willis ignored her husband's look of reproach. 'No, Norman, I'll not have it,' she said. 'It's bad enough we have to have her in the house to see to you. I'm not having her looking down her nose at my bairns too!'

'But I don't–'

'Don't give me that! I've seen you, looking round at my house like it's a pigsty. Just because we can't all live in a palace like you do!'

'Nettie, please. There's no need to talk like that.'

'No, it's all right, Mr Willis.' Agnes held up her hand to silence him. She could feel hot colour burning in her face. 'If Mrs Willis doesn't want me here, then I won't stay.' She looked at her watch. 'I am rather late anyway.'

'Aye, that's right. Make sure you don't outstay your welcome, won't you?' Mrs Willis' voice rang in Agnes' ears as she hurried away.

Chapter Thirty-Five

'It'll be Christmas soon, nurse!'

Bess glanced over her shoulder at Henry Slater. He was sitting up in bed, looking very cheery in spite of his failing health.

'I can't say I've been much for it since my Doris passed on, but this'll be the first Christmas in years I'll be spending wi' family. It makes a difference, doesn't it?' Henry beamed. 'But I daresay you already know that. I s'pose you'll be spending Christmas with your lass?'

Bess made a non-committal reply as she handed him his dose of digitalis. She and Polly hadn't spoken since their argument the night before last. They had bickered many times before, but this time there was real venom behind the words they'd spat at each other. This time the rift felt too wide to breach.

'Polly's such a nice lass, a real credit to you, nurse.' She drifted out of her reverie to hear Henry talking. 'It's a pity she doesn't come here so often, but I s'pose I'll still see her now and then, since she and Finn are courting...'

Bess stiffened at his remark. Luckily Henry didn't seem to notice as he handed her the medicine cup.

'I reckon Polly's good for him,' he went on. 'Finn was a right miserable beggar before he met her, if you'll pardon my language. But she's brought him out of himself. I reckon he's been good for her, too.'

That's a matter of opinion, Bess thought.

It was because of Finn Slater that Polly was about to make yet another big mistake in her life. She was on the edge of a precipice, about to step off, and his hand was at her back, pushing her.

But perhaps Bess was wrong about that. Because when she looked more closely, the only hand she saw at her daughter's back was her own.

She should never have given her that ultimatum, she realised. But Polly had seemed hell-bent on a course of self-destruction and all Bess had wanted to do was to shock her out of it, make her realise exactly what she'd be giving up again. Except it hadn't worked out that way. Polly had called her bluff, and now there was nothing Bess could do to stop the train of events she had set in motion.

She desperately wanted to back down, to tell Polly she was sorry, that she had never meant to push her into a corner. She'd tried to say it, several times, but each time her stupid pride got in the way. She was too stubborn to admit she was wrong. Even if it meant losing her daughter again.

But her concern over Polly's future faded into the back of her mind as she examined Henry and discovered a worrying oedema in his legs. The skin was stretched tight around his ankles where the flesh had swollen. It barely made a dent when she pressed it gently with the tip of her finger.

'Everything all right, nurse?' Henry was watching her closely.

'Your legs seem a bit swollen. How long have they been like this?'

'Oh, not long. Since yesterday, I think.' He stared down at his bare ankles, his face creased in concentration. 'Yes, I think it were sometime last night I first noticed it. Why? There's nowt wrong, is there?'

'It's probably nothing. But I'll keep an eye on it when I come back this evening. Now, do you think you could manage to use the bottle for me? I'd like to take a sample.'

Ten minutes later, Bess was coming into the kitchen just as the back door swung open and Finn staggered in under the weight of an enormous Christmas tree.

He stopped in his tracks when he saw her, the tree still slung like a caber across his broad shoulders. 'Oh! I thought you'd gone,' he mumbled. He'd started making a point of not being around when Bess visited.

'That's a nice tree,' she commented.

He looked embarrassed. 'I got it for the old man. He says he's not had one for a few years.'

Bess started to smile at his nice gesture, then reminded herself that this was the young man who wanted to ruin her daughter's life.

'I'm sure he'll appreciate it,' she said shortly.

She went to wash her hands, as behind her Finn struggled to sit the tree in a bucket of earth. Bess stood at the sink and watched him in the mirror as he worked intently. The top of the tree brushed the low-beamed ceiling.

She had to say something, she realised. And this was probably her only chance. If she couldn't get through to Polly, then perhaps she could appeal to Finn's better side. If he had one.

'Have you seen my daughter lately?' Bess asked.

He froze behind her, as defensive as a trapped animal. Finally, he said, 'No, I haven't.'

'You do realise she's planning to give up her nursing career for you?'

He didn't speak, but Bess knew she had his attention.

'I gave Polly a choice,' she said. 'Either leave her training and be with you, or leave you and carry on with her qualifications. And she chose you.' She tried and failed to keep the bitterness out of her voice.

Finn was silent for a long time. Then, just as Bess had given up on his ever speaking, he said, 'Why?'

'I don't know.' Bess shrugged. 'I suppose she's got this silly notion that the two of you are going to live happily ever after.'

'No,' Finn cut her off. 'I mean, why did you force her to make that choice?' He straightened up, his eyes meeting hers in the mirror. 'Why couldn't you let her have both?'

Bess was silent. He might not have much to say for himself, but when he did speak, Finn's words were as direct and deadly as a missile.

She couldn't think of a clever answer, so all she had to rely on was honesty. She looked down at her fingers, rubbing them with hard green soap.

'Because I don't think you're good enough for my daughter,' she said bluntly. 'Polly doesn't need someone like you in her life.'

'Someone like me?'

'You know what I mean.' Bess looked at him in the mirror and saw the colour rise in his face. He was staring at her, his eyes as hard as flint. Bess met his gaze fearlessly, knowing her daughter's future happiness depended on it.

'She's had a bad time, and now she's got a second chance to make something of her life. I don't want her to throw that away. I don't want her to lose everything she's worked so hard for. And nor would you, if you really cared about her...'

He'd stopped listening, she realised. He had turned away and was hard at work setting the Christmas tree in the bucket, back bent, head down, patting the soil around the trunk. He worked with great care, she noticed.

Bess wondered if her message had even sunk in. Or if it had, whether he would take any notice of it. There was no reason why he should. She had the impression that Finn Slater lived by his own rules.

Exactly the kind of man her Polly should avoid.

Bess rinsed her hands and dried them, then packed up her bag. Finn didn't turn round, or even acknowledge her presence.

'Right, I'll be off,' she said. 'I'll be in later to give Mr Slater his medication.'

Finn grunted in response, his back still bent over the tree, not looking at her.

As Bess reached the door, she turned and looked at him. She was sure he wouldn't hear her, but she had to try anyway.

'If you really love Polly, you won't want to be the one who ruins her future,' she said.

It was only as the door closed that she heard his gruff reply.

337

'Neither will you.'

'Come on, Chrissie love!'

Lil turned to look back at her daughter, her face full of exasperation. Christine was helping her mother deliver bundles of fresh laundry to her customers. But she had stopped pushing the barrow to massage her aching back again.

'Blimey, I reckon I could have finished this lot quicker on my own!' Lil sighed as Christine sat down on a low wall. 'What's the matter with you, lass? You're not sickening for owt, are you?'

'I – I'm just a bit tired, that's all.' She massaged the small of her back. It had been playing up for a while, but now she also had a dragging feeling in her belly that spread all the way into her legs. 'I just need to rest for a bit.'

Lil planted her hands on her hips. 'I don't know! And there was me thinking I'd get the job done quicker with your young legs to help me!'

'I'll be all right in a minute,' Christine promised.

'We've nearly finished anyway. I can do the rest of these myself.'

Lil picked up the bundle Christine had dumped at her feet. 'You get yoursen home.'

'There's no need–'

'Nay, lass, I've only got to drop this lot off down the hill. You go home and get t'kettle on.'

'All right, Ma.' Christine smiled gratefully up at her.

She watched her mother trudging off into the darkness, bundled up in layers of coats against the cold, washing bundles swinging from each gloved hand. She worked so hard, and rarely asked for anything in return. Christine desperately wanted to be able to help her, but her wretched body had let her down.

It was a freezing night and the pavements sparkled with frost in the lamplight. Christine pulled her coat tightly around her. Like her mother, she had bundled herself up in various layers to keep out the chill. But even through her woollen gloves, her hands throbbed with cold.

'Looks like it might snow,' a voice said behind her. She looked round and noticed the slight figure standing close by. Annie's Pilcher's small, pinched face peered out from between layers of woollen shawl wrapped around her head. The lamplight drained her skin of colour, giving her a pale, ghostly appearance.

'Want a sweet?' She proffered a brown paper cone.

'Thank you.' Christine started to take one but then hesitated, her hand halfway to the bag. Her mother would go mad if she saw.

'Go on, have a barley sugar. I won't tell!' Annie Pilcher's smile was mischievous, lighting up her face. Christine couldn't help smiling back as she reached for a sweet.

Annie perched beside her on the wall, sucking loudly on her barley sugar. 'You're Lil Fairbrass' lass, in't you?' she said at last.

'That's right.' Christine nodded, instantly wary. The whole of Quarry Hill knew there was bad blood between the two women after Lil had set about her.

Annie laughed. 'Don't look so afeared, lass, I don't hold no grudges. Not against you, at any

339

rate.' She looked sideways at her. 'How is your mum?'

'She's all right,' Christine said.

'What does she reckon to you being pregnant?'

The question caught Christine off guard. Blood sang in her ears and even though she opened and closed her mouth, no sound came out.

'She doesn't know,' Annie said. 'I thought not.'

Christine found her voice at last. 'I – I dunno what you're talking about.'

'Come off it, lass. You might be able to fool your mother, but not me. I've seen it all too many times.' Annie leaned back and gave Christine an assessing look. 'I daresay you can get away with it because you're so tiny. How many months gone are you? Four? Five? Maybe more,' she muttered, almost to herself. Christine didn't like the way Annie looked at her, as if she were a prize goose being weighed up for the pot. She put one hand over her belly in an automatic gesture. 'You won't be able to hide it for ever,' Annie said. 'Sooner or later that little bairn's going to pop out into the world. And won't that be a lovely surprise for your mum, eh? I'd like to see her try and look down her nose at the rest of us then!'

She gave a harsh, nasty laugh, revealing sharp little teeth. Christine shrank back from her, mortified. She started to get down from the wall but Annie put out a hand to stop her.

'Nay, lass, don't run off. I'm sorry if I spoke out of turn. I let my mouth run away with me sometimes, that's my trouble.' Her voice was soothing again. 'I expect you're scared enough without me going on, in't you? How old are you?'

'Sixteen.'

'Is that all? And I daresay the father's nowhere to be found?' Annie shook her head. 'It's a terrible shame, that's what it is. Men like that have their fun and expect us women to pick up the pieces.' She paused. 'But I could help you, you know.'

Christine suddenly heard Rene Wells' voice in her head.

She does favours for women.

'How?' She was curious in spite of herself.

Annie tapped her narrow nose. 'That'd be telling,' she said. 'Don't want to give all my secrets away, do I? Let's just say, I can sort it all out for you. You'd like that, wouldn't you, love? I can see it in your face. I could turn the clock back so that none of this ever happened. And your mum won't know a thing about it.'

Christine stared at her. This scrawny little women in her drab shawl might offer the answer to all her prayers.

But then another image came into her mind. 'You left Maisie Warren to die,' she said.

Annie's face changed. 'You don't want to believe everything you're told,' she snapped. 'Maisie Warren was nowt to do with me.'

'My mum says different.'

'From where I'm standing, I reckon your mum should keep her nose out of other people's business and start paying more attention to her own! Anyway,' Annie said, 'if you don't want me to sort you out then you only have to say. I've plenty of lasses who do want my help, I assure you.'

She got down from the wall and readjusted the layers of shawls around her head and shoulders.

341

'It's no skin off my nose one way or t'other,' Annie said carelessly. 'But if you do want my help, you know where to find me.'

She started off down the street, trailing shawls behind her. 'Just make sure you don't leave it too late, won't you?' she called back over her shoulder, her voice thin on the cold night air. 'From what I can tell, you in't got long left!'

Chapter Thirty-Six

It was a tradition that all the nurses attended Midnight Mass on Christmas Eve. Each year they visited a different church in the district, and as luck would have it this year it was the turn of St Martin's.

'I'm glad they didn't decide to visit the parish church in *our* district.' Phil shivered as they filed out of the church after the service. Agnes wasn't with them; at the last minute she had decided to catch a train down to London to visit her family. 'I wouldn't fancy cycling ten miles in the dark on a night like this!'

'Perhaps Father Christmas will bring you a motorcycle this year.' Polly smiled back at her.

'One can only hope!' Phil sighed. 'Just think, it's only another couple of months until we qualify. I can't wait, can you? I'm hoping they'll assign me somewhere a bit closer. Preferably with a decent bus or tram service!' She turned to Polly. 'How about you? Do you have any particular preference for where you want to go?'

Polly shook her head. 'I really don't mind.' But her heart was heavy. She didn't like lying to Phil, but she didn't want to tell anyone what had happened with her mother.

She was upset and furious that Bess had given her the ultimatum. Deep down, she knew it meant nothing; Miss Gale certainly wouldn't make her leave, whatever her mother might threaten. But Polly also knew she couldn't go on working alongside Bess when there was so much bad feeling between them.

In any case, her choice was made. Her future happiness lay with Finn Slater.

'Don't look now, but your friend is coming this way,' Phil hissed.

Polly looked round in a panic to see Matthew Elliott gliding towards her, looking angelic in his snowy white surplice, his light brown curls like a fluffy halo around his head.

'Polly,' he greeted her stiffly. 'How are you?'

He put out his hand but Polly ignored it. She couldn't bear to touch him or even look at him after all the trouble he'd caused.

Phil moved in smoothly, taking the curate's hand. 'I'm Phil,' she said. 'Phil Fletcher. We met at the dance?'

'Oh. Oh yes, of course,' Matthew replied absently, his gaze still fixed on Polly. She turned away from him and joined the slow tide of people moving towards the doors.

Phil caught up with her outside. It was bitterly cold, and the first tentative flakes of snow were beginning to drift out of the velvety black sky.

'That was a bit rude, wasn't it?' she said. 'You could have shaken the poor man's hand!'

'He was lucky I didn't punch him on the nose!' Polly replied with feeling.

Phil sent her a sideways look. 'Oh dear. What did he do to you?'

'You don't want to know,' Polly muttered.

As they passed the corner of the church, out of habit she glanced back over her shoulder towards the sexton's cottage. Her heart lifted with surprise and delight to see a light glowing in the window.

'You go on ahead,' she said to Phil. 'There's someone I need to see.'

'Now?' Phil looked at her watch. 'It's nearly midnight!'

'Please?' Polly begged.

Phil sighed. 'Oh, all right. You're lucky Dottie won't be locking the door tonight because of Midnight Mass. But don't be too late, will you?'

'I won't,' Polly promised.

'And remember, if you do get caught, you'll have to answer to your mother, since she's in charge while Miss Gale is away,' Phil warned.

'I know,' Polly said.

She watched Phil catch up with the other nurses and they all disappeared through the lych gate together. Then Polly turned and retraced her steps, back up the path past the church to Henry Slater's cottage.

Before she knocked, she looked in through the window. The curtains were open and she could see Finn sitting in his grandfather's old armchair, gazing moodily into the dying embers of the fire.

He looked distracted, as if he was a million miles away.

She tapped gently on the window, startling him out of his reverie. He jerked upright and swung round to stare at the window. When he saw her, a strange expression flitted across his face. If Polly hadn't known better, she would have sworn it was dread.

He came to the door and flung it open. 'What are you doing here?' he demanded.

'We've just been to church so I thought I'd call in and see you.' Polly smiled at him. She expected him to reach for her, to pull her into the warmth of his arms. But instead he stood rooted to the spot, his face a blank mask. 'Aren't you going to invite me in?' She shivered, stamping her feet to bring some life into them. 'It's rather cold out here.'

'I can't,' he said. 'Granddad's a bit restless tonight. I don't want to disturb him.'

Polly looked at Finn's rigid, expressionless face. Suddenly she felt cold seeping through her, and not just from the icy flakes that pattered against her face.

'I told my mother about us,' she said. He nodded, his face still blank. 'Aren't you going to ask me what happened?' He was silent. 'Finn?'

His silence frightened her. The past day or so had been horrible, and all she wanted was for him to hold her, to reassure her that he loved her and everything would be all right.

But he seemed cold, offhand, almost uninterested.

'Finn, say something!' She laughed nervously.

He looked at her, his expression bleak. 'I don't think we should see each other any more,' he said.

It took her a moment to realise what he'd said. But even then she couldn't bring herself to believe it.

'I – I don't understand. What are you saying?'

'I said it plainly enough, didn't I?' His voice was harsh. 'I don't want to be with you.'

Job pushed past Finn to greet her, nudging her gloved hand with his nose. Polly wanted to cry but she felt too numb. 'But I thought... You said you loved me.'

'I was wrong, wasn't I?'

Finn was staring down at the worn stone step as he said it.

'Look at me,' she said.

'Polly...'

'Look me in the eye and tell me you don't want to be with me!'

Even Job seemed to realise something was wrong. He stopped nudging Polly and sat on his haunches, looking up at Finn.

Slowly, he raised his gaze to meet hers. They were standing so close she could see the shadow of stubble on his strong jaw, and the inky rings that circled his stormy grey irises.

'I don't want to be with you,' he said.

She gazed into his eyes and saw something lurking in their depths. A look of utter wretchedness.

And then she knew.

'You've spoken to my mother.'

The fight seemed to go out of him, his broad shoulders sagging. 'I don't want this,' he said, his voice ragged. 'I don't want you to give up every-

346

thing for my sake.'

'But it's what I want.'

'It's not what *I* want. I couldn't live with myself if you did that. I can't let you give up your future.'

'You are my future,' said Polly, reaching for his hand. She felt the fleeting warmth of his touch before he pulled away.

'No,' said Finn. 'Not any more.'

He stepped away, putting distance between them. Polly felt him retreating from her, his warmth diminishing. 'You can't do this,' she pleaded. 'I love you.'

'And I love you too,' he said. 'That's why I have to do this.'

At three minutes past midnight on Christmas Day, little Ivy Jenkins came screaming into the world, much to the delight of her parents, Mary and Joseph.

'Can you believe it?' Ellen Jarvis marvelled as she and Bess made their way home, cycling carefully through the dark, frozen streets. 'A child born on Christmas Day to Mary and Joseph!'

'Not exactly in a stable, though,' Bess said. Although a tiny back bedroom in a Quarry Hill tenement wasn't much better, when she came to think about it. 'And no choir of angels either. Unless you count those drunks coming home from the pub!' Ellen laughed.

'I'm glad it wasn't a boy,' Bess said. 'Heaven only knows what they might have decided to call him.'

'Ivy's a nice name. And I daresay we'll be called out this time next year for Holly's birth, too!'

'Not me!' Bess shivered. 'This is the last time I do a night shift at Christmas. I'm getting too old for this lark.'

'Perhaps this time next year your Polly will have qualified as a midwife.'

Bess said nothing as they turned the corner into Steeple Street. The district nurses' house was in darkness, its steeply gabled roofs and Gothic pinnacles black on black against the night sky. Light from the street lamps caught the lazily drifting snowflakes.

'Looks like we'll have snow for Christmas,' Ellen said.

'It'll make the roads treacherous if we get called out.'

Ellen laughed. 'Bess Bradshaw! Don't you have any romance in your soul at all?'

Bess felt a stab of regret. 'It doesn't seem like it,' she said grimly.

She would have liked to go straight to her warm bed, but Ellen insisted they toast the arrival of Christmas Day – and baby Ivy with a glass of sherry.

They were just finishing their drinks when the other nurses returned from Midnight Mass, shivering and shaking the snow off their coats.

'Where's Polly?' Bess asked.

'She's – um – just following on behind.' Phil Fletcher looked away guiltily.

'Is she now?' Bess' mouth firmed. She had a very good idea where her daughter was.

'You mustn't worry about her, Bess. She's a big girl, she can take care of herself.' Ellen Jarvis laid her hand on Bess' shoulder. 'Here, have another

drink. This is turning into quite a party, isn't it?'
She offered the sherry bottle, but Bess put up her
hand.

'No, thank you,' she said. 'I'm off to bed.'

Ellen looked disappointed. 'Are you sure you
won't stay and celebrate with the rest of us?'

'Thanks, but I don't feel like celebrating. And
see you clear all those glasses away before Miss
Gale comes back tomorrow, or she'll never leave
me in charge again!' she added.

Bess left the other nurses laughing in the
common room and trudged up to bed. Part of her
wanted to wait until Polly came home so she could
hear what she had to say for herself. But deep
down she knew she was too exhausted to face another argument, and another part of her was
nervous that Polly might not come home at all.
For all Bess knew, she could be planning a second
elopement. The two of them might even be on
their way now, heading north through the snow...

Bess undressed quickly and got into bed, but
the heavy blankets offered no warmth and she lay
under them shivering with nervous anticipation
of what the next day would bring.

She didn't have to wait long to find out. Shortly
after the other nurses went to bed, their voices
ebbing and flowing on the landing as their doors
closed, she heard Polly come home.

Bess listened to her daughter's footsteps on the
stairs. She made no effort to tread softly. Bess
could feel anger emanating from every step.

She got up, pulling her dressing gown around
her just as the door opened.

Bess saw her daughter, and it was all she could

do to stop herself from rushing to her and gathering Polly into her arms. The poor girl looked distraught, her eyes red-rimmed in a white, bloodless face. But that wasn't Bess' way. So instead she retreated behind her familiar wall of bitterness and sarcasm. 'You're still here then?'

'Yes,' Polly muttered. 'I'm still here.'

'And will you be staying?'

'It looks like it, doesn't it?'

Bess' heart crashed against her ribs in sheer relief, but she daren't show it. She put out her hand to grip the bedpost. 'What made you change your mind?'

'As if you didn't know!' Polly's voice was harsh. 'You talked to Finn, didn't you?' she accused.

'Did he tell you that?'

'No, he wouldn't tell me anything. But I know it was you. You couldn't leave it, could you? You couldn't bear to let me be happy. You had to try to ruin it all.'

Bess lifted her chin. 'I don't like to see you upset,' she said calmly. 'But I'd be lying if I said I was sorry. He was no good for you, Polly.' She took a step towards her daughter. 'I don't want you to throw your life away. You're going to qualify soon, and then–'

'And then what?' Polly flung back at her. 'What do I have to look forward to? Growing old and bitter on my own like you?'

She looked around the room. Her expression had gone from distraught to full of dark, twisted malice.

'I don't want to live like this, in a mean little room with no memories. Look,' she said, gesturing at the bare walls. 'Look around you. You've got nothing, have you?'

'Polly–'

'It's true. This is all you've got.' She picked up the pot from the dresser and stared at it. 'Just some ugly little ornament. I bet you can't even remember where it came from, can you?'

'Polly, please. Just calm down, and–'

'I don't want to calm down!' Polly's voice rose. 'I'm sick of you ordering me about, telling me what I can and can't do, what I can and can't think, who I can and can't fall in love with. I'm not a child, and you can't treat me like one, not any more. I won't let you!'

Bess took a step back. She had never seen her daughter so angry. Her sweet, gentle Polly was gone, replaced by a furious demon.

'I could have been happy,' she said, her voice hoarse with anger. 'I had someone who loved me, but you couldn't bear that, could you? You had to go and ruin it all for me, just like you ruin everything!'

'I don't – I only want the best for you.'

Polly threw back her head and laughed. 'Don't make me laugh! You've never wanted the best for anyone in your life. All you ever do is make people as miserable as you are. You just can't stand to see anyone happy, can you? You always hated to see Dad laughing and joking with me, and now you don't want anyone to love me. You're only satisfied when I'm living here, where you can keep an eye on me, living a miserable little existence just like you. Well, I'm not going to do it. I'm sick of trying to please you. I hate you, and I hate everything about you!'

Polly threw the pot at the wall. It shattered into pieces, sending fragments of pottery and hairpins skittering all over the polished floorboards.

And then, all at once, the strength seemed to leave her and she sank down on the floor, her knees buckling under her, and started to sob; great keening sobs that racked her whole body.

Bess watched her, helpless in the face of such terrible grief. She had never seen her daughter like this.

Behind her, the door opened and Ellen Jarvis appeared in her nightgown.

'What is going on?' she said. 'I heard – Polly?' She looked at the sobbing girl on the floor. 'Oh Polly, my dear, what is it?'

Ellen immediately dropped down beside her and put her arms around the girl. Bess watched her rocking Polly in her arms like a baby.

Why couldn't she do that? Bess wondered. She desperately wanted to, and yet she couldn't allow herself to break down the wall she had built around herself. The wall that kept her safe, but also separated her from everyone she loved.

Finally, Polly calmed down, her sobs quietening to a whimper.

'What's going on?' Miss Goode whispered from the doorway. The other nurses had crowded in behind her. 'Is Polly all right?'

'She's quite well.' Ellen Jarvis took charge of the situation. She summoned Phil Fletcher forward with a wave of her hand. 'Miss Fletcher, would you take Polly away and help get her ready for bed, please? It might be as well if you stayed with her, since Miss Sheridan is away.'

'Yes, Miss Jarvis.'

Once Phil had ushered Polly away, the other nurses returned to bed and Ellen closed the door to Bess' room.

'Now,' she said. 'What on earth was that all about?'

Bess didn't look up from where she was kneeling beside her bed, carefully gathering up the broken shards of pottery. 'It was my fault,' she said. 'Polly was angry and I don't blame her.'

'Here, let me help you.' Ellen bent down beside her and started picking up the broken pottery. There seemed to be a million pieces, far more than Bess would ever have imagined for such a tiny pot.

'I take it it's over, then? Between her and the young man?' Ellen said. Bess nodded. 'You must be very relieved.'

Bess paused for a moment to examine her feelings. All kinds of emotions were going through her, but she wasn't sure if relief was one of them.

'I don't know about that. I'm beginning to think you were right,' she said. 'I shouldn't have interfered.'

Ellen Jarvis sat back on her heels. 'What's this? Are you going soft in your old age, Bess Bradshaw? It's not often you admit you were wrong.'

'Perhaps I should have done it more often,' Bess mused. 'Then happen I wouldn't be in this position.'

Ellen was silent for a moment and Bess tensed, knowing what was about to come.

'I was thinking,' she said slowly. 'Perhaps if you

353

told Polly about–'

'No,' Bess cut her off. 'I know what you're going to say, and the answer is no.'

'It might help her to understand?'

'No,' Bess repeated. Her hands shook as she picked up another fragment of pottery. 'I mean it, Ellen. I don't want her to know anything about it.'

'But it's so unfair...'

'Unfair or not, it's best Polly doesn't know. And I don't want you saying anything either,' she warned.

'Of course I won't, not if you don't want me to,' Ellen said. 'But I think you're making a mistake, Bess, I really do.'

'It wouldn't be the first time, would it?'

Ellen picked up a shard of pottery and considered it carefully. 'You know, I've always thought this was an odd little ornament,' she said.

'Polly made it at school, when she was a lass.' She'd made it for her father, but Bess had still treasured it.

Ellen smiled sympathetically as she handed the piece of pottery over. 'I'm sure it can be mended,' she said kindly. 'A bit of glue and it will be as good as new.'

Bess looked down at the fragments in her hand. It was a shame the same couldn't be said for herself and Polly.

There was an odd atmosphere in Steeple Street the following morning. Everything felt subdued and drained, like the morning after a heavy storm. Except unlike a storm the air hadn't been

354

cleared. It was still charged with electricity, as if something might happen at any moment.

It might have been Christmas Day for the rest of the world, but for the district nurses it was business as usual. It was a blessed relief for everyone when breakfast was over and they could escape on their rounds.

Only Bess was left behind. As Miss Gale was away, she had to stand in as Superintendent, so she had divided her round up among the other nurses. Ellen Jarvis was to look after Henry Slater.

'Do you want me to take over his case permanently, as he's in my district anyway?' Ellen asked.

Bess shook her head. 'No, I'll see him again in a couple of days.' She liked the old man too much to abandon him, and besides, it wasn't in her nature to back away from her responsibilities.

The house was empty apart from the sound of Dottie cursing over the Christmas dinner in the kitchen. Bess was in the Superintendent's office, trying to make sense of some of the paperwork Miss Gale had left her, when the telephone rang, shattering the peace.

Bess listened to Dottie's footsteps scuttling up the hall, then the sound of murmuring. A moment later there was a knock on the door.

'You're wanted on the telephone,' she said.

'Who is it?'

'Dunno.' Dottie shrugged.

Bess gritted her teeth, biting back a comment. Miss Gale had spent endless hours teaching Dottie how to take a message on the telephone, but she still hadn't fathomed it. 'I'd best come and see then, hadn't I?'

Bess stomped into the hall, muttering under her breath. If this was an emergency, and she was the only nurse available...

'Hello?'

'Is that Mrs Bradshaw?' enquired a haughty voice on the other end of the line.

'Yes, that's right. Who's speaking?'

'This is Sister Mary Helena of St Jude's. You wrote to me regarding Agnes Sheridan?'

It took a moment for Bess to place her name. So much had happened with Polly since she'd written the letter, she'd forgotten all about it.

'I appreciate your taking the time to telephone me, but it really isn't important now,' she said. 'I was just curious about Miss Sheridan's background, that's all.'

'And what makes you ask about Miss Sheridan?' The voice sharpened.

'As I said, it isn't important now. I was just wondering about her reference.'

'Reference? Whatever do you mean?'

'Miss Sheridan didn't bring a reference with her when she came here to train. I wondered if there might be a reason for that?'

There was a long pause. Then Sister Mary Helena said, 'I think there may have been a misunderstanding, Mrs Bradshaw. Are you under the impression that Miss Sheridan worked at St Jude's?'

Bess frowned. She disliked the other woman's tone. 'She said she was there for six months. We assumed she did her midwifery training–'

'Is that what she led you to believe? Well, I can't

say I'm surprised. Miss Sheridan always did have a rather devious streak.' Bess could hear the smirk in Sister Mary Helena's voice.

'I don't understand.'

'Mrs Bradshaw, Agnes Sheridan was never a nurse here. She was a patient.'

Chapter Thirty-Seven

It was just past ten o'clock on a bright, frosty Christmas Day when Agnes finally arrived in St John's Wood. She had slept fitfully on the night train from Leeds as it crawled down the country before depositing her early in the morning in a deserted King's Cross station. In her haste to get home Agnes had forgotten that no local trains or buses ran on Christmas Day, so she had had to walk the three miles or so to her parents' home.

She hadn't been back in nearly a year. Her life had changed so completely in that time, she was surprised to find the tree-lined road still looked just the same as when she'd last been there. It was still the same broad avenue of large, affluent houses, with sparkling bay windows and well-kept front gardens. The crisp, cold air tasted sweet after the tainted smog of Leeds. Agnes was so used to the dirty smoke that belched from the factory chimneys, she had almost forgotten what it was like to look up into a clear blue sky.

But as she approached her parents' house, she was in a state of complete terror. How had she ever thought this was a good idea? Her mother loathed surprises, and wouldn't take kindly to her wayward daughter turning up unannounced.

Agnes stood at the gate for a moment, and it was all she could do to make herself lift the latch. She took a deep, steadying breath. It might be a bad plan but she was here now and she had to see it through.

The maid looked startled when she opened the door. 'Miss Agnes!'

'Hello, Martha.' Agnes stepped past her into the hall. The house was in silence. 'Where are my mother and father?'

'They're at church, miss. They'll be back presently.' Agnes could see the maid's puzzled expression reflected in the mirror as she took off her hat and coat. 'Mrs Sheridan didn't mention you were coming home, Miss Agnes.'

'She doesn't know. I thought I'd surprise her.'

'Ah.'

Agnes caught Martha's apprehensive look. She clearly didn't think it was a good idea either.

But Agnes forced herself to smile as she handed the maid her hat and coat. 'I'd love a cup of tea,' she said, as brightly as she could manage.

'Of course, miss. I'll bring it in to you.'

Agnes went into the sitting room. It was a large, sunny room, with French windows at one end leading out to the garden. Her mother had decorated it beautifully. A welcoming fire crackled in the enormous fireplace, and the fragrance of burning logs mingled with the fresh resin pine scent of the Christmas tree.

Agnes sank down into the big, feather-filled

cushions of the sofa, so soft and welcoming after the hard couches in the nurses' common room, and breathed a sigh of relief. She was home at last.

Martha brought her tea and some home-made biscuits. Agnes took a few sips, but she was so tired after her long journey she must have dozed off next to the warmth of the fire. She snapped awake at the sound of the front door opening, and voices and laughter in the hallway.

Agnes sat up straight, smoothing down her hair. Her parents weren't alone. Vanessa and her husband Leo were with them, and some other people too. A surge of panic ran through her. She hadn't been expecting this.

'Come into the sitting room, we'll have a drink,' her mother was saying. 'I think we all need one after that interminable sermon. Martha!' she called to the maid.

Agnes shot to her feet as the door opened. Her heart was racing in her chest and suddenly all she wanted to do was to run and hide...

And then it was too late. There was her mother, standing in front of her.

Elizabeth Sheridan stopped dead, her smile freezing on her face.

'Hello, Mother,' Agnes said.

'Agnes?' Her father came in. Agnes was shocked at how he'd aged in the time she'd been away. Once a tall, well-built man, now his jacket seemed to hang off his stooped shoulders.

When he saw her, a slight look of bewilderment crossed his face. 'Good gracious, what are you doing here? I had no idea you were coming. Did you, Elizabeth?'

'No, indeed.' Her mother's smile stretched wider. 'Really, Agnes, you naughty girl. Why didn't you tell us you were coming?'

'I wanted to surprise you.'

'Well, you certainly did that!'

Her mother moved forward stiffly, as if propelled against her will. She gave Agnes the briefest of embraces.

Over her mother's shoulder, Agnes saw Vanessa's face, a frozen mask of dislike. Behind her stood her husband Leo, his face turned to the window. He couldn't even look at Agnes.

'You remember Mr and Mrs Pearson, don't you?' Her father introduced the couple who stood in the doorway, watching the scene with interest. They were roughly the same age as Agnes' parents, the man small and dapper with slicked-back hair and a round, smiling face, and his wife thin to the point of gauntness, with a wiry thatch of dark red hair and watchful dark eyes.

'Well, my goodness, she should remember us!' Mrs Pearson laughed. 'We've lived next door for the past ten years!' Her voice was high-pitched and girlish. 'How are you, my dear?'

'Very well, thank you,' Agnes replied politely.

'We should leave,' Mr Pearson said. 'We don't want to interrupt a family reunion.'

'Oh no!' Mrs Pearson looked disappointed. 'Must we? I do so want to hear all Agnes' news. I'm sure Elizabeth wouldn't mind if we stayed ... would you, dear?'

'No. No, of course not.' Agnes' mother's smile was so brittle, it looked as if her face might shatter like glass at any moment.

360

Mrs Pearson looked gratified. She was rather too made-up for church, Agnes thought. A bright crimson slash of lipstick looked clownish against her white-powdered face. Agnes couldn't imagine why her mother had invited her. She had never heard Elizabeth Sheridan say a good word about the Pearsons in all the time they had been neighbours.

But then, her mother always put on a good show in public.

The maid came in and served them all sherry. Mrs Pearson settled comfortably on the sofa beside Agnes. 'It is lovely to see you, my dear,' she said, patting her hand. 'Goodness, hasn't it been a long time? Where on earth have you been?'

'I–'

'Agnes has been in Leeds, training as a district nurse,' her mother answered for her. She was perched tensely on the edge of the armchair opposite, like a cat ready to spring. 'She's doing very well, actually.'

'A district nurse? How interesting.' Mrs Pearson looked thoughtful. 'What made you go all the way up to Leeds, I wonder? Don't they have district nurses around here?'

'The Superintendent in Leeds happens to be a friend of mine,' Elizabeth Sheridan jumped in again. 'So when Agnes said she wanted to train, it seemed the obvious place for her to go.'

She shrugged it off as if the matter was of no importance, but Mrs Pearson was like a bloodhound on the scent.

'You disappeared so suddenly we wondered what on earth had happened to you, didn't we?'

she said to her husband. 'One minute you were here and the next you'd been spirited away. Very mysterious!'

Agnes glanced across at her mother. Elizabeth looked utterly mortified.

'Well, I'm back now,' said Agnes.

'Yes,' her mother said quickly. 'Isn't it wonderful? Although I do wish you'd told us you were coming. We're hardly prepared for guests,' she added in a low voice.

Mrs Pearson laughed. 'Goodness, she's not a guest, is she? She's family. How long are you planning to stay, Agnes?'

She glanced at her mother. 'Well...'

'It's probably just a flying visit,' Elizabeth put in hastily. 'She's so busy with her training, she can scarcely spare us any time. Isn't that right, Agnes?'

She caught her mother's sharp stare. 'Yes,' she said. 'Yes, that's right.'

'Well, I suppose you'll be looking forward to meeting your new niece?' Mrs Pearson said. 'You'll adore her. She really is the sweetest little creature.'

Agnes looked at Vanessa. 'Is she here?'

Her sister's face was pinched with tension. 'She's upstairs.'

'I'd love to see her.'

'She's asleep at the moment. I don't want to disturb her.'

'Perhaps I could just creep in and look at her?' Agnes said. 'I won't wake her, I promise.'

'I said she's asleep!' Vanessa snapped. 'For goodness' sake, Agnes, when will you learn to take no for an answer?'

A brief, shocked silence followed her outburst. Mr and Mrs Pearson exchanged looks. Elizabeth turned her face to the fire, but Agnes could see the tide of colour sweeping up from her throat. Even though it had been Vanessa who had snapped, Agnes still sensed she was the one her mother blamed.

She longed for the Pearsons to leave so she could talk to her parents alone. But they showed no sign of going anywhere. Indeed, Mrs Pearson had settled back against the sofa cushions, sherry glass in hand, ready to enjoy whatever show presented itself.

Agnes glanced across at her father. He looked pleased to see her, at any rate. But his appearance still worried her. His hair was quite white now. He looked so much older than his fifty-five years. That was what the war and the loss of his son had done to him.

And she hadn't helped. All the troubles and heartache she had caused him over the past year must have contributed to his ill health. She noticed his hand trembling as he reached for his drink, and her heart went out to him.

'And what about you, Agnes?' She looked up to see Mrs Pearson's penetrating gaze fixed on her. 'When are you going to settle down and find a nice husband like your sister has?'

Agnes looked down into her glass. 'I – don't know,' she murmured.

'Oh, Agnes is far too busy for all that.' Her mother dismissed briskly. 'She has a vocation.'

'But there was someone, wasn't there?' Mrs Pearson persisted. 'I could have sworn there was a young man you were rather keen on?' Agnes cringed. She dearly wished Mrs Pearson would choke on her sherry. 'It was a doctor at the hospital, wasn't it? Now, what was his name...?'

'Daniel,' Agnes murmured. 'Daniel Edgerton.'

'That was it! I distinctly remember your mother telling me you were practically engaged. What happened to him?'

'He went up to Scotland to become a GP.'

'Really? What a shame. Is that why you broke it off? Or did he? I can't say I blame you if you did. I must say, I wouldn't fancy the idea of being a doctor's wife in the Highlands. Nothing for miles around except sheep!' Mrs Pearson's trilling laughter pierced like a drill.

Agnes put down her glass, unable to stand it any longer. 'Excuse me for a moment,' she said as politely as she could.

As she went up the stairs, she heard Mrs Pearson say loudly, 'Oh dear, I hope I haven't touched a nerve?'

Agnes locked herself in the bathroom and pressed her forehead against the mirror. The glass felt cool against her heated skin.

She shouldn't have come. She had thought it would be a good idea, but now she was here, all the bad memories were pressing in on her, enveloping her like a dark fog.

It wasn't just the talk of Daniel. Every room in the house seemed to open the door to another memory, like the pages in the book of her life, unfolding...

Even this bathroom, she thought. This was where she had locked herself when the storm was raging downstairs. She had stood in this very spot, staring at herself in the mirror as she listened to her parents arguing about what was to be done with her. She remembered looking at her mother's various bottles of pills lined up on the shelf and wondering if it would be easier on everyone if she just took them all, there and then...

She let herself out of the bathroom and crept across the landing to her old room. Her sanctuary, as it had been.

But not any longer. It was still her room, with its small cast-iron fireplace and a window overlooking the garden. But it had been transformed into a nursery, with pale pink walls and delicate white-painted furniture. And in the centre of it stood a cot, a confection of carved wood and frothy lace canopy, like something from a fairy tale.

Agnes started at the sight of it. As she stepped backwards, she collided with a lamp, knocking it off balance. She made a grab for it, but it fell to the floor with a crash.

Luckily it wasn't broken, but the noise was enough to wake the baby. Agnes froze, listening as the baby stirred. She waited for her to settle but she went on shifting restlessly, making strange gurgling, snuffling sounds that gradually changed into a little hiccupping cry.

Agnes set the lamp back down and edged forward to peer into the cot where baby Grace lay amid more frothy white lace. She looked so pink and plump and perfect, with her velvety dark hair and her tiny fists punching at the air.

Without thinking, Agnes reached down and gathered her up, breathing in the warm, milky smell of her.

The baby stopped crying immediately. She lifted her head to look straight at Agnes with serious dark eyes, focusing on her face as if she already had the measure of her.

'Put her down!'

Agnes swung round, startled. Vanessa stood in the doorway, eyes narrowed, hissing like a cat.

'She just woke up. I didn't know what else to do...'

Vanessa pounced and grabbed the baby out of her sister's hands, clutching the child so tightly to her own chest that the infant let out a wail of protest.

'I wasn't going to hurt her,' Agnes said, bewildered.

'How could you?' Vanessa spat, her voice rising above the baby's cries. 'I told you not to come. I said you weren't wanted here. But you had to come anyway, didn't you? Typical Agnes, always wanting to make trouble!'

'Shh, you're upsetting the baby,' Agnes pointed out quietly, but Vanessa was too angry to listen.

'Do you know how much embarrassment you've caused? Poor Mother is absolutely mortified. And in front of the Pearsons too. You know this will be all over St John's Wood by tomorrow!'

'I don't care,' Agnes said.

'Well, that's obvious. You don't care about anything or anyone but yourself, or you wouldn't be here!'

Grace's wails turned to screams of fear. 'Now see what you've done.' Vanessa sent Agnes an accusing look over the top of the baby's head. She turned away, shushing the child, crooning softly to quieten her.

'Can I help?' Agnes offered, but Vanessa backed away from her, colliding with the doorframe.

'Don't you come anywhere near her,' she warned.

Agnes stared at her, bewildered. 'Nessa, please. I won't hurt her...'

'I'm her mother. I'll look after her.'

There was something about the way she said it that hit Agnes like a dart to her heart. But before she could respond, their mother appeared on the landing behind them.

'Keep quiet, both of you!' she snapped. 'Our guests will hear you, and I think we've given them quite enough to talk about for today!'

'It's her fault,' Vanessa muttered darkly. 'I told her not to disturb Grace, but she came in here, poking around where she's not wanted.' She sent Agnes a baleful stare.

'I wanted to see my room,' Agnes protested. 'Or at least, what used to be my room,' she added.

Her mother had the grace to look guilty. 'We were just being practical,' she said, not meeting her daughter's eye. 'We needed a room for the baby when she comes to visit, and since you weren't using it...'

'How did you know I wouldn't be using it? How did you know I wouldn't be coming home? You said I could come home...'

'Yes, but we didn't expect you'd just appear out of nowhere, did we?' her mother snapped. 'Anyway, there's no need to be so childish about it. We've kept all your belongings quite safe. They're packed up in boxes in the attic, if you want them.'

Agnes looked around the room. She had been packed away, every trace of her removed from this house and their lives. Gone and forgotten.

'Anyway, why on earth would you want to come home?' her mother continued. 'It's not as if you can pick up your old life, is it? They'd hardly want you back at the Nightingale, not after everything that happened. And besides, we've told everyone you're living up in Yorkshire now. There would be too many awkward questions if you came back. You heard the Pearsons. Everyone would be far too curious.'

'That wouldn't do, would it?' Agnes couldn't keep the sarcasm out of her voice. 'We couldn't have anyone asking awkward questions, nothing that might embarrass the family.'

'I think you've embarrassed us more than enough, don't you?'

Agnes faltered at her mother's sharp tone. Elizabeth Sheridan's beautiful face was twisted with resentment. Do you really want to put us through even more than you have already? You've nearly cost this family its good name once already.'

'Is that all that's important to you ... your good name?'

Her mother lifted her chin. 'You may mock, Agnes, but your father is an important man in this community. As a doctor, people look up to him, respect him. If word had got out about your ... condition,' she suppressed a shudder, 'I dread to think what a terrible scandal it would have caused.'

'Is that why you sent me away?'

Her mother lowered her gaze. 'I did what was best for the family.'

'And what about me? How do you think I felt, being packed off to live in – in that place?'

Elizabeth sighed. 'Why do you have to be so melodramatic? We didn't send you to the workhouse, Agnes. St Jude's has an excellent reputation for looking after girls in your – situation.' Again, her slim shoulders shuddered delicately.

'Pregnant girls, you mean? It's all right, Mother, you can say it. Pregnant girls with no husbands, who are an embarrassment to their families. Those are the kind of girls who end up at St Jude's. And don't the nuns punish them for their sins!'

It haunted Agnes' dreams, even now. Sometimes she would wake up in terror, thinking she was still on her knees scrubbing the kitchen, or in the sweltering laundry, pounding away at washing in a dolly tub until her back ached and her hands were raw and bleeding.

'I'll never forget their cruelty,' she said. 'Did you know that they beat us? I've seen girls dragged across the room by their hair for nothing more than being late for chapel. One girl even had her skull fractured. Matron told her parents she'd fallen down the stairs, but we all knew better.'

'I'm sure you must be exaggerating,' her mother muttered, her gaze fixed on the floor.

'You didn't see it, Mother. You weren't there!' Agnes shook her head. 'I wanted you, but you weren't there,' she whispered sadly.

Elizabeth flinched. 'What else could we do? It was a difficult situation for all of us...'

'Difficult for *you*? You weren't the one who

cried herself to sleep every night because she was so scared of what was happening to her. I needed you, Mother. I needed my family around me!'

'You had a choice,' her mother rallied. 'You could have married Daniel. You were already engaged, everything was planned. You could have had a quiet, discreet wedding, and all this could have been avoided. But no, you had to do it your way. You decided you had to ruin everything by breaking it off with him.'

'I didn't love him,' Agnes said. 'It wouldn't have been right.'

Vanessa laughed harshly. 'And you think being unmarried and pregnant is right? How dare you come here, telling us your wretched stories and trying to make us all feel guilty, when you were the one who brought shame on us all in the first place!'

'Is everything all right up there?' her father's voice drifted up the stairs. 'We're getting worried about you!'

'We'll be down in a minute,' her mother called back in the trilling tone she always used in company. 'We're just having a little chat ... baby talk, you know.'

'Baby talk!' Agnes laughed at the irony. 'If only they knew.'

Her mother sighed. 'Is that what you want, Agnes? To tell everyone your secret?'

'No.'

'Then what do you want? Why exactly have you come here?'

Agnes swallowed hard. 'I want to come home.'

'You can't!' Vanessa put in.

'Is that what you really want?' Her mother's gaze was steady, her blue eyes cool. 'Because if it is, then I'm not going to stop you.'

'Mother!' Vanessa gasped, but her mother held up her hand, silencing her.

'Agnes is right, Vanessa. This is still her home. And if after everything she's done, and everything that's happened, she still feels she wants to come back regardless of the consequences, then that is her decision and we have no choice but to accept it.' She turned to Agnes. 'Now, I have to return to our guests. Come with me, Vanessa, and bring the baby. It might stop that wretched Pearson woman asking so many questions!'

She looked again at Agnes. 'I'll leave you to think about what you want to do. I trust you'll make the right decision – for everyone.'

After they'd gone, Agnes sat on a nursing chair in the room that had once been hers but now felt like a stranger's.

She reached into her bag and took out the teddy she had made in secret at St Jude's, cut from scraps of fabric she had found in the work-room. She had made it for her own baby, but he hadn't lived to see it.

She laid it in the cot, in the warm imprint where baby Grace had lain.

She didn't really blame her parents. They had done their best for her, under the difficult circumstances they had found themselves in. Her mother was right, she had caused so much trouble, one way and another. The least she could do was not to cause any more.

The sitting-room door was half open, and as

Agnes crept down the stairs she couldn't resist pausing halfway down to take one last look at her family. There were her parents, her sister Vanessa with the baby in her arms, Leo looking on proudly. They looked so happy together, like a tableau of the perfect loving family.

There was no room for Agnes any more.

Chapter Thirty-Eight

Lil Fairbrass had done her family proud as usual, serving up a Christmas dinner fit for a king. All Christine's brothers had gathered round the table to enjoy the feast together, and Tony and Eric had even managed to help Granddad Hollins down from the bedroom, so he wouldn't miss any of the fun. They had eaten turkey, and exchanged gifts, and pulled crackers, and laughed until their sides ached.

Or at least, her mother and brothers had. Christine had sat quietly through it all, too preoccupied to enjoy the festivities.

She wasn't the only quiet one. Maisie Warren's two small children sat at the table opposite her, wide-eyed at their surroundings.

'I bet they've never had a Christmas like it, eh?' Tony said to Christine.

She tried to smile back, but her face felt stiff. All she wanted to do was crawl away and lie down.

She had hoped no one would notice in the midst of all her brothers' loud laughter and joking, but as her mother stood up to clear away the plates, she said, 'You've hardly eaten a thing, love. What's the matter with you?'

'I'm not hungry,' Christine said.

'All the more for us then!' Alfie went to snatch a roast potato from her plate, but his mother rapped him smartly on the knuckles with a spoon, making him howl in pain.

'I reckon I should take you to the doctor,' she said to Christine. 'You've not been right for a while, have you?'

'I'm all right, honestly.'

'I don't think you are. You're off your food, tired all the time. And I know you're awake most of the night, tossing and turning.'

'Leave the lass alone, Ma!' Tony said. 'You fuss over her like she's a china ornament.'

Lil sighed 'I can't help it, can I? She's my baby.' She slowly dragged her gaze away from Christine.

'Right, where's the Christmas pud?' Adam asked.

'Greedy little beggar! You couldn't eat another thing five minutes ago!'

'Yes, well, I'm a growing lad, in't I?'

The next minute they were all laughing and joking again. Christine was thankful for their high spirits, as it took their mother's attention away from her.

She shifted in her seat. Sitting for too long pressed on her back and made her uncomfortable.

'I'm going to the privy,' she said.

'Again?' Ernie said. 'You only went five minutes ago.'

'I didn't know you were keeping count!'

Christine flicked the back of her brother's head as she passed, making him yelp.

In the privy she carefully adjusted her layers of clothing to hide her bulging belly. She was really beginning to show now. She was just glad that the weather was cold enough that she could conceal herself under various woolly jumpers.

But she didn't know how much longer she could go on hiding.

Annie Pilcher's mocking words came back to her: *Sooner or later that little bairn's going to pop out into the world. And won't that be a lovely surprise for your mum, eh?*

Christine picked her way back across the snow-covered yard to the welcoming warmth of her mother's bright kitchen, to find the rest of the family gathered around the table in a state of high excitement.

When she came in, they all clustered together, as if they were trying to hide something.

'What is it?' She looked from one laughing face to another. 'What are you lot up to?'

'We'd best show her,' Lil said. She and the boys stepped aside, to reveal a large, brightly wrapped package sitting on the kitchen table.

Christine blinked. 'What is it?'

'What does it look like?' Ernie said, exasperated. 'It's a present, dafty.'

'For you,' Alfie added.

'For me?' Christine stared at it. 'But we opened all our presents this morning?'

Her mother smiled. 'We kept this one back, 'cos it's special.'

'What is it?'

'You'd best open it and find out, hadn't you?'

They gathered around her, and Christine could feel their eyes watching her eagerly as she pulled off the wrapping paper. 'I still don't understand why–' She stopped dead when she ripped off a piece of paper to reveal a leather-bound book with gold lettering on its spine. 'No,' she murmured. 'It isn't ... it can't be.' She tore at the paper, pulling it away to reveal yet more books. Five in total.

'It's that set of encyclopaedias you wanted!' Alfie shouted, unable to stand the suspense any longer. 'The ones from the pawn-shop window.'

'She can see that, you daft ha'porth!' Tony cuffed his brother. 'Ma said you've had your eye on them for a while,' he explained to Christine. 'She's been putting money away every week to buy them for you.'

'And we've been putting from our wages too,' Ernie said. 'I've been smoking nowt but dog-ends this past three months!'

'I know they're not brand new,' Lil said. 'But they'll do, won't they? For your schoolwork?'

'They're beautiful,' Christine breathed, running her finger over a tooled leather spine. She had never owned anything so wonderful. 'But you shouldn't have spent all your money on me.'

'It'll be worth it,' Lil said, 'when you're a teacher one day.'

Christine looked up at her mother, her face shining with quiet pride, and suddenly it was all too much for her.

'Nay, lass!' Lil rushed to embrace her as she sobbed. 'Don't take on so.'

'I've never seen anyone cry at a Christmas

375

present before!' Alfie scoffed.

'Don't tease her,' Lil warned. 'She's just crying 'cos she's happy, that's all. In't that right, love?'

Christine buried her face in her mother's shoulder, breathing in her warm, comforting scent. She wished she could stay there for ever, and never have to face anyone or anything else again.

Her mother had no idea that Christine was crying out of shame.

When Agnes arrived back at Leeds station the following day, the first person she met was Miss Gale.

At first Agnes didn't recognise the well-dressed little woman who approached her outside the station.

'Good afternoon, Miss Sheridan,' she greeted Agnes cheerfully. 'I trust you had a pleasant Christmas?'

'Yes – thank you.' Agnes looked her up and down. The Superintendent seemed so different out of her crisp grey uniform, a rather fetching red felt cloche hat pulled down over her grey hair.

'You've been to see your family, I assume?' Agnes nodded. 'That must have been nice for you, being able to spend time with your mother and father.'

Agnes was silent. No need to tell anyone that she had spent most of yesterday scouring the streets around King's Cross, looking for a cheap bed and breakfast. She had finally found one so squalid it wouldn't have looked out of place in Quarry Hill, where she had spent a sleepless night in a cold, draughty room, watching bugs crawling up the wall while she waited until she could catch the first train home.

Home. She frowned at the word that came into her mind. When did she start thinking of this place as home?

Perhaps when she realised she had nowhere else to go.

Miss Gale insisted that Agnes share her taxi back to the district nurses' house. Agnes was embarrassed, wondering how she was going to pay when she'd spent all her money on a place to stay the previous night, but Miss Gale said it would be her treat.

'I wouldn't hear of you walking all the way back to Steeple Street in the snow,' she said. 'Besides, I want to hear about your visit. How was your mother?'

Fortunately, Agnes was able to steer the conversation away from that subject towards Miss Gale's Christmas with her own family. The Superintendent had a great deal to say about her sister, her children and all their various offspring.

'Honestly, it was a mad house,' she declared. 'I tell you, Miss Sheridan, I shall be relieved to return to Steeple Street, just for some peace and quiet. Although my niece did buy me this hat for Christmas,' she added. 'I wouldn't usually wear red, but it's rather dashing, don't you think?'

They returned to Steeple Street to find a noisy game of gin rummy going on in the common room, and the telephone ringing in the hall.

'Oh dear,' Miss Gale said. 'Perhaps I was wrong about the peace and quiet!'

She headed for the telephone just as Dottie

appeared in the hall, a glass of brandy in her hand. She took one look at Miss Gale and ducked back into the kitchen.

'I hope that is for medicinal purposes, Dottie!' Miss Gale called after her as she picked up the telephone receiver. 'Hello? Steeple Street District Nurses, Susan Gale speaking. Oh, hello, Dr Branning. No, I've just this moment returned myself... Miss Sheridan? Yes, she's here. She came with me from the station as a matter of fact...'

Agnes was halfway up the stairs but she stopped and turned at the sound of her name.

'Oh dear, that's unfortunate.' Miss Gale frowned into the receiver. 'And you say he's been taken to the Infirmary? Yes, I'll inform her right away. Thank you for letting us know, doctor.'

She hung up the telephone, still frowning. Agnes came slowly down the stairs.

'Did I hear you mention me, Miss Gale?' she asked.

'Yes. Yes, you did. You treat the Willis family, don't you?'

'That's right. Why, what's happened? Has Mr Willis been taken ill again?' Agnes' heart sank. Poor Mr Willis, she thought. And just as he was starting to recover, too.

Miss Gale shook her head. 'Not this time. Apparently one of the Willis children has been taken to hospital with suspected diphtheria.'

Chapter Thirty-Nine

'They called Dr Branning out to the house this morning. Apparently the boy was taken ill with a sore throat and fever a few days ago.'

A strange sinking feeling came over Agnes as she listened to the Superintendent.

'What is it, Miss Sheridan?' Miss Gale said. 'You look quite pale.'

Agnes paused. 'Mr Willis asked me to see the boy,' she said.

'Did he? When?'

'A couple of days ago. When I called in to treat his leg.'

'And how did he seem to you?'

'I – I don't know, I didn't see him. Mrs Willis wouldn't allow it.'

'Wouldn't allow it? Why on earth not?'

Agnes could feel herself blushing. 'She doesn't like me, Miss Gale.'

'I see. Well, I knew you and Mrs Willis have had your difficulties, but I didn't realise the situation had become so bad.' Miss Gale looked grave. 'I must say, that does make it rather difficult for you to carry out your duties. It's extremely important for a district nurse to win the trust of her patients and their families if she is to do her job properly.'

'I know,' Agnes said miserably. Bess Bradshaw had said the same thing to her many times.

Miss Gale looked thoughtful. 'I shall have to consider this matter very carefully,' she said.

'Perhaps if I went to see her again?' Agnes suggested. 'If I talked to her, it might–'

'No,' Miss Gale cut her off firmly. 'No, I don't think that would be a very good idea at all. Believe me, it would only make matters worse.'

In spite of Miss Gale's dire warnings, Agnes decided to go to the Infirmary. It wasn't just that she wanted to talk to Mrs Willis; little John Willis was one of her patients and she was genuinely concerned about him. It didn't feel right to sit at the district nurses' house waiting for Dr Branning to telephone with news, especially when she might be of some practical help.

It felt strange to be back in a hospital again, to breathe in the antiseptic smell that had once been so familiar to her. It seemed like so long since she had walked down a hospital corridor, her shoes squeaking on the polished floor.

A ward sister walked purposefully by, her chin up, immaculate in her starched uniform. Agnes averted her eyes out of habit, and almost walked into a pair of staff nurses hurrying along, doing the rapid heel-toe walk that all nurses perfected because they were forbidden to run.

Mr and Mrs Willis were sitting outside the double doors to the Children's ward. Mrs Willis was crying in her husband's arms.

Mr Willis saw Agnes first, turning his head at her approach. 'Nurse?' He frowned at her, his face pale with tension. 'What are you doing here?'

'I came to ask after your son. Is there any news?'

Mrs Willis' head shot up at the sound of Agnes' voice. Tears had ravaged her features, making them blurred and puffy. 'You!' Her voice grated with loathing. 'Come to gloat, have you?'

'Nettie, calm down. You're not helping matters, getting in a state.' Mr Willis turned back to Agnes. 'He's holding on, nurse. But they're worried about him. They reckon the next few hours will be touch and go.'

'I came to see if there was anything I could do.'

'You can go away and leave us alone. We don't want you here.'

Agnes fought to control her rising temper. Mrs Willis was only lashing out because she was frightened, she told herself. 'It isn't my fault your son is ill, Mrs Willis.'

'That's right, rub it in! My son's dying and all you can do is stand there and tell me it's my fault!'

'I didn't say that–'

'Nettie, stop it,' Mr Willis joined in. 'Don't have a go at the nurse. She's been kind enough to come all this way to see us...'

'Kind? Kind, you say? That snotty cow hasn't a kind bone in her body. She in't even fit to call herself a nurse!' Nettie's lip curled as she addressed Agnes. 'If you really want to help, you'll clear off and leave us all alone. No one in Quarry Hill likes you. You're best off going back where you came from!'

She slumped back in her chair, her rage spent. Mr Willis looked up at Agnes. 'It might be best if you left us to it, nurse,' he said quietly.

'Are you sure? Perhaps I could have a word

with the ward sister, see if I can find out anything for you? She might talk to me...'

'Why? Because you're so much better than the rest of us?' Mrs Willis' voice was raw with contempt.

Agnes glanced at Mr Willis. He shook his head. 'Like I said, nurse, you'd best leave it for now.' He gave her a sad smile.

'Very well,' she said quietly. 'But you will let me know if there's anything I can do?'

'Just go, will you?' Nettie spat. 'How many times do we have to tell you, no one wants you here!'

'I beg your pardon?' Miss Gale blinked at Agnes from behind her spectacles. 'You want to do what?'

'I want to resign, Miss Gale.' Agnes held herself upright, staring out of the window beyond the Superintendent's shoulder.

'And may I ask what has brought this on?'

She in't even fit to call herself a nurse, Nettie Willis' voice hissed in her ear. It wasn't just Nettie who thought that either. Agnes had heard the other nurses discussing it in the common room when she'd returned from the hospital the previous evening.

'Can you imagine, not being allowed to see the poor bairn?' she heard Miss McLeod saying as she passed the half-open door. 'I wonder what she did to upset the family?'

'Wait until Bess Bradshaw hears about this,' Miss Goode said with relish. 'I wouldn't care to be in Miss Sheridan's dainty shoes then!'

'Well?' Miss Gale's sharp voice brought Agnes

382

back to the present.

'I don't think I'm cut out for district nursing, Miss Gale.'

'Well, I'll admit you've had a few problems, but I thought you were beginning to get to grips with the work.' Miss Gale paused and considered. 'So what will you do?' she asked.

Agnes looked at her blankly. 'I beg your pardon?'

'What will you do if you leave district nursing? Will you go back to hospital work?'

'I – I don't know.' Agnes hadn't thought much beyond walking into Miss Gale's office and handing over her letter of resignation. She was in such a deep fog of misery and self-recrimination, she couldn't see what lay ahead of her.

But now she did think about it, she had no answers. Growing up, she had always had a plan, a clear path of goals she wanted to achieve. She would train as a nurse, gain her qualification, work as a staff nurse, then as a sister, and ultimately become a matron.

But becoming pregnant had thrown her carefully laid plans off course. She had been discreetly but humiliatingly dismissed from the Nightingale, and from that moment on her life had fallen apart.

Then, after St Jude's, a new plan had been formed. It was mostly of her mother's making, but Agnes could see another clear path laid out for her. Train as a district nurse, then qualify, and slowly but surely earn back the respect she had lost.

But now that plan had also crumbled, and once again Agnes was left standing in the rubble of her ruined life, with nowhere else to go.

And there was no one to help her this time. She couldn't even go home, she realised.

Her utter despair must have shown on her face because Miss Gale said, 'I don't think I'll accept your resignation just yet.' She pushed Agnes' letter back across the desk towards her. 'I want you to go away and think about it. Sleep on it, if you will.'

'But I've already made up my mind.'

'Sleep on it,' Miss Gale insisted. 'And if you still want to resign in the morning, come back and see me and we will discuss it further.'

Agnes went to her room with a heavy heart. For only the second time in her life, she truly didn't know what to do. She almost wished Miss Gale had accepted her resignation there and then, because at least some kind of decision would have been made.

Even if it was the wrong one.

Except it wasn't the wrong one, Agnes told herself. She didn't fit in here. Everyone – Bess Bradshaw, Lil Fairbrass, Nettie Willis – had been telling her so since the day she had arrived. But she had been too stubborn, too determined to do things her way, to listen.

But now all she could hear were their voices in her head, ringing out loud and clear, shutting out everything else.

You don't belong here...You'll never understand the people of Quarry Hill...You in't even fit to be a nurse...

Her bag was still on the bed where she'd dumped it before she went to the Infirmary. Agnes wondered if she should even bother to unpack it. Perhaps she should pack the rest of her things, in anticipation of leaving?

She looked around the room. She would miss it, she realised. In a few short months this place had become home to her. She liked the other nurses, and Dottie's hit-and-miss housekeeping. She liked the familiar routines and the lively conversations at mealtimes, gently teasing Miss Hook about her poetry and Phil about her endless quest for a motorcycle. She liked sharing a room with Polly, even though she could be maddeningly untidy sometimes...

Agnes stopped short, suddenly noticing something. Polly's belongings weren't scattered all around the room as they usually were. Her bed was neatly made, too, as if it hadn't been slept in.

And come to think of it, Agnes couldn't remember setting eyes on her roommate since she'd returned.

She asked Phil about it when she wandered in a moment later. Agnes was still standing in front of her open bag, dithering over her unpacking.

'Oh, you won't have heard, will you?' Phil said. 'She and her mother had an almighty row. Shouting, screaming, smashing pottery ... it was absolute mayhem.'

'No!' Agnes was horrified.

'It's true!' Phil said. 'You should have seen it. Talk about the worm that turned.'

'Why did they argue?'

'Why do you think?' Phil looked worldly wise. 'Man trouble, obviously.' She rolled her eyes. 'From what I can gather, Bess Bradshaw put her foot down about Polly courting some young man, and Polly didn't like it.'

Agnes recalled the conversation she'd had with her roommate, when Polly had confided that she'd fallen in love with Finn. She had predicted her mother might try to cause trouble for her, and it looked as if it had all come to a head.

It was a shame, Agnes thought. Polly had seemed so happy and in love. Why couldn't her mother just be happy for her, instead of trying to ruin it?

'Anyway, Polly has gone off to stay with a cousin for a few days, to give her a chance to cool down,' Phil went on.

'What about Bess?'

'Oh, she's still here, worse luck. And as you can imagine, all this has put her in the most marvellous of tempers. She's even more like an enraged bull than usual.'

'Careful, Miss Fletcher. That enraged bull might just charge in your direction.'

Bess Bradshaw stood in the doorway, arms folded across her bosom. She did look even more bad-tempered than usual, Agnes thought, her brows low over her flinty eyes. Phil turned instantly to stone. 'I – I–'

'Oh, do stop trying to speak, lass. You look like a stranded goldfish!' Bess dismissed her impatiently. 'And don't look so worried. It isn't you I'm after this time. It's Miss Sheridan here. Now make yourself scarce, if you please.'

Phil's relief was palpable. She was out of the room before Agnes could say a word. Traitor, Agnes thought.

She turned to face Bess. She was leaving, and

the Assistant Superintendent no longer held any fears for her. Within a couple of weeks she would be gone, and Bess Bradshaw would be nothing more than an unpleasant but distant memory.

'You wanted to speak to me?' Agnes said calmly.

Bess stepped into the room and closed the door behind her. 'I've had a word with Miss Gale, but I just wanted to hear the good news for myself,' she said. 'Do my ears deceive me or is it true we're finally getting rid of you?'

Agnes lifted her chin. Bess was trying to goad her, but she refused to rise to it. 'It's quite true,' she said. 'I handed my letter of resignation to Miss Gale an hour ago.'

'And she refused to take it, is that right?'

'She told me to wait until the morning and then reconsider.'

'More fool her,' Bess said grimly. 'If it were me, I'd have you out of that door before you had a chance to change your mind.'

Anger pricked Agnes, but still she wouldn't rise to the bait. 'I'm sure you would,' she said.

Bess prowled around the room. Agnes watched her out of the corner of her eye. Even though she told herself she had nothing to fear, the Assistant Superintendent still made her uneasy.

'So what made you finally decide to go?' Bess asked.

Agnes swallowed. 'I realised I don't belong here.'

'It took you long enough to work that out!'

'I'll never understand the people of Quarry Hill,' Agnes continued. 'And they'll never accept me either.'

'Aye, you might be right.' Bess picked up a

comb Polly had left on her bedside table and stared at it for a moment. 'I suppose this is to do with the Willis lad?' she said.

'No.'

'Are you sure?' Bess turned to face her.

'Not entirely,' Agnes amended. She studied her hands. 'I went to the Infirmary to see him.'

'Why did you do that?'

'I wanted to see if I could help.'

'That was brave of you, to face Nettie Willis like that. A bit daft too. I'm surprised she didn't rip your hair out by the roots.'

Agnes put up her hand to smooth her hair, reassuring herself it was still there. 'She might have done, if her husband hadn't been there.'

'Oh yes, her husband.' Bess looked thoughtful. 'He's a lot better, I hear?'

'Yes.' Agnes smiled in spite of herself. 'He's working again, doing some odd jobs. It's done him the power of good.'

'You had a little chat with him, I understand? About your brother and your dad.'

Agnes blushed. Was there anything Bess hadn't heard? 'We just talked about the war,' she said quietly. 'He needed to talk, but I don't think anyone's ever listened to him before.'

'But you did.'

'Yes.'

Agnes opened her drawer and took out some of her folded underclothes, then moved to put them in her bag. All the time she could feel Bess' gaze on her.

'I'll tell you who else I saw recently. Little Mr Shapcott. Not that I recognised him,' Bess said.

Agnes smiled again. 'He's quite transformed, isn't he?'

'Transformed? He's a different man altogether.' Bess tilted her head consideringly. 'How did you manage it I wonder. How did you succeed where the rest of us failed?'

Agnes shrugged. 'It wasn't difficult, once I found out what he was scared of.'

'And there we all were, thinking he was just a dirty little beggar!' Bess marvelled. 'You've got a way of getting people to tell you their troubles, haven't you?'

Agnes sent her a sideways look. 'What are you trying to say?'

'What I'm trying to say is that you're not as bad a nurse as you might think. Don't get me wrong, you're not perfect,' she said. 'You put your foot in it more times than a drunken dairyman in a cow field. But you've also got a knack for getting in here.' She tapped her temple. 'You can fathom out what's really troubling people, beyond all their aches and pains. And that's a good thing in a nurse.'

Agnes stared at her. She didn't think she had ever heard a word of praise fall from Bess Bradshaw's lips before. Agnes hadn't thought her capable of giving anything but criticism.

But even Bess' approval wasn't enough. 'People still don't like me. Nettie Willis said I was stuck-up.'

'Nettie Willis doesn't know everything. I'll let you into a little secret, shall I?' Bess said. 'When I took over your round while you were ill, all anyone wanted to know was where the real nurse was.'

'Really?'

Bess nodded. 'Right got on my nerves, I can tell you! But it just goes to show, you're not as bad as you thought.'

The bubble of hope that rose inside Agnes quickly burst again. 'Tell that to Nettie Willis and Lil Fairbrass,' she said miserably.

'Nettie and Lil are mothers, fearful for their bairns. Of course they're going to lash out. You get between a mother and her child, Miss Sheridan, and you'll know about it!'

Agnes flinched from the fierce fire in Bess' eyes. Was that the root of the problem with Finn Slater, she wondered.

'But they'll come round,' Bess went on. 'They'll accept you in time, just like Mr Willis and Mr Shapcott and all the other people you've won round. You've just got to earn their respect.'

'I don't think I can,' Agnes said wearily.

'Then you're not the lass I thought you were.' Bess planted her hands on her hips. 'You disappoint me, Miss Sheridan. I had you down as a fighter. You've certainly given me a run for my money a few times!' She smiled grimly.

'Perhaps I'm just not up to this fight?'

'This? This is nothing compared to what you've been through already. Anyone who can get through six months at St Jude's is made of sterner stuff than that, I reckon.'

Agnes felt the blood drain from her, leaving her lightheaded with panic. 'I don't know what you mean...'

'I think you do.'

Agnes caught Bess' frank gaze and her throat

dried. 'How – did you–?'

'I made it my business to find out. Nay, lass, don't look so afeared, no one else knows. And they won't neither. Not from me, at any rate.' Bess' eyes were suddenly gentle, the gleam of combat gone. 'We all have our secrets, and what happened in your past is your business and no one else's. All I'm saying is that if you can get through what you've had to face, then I reckon Quarry Hill should hold no fears for you.'

Agnes stared at her. Her secret was out, and to Bess Bradshaw of all people. She should have been afraid, but somehow she knew Bess could be trusted to take this one to the grave. The Assistant Superintendant wasn't looking at her with contempt, either. There was almost a grudging respect in her expression.

One day, thought Agnes, she might tell her everything that had happened. But now was not the time. She wasn't ready to share it with anyone.

'So you really think I have what it takes to be a district nurse?' she ventured.

Bess grimaced, all her tenderness suddenly gone. 'You're too posh, too impatient, and you never do as you're told,' she said. 'But I daresay we can knock that out of you in time. And let's face it, who else would have you?'

Agnes smiled. Bess might have meant it as a joke, but she really had nowhere else to go. Steeple Street was her last chance, and she had no choice but to stay and fight.

'Anyone would think you were trying to persuade me to stay.' she said.

'Nay, lass.' Bess shook her head, but there was

391

a twinkle in her eye, and the hint of a smile on her lips. 'Why would I do that? If anyone asks, I'll tell them I can't wait to see the back of you. But if I know you, you'll probably stay to spite me. Won't you?'

Chapter Forty

Bess was surprised to see Finn waiting for her when she arrived at Henry Slater's cottage the following morning. Usually he took pains to make himself scarce during her thrice-daily visits.

But today he was standing outside the door as she came up the path, his faithful black dog by his side as usual. He was busy chiselling the crumbling mortar from around a loose brick, but Bess knew that he was waiting for her.

'Good morning, Mr Slater,' she greeted him politely.

Finn didn't turn round. 'Granddad's had a bad night,' he said in a low voice.

Would it really hurt you to say 'good morning'? Bess thought. 'You mean he couldn't sleep?'

'Not just that. He was raving. Not bad dreams or anything like that. He was wide awake but he was making no sense.' Finn flicked a glance at her over his shoulder, and she saw the fear he was trying to hide. 'That in't right, is it?'

No, Bess thought with a sinking heart. It isn't right. But she pasted her most professional smile on her face and said, 'Let's go and have a look at him, shall we?'

Even without examining him, Bess could see Henry's condition had worsened. There was no smile of greeting for her when she walked into the bedroom. He lay there scowling, his face grey with exhaustion.

Finn followed her into the room. He kept himself to a corner, but she could feel him watching.

'How are you today, Mr Slater?' she asked Henry with a bright smile.

'You're the nurse, you tell me!'

'Granddad!' Finn muttered.

'And you can be quiet an' all,' Henry turned on him. 'What are you doing hanging about here anyway? In't you got nothing else to do? There are bulbs to be planted tha knows. And those apples want getting in.'

'It's December, Granddad.' Finn's voice was patient. 'There in't no apples to get in, and the bulbs are already–'

'Don't argue with me! Don't you think I know this land? I should do, I've been tending it for longer than you've been on this earth. Useless article!' He turned back to Bess. 'Have you got any children, nurse?'

Bess glanced at Finn, standing in the corner. His face was expressionless. 'Let's have a look at your legs, shall we?' she said to Henry.

The oedema was much worse than before. His legs were shockingly swollen and engorged with fluid. The digitalis hadn't worked; neither had the other diuretics the doctor had prescribed.

'When am I going to be allowed to get up?' Henry demanded.

'Soon, Mr Slater.' Bess pulled the covers back over him. 'I'll have a word with the doctor and we'll see what is to be done, shall we?'

She took his temperature and pulse, and checked his respiration. It was very poor. The old man's lips were tinged with blue and he fought for every breath. As Bess prepared his medication she was aware of Finn watching her closely. He wasn't being hostile, she realised. He was afraid.

'Right, that's all done.' She stepped back. 'Now, have you had any breakfast this morning?'

'No.'

'I brought you tea and a bit of toast earlier,' Finn reminded him.

'Did you? I don't remember it.' A look of fear flashed into the old man's eyes. 'Are you sure, lad? Why can't I remember?'

'It's all right, Granddad. Everyone gets a bit forgetful sometimes.' Finn stepped forward. 'Here, let me make you more comfortable.' He moved to plump up the old man's pillow, but Henry shrank back from him.

'Don't you touch me!'

'But I only wanted to help...'

'I don't want any help from you!' Henry lashed out and seized one of his grandson's wrists, holding him fast. 'You see these hands, nurse? These are killer's hands!'

Finn flinched as if he'd been struck. He snatched his hand away and left the room, slamming the door behind him.

He was in the kitchen when Bess walked in a few minutes later. He stood at the window with his back to her, but she could see the dark crimson

394

flush on the back of his neck.

She said nothing as she went over to the sink to wash her hands. She'd never thought she would feel pity for Finn Slater, but she did now.

'Granddad's dying, isn't he?' he said.

Bess went into her automatic response. 'I'll telephone the doctor, get him to come out and see him again,' she started to say, but Finn cut her off.

'Tell me the truth, nurse. Please?'

Finn turned to face her, and Bess saw the anguish he was trying so hard to conceal. She couldn't bring herself to lie to him. He deserved her honesty.

'Yes,' she said quietly. 'Yes, I believe he is.' She started to explain what was happening to Henry, how his failing heart was causing his other organs to struggle and fluids to build up in his body. Finn listened carefully, his face devoid of expression. But Bess could see him fighting to hold himself together.

'How long has he got left?' he asked.

'I don't know.'

'But he's going downhill fast?'

'Yes.'

'So is it days or weeks, d'you reckon?'

'I couldn't...' Once again, she saw Finn's face and her professional response failed her. 'Days,' she said.

Finn nodded, taking it all in. 'Thank you,' he said quietly.

He was just a lad, Bess thought. He was doing his best to appear calm, but underneath his gruff exterior she could see a lost little boy. Her motherly instincts came rushing in and it was all she could do to stop herself from putting her arms around him.

He sat down at the table and pulled on his work boots.

'Are you going out?' Bess said.

'Can't stay here. Granddad's right, there's work to be done.' His voice was hoarse.

Bess glanced out the window. Snow still laced the bare branches of the trees. She couldn't imagine there was much to be done on the iron-hard ground, but she appreciated that Finn needed to keep himself busy.

'There's a patch of earth round the back, outside Granddad's window,' he went on. 'I'll tidy that up, make it nice. I want him to look out and see I've kept it looking like he would have wanted.'

He looked so determined to please the old man, a lump rose in Bess' throat.

As Finn was letting himself out, she said, 'Thank you.'

He paused. 'What for?'

'For what you did.'

She didn't have to say any more. He knew what she meant. It was written in every rigid line of his body.

'I didn't do it for you. I did it for her.'

'I know.'

'Like you said, I didn't want to be the one who ruined her life.'

Bess flinched as he parroted her own words back at her. Had she really said that? She was horrified by her own cruelty.

She had thought she was protecting her daughter from harm, but now Bess realised she herself was the one who had ruined everything, not Finn. She was the one who had caused the rift.

'I – I know you were fond of her...' She wanted to speak, to explain why she had done what she had. She wanted Finn to understand, even if Polly didn't.

'It's all right, nurse, you don't have to say anything,' Finn told her. His voice sounded surprisingly gentle. 'You were right, I would never have been good enough for her. Polly deserves someone far better than me.'

He left the cottage, his dog at his heels, closing the door behind him. Bess made Henry a cup of tea and went back to check on him, then packed up her bag and let herself out.

As she trudged down the path, she looked back over her shoulder and saw two figures in the snow. Finn was sitting on a white-shrouded tree trunk, slumped over, head down, shoulders shaking. His dog was close to him, black head pressed into his master's chest, as if to comfort him.

Bess' heart lurched. They said dogs were better judges of character than most people.

Better than she was, at any rate.

Chapter Forty-One

'I knew I'd see you again sooner or later.'

Annie Pilcher's smug tone made Christine cringe. The woman sat by the fire, her narrow face illuminated by the flickering flames. She didn't

397

seem quite so mousy and harmless in the dark, shadowy warmth of her own cottage, with its strange earthy smells and shelves lined with glass jars of herbs.

Christine wished she'd never come and yet she knew she had no choice.

'So what can I do for you?' Annie said.

Christine dropped her gaze to the skinny ginger cat that insinuated itself around her legs. Its lean, snaking body made her shudder, and she fought the urge to kick out at it. 'You know,' she murmured.

'You want to get rid of it, then?'

Christine put a protective hand over her belly and felt a hard kick in response. She couldn't bring herself to say the word, could only nod in response.

I'm sorry. She closed her eyes and let the apology fill her mind. *If there was any other way...*

'It'll cost you.' Annie's voice broke harshly into her thoughts.

Christine opened her eyes. 'How much?'

Annie laughed. 'Don't look so shocked, lass. Did you think I'd do it for free?' she mocked. She took a long drag on her cigarette. 'Two quid,' she said finally.

Christine gasped. 'But I don't have that kind of money!'

'Reckon you're in a bit of a pickle then, in't you?' Annie sent her an assessing look through the plume of smoke that escaped between her thin lips. 'All right, a pound. But I'll not do it for less than that. I'm robbing myself as it is. You don't know the risks I have to take...'

Christine had ceased to listen, her ears ringing with panic. A pound was more money than she'd ever had in her life. Even her mother didn't earn that much, nor any of her brothers come to that.

She felt tears spring to her eyes. She had been so sure that Annie Pilcher was the answer to her prayers.

'I don't know what to do,' she whispered.

Annie sighed angrily. 'It's no use you turning on the waterworks, expecting me to feel sorry for you!' she snapped. 'You in't the first lass who's tried that wi' me!'

'I – I'm not trying anything.' Christine rubbed away her tears with the heel of her hand.

There was a long pause. Then Annie said, 'All right, what have you got?'

'I don't–'

'If you in't got money, you must have summat else. Jewellery? An old clock? A decent pair of shoes? Come on, lass, think. Even Lil Fairbrass must have summat I can take down the pawn shop.'

The pawn shop. A sudden image came to Christine's mind of herself, standing with her nose pressed against the shop window, admiring a set of leather-bound encyclopaedias...

No. Her mind rejected it. She couldn't do it, she wouldn't. It would be the worst betrayal, her mother would never forgive her...

She won't forgive you if you bring a bastard child into her house either.

Christine started, not sure if she'd spoken the words out loud.

'Well?' Annie said. 'What's it to be? You got anything or not?' Christine nodded. 'Good.' Annie stuck another cigarette between her sharp little teeth and rubbed her hands together. 'Then it looks like we've got a deal, doesn't it?'

Against all odds, and the doctor's predictions, within three days John Willis' diphtheria had responded to the antitoxin therapy.

'I thought you'd like to know.' Bess delivered the good news as they prepared for their rounds in the district room. 'Since you've taken such a personal interest.'

'That was good of you.' Agnes stood at the store cupboard, surveying the identical rows of bedpans. All she needed was to select one for Mrs Pinker to borrow, but for some reason suddenly she couldn't seem to choose between them.

'Is that it? I thought you'd be more pleased. You've been on pins these last three days, jumping every time the telephone rings.'

'I am,' Agnes said. 'It's just...'

'Come on, out with it.'

Agnes sighed. 'I can't help blaming myself for the fact that the poor boy didn't get treatment sooner. If only I'd insisted on seeing him, instead of letting Mrs Willis scare me away...'

Bess snorted. 'Nettie Willis would scare anyone! You mustn't blame yourself. You did what you could. Just be grateful the little lad is getting better.'

'Yes, but if only–'

Bess cut her off. 'We could all drive ourselves mad with if onlys,' she said firmly.

The Assistant Superintendent looked thoughtful when she said it, and Agnes wondered if she was driving herself mad too. Polly was due to return soon from staying with her cousin, and Agnes could tell Bess was apprehensive about seeing her again.

How things change, she thought. A couple of days ago she would have had no sympathy with Bess Bradshaw. But ever since their heart-to-heart, they had built some kind of bond.

'I think I might pay Mrs Willis a visit, just to clear the air,' Agnes said.

Bess let out a low whistle. 'I dunno if that's such a good idea. I'd leave well alone if I were you.' Then she looked at Agnes and said, 'Although I dunno why I'm wasting my breath. You've already made up your mind to go, haven't you?'

Agnes smiled. 'May I borrow your bicycle, as it's raining and you're not going out?'

'Certainly not!' Bess said. 'You're not having anyone's bicycle until you've learned not to be so careless with your own.'

'But I don't have one of my own, do I?' Agnes pulled a bedpan from the shelf with a clatter. 'And I don't know when I'm going to get one, either.'

'Then you'll just have to be patient, won't you?' Bess replied maddeningly. 'In the meantime, the walk will do you good.'

If it doesn't give me pneumonia! Agnes thought as she hurried down to Quarry Hill, rain dripping off her hat. She'd never have guessed how much she'd miss her old boneshaker of a bicycle until it was gone. She still didn't know who had stolen it, but she had seen a couple of kids towing a cart

401

made out of an old orange box and a couple of wheels that looked very familiar.

On the way, she stopped off at the newsagent's and bought a couple of comics for John. He would be in hospital for some time, and she knew from her nursing experience how boring it could be for children isolated on the fever wards with no friends to play with.

Norman Willis opened the door to her. He was wearing an old pair of overalls, and his face and hands were stained black with oil. But he looked more cheerful than Agnes had seen him in a long time.

'Hello, nurse. We weren't expecting you. Come in.' He stood aside to let her in to the kitchen. 'Nasty weather, in't it? Take off your coat. I'd hang it up for you, but I don't want to get oil all over it.'

Agnes took off her wet coat and put it on a chair, folded round so the lining faced out.

'Who was that at the—' Nettie came out of the scullery and stopped short when she saw Agnes. 'Oh, it's you. I thought you'd show your face sooner or later.'

Norman shot his wife a warning glare, then said, 'Would you like a cup of tea, nurse?'

'I—' Agnes started to reply but Nettie cut in.

'It's no use offering her one, she'll not drink it. She thinks we're too dirty and ignorant for her to drink out of our cups.'

Norman Willis turned to his wife. 'Will you give over sniping, Nettie?' He looked back at Agnes. 'What can we do for you, nurse?'

'I just came to see how John is getting on – and to give him these.' She proffered the comics, but

402

Nettie stepped in again.

'We don't want your handouts!' she snapped. 'We can buy our own comics, thank you very much!'

'Nettie!' Norman Willis raised his voice, shocking them both. 'Will you give the poor lass a chance?'

'No.' His wife looked mutinous.

'I'm telling you, Nettie, and you will listen. Miss Sheridan has come all this way in the rain. The least you can do is stop shouting the odds and hear what she has to say. Or she won't be the only one as thinks you're ignorant!'

Nettie and Agnes both stared at him. Agnes didn't think she'd ever heard Mr Willis raise his voice above a murmur before.

'Now,' he said, 'I'm off to the workshop to finish that job I'm doing. And I want you two to sit down and settle your differences. I mean it, Nettie,' he warned his wife, as she opened her mouth to speak. 'I won't be responsible for my actions if I find out you've chased Miss Sheridan off again. Remember what happened last time. Our John nearly paid for it wi' his life.'

He left. Nettie stood as still as a statue, staring at the back door, her mouth closed like a steel trap.

Agnes realised Mrs Willis wasn't going to utter another word, so she made a start at conversation.

'I hear John is getting better. You must be relieved?'

Nettie swung round to face her. 'Is that why you've come? I might have known!' She plonked

403

herself down at the kitchen table. 'Come on then, let's get it over with.'

Agnes frowned. 'I don't know what you mean.'

'Oh, don't act the innocent wi' me. I bet you couldn't wait to come here, could you? As I said, I'm surprised you in't shown your face before. Want to rub it in, do you? Tell me how I nearly killed my own son because I didn't listen to you?'

'No, not at all.' Agnes stared at her. 'Actually, I came to say I was sorry.'

Nettie stopped talking, her brow creasing in a frown. 'I beg your pardon?' she said slowly.

'I'm sorry I let you down. The only reason you didn't let me see your son was because you didn't have any trust in me. And if you didn't trust me, it's because I haven't done a very good job of earning it. So I'm very sorry for that.'

Nettie sat back in her seat. For a moment she could do no more than look at Agnes, speechless. Then she said, 'Well, in all my born days! I never expected you to say that. Imagine, you saying you're sorry...' She shook her head, marvelling at it. 'I always thought you reckoned yourself better than the rest of us.'

'Perhaps I did – at first,' Agnes admitted. 'But it was only because I knew nothing about you. I'd never met anyone from – a place like this.' She saw Nettie's frown deepen and knew she was straying on to dangerous ground. 'But I've come to realise I was wrong,' she went on quickly. 'And I'd like another chance. You know – to make a fresh start?'

Nettle said nothing for a moment. She sat studying her work-worn hands. 'Happen I was a bit harsh on you,' she said finally. 'But the truth

404

is, I've been feeling bad about the way I acted. I let my stupid pride get in the way, and it nearly cost me my son.' Her voice shook, and Agnes could see the other woman was fighting to hold her emotions in check.

'I think we're both guilty of a bit of misplaced pride,' Agnes said gently.

'Aye, that's true enough.' Nettie sniffed back her tears. 'Happen we're not so different after all,' she said ruefully. She looked at the comics. 'Did you really bring those for our John?'

'If you think he'd like them?' Agnes handed them over. 'It's not charity, honestly,' she said. 'I just thought they'd keep him occupied.'

'That's very thoughtful of you. Thank you.' Nettie took the comics and settled them on her lap. 'And I also want to thank you for what you've done for Norman,' she said.

'He does seem a lot brighter.'

'Brighter? He's like a new man. He's really come out of his shell. Happen a bit too much.' She frowned. 'Did you hear what he said to me? Raising his voice to me indeed! I've never heard the like.'

Agnes smiled. 'You'll have to have a word with him.'

'Oh, don't worry. I will!'

'Well, I'd better be off.' As Agnes went to pick up her coat, Nettie said, 'Would you like a brew before you go?'

It was a casual enough question. But Agnes saw Nettie's face and recognised the meaning behind it.

'Yes,' she said. 'Yes, I think I would.'

Chapter Forty-Two

'Cousin Polly! Cousin Polly, look at me!'

Polly turned round, and a second later felt the frozen thwack of a snowball hitting her square in the face.

'You little monsters!' she called out as the culprits disappeared, giggling, into the house. 'Just for that, I've a good mind not to help you make this snowman!'

She straightened up, brushing the snow out of her hair. She knew it wouldn't be long before the children came back. Her cousin Gertie would send them straight out of the house as soon as she saw the mess they were making on her newly polished floor.

But at least for now Polly could enjoy a brief respite. She loved her cousin's two children dearly, but she'd had no idea when Gertie invited her to stay that she would end up acting as their unpaid nanny. Gertie had recently had her third baby, and was making the most of the extra help Polly could provide.

Not that she really minded. Playing with trains, and dolls' tea parties, and dressing up as pirates, had all helped to take her mind off what had happened with Finn and her mother.

Now the white heat of her anger had cooled, Polly felt sorrow for what she had done. She should never have lost her temper with her mother, or said such hurtful things. It was so completely unlike her, she had shocked even herself.

But she still couldn't forgive her mother for what she'd done. As far as Polly was concerned, Bess had set out to ruin her life for no other reason than that she couldn't bear to see her happy. All Polly wanted was to finish her training and enjoy her romance with Finn, why that should be impossible.

Her mother claimed she wanted the best for her, but Polly could see now that Bess didn't really love her. She only wanted to control her.

The children appeared again, two little figures ducking around the side of the house as they circled for another attack. Polly smiled to herself, and bent to gather a ball of snow between her gloved hands. She would be ready for them this time.

She waited, snowball poised, the cold air tingling against her face. The children had disappeared off to her left, but she knew from past experience that they would be sneaking out of the side gate into the street, to pop up behind the snow-covered front hedge to her right.

Sure enough, a moment later she heard the sound of footsteps, muffled by the snow, following the line of the high front hedge.

Polly swung her arm back to take aim, and as soon as she caught sight of a gloved hand reaching for the front gate, she launched her snowball full force.

'Got you!' she shouted in triumph, then realised with horror that it wasn't the children at the front gate – it was her old friend Ellen Jarvis.

The missile ricocheted off her shoulder and exploded, showering her with snow and knocking her off balance.

'Miss Jarvis!' Polly ran towards her, boots crunching through the snow. Behind her, she could hear the children giggling. 'Oh, I'm so sorry. Are you all right?'

'I think so.' Miss Jarvis brushed the snow off her coat. 'What a good thing you're not a better shot, my dear, or you could have had me clean over!'

'Here, let me help you.' Polly patted her with gloved hands, but only managed to cover her with even more snow.

'It's quite all right. No harm done.' Miss Jarvis smiled at her. 'I'm pleased to see you're making the most of the weather, at least!'

'I promised Tom and Daisy I'd make a snowman with them. But I'm not sure I want to keep my promise now.' Polly shot a quick, venomous look over her shoulder at the children, now helpless with laughter. 'Are you sure you're all right?'

'Quite all right, thank you. It's you I'm concerned about.' Miss Jarvis finished dusting off her coat and brushed the snow from her gloves. 'I came to see how you were getting on.' She looked past her towards the children. 'You seem to be having fun, at any rate?'

'I don't know about that!' Polly grimaced. Then, remembering her manners, she added, 'Won't you come in? You must be cold.'

She sent the children to the care of their mother – 'It won't hurt Gertie to look after them for once!' she told Miss Jarvis – then asked the maid to bring them some tea.

'What a beautiful house,' Miss Jarvis commented as they sat in the sunny breakfast room, overlooking the garden. 'Your cousin has done very well for herself.'

And don't I know about it? Polly thought. Gertie had married a junior bank manager, and now lived in Beeston, an affluent suburb of Leeds. Scarcely a day went by when she didn't make some comment to Polly about how their lives had diverged.

'Just think, Pol. When we were children we used to pretend we had husbands and lived in a house like this. And now look at me! Married with three children. Can you imagine it?'

But Polly didn't have to imagine it when it was presented to her every day. She was devoted to Gertie and didn't begrudge her her good fortune in the slightest, but she only wished she didn't have to be constantly reminded of it.

The maid brought their tea and Polly served it. It seemed so strange to see Ellen Jarvis here, away from Steeple Street. They had been friends ever since Polly had started her district nursing, but she knew Ellen had been her mother's friend for a great deal longer.

No prizes for guessing what had brought her here, then.

'I suppose my mother sent you?' Polly said, handing her a cup.

'On the contrary,' Miss Jarvis said. 'I expect she would be furious if she knew I was here.'

That shook Polly. 'You mean she doesn't want me back?' The words were out before she could think about them.

'Bess would dearly love you to come back, as would we all. Except your mother would never admit it.' Miss Jarvis smiled at Polly over the rim of her teacup. 'You two are very alike in that respect. Neither of you will ever admit when you're wrong.'

Polly stiffened. 'I'm nothing like my mother!'

'Aren't you?'

'Not at all. Don't you think that's half the problem? I take after my father too much, and my mother can't bear it.'

'Perhaps you're right,' Miss Jarvis agreed. 'You certainly look like him. Albert Bradshaw was a very handsome man, as I recall'

Polly smiled, remembering. 'Yes, he was.'

'What else do you remember about him?'

It was an odd question, Polly thought. She couldn't recall anyone ever talking to her about her father before. 'I remember he was always laughing,' she said. 'He used to make me laugh too, with all his silly songs and stories. And he used to lift me up in his arms and dance around the kitchen.' She could still remember it now, the dizzying feeling of being whirled around and around, the room spinning by. 'Until my mother appeared and put a stop to it,' she grimaced. 'She would always put a stop to our fun.'

'Didn't you ever wonder why your mother didn't laugh and sing and dance around the kitchen too?'

Polly frowned. The very idea was too odd for her to imagine. In all her childhood memories, her mother was always looking on from the sidelines, a scowl on her face. 'She wouldn't have wanted to,' she said. 'She never wanted to join in.' She looked at Miss Jarvis enquiringly. 'Why are you asking me this? You've known my mother for years. And you knew my father, too. Surely you knew what he was like?'

'Oh yes, I knew all right.'

There was something about the way Miss Jarvis said it that made Polly feel wary.

'So why have you come here?' she asked. 'This isn't just a social call, is it?'

'No,' Miss Jarvis said heavily. 'No, it isn't.' She put down her teacup. 'I told you your mother would be furious if she knew I was here. And she would be even more furious if she knew what I was about to say to you. But I felt I needed to come. I couldn't stand by and watch my dear friend lose everything she treasures, just because she has too much pride to defend herself.'

Polly frowned. 'What do you mean? I don't understand–'

'No, my dear, you don't. You don't understand at all.' Miss Jarvis sent her a level look. 'I have a few things to tell you, Polly. And I'm afraid you're not going to like them.'

Chapter Forty-Three

Fear prickled down Polly's spine. 'Go on,' she said.

Miss Jarvis hesitated. Now she didn't seem to know where to begin.

'As you know, your mother and I have been

411

friends for many years,' she said at last.

Polly nodded. Bess and Ellen Jarvis had grown up together. It was Miss Jarvis who had helped Bess get her start in nursing after Polly's father was killed in the war.

'But I have to tell you, the Bess I knew when we were young was very different from the one you know – or think you know,' Ellen amended. 'She was lively, she loved to laugh. She liked to dance too, as I recall.' She smiled fondly at the memory. 'Oh yes, Bessie did love to dance.'

It was such an unlikely picture that Polly couldn't help laughing. 'That doesn't sound like Ma! I wonder what happened to her.'

'I'll tell you what happened to her.' Miss Jarvis' expression suddenly grew solemn. 'She met your father.'

Polly had been stirring her tea, but she let her spoon drop into the saucer with a clatter. Miss Jarvis barely seemed to notice as she went on with her story.

'You're quite right, Albert Bradshaw was a charmer. He could light up a room just by walking into it. And so handsome! All the girls loved him. Of course, he had his faults,' she said. 'He could be a bit reckless sometimes, especially when he'd had a drink. And he had a bit of a temper on him, even then... But he had a way of looking at you that made you forgive him everything.' She smiled at the memory. 'Anyway, he swept your mother off her feet. Within three months they were married.'

Polly stared at her. 'I didn't know that!'

'Oh yes, it's quite true. You see?' she said. 'I told you the two of you were similar. And I'll tell you something else, too. Your grandmother was as dead against the match as your mother was about you and Frank.'

Polly could scarcely remember her grand-mother. She had rarely seen her when she was growing up, and her mother never talked about her. Now Polly could understand why.

'She said Albert was no good for her daughter, that he'd come to a bad end and drag Bess down with him,' Miss Jarvis went on. 'But of course your mother wouldn't listen. She was in love, and that was all that mattered.'

'I'm surprised Ma took against Frank so much, if she'd done the same thing.' Polly said.

'Perhaps she didn't want you to make the same mistake.'

Polly looked up sharply. 'Mistake?'

'Your father wasn't the man she thought he was, Polly. And I'm afraid he wasn't the man you think him either.'

No! A feeling of dread washed over her. Suddenly she wanted to run away, not listen to what Miss Jarvis had to say. But something kept her rooted to her chair, eyes fixed on the rug.

'Things went well for the first few months,' Miss Jarvis said. 'But after a while, I started to notice a change in my friend. She wasn't the Bess I once knew. She was quieter, more subdued, especially when Albert was around. And she would watch him all the time. Even when she was doing some-thing else, she would always be watching him out of the corner of her eye. It didn't take me long to realise why. She was afraid of him.'

'No!' The fierce denial burst from Polly. 'It

413

wasn't like that. He was the one who was afraid. You didn't see them together, you didn't know...'

Miss Jarvis shook her head. 'It's the truth, Polly.' She paused then said, 'You know that scar she has on her wrist?'

'The one where she burned herself on the hot stove?'

'Bess didn't burn herself. He held her hand down on that stove because she'd accidentally ruined his dinner. He held it until she could smell her own charred flesh.'

'No!' Polly shot to her feet. None of this made sense to her. Her father had been a laughing, gentle giant, not the monster Miss Jarvis was trying to make him out to be. 'I don't want to hear any more.'

Miss Jarvis regarded her calmly. 'I really think you should.'

'But it's not fair! My father isn't here to defend himself, and she's making up terrible lies about him.'

'They're not lies, Polly.'

Polly lifted her chin. 'Why didn't she leave him, if he was that bad?'

'Because she had too much stupid pride to admit she had made a mistake, I suppose,' Miss Jarvis said. 'And, of course, there was you,' she added.

'Me?'

'Bess was pregnant with you by then. She truly thought being a father would change Albert, stop him drinking and calm him down a bit. And she was right – for a while.' Ellen smiled. 'He doted on you. Those memories you have of him are quite true. You were the apple of his eye, his little princess. But he was jealous, too. He couldn't stand to share you with anyone – not even your own mother.' The smile faded. 'Bess wasn't allowed to pick you up, or cuddle you, or even smile at you while he was watching. She could feed and change you, give you a bath and look after you, but if she showed you any kind of affection...' Ellen's voice trailed off.

Polly stood rigid, her hands pressed together as if in prayer. She wanted to deny it all, but even as her mind rejected it, a fleeting memory came into her mind. Her mother's quick, fierce hug, face buried in Polly's hair, breathing in the smell of her. A bedtime story whispered at a breathless pace as she tucked her in.

Don't tell your dad...

Polly had always thought it was because her mother was busy, didn't have time for her. But now...

Still her mind pushed the thought away. 'I don't believe you,' she said flatly. 'My father didn't hit my mother.'

'No, he didn't hit her.' Miss Jarvis' voice was a fierce hiss. 'He beat her. Broke her ribs, blacked her eyes. He'd always go too far when he'd had a drink. And she'd always come to me to patch her up.'

More images were flitting through Polly's mind – long-buried, broken fragments of memory that gradually coalesced as they came into the light. Her mother wincing as she bent to help Polly fasten her shoes. Her father laughing– 'Your ma's fallen down the stairs, Pol. What a daft bat!' Polly had even laughed with him at her mother's clumsiness.

And then there was the look on her mother's face when her husband came reeling in from a night at the pub. Polly had always thought it was disapproval, but now she recognised it as fear and despair.

'She could have left him.' She held on to that one simple fact. 'Why did she stay, if it was that bad?'

'Because of you,' Miss Jarvis said simply.

'Me?'

'You loved him. Bess knew you would never go with her, even if he'd allowed her to take you. She either had to stay, or never see you again. And so she stayed.'

And so she stayed… The words burned in Polly's brain. Every day must have been torture for her, but she had endured it for her daughter's sake.

'What about after he died?' she said.

Miss Jarvis paused for a moment, and Polly sensed she was choosing her words carefully. 'I know it's wrong to speak ill of the dead, but it was the best thing that could have happened to Bess. It was as if she had been released from prison.'

'But she didn't change,' Polly said, turning to face her. 'If what you're saying is true, then surely she would have changed once he'd gone.'

'Old habits die hard, I suppose,' Miss Jarvis said sadly.

Was she right? Polly wondered. Even now, she sometimes caught her mother watching her with a yearning look in her eyes. But the next minute Bess would be back to her brisk, critical self.

'I know Bess hoped things would change,' Miss

Jarvis continued. 'She so wanted to be close to you... But you were your father's daughter by then. All you wanted was your dad, not her. I suppose it must have seemed very unfair to her, as if Albert was still taking you away from her even after he was dead. So she threw herself into something practical, making a good life for you both.'

'She was always working,' Polly recalled.

'She had to,' Miss Jarvis said. 'Your father was never a rich man, but he'd died leaving a great many debts. Your mother had a struggle on her hands to pay them off and keep a roof over your heads.'

'I never knew.'

Miss Jarvis' mouth curved. 'Forgive me, but there is a great deal you didn't know.'

Polly was silent. It was true, she thought. She hadn't wanted to believe it, but suddenly so many things began to make sense.

'It was the happiest day of Bess' life when you decided to become a nurse,' Miss Jarvis said. 'She truly thought it must mean something, that you'd decided to follow in her footsteps.'

She hugged me, Polly thought. What did it say about them both that she could remember each and every time her mother had put her arms around her? She looked at Miss Jarvis 'I did it because I wanted her to notice me.'

Miss Jarvis' smile wobbled. 'Oh Polly,' she said, her voice choked. 'If only you knew how desperately she wanted the same thing.'

'But then Frank came along?'

'Indeed,' Miss Jarvis sighed. Polly watched her pouring more tea, refilling their cups. 'Now do you understand why she was so set against him? Not only did she think she might lose you again, she could see history repeating itself.'

'Frank wasn't like my father! He would never—'

'I know.' Miss Jarvis set the teapot down. 'But your mother didn't. All she saw was another handsome, feckless charmer who was going to break your heart and ruin your life just as hers had been ruined.'

'She wouldn't have thought that if she'd got to know him,' Polly said resentfully.

'No one ever said your mother was a saint, Polly. You know as well as I do that Bess Bradshaw speaks before she thinks most of the time.'

'Like I do,' Polly murmured. Miss Jarvis raised her eyebrows but said nothing.

It seemed odd to be sitting down and sipping tea when her life had been turned upside down, but Polly didn't know what else to do. Miss Jarvis' revelations had put her mind in turmoil, changed everything about the way she viewed the world.

'Why didn't she ever tell me?' She hadn't realised she'd spoken the question aloud until she saw Miss Jarvis smile.

'Because she knew how much you adored your father, and how much it would hurt you to hear the truth.'

Polly lifted her gaze. 'Then why are you telling me?'

'Because I think you deserve to know,' Miss Jarvis said simply. 'And I can't stand by any longer and watch you hating your mother when all she's done is try to love and protect you.'

Polly stared down into her cup. There was simply nothing she could say to that.

Miss Jarvis set down her cup and stood up. 'I can see there is a lot for you to take in,' she said. 'So I'll leave you in peace to think about what I've said. I hope I can trust you not to tell your mother about our conversation? Bess would be heartbroken if she thought you knew.'

'I won't say anything.'

'Good. She's a proud woman, Polly. That's half her trouble. She would rather blunder on and get herself into an even bigger mess than ever admit she was wrong.'

Polly smiled in spite of herself. 'That sounds like my mother!'

'And perhaps like you as well?'

As Polly showed her out, Miss Jarvis leaned in to brush her cheek with a fleeting kiss. 'Take care of yourself,' she said. 'I hope we'll see you in Steeple Street soon?'

'I – I can't say.' Polly dropped her gaze.

Miss Jarvis sighed. 'Look, I don't know if anything I've told you will make a difference to you. I can't tell you what to do, or whether to come back to nursing. But whatever you do, I hope you can forgive your mother. After everything she's been through, I think she deserves that at least.'

Chapter Forty-Four

'And what are these supposed to be?'

Annie Pilcher looked at the pile of books with as much distaste as if Christine had dumped a dead rat on her kitchen table.

'Encyclopaedias,' Christine said. 'They're worth a lot of money, honest,' she added, seeing Annie's expression. 'My ma saved up ages to buy them.'

Her voice faltered. She couldn't bear to remember Lil's face, shining with pride and love on Christmas Day as she'd handed them over.

'Did she indeed?' Annie arched one eyebrow. Christine cringed as she watched the woman flicking through the pages with her grubby, pointed fingernails. 'Well, they in't my cup of tea, but I s'pose they might fetch a few bob.' She shrugged and looked at Christine. 'We'd best get on with it then, hadn't we?'

'Could I sit down for a minute?' Christine said. 'I'm not feeling very well.'

Annie was instantly on her guard, eyes narrowed. 'What's the matter with you?'

'Nothing. I – I've just got a bit of backache, that's all.'

'That'll be the baby, pressing on your spine.' Annie nodded knowingly. 'How far gone did you say you were?'

'I don't know.'

'You mean you don't know when your monthlies

stopped?' Christine shook her head. 'Honestly, you girls! You're as ignorant as lambs, the lot of you. Some of the lasses I've seen don't even know how they ended up pregnant in the first place!' Annie cackled. Christine looked away, hoping she couldn't see her blush in the dim light. 'Anyway, we'll soon sort you out,' Annie went on. 'Go into the other room and get up on the bed while I wash my hands.'

Christine hesitated in the doorway. 'Will it hurt?' she asked.

'I daresay. But it'll be worth it in the end. I can give you a nip of brandy to help the pain, if you like?'

'No, thank you. I don't drink.'

'Proper little saint, in't you?' Annie laughed harshly. 'Well, don't just stand there gawping, lass. Go and get yourself comfy. I'll be in in a minute.'

The other room, as Annie called it, was the front parlour. Heavy chenille curtains were pulled over the windows, blocking out the light. In the centre stood a bed, covered with a stained brown mackintosh sheet.

Christine felt her belly cramp in protest at the sight of it. She cradled the softly rounded shape she had grown so used to. She couldn't allow herself to think of it as a baby, not now. Just as she never allowed herself to think of Oliver, and how he used to love her, and how different everything might be if he still did.

'I'm sorry,' she whispered. 'I'm so, so sorry.'

Beside the bed was a small table. Arranged on it was a length of rubber tubing, a jug and bowl, and various bottles.

Christine picked up the nearest one, pulled out the cork stopper and sniffed it. The pungent aroma of disinfectant nearly knocked her sideways.

'Now then, what are you doing?'

Annie's voice startled Christine so much she nearly dropped the bottle. The older woman stood in the doorway, a steaming mug in her hand. Christine caught a strong whiff of earth and rotting vegetables. 'I was only looking.'

'Nosing around more like. Always curious, in't you? Always asking questions.' She put the mug down, then took the bottle from Christine, replaced the cork and put it back on the table. 'But you don't have to look so worried. I won't be using that lot on you.' She nodded towards the equipment. 'Not if you're as far gone as I think you are.'

Christine stared at her in dismay. 'Then what–'

'I've brewed you one of my concoctions!' She picked up the mug and held it out to her. 'A few swigs of this will sort you out in no time.'

Christine peered into the murky brownish-green liquid. It looked and smelt as if Annie had skimmed it from the canal. 'What's in it?'

'Never you mind! All you need to know is that it will work. Now drink it down, then I want you to go home and take yourself straight to bed.'

Christine eyed her fearfully. 'And then what?'

'Let nature take its course.'

'But I can't go home!' Christine's heart thudded in panic.

'Well, you can't stay here!' Annie snapped. 'I

422

don't want no lasses giving birth on my doorstep, thank you very much!' She tutted. 'Look, you'll have to find somewhere,' she said impatiently. 'Now, come on. Be a good girl and drink it down. The sooner you do it, the sooner all this will be over.'

'Man o' War. Now there was a horse if ever there was one. Do you know, he won the Belmont Stakes by twenty lengths?'

'Really?' Agnes did her best to sound interested. Isaiah Shapcott was in one of his talkative moods, and she knew there would be no stopping him.

'It's true. And he won the Kenilworth Park Gold Cup by one hundred lengths. A hundred lengths! Can you imagine? By the time he finished his career, no other trainer would put their horses up against him. Well, you wouldn't, would you?'

'I suppose not.'

Agnes let her attention drift towards the window as Isaiah chattered on. She didn't mind listening to him at all, but sometimes wished he would talk about something other than racehorses.

The snow had thawed to an unpleasant slurry of ice and slush that rendered the cobbled yards completely treacherous. Agnes could feel the icy dampness seeping through her shoes as she sat at the kitchen table, writing up her notes.

Meanwhile, on the other side of the screen, Isaiah chattered on. They had exhausted her limited knowledge of horses some weeks previously, so now their weekly meetings consisted of Agnes reading the *Sporting Life* to him from cover to cover, then settling back for a lecture on bloodlines, or trophies, or whatever racing-related topic Isaiah saw fit to discuss that day.

But at least she could catch up with her work. Isaiah didn't seem to mind that she didn't join in with any opinions of her own, as long as she was there to listen to him and supply the odd interested 'ooh' and 'ah'.

'It was a terrible shame when he retired five years ago,' he was saying. 'I would have liked to see him race in the flesh, instead of just reading about it and looking at pictures. You can't really get an idea from pictures, can you?'

'I suppose not.'

'Still, I daresay he'll sire a few more champions before long.'

'I daresay he will.' Agnes had paused for a moment in the middle of writing up an account of Miss Wheeler's phlebitis when a movement outside caught the corner of her eye.

She looked up to see a girl staggering across the yard, red hair streaming like a bright flag in the wind. She was bent nearly double, her arms wrapped around her middle.

'Christine!' Agnes shot to her feet and ran to the door, throwing it open. 'Christine Fairbrass?'

Christine froze for a moment and looked round. She saw Agnes and hurried away, her boots slipping and sliding over the slushy cobbles in her hurry to escape.

'Oi! Close that door, you're lettin' all the cold in. D'you want me to catch me death?'

Agnes turned to see Isaiah emerging from behind the makeshift screen, his teeth chattering, a thin towel wrapped around his narrow white body.

424

Agnes took one last look outside, but Christine had disappeared up the alleyway. She closed the back door.

'I should think so too,' Isaiah huffed. 'I do have some modesty to protect, you know. I don't want all the neighbours looking in. What were all that about, anyway?'

'I just – saw someone I knew.'

'In the yard? I shouldn't think you did. Half the houses roundabout are falling down, in case you hadn't noticed. In't no one lives here except me and – her.' His mouth curled.

'Who?' Agnes asked.

'I don't like to say. It in't right. Not right at all.' Isaiah tapped his temple. 'They reckon I'm daft, but I know right from wrong, y'know. And what she does – well, I don't hold with it. Not at all.'

'Don't hold with what, Mr Shapcott?' Agnes tried to be patient, even though her mind was screaming. 'Who are you talking about?'

'Her.' Isaiah moved to the window and twitched aside the curtain to peer out. 'Annie Pilcher.' He nodded towards the cottage opposite, the only other dwelling still standing intact in the tumble-down yard. 'She kills babies.'

Agnes finished attending to Isaiah as quickly as she could then dashed off to look for Christine.

It was growing dark and the snow was falling again, flurries that struck her face like tiny, frozen knives while she searched the warren of alleyways. Freezing slush filled her shoes as she splashed through ankle-deep puddles. In her haste to get away, she had left her gloves at Mr Shapcott's and

425

her fingers throbbed with cold.

Back at Steeple Street the nurses would be settling down for their tea and wondering where she was, but Agnes didn't dare abandon her search. She was too haunted by the vision of a distressed Christine staggering from Annie Pilcher's house, clutching her belly.

That picture of fear and pain and loneliness stuck vividly in Agnes' mind, because she knew only too well what it was like.

Perhaps Christine had gone home? If she was afraid and in pain, it made sense for her to seek help there.

Agnes knew she should go to see Lil Fairbrass at any rate. Even if Christine wasn't there, Lil still needed to know what was going on. But Agnes could barely face the prospect, not after what had happened last time.

Lil had been angry enough when she'd thought Agnes was wrong. How angry would she be when she knew the nurse was right?

Lil's house looked deceptively welcoming, with bright light streaming out into the yard. When Agnes peered through the window she saw Lil's five sons sitting around the table with Lil at its head, dishing up food on to plates.

Christine's place was empty.

Ignoring everything Bess had told her about being a guest and waiting to be invited, Agnes lifted the latch and let herself in. Lil probably wouldn't allow her over the threshold anyway, if she knocked.

Six heads turned in her direction.

'Oh, here we go. Seconds out, round two!' one

426

of the boys laughed, nudging his brother next to him.

Lil straightened up, gripping the ladle like a weapon. She was a terrifying sight, tall and broad as a man, a tangle of faded coppery hair hanging around her red face. 'What do you want?' she boomed. 'You've got a bloody nerve, showing your face–'

'Where's Christine?' Agnes cut her off.

Lil's eyes narrowed to slits. 'What do you want to know that for?'

'Just tell me, is she here?'

'She's at the library.' One of the boys, the eldest and most sensible in Agnes' opinion, joined in. He must have seen the concern in her face, even if his mother was too angry to notice anything. He pushed back his chair and stood up. 'Why? What's happened?'

Agnes drew in a deep, steadying breath. 'She isn't at the library,' she said. 'I've just seen her coming out of Annie Pilcher's house.'

Lil dropped the ladle with a clatter. 'Annie Pilcher? But what would Christine be–'

Agnes watched the look of horror slowly dawn on Lil's face. The high colour drained away, leaving her deathly white.

'Now do you see why we've got to find her?' said Agnes.

Lil sprang into action, mustering her sons.

'Ernie, you go and look round the church... Tony, you search down by the goods station. Alfie, you'd best go round the market...'

'What about my dinner?' one of the younger

427

ones protested.

Lil clipped him smartly around the ear. 'Didn't you hear what the nurse said? Your sister's gone missing.' Her voice was choked.

'Where shall I go?' Agnes asked.

Lil stared at her blankly for a moment, as if noticing her for the first time. Then she said, 'You don't have to trouble yourself, nurse. You've already done enough. Thank you for letting us know.' She sounded stiff and overly polite, as if she was holding on to her manners with the last of her self-control.

Agnes shook her head. 'Oh no,' she said. 'I'm staying.'

'But won't they be expecting you back at the nurses' home?'

'It doesn't matter. I want to help find Christine. You might need me,' she added quietly.

She didn't have to say any more. Lil stared at her for a moment and Agnes could see the other woman's mind working. If Annie Pilcher had done her worst, then they would indeed need a nurse.

'Aye, you're right,' Lil said at last. 'You'd best come wi' me.'

They searched for Christine for the best part of an hour, trudging through the freezing streets, their heads down against the cold. Neither of them spoke.

Lil was in a state of shock and disbelief. Agnes could see it written all over her grim profile as she walked beside her. She wished she could say something to comfort the woman but knew nothing she said would be welcome. The best Agnes could offer was her silence.

They must have scoured every inch of Quarry Hill. Every lane, every alleyway, every yard and terrace, they searched it all. They even ventured into some dark, ruined corners that Agnes had never seen before. Sinister, desperate-looking characters lurked in the shadows, and Agnes could feel their gazes following them. But Lil marched on, utterly fearless. She was a lioness searching for her cub, and nothing would stand in her way.

'I can't think where she might have gone,' she muttered. 'It's not like Christine to stray far from home like this.' She stopped dead, pressing her lips together. Once again, Agnes could read the thoughts going through her mind. After what had just happened, Lil must be wondering if she knew her daughter at all.

All Agnes could think about was the state Christine might be in. If she was anything like poor Maisie Warren, had been she could be bleeding in a freezing ditch somewhere.

Lil seemed to be haunted by the same thought. 'If Annie Pilcher has harmed one hair on my little girl's head,' she hissed, 'I'll have her. As God is my witness, I'll have her!'

'Let's just concentrate on finding Christine, shall we?' Agnes said gently.

They continued on in silence. They met Tony and hope flared in Agnes, only to die when he said there was no sign of Christine at the goods yard, or around the library, or the school.

'Why don't you go home, Ma?' he suggested gently. 'You never know, she might be there?'

But Lil shook her head. 'You go,' she said. 'I'm going to keep looking for her.'

429

'But Ma–'

'I'm going to keep looking for her!' Lil repeated tautly.

He clearly knew better than to argue with his mother. 'All right,' he said quietly. He glanced at Agnes. 'Let me know if there's any news, won't you?'

'We will,' Agnes promised.

They went on their way, plunging into the darkness of another narrow alleyway. The ice underfoot made it difficult to walk, but Lil ploughed on ahead, heedless of everything.

'I should have known,' she kept murmuring under her breath. She seemed more angry with herself than with her daughter. 'I'm her mother, I should be able to tell these things...'

Agnes cleared her throat. 'It wasn't your fault you couldn't see it. She was barely showing.'

'You knew!' Lil turned on her, her face blazing. 'You could tell.'

Only because I was once in that position myself, Agnes thought. Hiding her shame under layers, afraid to admit the truth, even to herself.

'But why didn't she tell me?' Lil was saying. 'She could have come to me, surely?'

'Perhaps she didn't want to disappoint you?'

Lil stared at Agnes, her face shocked. 'Disappoint me?'

'You had such high hopes for her. Perhaps she didn't want you to think she'd failed you.'

'But how could she ever fail me? She's my little girl.'

It was such a simple question, and yet it was as if someone had pierced Agnes' heart with an arrow, stopping her briefly in her tracks.

Luckily, Lil didn't seem to notice. 'I suppose I owe you an apology,' she said stiffly. 'The way I behaved when you tried to tell me before ... I shouldn't have flown off the handle like that. I should have listened.'

Yes, Agnes thought. Yes, you should have. Part of her still felt angry and humiliated over the way Lil had treated her. But seeing the poor woman's face as she stood before her now, so full of anguish, Agnes couldn't find it in her heart to punish her any more.

'It doesn't matter now,' she said quietly. 'What matters is that we find Christine.'

'You're right,' Lil said. They trudged on in silence for a few moments, but Agnes sensed Lil had something on her mind.

Finally, she said, 'How did you know? About her being – you know?' She sent Agnes a sideways look. 'I s'pose you can tell these things, with being a nurse?'

Lil was looking for comfort, to make herself feel better for not seeing the signs. She was still blaming herself, though, wondering how a stranger could see what had been staring Lil in the face so plainly.

'It was – experience,' Agnes said, choosing her words carefully. 'But I also saw her once, with her young man.'

Lil's face darkened. 'Young man? Do I know him? Is he a local lad?'

'I – I don't know,' Agnes faltered in the face of Lil's simmering anger. 'All I know is that I saw them coming out of...'

431

'What?' Lil said. 'What is it?'

Agnes turned to her. 'I think I know where Christine might be!'

Chapter Forty-Five

The landlady of the bed and breakfast eyed them suspiciously.

'What do you want? If it's a room you're after, they're all taken.'

She went to close the door, but Agnes put out a hand to stop her. 'We're looking for someone,' she said. 'A girl with red hair? She's been here before, with a young man.'

The woman's eyes narrowed. 'What about her?'

'Is she staying here?'

'None of your business,' the woman snapped. 'I run a discreet establishment.'

She went to close the door again, but Lil shouldered her way in.

'That girl is my daughter,' she growled, squaring up to the landlady. 'She's in trouble, and if you don't tell me where she is—'

'Room three,' the woman quavered, her eyes bulging with fear. 'Top of the stairs, on the left.'

Lil started up the stairs, with Agnes following. The landlady trailed behind.

'What's going on?' she demanded, keeping a safe distance between herself and Lil. 'I want to know. I have my good name to protect, you know! You ask anyone, Maud Pettman is the soul of respectability...'

Lil found the door and rattled on the door-knob. 'It's locked,' she said.

They both turned expectantly to Mrs Pettman. She must have found the courage from somewhere because she shook her head.

'I can't let you in. It's against my rules. As I said, I run a discreet–'

She was interrupted by the sound of a low, anguished moan coming from the other side of the door.

'Christine!' Lil was instantly galvanised, pounding on the door with her fists as if she could break it down with her bare hands. 'Christine love, can you hear me?'

The landlady stepped forward, reaching for the ring of keys that jangled at her waist. 'I'm warning you,' she said, 'if there's been any funny business–' She threw open the door and gaped in horror. 'Oh my God! What's this?'

It was like opening a door into a horrible flashback. Christine lay on the bed, her red hair plastered to her white, sweating face. Her clawed hands clutched at the bedsheet, bunching it tightly between her fingers as she gritted her teeth against the pain.

The world suddenly tilted on its axis and Agnes felt herself go with it, the ground sliding from underneath her feet. She grasped the doorframe to keep herself upright as her knees buckled.

'Nurse?' Mrs Pettman's voice seemed to come from the end of a long tunnel. Agnes turned and groped towards the sound. Her vision cleared and she saw the picture as it really was, with Lil sitting at her daughter's side and the landlady standing in the doorway, staring at Agnes.

They expected her to take charge, she realised. Her nurse's uniform gave her instant authority, even if she didn't feel able to wield it.

She managed to hold herself together enough to give Mrs Pettman instructions to telephone the district nurses' home for the emergency nurse.

'Tell her there's a girl in labour,' said Agnes. She couldn't allow herself to voice the other awful possibility: that poor Christine might be in the throes of a miscarriage. 'Don't just stand there. Hurry up!' She snapped, tension getting the better of her as the landlady remained rooted to the spot.

The woman went off in a huff, still muttering about her reputation, and Agnes closed the door behind her.

Christine clutched her mother's hand as if her life depended on it. Her eyes were feverishly bright in her bloodless face.

'I'm sorry,' she kept saying, over and over again. 'I couldn't do it. I thought I could, but – I ran away. I'm sorry I wasn't brave enough, Ma!'

'It's all right, my love. You're safe now.' Lil gathered the girl into her arms, rocking her gently. 'Everything's all right now. I'm here. I'll look after you.' She looked at Agnes over the top of her daughter's head. 'Well? In't you going to do something?' she hissed.

Agnes stared back at her blankly. 'What?'

'Get ready to deliver this baby, for one thing!'

'I can't!' Agnes was aghast. 'I've sent for the nurse.'

'You are a bloody nurse, in't you?'

'Yes, but...' She winced as Christine let out another wail of agony. 'We need to wait.'

'I don't think we've got any choice in the matter.' Lil held her daughter tighter as her cries subsided. 'It's all right, love. I know it hurts, but it'll be over soon.'

Agnes stood frozen to the spot. She wanted to run away, close the door, put as much distance as she could between herself and Christine's pain.

Mrs Pettman returned. 'Both the emergency nurses are out, but they say they'll send someone as soon as they can,' she announced.

Agnes looked at Lil, still holding on to Christine as if she would never let her go again.

She was right. They had no choice in the matter.

Agnes took a deep breath and turned to the landlady. 'Right, we're going to need boiling water, as much of it as we can get,' she said. 'And bowls, and jugs, and plenty of newspaper, and–'

'Don't you worry, love.' The landlady patted her arm reassuringly. 'I've had three kids. I know what to do.'

I wish I did, Agnes thought as she watched Mrs Pettman hurry off.

Agnes scrubbed her hands at the tiny wash-basin in the corner of the room, rubbing the soap under her nails. She was putting it off, delaying the moment when she would have to step forward, take action.

But in the end she couldn't avoid it any longer.

She turned to Christine with her most professional smile in place. 'Right,' she said. 'Let's have a look at you, shall we?'

Christine looked up at her with pleading eyes. 'I'm sorry,' she whispered. 'I'm sorry I let everyone think you were lying about me...'

Agnes glanced at Lil who had her eyes cast down, not looking at her. 'It doesn't matter now,' she said.

There was no doubt the baby was well on its way. 'You're almost fully dilated,' Agnes said, when she'd finished examining her.

'I've been having pains for a while,' Christine said. 'I didn't know what was happening to me, I didn't realise...' Her eyes glittered with tears. 'I shouldn't have gone to Annie Pilcher,' she sobbed. 'I didn't want to, but I didn't know what else to do.'

'Did she do anything to you?' Agnes asked.

Christine shook her head. 'She tried to give me something to drink, but I – I couldn't do it.'

'Thank God you didn't,' Agnes murmured. She knew about the concoctions some old wives swore by. One of the girls at St Jude's, driven to despair by fear and shame, had concocted a brew of tansy and pennyroyal, with disinfectant added. By the following morning she was dead.

Lil Fairbrass seemed to read her thoughts. 'By God, I'm going to string that woman up!' she hissed.

'Let's just worry about Christine, shall we?' Agnes said, seeing the look of helpless distress on the young girl's face.

'Aye, you're right.' Lil squeezed her daughter's hand. 'At least you're all right, lass.' Agnes looked away so they wouldn't see her troubled expression. She wished she could say the same about the

436

child she was carrying. The fundus measurement was so small, no wonder no one had spotted Christine was pregnant. She could barely be more than seven months, if that.

The baby would be lucky to survive.

A feeling of dread began to gather inside Agnes. Christine's baby was going to be born dead, just like Agnes' own precious little one.

She couldn't bear that, not again. A wave of panic rose like a wave, engulfing her until she couldn't breathe.

Mrs Pettman came back, carrying a tray laden with jugs and bowls, clean towels and various other items.

'I've boiled and sterilised everything as best I can,' she said, setting the tray down on the dressing table. 'I've brought scissors to cut the cord. See, they're in this jar, steeping in disinfectant.'

'Thank you,' Agnes said shakily.

'And I've brought some clean sheets for the bed, and some newspaper like you asked.'

The three of them worked busily, laying down newspaper and changing the sheets. There was no mackintosh, so they laid more newspaper over the mattress. The landlady seemed quite tickled by the idea of a baby being born in one of her guest rooms, once she'd got over the shock.

'And I suppose the father's nowhere to be found?' she whispered to Agnes, as they made the bed together. 'I always knew he was a wrong 'un,' she declared. 'A bit too pleased with himself for my liking. Poor lass.' She shook her head in sorrow. 'Still, she's not the first to get caught out and I daresay she'll not be the last. Eh, nurse?'

But Agnes wasn't listening. Once again her mind was full of the image of another room, and another girl on a bed in the throes of labour.

Like Christine, Agnes' pains had begun when she was alone. She had escaped from St Jude's to go walking in the grounds. They were the only beautiful thing about the place, acres of gardens giving way to wild meadows and a small wood with a stream running through it. Agnes loved to go down to the stream, far away from the nuns and their strict, punishing daily routines. She would sit on the bank and try to remember a time when she was happy, fishing with her brother and her father.

But on this particular afternoon, her waters had broken and the niggling aches she had been feeling all day suddenly gathered force, taking her breath away.

Agnes had tried to get back but it was a long walk, especially when she had to keep stopping every few minutes to deal with the painful spasms that racked her body. By the time she made it back to St Jude's, there was barely time to rush her to the delivery room before her baby came into the world.

Afterwards, they blamed her. It was her long walk that had brought the baby on too soon. If she hadn't taken it into her head to go wandering off by herself, they might have been able to save him.

Agnes knew nothing about that. All she could remember was the silence as she held him in her arms...

'Why isn't he crying?' she had asked. Then hands had come out of nowhere, grabbing him

438

from her. He was whisked away and she never saw him again.

There's nothing anyone can do for him. Now stop crying, you silly girl. No one cares about your tears.

'Nurse!' Lil shouted at her, bringing her back to the present. 'Do something, for God's sake!'

Agnes looked round at Christine. Her knees were drawn up, her face contorted as she pushed with all her might. One hand was wrapped around her mother's, gripping it so hard her knuckles were white. But Lil didn't seem to notice as she urged her on, glued to her daughter's side by love, whatever she might think of what she'd done.

Agnes' mother hadn't been there to help her during her birth. She wasn't there afterwards, when the puerperal fever took hold and Agnes lingered for days between life and death.

The only time Agnes saw her was days later, when her fever had finally, broken. She'd woken to find her mother at her bedside with the news that the baby had died.

'Perhaps it's for the best,' were the only words of comfort she had offered. 'After all, God works in mysterious ways.'

'The head's coming!' Lil shouted.

Agnes snapped herself back to the present. She had to concentrate, to focus. She had to do this right, couldn't afford to make a single mistake.

Thankfully, it was a quick, straightforward birth. Within half an hour the baby emerged, perfect and tiny as a doll. It slipped into Agnes' hands and she could only stare at it, dazed by the miracle that had just happened.

'It's a girl,' she said.

'A girl!' Lil beamed with pride. 'You've had a little girl, lass.'

Suddenly everyone seemed to be celebrating. Christine was weeping and laughing, and Lil and Mrs Pettman were embracing each other as if they were old friends.

But in the middle of it Agnes stood very still, staring at the baby in her hands. No, she thought, dread washing over her. No, no, no...

Perhaps it's for the best... After all, God works in mysterious ways.

Who would miss another unwanted little soul, who didn't deserve to be born and had no place in the world?

Then Christine spoke up. 'Why isn't she crying?' she asked.

Suddenly all eyes were on Agnes and the lifeless little form in her hands.

She looked back at their beseeching, hopeful faces. The baby wasn't unwanted by them. She might not have been expected, but she already had a place in their world, whether she knew it or not.

Unlike Agnes' own poor baby, who had slipped out of the world unloved and unmourned by anyone but her.

She hadn't managed to save her own baby, but she would do her utmost to save this one. Perhaps if she could save Christine's little girl, she could forgive herself for the death of her own child.

She turned to Mrs Pettman. 'Stoke up that fire,' she said. 'And bring me extra blankets. We need to make her as warm as we can.'

As she tied and cut the cord and swaddled the baby up in the blanket the landlady had brought warm from the airing cupboard, Agnes tried to remember what Bess had told her on the night they had delivered the Rankin baby.

The child had gone into shock, and Agnes had to try and revive her.

She set the baby down beside the fire. 'I need you to help me,' she said to Lil. 'Come and hold the baby's feet.'

'Why? What are you going to do?'

'Just do as I say, will you?' Tension made her snap.

Lil looked shocked – Agnes suspected no one had spoken to her like that before – but did as she was told, kneeling down on the rug opposite Agnes.

'Now what?' she whispered.

'Shhh. I need to think.' Agnes grasped the baby's tiny arms between her fingers, trying to remember how Bess had done it. She gently circled the arms, opening up the chest, just as Bess had for the Rankin baby.

But the Rankin baby didn't survive, did she? A small voice taunted Agnes. She died, just like your baby died.

'No!' The word burst out of Agnes, taking Lil by surprise. The heat from the fire was burning her face, but she kept on, willing this baby to live.

And then, suddenly, a miracle happened. The baby took a gulp of air and started to cry, a thin reedy cry that was the sweetest sound Agnes had ever heard in her life.

'You did it!' Lil's voice was hoarse. 'You did it, nurse. You saved her.'

441

Bess Bradshaw had attended some odd births in her time, but she'd never expected the scene that greeted her when she arrived at the bed and breakfast. Who could have imagined little Christine Fairbrass sitting up in bed like a princess, her mother at her side and her baby daughter in her arms?

'Look at that red hair,' Bess said. 'She's a Fairbrass all right!'

She caught Lil's eye when she said it. The new grandmother's expression gave nothing away. 'Aye,' she muttered through tight lips. 'She is that.'

Bess looked at her sympathetically. Poor Lil looked dazed. If the sight of Christine with a baby in her arms was a shock for Bess, she couldn't imagine what it must be like for the girl's mother. 'I'm only sorry, I couldn't get here sooner, to help with the birth,' she said, and looked around. 'Where is Miss Sheridan?'

Lil frowned. 'I think Mrs Pettman's taken her off to have a cup of tea and calm her down. You should have seen the state she was in. Shaking like a leaf she was. Mind you, I'm not surprised,' Lil went on. 'It was a shock to all of us.'

She glanced at her daughter when she said it. Her expression was still unreadable. Christine looked away, her face flushing.

'Anyway, that lass was a proper heroine today,' Lil said. 'I don't mind admitting, I was wrong about her, nurse.'

I reckon we all were, Bess thought.

She touched the baby's soft cheek with the tip of her finger. 'What are you going to call her? Have you decided yet?'

There was a silence.

'I want to call her Lilian Agnes,' Christine announced.

Bess nodded. 'She'll grow up strong, then.' Lil said nothing, but stared down at her own rough hands.

After Bess had checked Christine and baby Lilian to make sure they were well, she and Lil walked downstairs together.

'You'll have to let your boys know there's a new addition to the family,' Bess said. 'I expect they'll be shocked, won't they?'

'I daresay they will, nurse.'

Bess sent her a sideways look. Poor Lil. Her face gave nothing away, but Bess could only imagine the turmoil she was going through inside.

'And how do you feel about it all, Lil?' she asked gently.

Lil frowned. 'I dunno what to think,' she said.

'It's not what you wanted for Christine, is it?'

'No,' Lil conceded. 'No, it isn't. But she's still my daughter, when all's said and done,' she said bracingly. 'And I'll stand by her, whatever happens.' She looked at Bess. 'It's what a mother does, in't it?'

An image of Polly came to mind.

'Yes,' Bess said heavily. 'Yes, I suppose you're right.'

Chapter Forty-Six

As the year 1925 drew to a close, Henry Slater's life seemed to be ending with it.

Bess spent every moment she could at the sexton's cottage, for Finn's sake more than anything. Henry had passed into a delirious state and had long since ceased to notice if she was there or not.

But Finn was a worry to her He was constantly at his grandfather's bedside, reading to him, sponging his face and wetting his lips, or else just sitting quietly watching him. Bess had taught him to carry out simple nursing jobs, and she knew the old man was in good hands when she wasn't there.

But Finn didn't seem to give any kind of care to himself. He went for hours and days without eating or sleeping, unless Bess was there to insist on it.

'You'll make yourself ill,' she had warned him, but he only shrugged and said, 'It doesn't matter. Granddad needs me.'

Then, on the last day of the year, Bess arrived at the cottage to find a young woman washing up dishes at the kitchen sink.

'Oh, hello.' She reached for a tea towel to dry her hands. 'You must be Mrs Bradshaw? I'm Isabel, Finn's sister.'

'How d'you do?' They had the same grey eyes and black hair, Bess thought. But Isabel was pertly pretty, with none of her brother's rough edges. Her hair hung in a shiny curtain to her shoulders, held off her face by a mother-of-pearl barrette.

'Finn wrote to let us know about Granddad,' Isabel said. 'I came to see if I could help.'

'Have the rest of your family come too?'

'No. It's just me.' Isabel's lowered gaze spoke volumes. 'I expect my parents will come after...'

After he's dead, Bess finished for her silently. What a charming family they must be, not to want to say goodbye to an old man who had been father and grandfather to them. Or to support their grieving son, come to that.

'Well, it's good that you're here anyway.' She smiled at Isabel. 'I daresay your brother will welcome the company.'

'Will he? It's always so hard to tell what's going on in Finn's mind.' Isabel's pretty mouth turned down. 'I don't even know if he wants me here or not. He's barely uttered a word to me since I arrived.'

'Surely he wouldn't have written to you if he didn't want you to come?' Bess reasoned.

'I suppose not.' She looked up, and Bess could see the tears glazing her grey eyes. 'How is Granddad?' she asked. 'Really, I mean?'

'He's very poorly.' Bess started the automatic response, but Isabel lifted her hand.

'It's all right, Mrs Bradshaw. I'm a trained nurse myself. You can tell me the truth. He's going to die, isn't he?' Bess nodded. 'That's what I thought. I mean, Finn did tell us in his letter, but I must say I was shocked when I saw Granddad for myself... He doesn't have long, does he?'

'No,' Bess said heavily. This was always a difficult part of her job, preparing relatives for the inevitable. Not that it was ever possible to prepare anyone for the loss of a loved one.

She looked at Isabel. The poor girl looked so downcast, Bess' heart went out to her.

'Let's go and see him, shall we?' she said quietly.

Finn was in his usual place at his grandfather's bedside. Job lay beside him. The hound's heavy tail beat up and down on the rug when he saw Bess but he didn't move from his master's side.

Bess let her gaze skim past him. She didn't approve of dogs in a sick room, but Finn was adamant that Job should stay. Bess knew when she was beaten. Besides, the dog obviously gave Finn comfort, which he badly needed.

'How is he?' she asked.

'No change. But I gave him a drink earlier, and he managed to sip it. And when I read the paper to him, he looked as if he was taking it in...'

Bess looked at the spark in the young man's eyes. Even now, he was still clinging to any shred of hope he could find.

'We've just given him a nice wash and put on some clean pyjamas,' Isabel chimed in. 'And I've taken his TPR,' she added.

Bess suppressed her irritation. The girl was only trying to be helpful, she told herself.

'Well, I'll just do it again, to make sure,' she said.

As she reached for the thermometer, Bess said to Finn, 'And how are you, young man?'

He looked up, dazed at the question.

'Have you eaten since I saw you yesterday?' Bess pressed him.

'I don't know. It doesn't matter anyway,' he replied carelessly.

'I've been trying to persuade him to go out and get some fresh air,' Isabel said.

'That sounds like a good idea.'

'I don't want to go,' Finn said in a low voice.

'But it will do you good.'

'I told you, I don't want to go!' Finn rounded on his sister. 'I would never have sent for you if I'd known you were going to nag me!'

Bess saw poor Isabel's mouth tremble, and stepped in quickly. 'Why don't you just go for a walk around the churchyard?' she suggested. 'Then you won't be too far away if we need to fetch you back.'

Finn looked from one to the other, his expression mutinous. Then, without a word, he stood up to go.

When he reached the door he turned and said, 'You will fetch me, won't you? If – anything happens?' His gaze was fixed on Bess as he said it.

She nodded. 'I promise.'

He left, and Isabel turned to her. 'Well,' she said. 'He certainly likes you.'

Bess frowned. 'What makes you say that?'

'I can just tell. He trusts you. And that's a real compliment, because Finn hardly trusts anybody.'

I can't think why he would, Bess thought. After the way she'd treated him, the last thing she would have expected was for Finn to like her.

Suddenly she felt awkward. 'Come on,' she said to the girl. 'Since you're a nurse, you can help me change this bed.'

They talked as they worked. Bess found out

Isabel was twenty-three years old and worked as a nurse in Huddersfield, where their parents lived. But like Finn, she remembered spending her school holidays with her grandfather in Leeds.

'I'm glad I managed to get here in time,' she said. 'I've always loved Granddad Henry. Not that I knew him as well as Finn did. He was closer to him than anyone. I suppose that's why he came here after...' Her voice trailed off. 'Poor Finn. What's he going to do when the old man dies? He's going to take it badly, I know he will. And he'll be all on his own.' She chewed her lip worriedly.

'He'll have the rest of the family, won't he?'

Isabel shook her head. 'Hardly. Why do you think they're not here now? They want nothing to do with Finn, not after...' Once again, her voice trailed off.

'After he was sent to prison, you mean?'

Isabel looked at Bess sharply. 'Finn told you that? Goodness, he really does trust you, doesn't he?' she murmured.

Bess didn't reply. She was too embarrassed to admit she had heard it all third-hand from a malicious curate. It really wasn't like her to snoop into other people's business.

'So I suppose he must have told you the whole story?'

'Well–'

'Then you'll know how unfair the whole thing was,' Isabel went on, not waiting for a reply. 'I do wish our parents hadn't turned their backs on him,' she sighed. 'I know Finn can be a bit surly and difficult sometimes, but he needs them, even

448

if he won't admit it to himself. I'm sure they'd find it in their hearts to forgive him if they only knew the truth.'

'The truth?' Bess said.

Isabel blushed. 'I thought you said you knew all about it?'

'I know he's done time in prison for stabbing a man.'

'Oh Lord,' Isabel said. 'So you don't know the full story after all?'

'No,' said Bess. 'But why don't you tell me?'

'I can't.' Isabel bit her lip. 'I swore to Finn I'd never tell...' Her grey gaze fixed on Bess, as if trying to weigh her up. 'But I suppose if Finn trusts you, then I should too.' She was silent for a moment. Then she said: 'Finn didn't stab that man. Amy did.'

'But I don't understand,' Bess said. 'He confessed to the police. They found him standing over the body with a knife in his hand...'

'Finn was the one who found him,' Isabel said. 'But it was Amy who did it.' She paused, glancing around the room as if to check no one was listening. 'I'm the only one who knows,' she said in a low voice. 'I thought Finn had told you, otherwise I would never have said anything.' Her eyes flew to the old man in the bed, murmuring to himself, caught between one world and the next.

'He won't say anything and neither will I,' Bess said. 'Tell me what happened.'

Shakily, Isabel explained how their young sister had changed after she was attacked.

'She was always jittery, couldn't settle to anything,' said Isabel. 'She used to love to paint and draw, and play the piano, but suddenly she couldn't sit down for more than a minute at a time. She was always restless, looking over her shoulder... And her temper!' Isabel went on. 'Overnight she turned from being the sweetest, most biddable girl you could ever meet to being – well, like a wild cat. She was ferocious.'

I'm not surprised, Bess thought. A shocking and terrifying ordeal like the one Amy had suffered would scar anyone for life.

'My parents sent her to all kinds of doctors. There was even talk of sending her to the asylum.' Isabel shuddered. 'I know they wanted to send her away, but Finn talked them out of it. I don't think he could bear the idea of Amy being locked up. But even he could see she was slipping out of control. She became obsessed by the monster who had – done that to her.' Isabel chose her words delicately. 'She would watch him, follow him... Finn was constantly searching for her and bringing her back home before our parents found out what was happening.

'And then one night he went out looking for her and found her standing over his body. Amy didn't mean to do it, I'm sure she didn't.' Isabel pleaded for Bess' understanding. 'She was so lost and fragile... Finn could see that too. He knew it would kill her if she was locked up, so–'

'So he took the blame for it himself?' Bess' voice was hoarse.

'He told Amy to run,' Isabel said flatly. 'He gave her enough time to get away, then he telephoned the police and confessed.'

450

'And how do you know it wasn't really him?' Bess asked.

Isabel frowned at her. 'Why would he lie about it, if he was going to take the punishment anyway?' she reasoned. 'And besides, you've seen him with Granddad. Finn might look tough, but he's a gentle soul. He would never hurt anyone.' A smile curved Isabel's lips. 'And if he had set out to hurt that man, then he would have finished the job,' she said simply.

Bess was silent, accepting the truth of what she'd heard. 'What happened to Amy?' she asked.

Isabel's smile faded. 'That's the truly sad thing,' she said. 'Finn took her place to give her the chance of a life, but instead she killed herself after he went to prison. I suppose she couldn't live with the guilt of what she'd done.'

To the man who'd molested her or to her brother? Bess wondered. It didn't matter, either way. Poor, tragic Amy was dead, and Finn had been punished for it. Meanwhile the monster who'd assaulted her was still walking the streets, a free man without a stain on his character.

The world could be a cruel, unfair place sometimes, Bess reflected.

'Why didn't you ever tell anyone?' she asked.

'Because Finn made me promise not to,' Isabel replied. 'Even now, he's still protecting Amy's memory.' She smiled sadly. 'That's Finn. Poor, loyal Finn, always protecting everyone but himself.'

Bess left the cottage, promising Isabel she would return in a couple of hours. She also left strict

451

instructions that the girl should telephone the district nurses' house if Henry's condition grew worse before then. From what Bess had seen, she didn't expect him to make it through the night.

Finn was a distant figure on the far side of the churchyard, beyond the church, busying himself mending a fence that had come down over the winter. Job lay on the ground, watching him.

Bess paused by the lych gate to watch Finn at work. He had his back to her, swinging the sledgehammer, driving the loose fence posts back into the ground as if his very life depended on it.

Perhaps it did, she thought. He was putting all his rage, all his despair, and all his energy into each swing of the hammer, exhausting himself so he didn't have to feel any more.

'Hello, Ma.'

Bess was so absorbed in watching him she didn't hear anyone approaching. She swung round and there was Polly, her Polly, standing there, framed by the lych gate.

'Polly!'

She looked pale, Bess thought. Too pale. Without her usual pink lipstick, her face was drawn and washed out.

But Bess didn't think she had ever seen a more beautiful sight.

'I went to Steeple Street,' Polly said quietly. 'They told me I'd find you here.' She lifted her gaze, and Bess saw her lips tremble. 'Oh Ma, I'm so–'

Bess didn't even wait to hear what she had to say. Breaking all the district nursing rules, she dropped her Gladstone bag on the ground and flung her arms around her daughter. She felt Polly stiffen with surprise at first, her body as unyielding as a poker. But then, gradually, she began to relax and her arms went slowly, tentatively around Bess.

'I'm sorry,' she whispered.

Bess closed her eyes, for once not ashamed of the tears that squeezed between her lashes. 'So am I, lass. So am I.'

She held on to her daughter, clinging to her fiercely. She didn't count the seconds or look over her shoulder. She didn't even care that she might make herself look weak or vulnerable, because she was. And it didn't matter any more.

Lil's words came back to her. *She's still my daughter... And I'll stand by her, what ever happens... It's what a mother does.*

Finally Bess collected herself and released Polly, stepping back to wipe away a tear with the heel of her hand.

'I've brought you a present,' Polly said, holding out a small package.

'For me?' Bess frowned as she took it. 'It in't my birthday, is it?'

She unwrapped the package, aware of her daughter's eyes on her. Inside was a small china pot.

'It's to replace the one I broke,' Polly said.

'You didn't have to bother, I mended the old one–' Bess started to say, then pressed her lips together. 'It's lovely,' she corrected herself.

Polly smiled. 'Now you've got two,' she said. 'You could start a collection?'

'I might just do that.' Bess smiled back. 'It might be nice to have a collection on the dresser.

Two instead of one.'

'Two's always better than one,' Polly said. 'One's such a lonely number.'

They looked at each other for a long time.

'Aye,' Bess agreed, her smile trembling. 'You're right.'

Polly linked her arm in her mother's. 'Shall we go home?' she said.

Bess shook her head. 'Nay, lass. It wouldn't be right.'

Polly's confusion and dismay were written all over her face. 'But I thought–'

'It wouldn't be right because there's someone who needs you more than I do at the moment.'

She nodded back towards the churchyard, to where Finn was still working away, a small figure in the distance, wielding his sledgehammer. Polly looked over at him and Bess saw her expression change, soften with longing.

'Go to him, Pol,' Bess said.

Polly dragged her gaze from Finn to her mother. 'But–'

'Go to him,' she repeated softly. 'He needs you.'

She watched Polly walking up the path. Job saw her first. He lifted his black head and got to his feet. Then Finn turned to see what had attracted his dog's attention. He saw Polly and froze for a moment.

'Go on, lad,' Bess urged him softly. 'Don't be proud. Don't make the same mistake I did.'

But there was no danger of it. A moment later Finn let the hammer fall to the ground with a thud and they were running into each other's arms.

Bess watched them for a moment. Polly was

right. Two was always better than one. And now she, Finn and Polly all had two people to care for and to look after them.

Satisfied with her work, Bess picked up her bag and headed back to Steeple Street.

Chapter Forty-Seven

The nursing badge felt heavy and solid, and Agnes couldn't stop looking at it. It bore the letters QVJI, the initials of the Queen Victoria Jubilee Institute, named after the monarch whose generous donation had allowed the first district nurses to go out and do their work.

On the back it was engraved with a special number. Miss Gale had explained that every district nurse had her own number, and when she left the service her badge – with its number – was passed on to someone else.

Agnes couldn't help wondering about the district nurse who'd had her badge before her. She liked to think it had a happy story attached to it.

'It's a proud moment for you, I daresay, to be able to call yourself a Queen's Nurse at last?' Miss McLeod said. They were gathered around the table in the dining room for a celebration tea, as they always did when a student nurse gained her badge. Phil and Polly had celebrated theirs a month earlier.

'Yes,' Agnes agreed. 'Yes, it is.'

There was a time when she might have scoffed

at the very idea. When she'd first arrived – was it only six months earlier? It felt like a lifetime – she couldn't imagine that the nurses of Steeple Street had anything to teach her.

But now...

As if she could read her thoughts, Bess said, 'Well, Miss Sheridan? Do you still think it's just a matter of changing dressings and giving injections?'

Agnes cringed. How naive could she have been? In the past six months she had seen and experienced more than she would if she'd stayed at the Nightingale for six years. She'd learned a great deal more about human nature, too.

But conscious that it was Bess Bradshaw asking the question, she smiled sweetly and said, 'Oh yes. You've taught me there's much more to it than that.'

Bess' brows rose. 'Oh?'

'Yes, indeed. There's drinking tea as well.'

Everyone laughed. Even Bess' mouth twisted wryly. 'I'm glad we could teach you something, at least. Especially since you trained at London's most prestigious teaching hospital!' she mimicked Agnes' accent as she helped herself to a slice of seed cake.

Agnes blushed. 'Was I really that pompous?'

'Lass, if you were any more puffed up, we could have pricked you with a pin!'

'Take no notice of her,' Polly said from across the table. 'She's teasing you, as usual.'

Bess turned on her daughter. 'Your collar's crooked,' she said.

'You see?' Polly shrugged. 'She doesn't have a

good word to say about anyone. I shan't miss her at all when I'm away doing my midwifery.'

'You won't last the six months,' Bess said.

'I shall have to prove you wrong, won't I? As usual.'

Agnes saw the smile that passed between them. Polly had changed a lot in the past six months too. There was a time when she would have crumbled under her mother's stinging remarks. But now she calmly gave back as good as she got.

That must be what being in love does to you, Agnes thought.

But seeing Polly and her mother on such good terms made her feel the loss of her own mother more keenly. Agnes hadn't heard from any of her family since Christmas and she had long since given up looking in her pigeon hole and hoping for a letter.

Part of her wished it didn't have to be this way. Surely if even Polly and Bess could make up their differences, she and her mother could do the same?

But the difference was that both Polly and her mother wanted to build bridges. It took two, and Agnes' mother had no interest in even trying. Her father might have interceded for her, if he hadn't been so frail himself. As it was, Agnes had to admit to herself that her family was lost to her. For the time being, at least.

It was time to stop hoping and wishing for a miracle, she thought. And it was also time to stop blaming herself. She had made a tragic mistake, but she shouldn't have to spend the rest of her life paying for it.

Seeing the way Lil Fairbrass and her sons had rallied around Christine and her baby had made Agnes realise how cold and uncaring her own family had been.

She looked around the table at the ring of smiling faces, all wishing her well. Over the past six months, she and the other district nurses had laughed and cried together. They had argued and sniped and sulked, and celebrated and commiserated together. These people were her family now, Agnes thought. Together with Christine and Lil Fairbrass, and Queenie Gawtrey, and Isaiah Shapcott, and all the other quirky characters she'd come to know and – in spite of what she'd at first believed – actually love. She would miss them all desperately when the time came for her to leave Quarry Hill and go to her new district.

Miss Gale tapped her teaspoon on the side of her cup for silence.

'Of course,' she said, 'now you've got the badge, you really should have a bicycle to go with it.'

Agnes sat up straight, hope lifting her heart. 'Did the Association buy me one?'

'I jolly well hope not!' Phil muttered. 'My motorcycle is top of the list!'

'Unfortunately not,' Miss Gale said. 'There are no funds for either of you, I'm afraid. But someone else has come to your rescue at least, Miss Sheridan.'

Miss Gale met Bess' eye across the table. Agnes could see they were both trying their best not to smile.

Just then the loud ringing of a bicycle bell came from outside.

'Right on cue.' Miss Gale smiled round at them all. 'Shall we go?'

The Superintendent led the way out to the front garden, just in time to see Norman Willis pushing a bicycle up the path. His wife Nettie followed behind.

Agnes stared at them. 'What's this?'

'What does it look like? A camel?' Like Bess, Nettie Willis could never resist a sly dig even if she and Agnes had made their peace.

Agnes ignored her. 'Is it for me?'

'If you want it,' Mr Willis said. 'We just thought – that is, the wife and I – and a few of the others round Quarry Hill – we thought–'

'We were sick of watching you trudging along with that bag of yours,' Nettie finished for him.

'It in't brand new,' Mr Willis said apologetically. 'I put it together myself, from bits and pieces I found at the workshop.' He looked shyly at her. 'Well? Will it do, nurse?'

It was a Frankenstein's monster of a bicycle, and Agnes had no doubt she would be teased about it wherever she went, but she felt a lump in her throat when she looked at it.

'It's beautiful, Mr Willis,' she said. 'And I wouldn't have a new bicycle now, not even if the Association gave me one plated in gold.'

'They'd better not!' Phil muttered.

'I hope it'll stand you in good stead at any rate. Wherever they send you next,' Mr Willis said.

'That's a point,' Miss Goode spoke up. 'Do you know where you'll be going yet?'

Miss Gale and Bess Bradshaw looked at each other. 'As a matter of fact, we were just dis-

459

cussing that very matter,' Miss Gale said.

'Oh yes?' Agnes looked up hopefully.

Bess grinned. 'I hope you're ready for a challenge?'

Agnes rang the bell on her new old bike and the other nurses jumped back in horror, covering their ears. She wasn't sure what kind of bell it was, but it was loud enough to scare the birds out of the trees.

'After the six months I've just had, I think I'm ready for anything,' she said.

The publishers hope that this book has given you enjoyable reading. Large Print Books are especially designed to be as easy to see and hold as possible. If you wish a complete list of our books please ask at your local library or write directly to:

Magna Large Print Books
Magna House, Long Preston,
Skipton, North Yorkshire.
BD23 4ND

This Large Print Book for the partially sighted, who cannot read normal print, is published under the auspices of

THE ULVERSCROFT FOUNDATION

THE ULVERSCROFT FOUNDATION

... we hope that you have enjoyed this Large Print Book. Please think for a moment about those people who have worse eyesight problems than you ... and are unable to even read or enjoy Large Print, without great difficulty.

You can help them by sending a donation, large or small to:

**The Ulverscroft Foundation,
1, The Green, Bradgate Road,
Anstey, Leicestershire, LE7 7FU,
England.**
or request a copy of our brochure for more details.

The Foundation will use all your help to assist those people who are handicapped by various sight problems and need special attention.

Thank you very much for your help.